# MONEY GRAB

# MONEY GRAB

## Frances Aylor

A Robbie Bradford Novel

Hastings Bay Press

Cover by Vince Robertson of VIROART.COM

Hastings Bay Press
P. O. Box 2863
Mechanicsville, Virginia 23116

Printed in the United States of America

First Printing May 2017

10 9 8 7 6 5 4 3 2 1

ISBN: 978-0-9987959-0-4

# Acknowledgements

Many thanks to everyone who helped in the writing and publishing of this book.

First, to my husband and children, my sister, family and friends who read countless drafts and were unwavering in their encouragement.

To my investment friends, including Jeff Markunas, IronOak Advisors, Jeff Chapman, CFA Institute, and CFA Society Virginia.

To James River Writers and Sisters in Crime, especially Maya Bality, Michael Sumner, Mary Miley Theobald, Jim Bacon, Susan Campbell, Mary Dutta, Marilyn Mattys, Ron Sterling, Rosemary Stevens, Sandie Warwick, Heather, Weidner, and Judy Witt.

To Colonel David R. Hines and the Hanover County Sheriff's Department, especially the Hanover County Citizens Police Academy.

To my social media coach Kristi Austin of Tuck Austin Associates.

To Diane Beirne and Crystal Garthaffner of The Woman's Club and Kelly Justice of Fountain Books, who organized my very first book signing.

# CHAPTER 1

WHEN HE SMILED, I knew I had him.

Nobody had thought I could pull it off. Maybe not even me.

The three of us were sitting in a secluded booth at Terence's, one of those dim, intimate restaurants where deals got done over double-cut filets and gigantic slabs of prime-aged Porterhouse.

Judge Edmonton's body language told me he was almost ready to commit. He nodded agreeably during dinner, shoulders relaxed, fingers casually wrapped around his wine glass. But there was a certain hesitation in his eyes. He wasn't totally convinced. I needed to change that.

Over the past six months I'd spent my entire year's entertainment budget on the judge and his wife Barbara, trying to persuade them to move their twenty-million-dollar investment account over to me and my team at Fairburn, Crandall. Shep Fairburn told me I was wasting the firm's money. That I was too young, too green and too unconnected to win the account. And too female. Shep thought Judge Edmonton was much too traditional to have his money managed by a woman, especially one in her mid-thirties.

I was willing to chance it. The fees from this account would make me one of the highest revenue generators in the firm. And it would prove I was partner material, a rainmaker who could bring in significant new business. I had lusted after that partnership ever since I joined Fairburn, Crandall five years ago. It would mean more money. Wealthier clients. A bigger office. But even more important, making partner meant public recognition that I was at the top of my game as a financial advisor. That all the sacrifices I had made to get here were finally paying off.

"So tell me again about this team of yours," the judge said, carving off a last slice of prime rib. "The one that is going to take such good care of my money."

We had already been through this, but I patiently laid it out again. "You've met some of them," I said. "Bradley Pearson is our tax strategist. And Devon Michaels focuses on estate planning. They've both got some great ideas for you." I smiled, determined to keep the desperation out of my voice, ignoring my churning stomach and sweaty palms. If I didn't land this account, I was totally screwed. I'd neglected all the other leads in my pipeline to concentrate on this one. "And you met Shep Fairburn at the horse races this summer. He's one of our founding partners. His long term stock performance is at the top of the charts."

"Oh, yes," he said, nodding as he chewed. "Good man. We talked for quite a while."

"We can make more money for you," I said, looking him straight in the eye, my voice firm. "A lot more."

My cell phone suddenly vibrated in my lap. I let it go to voicemail. Everyone I cared about knew that I was closing this deal. Anyone else could wait.

The waiter cleared our plates and inquired about dessert. We all ordered coffee.

"Robbie, I like the things you're saying. And it sounds like you've got a great team." There was the slightest tinge of uncertainty in his voice.

I frantically searched for the right words to clinch this deal. I knew the judge had checked us out thoroughly, our people, our investment track record. He probably knew as much about our firm as I did.

His long-term advisor had dropped dead of a heart attack two years ago. His new advisor had given him some bad advice that cost him big money. But more than that, the new guy did not give him the high level of attention he was used to. The judge wouldn't have that problem with me. There were not that many twenty-million-dollar clients in the southern city of Hastings. I would wash his Mercedes with my tongue if it would get me the account.

"Anyone else I should know about?" he asked. "A backup in case you're not available?"

My cell phone vibrated again. I ignored it.

"Of course. There are other managers who can be brought in on an as-needed basis." I thought of Vivian Sutherland, another financial advisor at our firm, who was terrific at picking out small stocks on the cusp of accelerating growth. Shep had been playing Vivian and me off against each other all year, watching us compete for the partnership. I wouldn't let her get near the judge until all the paperwork was signed and I was officially his account manager. "Judge, Barbara," I said, focusing for a long moment on each of them, "I promise you, nobody will be more dedicated to you and your account than I will. I care about you both. I want to protect your money and help you grow your investments. And I will always be there for you."

He glanced at his wife. "Well, this all sounds good. What do you think, Barbara?"

I held my breath. I had invested a lot of time in Barbara, taking her shopping, to the museum, to the spa. We would relax together after our massages, sipping Pellegrino as we got mani-pedis. Barbara was fifteen years younger than her husband and wanted someone to look out for her and her two small sons, to protect them from the judge's vengeful ex-wife. I had promised to fill that role.

She glanced at me. "I think Robbie will do an excellent job for us," she said, patting his hand.

I slowly exhaled. I would have to give the masseuse a bigger tip next time.

"Let's do this," the judge said, smiling. And there it was. I had him.

"So, can I bring the paperwork by your office on Monday morning?" I asked.

"Absolutely," he said. "I'm ready to make the move."

I sat up straighter, trying to remain calm, to stay in the leather booth and not dance madly around the restaurant. I took a long, slow sip of chardonnay, letting its fruity crispness caress my tongue. This was a night for celebration. Everything I wanted was coming to me. This account. The partnership. It was mine.

The phone vibrated a third time. Annoyed, I reached for it, pretending I was adjusting my dinner napkin. There were three text messages from Fontaine. "Call me immediately."

I smiled at the judge. "Please excuse me for a moment. I'll be right back."

He nodded. I walked out into the hallway to call Fontaine. "Did we win?" I asked as her voice came on the line.

Our college football team was playing for a bowl bid. My best friend Fontaine and her husband Nate had tailgated with Rolfe and me for years, the four of us rarely missing a home game.

"What do you mean, you're not going?" Rolfe had asked a few weeks ago, his dark eyes flashing, when I told him about my dinner with the judge.

"I've got to lock up this account, Rolfe," I said.

"Find another night."

"There is no other night. We're too close to year end. His calendar is booked."

"Don't do this, Robbie. Don't put your career ahead of us. Not again."

We glared angrily at each other, arms tightly crossed, lips pressed in a thin line, neither willing to give in. Finally, he had grudgingly agreed to take our three-year-old son Jason in my place.

I kept an eye on Judge Edmonton and Barbara as I walked down the hallway of the restaurant, my phone pushed hard against my ear. There was a lot of background noise. Car horns. Shouts. "Fontaine, I can't hear you. Did we win?"

"There's been an accident," she said. "It's Rolfe."

It couldn't be more than a fender bender. Rolfe was one of the safest drivers I knew. I often teased him about driving like a little old lady. I was the one with the heavy foot, always glancing in the rear view mirror for patrol cars. "Are he and Jason all right?"

"You need to come here," Fontaine said.

I could see the waiter at our table, pouring coffee. "It's nothing serious, is it? I'm winding everything up. Just give me a few more minutes."

"No. It's bad. You need to come right now."

Her sense of urgency scared me. "What happened? Where are you?"

"Eastbound on the interstate a few miles out of town. Past the Sheldon Road exit. The police just got here. You need to hurry."

"I'm leaving now." I slipped back into the dining room to tell Judge Edmonton that I had a family emergency. "I've settled the check with the waiter. Let him know if you want anything else."

He stood up. "Is there anything we can do to help?"

"No, I'm sure we'll be fine." I shook his hand and gave Barbara a quick hug. "I'll bring the papers to your office on Monday."

"I look forward to seeing you," he said.

Outside the restaurant the whipping November wind drove icy rain into my face. I pulled my coat more tightly around me, waiting for the valet to bring my car around. I tipped him and settled in behind the wheel. The tires spun as I accelerated away from the curb.

Westbound interstate traffic was backed up, barely moving, as I neared the Sheldon exit. "It's just a fender bender," I told myself over and over, trying to stay calm as I slowly rolled toward the brake lights of the minivan in front of me. "Rolfe is a safe driver. They're fine." But the eastbound lanes across from me were completely bare. Rolfe's accident had stopped three lanes of traffic. No fender bender did that.

Desperate to get to Rolfe and Jason, I pulled to the left shoulder, blowing my horn impatiently, forcing the stopped cars to squeeze to the right. Even on the shoulder, it was slow going. I had crept along for maybe half a mile, searching through the tall pine trees clustered in the median, when I finally saw the flashing blue lights of police cars in the eastbound lanes. At the first access road, I cut across and headed back, bouncing along the edge of the road, horn blaring, cursing at the cars who begrudged giving me room.

The shoulder gave out at a concrete berm. I tried to edge onto the asphalt, impatiently scraping the bumper of a huge pickup truck as I forced my way into the lane. The driver climbed down from his seat and stomped toward me. "Are you crazy?" he yelled, shaking his fist. "We're packed in here. There's no place to go."

"It's my family," I screamed, jumping out of the car and running.

Bursting through the solemn crowd that had gathered to watch, I stopped abruptly at the row of fire trucks. Their blood red lights throbbed into the night sky, strobes that transformed the urgent scrambling of the rescuers to robotic slow motion.

Rolfe's car had flipped upside down, a tire bent inward, undercarriage exposed. One lone headlight fought the night. The other was smashed beyond repair. The car perched precariously at the side of the road, the rear end extended over black space, ready to slide down the embankment. Pieces of metal were scattered across the roadway. Firefighters crouched beside the car, peering inside, attaching chains and blocks to stabilize it. My feet crunched across broken glass as I ran screaming toward them.

A policeman grabbed me roughly by the arm. "You can't go there," he said.

"It's my husband. And my little boy."

"I'm sorry, ma'am," he said, more gently. "It's not safe over there. The best thing you can do is wait here until the firefighters get them out of the car."

Fontaine rushed up and grabbed me. "Robbie, Robbie," she said, tears running down her face, "I'm so sorry."

"Fontaine, what happened?" I asked.

"We were coming home from the football game," she said, her voice wobbly. "Rolfe was several car lengths in front of us. Suddenly he swerved and slammed into the trees." She pointed to the dense stand of pines lining the right side of the roadway. "The car flipped over and skidded toward the ravine."

Nate walked up and hugged me. "Robbie, thank God you're here."

"This is just crazy," I said. "Rolfe's never had an accident. He's never even gotten a speeding ticket."

Nate moved me toward the side of the road, his arm firmly around my waist. And then I saw them. A doe and her fawn, stretched out on the side of the road. Their necks twisted, stomachs torn open, blood pooling on the asphalt. "They must have run out in front of him," Nate said.

A pounding noise made me jump.

"It's a generator. For the jaws of life," Nate explained. "The firemen need to cut the doors off so they can get to Rolfe and Jason."

I watched as the firefighters attacked the side door with what looked like giant pliers. The door was wedged in tight and stubbornly resisted, but finally fell to the ground. I could see the white of the collapsed air bag.

The crowd around me had grown larger. Drivers had switched off their cars and walked up to watch the action. Someone beside me muttered, "Jeez, that car's flat as a squashed beer can. Ain't nobody still alive in that thing."

I turned toward him, ready to fight. Fontaine grabbed my hand and pulled me away. "Why don't they get them out?" I asked. "What's taking so long?"

I held my breath as they slowly pulled Rolfe from the car and laid him on a waiting stretcher, buckling him in place. I rushed up and knelt beside him in the mud, gripping his hand.

"I'm sorry," he said in a hoarse whisper.

"It'll be all right," I answered, bringing his hand to my lips. "I love you."

"Jason?" he asked.

I turned to the car. They carefully pulled my little boy from the back seat, then buckled him onto a stretcher and moved toward us. He looked so tiny, his hair matted to his head by the icy rain. My stomach heaved as blood oozed from a gash deep enough to expose the bright white of his skull.

"It'll be all right," I repeated, determined that Rolfe not see how scared I was.

"Stay with Jason," he said.

I watched as rescue workers loaded Rolfe into a waiting ambulance, then scrambled up beside Jason as he was loaded into the next one. I perched on the edge of the bench as paramedics crowded around him. We pulled away, sirens screaming into the night. I held Jason's limp hand in mine as I closed my eyes and started to pray.

§§§

I went back to work four days after the funeral.

It was too soon.

I thought it would help, to get out of my deserted house, to get back into the routine of the office. Monitoring clients' accounts, checking the activity of the markets, making customer calls. Anything to blot out the image of that crumpled car, the strained expression of the doctor when he gave me the horrible news. But it didn't work. At the end of each day, I couldn't remember who I'd talked to or what I'd said.

The twin sisters of guilt and grief took over my mind, unshakeable companions who stalked me by day and snuggled up against me at night, dragging me down into tortured dreams, making me wander through endless labyrinths of twisted memories. I should have been in the car with Rolfe instead of Jason. I would have spotted the deer. Grabbed the wheel. Steered us to safety.

But I wasn't there. Instead I had been entertaining my new client. Celebrating the closing of my big deal. Sipping expensive chardonnay.

Each morning I woke exhausted and confused, barely able to dress myself and get into the office. Usually I was so good at reading the stock market. Its heartbeat flashed rapidly on my computer monitors, green, then red, then green again, as stock prices moved up and down, powered by the hopes and dreams, the fear and greed, of investors all over the globe. I could see the patterns, feel the tempo, know when a stock was ready to start a move up, when it had peaked and was starting to roll over.

But not now. Now there were no patterns. There was no rhythm. The stock quotes on my screen were an indecipherable jumble of swirling color. All I could see were two burnished mahogany coffins, one full size and the other impossibly tiny, being lowered side-by-side into the muddy earth.

Fontaine convinced Shep to give me a leave of absence. She watched out for me, long after all the calls and emails from friends and co-workers had tapered off. After my four sisters and their families had gone back to their homes. After Rolfe's parents had retreated tearfully into their rambling mansion. She settled me in her guest room and rushed to my bed night after night, to grab my hand and pull me back, sweat-slicked and screaming, from the abyss of my dreams.

When I went back to work a few weeks later, I found that Judge Edmonton had called often to check on me. Vivian had taken his calls. Vivian with that long mane of golden curls that she liked to swish back over her shoulder. With those exotic high cheekbones and piercing blue eyes. With that smoky seductive voice that could persuade every man in a room to do what she wanted. A voice that convinced the judge to sign the paperwork that transferred that twenty-million-dollar account to her.

He was apologetic, almost sheepish, when I finally got in touch with him. He said he was still counting on me as part of the team at Fairburn, Crandall. But he had gotten to know Vivian over the past month and felt very comfortable with her. So he would let her remain the lead manager on his account. That meant she got all those big fees, for the account that I had worked so hard to capture.

I felt empty and trampled. All the anger, all the guilt and grief I had been feeling for weeks, I directed at Vivian. The more I watched her bounce her tight ass through our offices each day, the more I hated her. And I swore that someday I would make her pay.

# CHAPTER 2

THAT FAMILIAR RUSH OF POWER washed over me as I pushed open the heavy glass doors of Fairburn, Crandall the first week of the new year. The expensive antiques, darkened oil landscapes and gently-aged oriental rugs in our spacious reception area all screamed old money in a tasteful whisper. Floor-to-ceiling windows gave expansive views of downtown Hastings and the ice-rimmed river far below us, where a lone jogger, bundled up against the cold, pounded silently beside the gray water.

Shep Fairburn and Vince Crandall had started the firm over thirty years ago. Working for a major brokerage firm, the two of them had been restless, bored and tired of having other people tell them what to do. They quit their jobs and wheedled start-up money from family and friends. Big bets on a few excellent stock picks led to spectacular performance. When their faces hit the covers of business magazines, new money gushed in. Fairburn, Crandall gradually became one of the most respected wealth management firms in the Southeast.

The opportunity to work with the legendary Shep Fairburn had helped persuade me to move south to Hastings after Rolfe and I got married. Fortunately, most of my New York clients stuck with me after the move. And once we arrived, the Bradford family's standing in the community opened a lot of doors for me. So I had built quite an attractive customer base since I joined the firm, one that I was convinced put me in contention for the partnership.

This morning the office smelled faintly of lemon, that clean orderliness of hope that the first few days of January always offered up, when the holiday clutter was packed away and bold New Year's resolutions made a fresh start seem possible. The market even had a name for it -- the January effect -- when fresh investor optimism, the end of the previous year's tax selling, and new money flooding into retirement accounts often sent the stock market soaring.

I couldn't see January bringing much of a fresh start for me. A year ago Christmas had been an exuberant whirl of parties, a mad scramble to get ready for Santa. This holiday had been numbly endured, my only celebration a disastrous Christmas Eve dinner at Fontaine's. My resolution for the new year was to focus on work. Even though the odds were against me, I still desperately wanted the partnership. It was all I had left.

The investment committee members were already squeezed into the war room when I walked in, crowded around a chipped veneered conference table branded with the rings of countless coffee mugs. Shep sat at the head of the table with Vivian Sutherland in her usual spot to his right. Hardy Allenstone, Charlton Madison and Lyman Reedmon were seated on the far side of the table. I slipped into a chair beside Murphy Greeley, who had been a mentor to me when I first joined Fairburn, Crandall, a tiny oasis of support in a cut-throat firm.

"So what the hell is wrong with Bovender?" Shep slapped his palm against the arm of his chair, a gold cuff link peeking from the sleeve of his custom-made suit. In his late sixties, he was still an attractive man, with silver hair and a chiseled jaw that was just beginning to soften with age.

Bovender's stock price chart lit up the enormous wall-mounted flat screen monitor at the end of the room. For more than five years, Bovender's price had moved up as sharply as a mountain climber attacking K2. But in the past three months the price had plateaued, a desperate climber stumbling in place, low on oxygen.

"Murphy, this one is your baby. What do you think?" Shep asked.

Murphy pushed his heavy dark-rimmed glasses a little higher on his nose and rotated toward the screen. "It's fine," he said. "I'm expecting strong earnings this quarter. Nothing to worry about."

Shep scowled. "What about the rest of you? We have a huge position in this one. We can't afford to be wrong." A couple of missteps had caused our investment performance to slip last year, and we badly trailed both our benchmarks and our peers. A few clients had already pulled their money away from us. Shep restlessly roamed the halls at year end, pressuring all of us to bring in new business.

Charlton Madison looked up from the Wall Street Journal folded neatly in front of him. In his late fifties, slightly stocky from too many client lunches over the years, he had a loyal client base that allowed him to spend as much time on the golf course as he did managing portfolios. "The price softness is probably a good buying opportunity."

"Hardy, what do you think?" Shep asked.

Hardy Allenstone was hunched over his laptop, his handsome face bronzed from his annual Caribbean year-end holiday on the family sailboat. He was only half listening, multitasking as usual, his fingers moving quickly over the keyboard. He kept a privacy screen over his monitor, making the screen look a blurry gold to anyone seated beside him, designed to keep his neighbors on an airplane, or a train, or especially in one of our conference rooms, from seeing what he was doing. In his mid-forties, he was generally considered on the fast track to take over the firm once Shep retired. "I'm fine with Bovender," he mumbled, keeping his eyes on his monitor.

Vivian shot disapproving looks at Charlton and Hardy. "You're kidding, right? Bovender's screwed. We need to sell it all, right now."

Murphy gave me one of those "here we go again" glances, the corner of his mouth scrunched in that frustrated expression he so often had around Vivian. "And why is that?"

She arched her left eyebrow. "Because their main drug is going off patent next year. They're depending on their new drug to jumpstart earnings growth. But clinical trials aren't going well. They won't get FDA approval."

Murphy shook his head. "That's not true. I talked to management a few weeks ago. Everything is on track." Murphy had covered the company for years and had developed a close relationship with the CEO.

Vivian shook back her long blond hair as she reached for the keyboard. "What we need to buy is Hawthorne Medical," she said, bringing up Hawthorne's price chart on the big screen. "It's a small biotech company with a terrific pipeline. It has several drugs near final stages of approval."

"That's a good looking chart," Hardy said, looking at the screen. "How about their financials?"

"Hawthorne's not making money yet," Vivian said. "They're still in cash-burn stage, which is typical of start-up companies. But revenues will pop when they get approval for their new drug. It causes the body to regenerate cartilage. Just imagine the potential. Professional athletes could have their careers extended for years, pain-free. Aging baby boomers could keep on jogging or skiing or playing tennis, with no more hip or knee replacements."

"You think it will really work?" Lyman Reedmon asked. He was one of the oldest partners and had limped around the office for months after a botched knee replacement, putting off surgery on the second knee until the pain was almost unbearable.

"I'm sure of it." Vivian leaned toward him. "What would you have given not to go under the knife?"

"Just about anything," Lyman said.

"This could easily be a multi-billion dollar drug," Vivian said. "We've got to get in on it."

"I don't know." Hardy hesitated. "Hawthorne doesn't have any drugs already on the market. If this one isn't approved, they've got nothing."

"Bovender's our kind of stock," Murphy insisted. "Solid company. Good balance sheet. Our clients have made a lot of money in it."

"Bovender's not as solid as you think," Vivian said. "Debt has been going up for the past three years. And profit margins have been going down."

"What about that, Murph?" Shep asked.

Murphy ran an anxious hand through his faded red hair. "Bovender is making a lot of money. So maybe the profit margins have bounced around a bit. That's nothing to worry about."

"Maybe you need to take a closer look at the financials," Shep said. "Just to make sure we're on solid ground here."

Vivian snorted. "Murph wouldn't know what to do with a financial statement if it jumped up and gave him a lap dance."

Charlton, Murphy, Vivian and Hardy all started to talk at once, their voices escalating. Trying to get this group to agree was like herding cats. Team decisions were supposed to represent best ideas, the polished result of careful consideration and negotiation, an optimal solution eagerly supported by the group after disparate points of view were thoughtfully mulled and culled. Or at least, that's what they taught us in business school. But for our dysfunctional group, team decisions were often the opinion of whoever talked the loudest.

I tuned them out, absently fingering the gold charm bracelet I always wore on my left wrist, my thumb massaging the angular Eiffel Tower charm that Rolfe bought me during our honeymoon in Paris. The two of us had stood on the top level of the tower, arms wrapped around each other, mesmerized by the magical city that stretched out below us. We were so much in love and so sure that all our dreams were possible. That all we had to do...

"Robbie, what do you think?"

Shep's stern voice startled me out of my reverie. I hesitated, struggling to come up with a reasonable answer when I wasn't quite sure of the question.

Vivian jumped in. "It's probably not fair to put Robbie on the spot," she said. "After all, she's missed a lot of time from work in the past two months, coping with her *personal* issues. She probably hasn't even had time to think about Bovender."

I glanced up just in time to catch the sly smile that flickered at the corners of her mouth. She had been making jabs ever since the accident, trying to chip away at Shep's confidence in me. But this time her strategy backfired, giving me time to put together my response. "I appreciate your concern," I said quickly. "But actually, I've already sold all my Bovender. It was starting to look a bit top-heavy to me." I smiled innocently as her lips pressed into a tight line.

Murphy's eyes widened in disappointment. Usually we voted together in these meetings, and it was obvious he had been counting on me. "We can't dump this stock here," he insisted. "Our firm is one of the largest institutional holders of Bovender. If word gets out that we're selling, it will kill the stock price."

"I disagree," Vivian said. "There's plenty of liquidity in this name. Our traders can ease us out of it without impacting the market."

"Bovender fits our investment strategy," Murphy insisted, his cheeks flushed. "Hawthorne doesn't."

"My investment strategy is to pick stocks that win," Vivian snapped. "And Bovender just doesn't make the cut."

Murphy looked desperately around the room, seeking support. "I'm sticking with Bovender," he said. "We know this company. Its products. The management team. I refuse to put a speculative stock like Hawthorne in my clients' accounts. There's just too much risk."

"Man up and grow a pair, Murph," Vivian said. "Hawthorne's a winner. Bovender's going nowhere but down."

Shep frowned, his bushy eyebrows drawing close together. "So what's it going to be? Do we sell Bovender?"

The room was silent.

"Charlton, what do you think?" Shep asked.

Charlton's strategy was always to vote with the boss, and he was struggling to figure out which way Shep was leaning. "I guess I could trim a little Bovender."

"Lyman?"

Lyman's bald head glistened in the fluorescent light. "Sell the Bovender and buy Hawthorne."

"That's ridiculous," Murphy said, glaring at Lyman. "We don't know anything about Hawthorne."

Lyman shrugged. "Vivian thinks it's a good buy, and I trust her judgment."

"Hardy?"

"I'm fine with trimming Bovender," Hardy said, "but I need to dig more into Hawthorne before I buy that one."

Shep glanced back at the screen. "Let's take a closer look at both of these before we decide. Vivian, get us some more information on Hawthorne. Murph, you double check with all your sources about the FDA issue. I don't want Bovender to blow up on us."

The meeting dragged on as we went through several other names in the portfolio. It was close to noon when we finally finished. The other portfolio managers hurried from the room. I lingered behind, wanting to explain my position to Murphy. But Vivian was there first, leaning down, murmuring in his ear. "I tell you what, Murph," she said, her voice loud enough for Shep and me to hear. "I'll pick up some super glue for you when I'm out at lunch today."

He turned toward her, puzzled. "Super glue?"

"Sure. And if you can find your balls while I'm gone, I'll help you stick them on when I get back."

# Chapter 3

MURPHY WAS WAITING for me when I returned to the office with my double bacon cheeseburger and a large order of chili fries. January was the start of earnings season, a high-stress time when companies reported their fourth quarter and year-end results, and for the next few weeks I would need a lot of comfort food. Companies that beat Wall Street analysts' estimates could see their stock price soar. Those that missed, even by a penny, faced major downside risk. Getting our clients' portfolios correctly positioned before the earnings release meant the difference between beating our benchmarks and lagging painfully behind them.

"Thanks for having my back this morning, Robbie," Murphy said as he leaned against the door frame. "Really appreciate it."

"Sorry, Murph," I said, edging past him and setting the bag on my desk. The winter sun glared onto my computer monitor, reflecting back the sharp angles of my cheekbones and my spiky dark hair. I tugged at the short wisps at the nape of my neck, a fruitless attempt to stretch them longer. It would be years before my hair grew back to its regular length.

He settled into the chair across from me. "I can't believe you sold your Bovender. What were you thinking?"

The scent of grilled meat filled the room as I unwrapped my burger. "It just got too rich for me, Murph. Bovender's trading at forty times next year's earnings estimate. That's priced for perfection." I offered him a chili fry, but he shook his head. "And if Vivian's right, if they're having trouble getting that drug approved, then there's no way it's holding here."

"She's not right. I don't know where she got that information." He pulled a copy of *The Economist* off my desk and began to flip through it. "So how can I convince you to get back into Bovender? You know it's a great company."

"A great company is not necessarily a great stock," I mumbled, my mouth full. "Isn't that one of the first things you told me when I started here?" I pulled the pickles off my burger. "You know I like stocks with low valuations and solid dividends. Something you can count on. Comfortable. Dependable. Like a pair of elastic-waist sweatpants that still feel good even after that second pint of ice cream."

"But we've all made a lot of money in Bovender," he protested.

"Risk management, Murph. Buy low, sell high. I sold high."

He tossed the magazine back on my desk. "If Vivian's right, then I am completely screwed. I've got heavy concentrations of Bovender in all my accounts."

"Why don't you sell some? Lock in some profits?"

He leaned forward and rested his elbows on his knees. "My clients would have to pay huge capital gains taxes if I sold. If there's one thing they hate more than losses, it's stroking a big check to the IRS. I'd never hear the end of it." He curled his lip. "That woman is so irritating. She thinks she's so much smarter than the rest of us."

"She probably *is* smarter than the rest of us, Murph," I admitted reluctantly.

"Not any smarter than you," he said. "Both of you did stints on Wall Street. And you've both got that long string of initials after your name." He glanced toward the framed certificates on my office wall. Master of Business Administration. Chartered Financial Analyst. Certified Financial Planner. Both Vivian and I had invested a lot of time learning how to give our clients the very best financial advice.

He picked up my nameplate from my desk and slapped it restlessly against his palm. "Vivian told Shep I was a weak link. That I'm losing accounts and he should push me out." He gripped the nameplate so tightly that his knuckles turned white. "I can't let that happen. I'm too old to start over."

"That's ridiculous. You're a partner. You guys have been together a long time. He'd never do that."

"I don't know. I'm close to losing another big account. John Drake. He's been with me for over twenty years."

"What happened?"

He set the nameplate back on my desk and walked behind me to the window, staring out toward the snow-slicked streets below. "Drake had some losses in the market. Got cold feet and cancelled an around-the-world cruise that he'd planned to celebrate his fiftieth wedding anniversary. Sandra went ballistic. Insists he move the account."

"I'm so sorry, Murph."

Murph pounded the metal window frame. "The thing is, the guy's got millions. He could easily afford that cruise. But he's running scared. Afraid he'll lose all his money."

I poked at a thin slice of tomato sliding off my burger. "So what's the plan?"

"I'm taking them to the Winter Ball in February. Sandra is really looking forward to it. I'm hoping some steak and crab cakes will put her in a good mood. Give me a chance to win her back."

The Winter Ball was the most prestigious event on the charity carousel, that endless round of fundraisers where the wealthy greeted each other over and over throughout the year, giving generously to innumerable worthy causes. Fairburn, Crandall was sponsoring two tables for our best clients.

"I need to do some fence-mending of my own at the ball," I said.

"Oh, yeah?"

I nodded. "Nate Thornton, Fontaine's husband. He's furious with me."

"I thought you and the good doctor were best buddies."

"We were. But Nate hasn't talked to me since his account nose-dived in December. Won't return any of my calls." The chili fries had gotten cold. I tossed the last of them into the trash.

"How much did he lose?"

"Five million."

"Whoa. I can see why that might put him off his game. What happened?"

I swiveled around to face Murphy. "He had his money concentrated in a few high flyers his golf buddies kept bragging about. I'd been after him for months to sell and lock in profits, kept telling him that trees don't grow to the sky. But he wouldn't listen. Said there was plenty more upside. And now he blames me. Says if I hadn't been so distracted after the accident, I would have gotten him out of those stocks."

Murphy crossed his arms over his chest. "I'm sure you'll bring him around. He's been with you for a long time."

"I'd like to think so." I crumpled up my burger wrapper and wiped my greasy fingers. "But Vivian's been sniffing around the account. You know she can always smell blood in the water. If she pulls it away from me, there's no way I'm making partner. Not after what happened with Judge Edmonton."

He leaned back against the low filing cabinet under the window. "Nate would never move that account from you. Fontaine wouldn't let him."

I shook the ice in my cup, then sucked hard on the straw to pull up the last drops of liquid. "I'm not sure Fontaine could stop him. You know Nate can't resist a pretty face. But I tell you, if she steals that account..."

"Yes?"

I tossed my cup into the trash. "I swear I'll kill her."

# CHAPTER 4

FONTAINE THORNTON'S SEQUINED designer gown glittered in the soft light as she stood on the balcony of the Hastings Museum, looking down at the couples twirling on the crowded ballroom floor. The pulsating bass notes of the band rattled the stained glass windows of the domed ceiling above us. "Robbie, this is fantastic," she said. "I think it's our best crowd yet."

"Lots of rich people, all in a good mood, ready to spend money," I said, clinking my champagne glass against hers. "Congratulations, Madam Chairman. This year's Winter Ball will raise even more than last year's."

Fontaine had spent an entire year scrutinizing spreadsheets and checklists, twisting arms and calling in favors to bring in sponsors and donations. This year the ball targeted neonatal research. No one could hear Fontaine's descriptions of those tiny premature babies at the hospital without holding a hanky in one hand and their outstretched checkbook in the other.

"I'm just so glad the snow held off," she said. "There's another front coming through tonight. I was really worried we might have to cancel."

"Are you kidding me? Even Mother Nature wouldn't dare interfere with the Winter Ball."

Fontaine set her champagne flute on the balcony railing. "I'm a little worried about the live auction. I don't think the things we're selling are quite as glitzy as last year. You remember that bidding frenzy we had on cosmetic surgery. Brought in forty thousand for us."

I leaned over the railing to watch a smiling redhead dance enthusiastically, her arms swaying above her head. "Yes, I can see Annabelle Scotland's new boobs from here. Her husband obviously believes they were worth every penny."

Fontaine laughed and adjusted the diamond combs that sparkled in her dark hair. "I'm expecting our best seller tonight to be the Dardishay painting. He's one of the hottest artists in New York this season. I can't believe I got him to donate one of his pieces to us." She picked up her glass. "He's a bit of an acquired taste, though. What if this crowd doesn't like it? What if no one bids on it?"

"I'll bid on it," I assured her. "And so will everyone else. Now would you relax? Everything is just perfect."

"What would be perfect," she said, wrapping her fingers around the champagne stem, "would be for you and Nate to somehow make peace. This situation between the two of you is driving me crazy."

I shrugged. "Fontaine, you know I've been trying. But he won't take my calls. Won't return messages. I even tried camping out at his office, but he refused to see me. What else can I do? Should I sit in your driveway and throw rocks at the window to get his attention?"

She sighed. "That wouldn't help. He's turned absolutely paranoid. Upgraded our security system. Even got a stupid guard dog that does nothing but pee all over the kitchen floor."

"A guard dog? To protect him from me?" I stepped back from the railing. "My God, Fontaine, it's not like I'm stalking the guy. I'm not the enemy here."

"I know that, Robbie. And so does he. He knows he's the one who screwed up. He just doesn't want to admit it."

I tilted my glass to drain the last few drops of champagne. "So what do we do now? Any suggestions?"

"Try him again tonight. He knows how much the ball means to me. How hard I've worked to pull it all together. So I think he'll be in a more forgiving mood. After all, friends shouldn't let something like money come between them."

It was easy for her to think that. Fontaine's family had been wealthy for generations. But Nate came from a much scrappier background, long-suffering from the slow burn of lusting after things he could not afford. Fontaine and I met him when we were college sophomores and he was a struggling medical student working two jobs, desperate to hold onto his scholarships. Losing money was not something he could take lightly.

"I'll do my best."

"Good. I know you can fix this." She waved to a woman on the dance floor. "Oh, there's Leanne. She's our ticket chairman this year. I need to check with her on our final headcount." She gave me a hug. "Go take a look at the Dardishay. Let me know what you think."

I watched the crowd for a few minutes after she left, then headed down the spiral staircase to the main floor. Halfway down I heard a sharp, accusing voice. "You didn't really think you could get away with this, did you?"

I peered over the railing. Vivian stood at the bottom of the steps, wearing a shimmering coppery silk dress with a deep V neckline that dipped almost to her navel.

"It was an honest mistake, Vivian. No harm meant," Murphy said. He stood close beside her, his face flushed.

I flattened myself against the wall. There was no way I would step in between those two. They had been open enemies ever since Bovender's earnings release in mid-January, when the company announced a delay in FDA approval for its new drug. The stock immediately plunged thirty-five percent.

Murphy kept buying as the stock dropped lower. Shep obviously was not on board. He camped out in Murph's office, door closed, their angry voices zinging through the thin walls. The stock finally began to scrape its way back, rallying up five percent one day, four percent the next, gaining traction. Several of the portfolio managers followed Murphy's lead and jumped in, thinking the worst was past, convinced it was a great buying opportunity.

But it was only a dead cat bounce. Suddenly the stock went down, then up, then down again, quivering like a screaming bungee jumper, making lower highs and lower lows. The stock couldn't break through resistance on the upside. And it couldn't hold support on the downside. With that kind of price chart, no prudent investor would come near it. Nobody wanted to catch that falling knife.

It was a disaster for our firm, one that could put a serious dent in our year-end bonuses. Everyone was angry, especially Vivian, who kept reminding us that she told us to sell the stock.

Murph's voice now floated up the spiral steps as he pleaded with Vivian. "Listen, I can fix this. First thing Monday."

"It's much too late for that," she said. "You really screwed yourself this time. When Shep hears about this, you'll be tossed out on that fat ass of yours. And it will be long overdue."

"Don't do it, Vivian. I'm warning you."

"Just try to stop me." Her curls bounced against her shoulders as she stomped down the hallway.

I waited before I started back down, giving Murphy enough time to move away. But he was still at the bottom step, tightly gripping the wrought iron railing. "Vivian spreading peace and love?" I quipped.

He started at my voice and glanced up, grimacing. "You heard that?"

"Are you kidding? Everybody within five miles heard it. The two of you weren't exactly whispering."

He took off his heavy glasses and massaged the bridge of his nose. "It was nothing. Just a misunderstanding."

"Still arguing about Bovender?"

"Something like that."

"It's been a tough situation, Murph. I'm really sorry."

He polished his glasses on his sleeve, then put them back on. "Don't be," he said as he squinted through the thick lenses. "These things just take time. It'll all work out." He tugged on the lapels of his tuxedo. "And now, if you'll excuse me, I think I need a drink."

As he walked off, I headed across the hall to the silent auction, a maze of tables loaded with designer handbags, shoes and accessories. The frenetic din of women discovering new treasures from Christian Dior, Fendi and Prada reminded me of market day in Marrakesh.

I wandered along the display tables, stopping to put in a bid on a striped twill Hermes scarf in royal blue and a Fendi python clutch bag too small to hold much more than my car keys and a credit card. Then I heard a familiar laugh. Nate stood several aisles away, in front of a big display of Ferragamo oxfords, chatting with several doctors from his practice. Threading my way through the shoppers, I walked up behind him and put my hand on his arm. "Nice to see you, Nate."

He stopped in mid-sentence and turned slightly at my touch. Realizing it was me, he scowled and swatted my hand away, then turned back to his conversation.

So much for Nate being in a forgiving mood. But this was the closest I had gotten to him in a month. I had to keep trying. "Fontaine's done a great job on the ball," I said. "I know you're proud of her."

He rattled the ice in his glass. "Leave me alone."

"Come on, Nate. Let's talk about this."

"You want to talk?" The drink in his hand was obviously not his first of the evening. His breath smelled strongly of bourbon, and he seemed a bit unsteady on his feet. "Then talk to my lawyer. You cost me a shit load of money, and I plan to sue you and Fairburn, Crandall to get back every penny."

My face went hot as the people around us leaned in, finding us much more interesting than the Burberry scarves on the table behind me. "You don't mean that."

"The hell I don't. I pay you all those big fees to manage my money, and you just make it disappear. Obviously, you don't know what you're doing."

I knew I should walk away, wait until he sobered up, try to reason with him when it was just the two of us. But his ranting made me angry. The four of us had been best friends for years. He and Fontaine had been Jason's godparents. And now he was ready to destroy my career with a few careless words. "Nate, you are such an asshole."

His face turned red and he took a step toward me. Murphy suddenly appeared and grabbed my arm, pushing his body between me and Nate. "Robbie, that's enough."

I pulled back, struggling to get free. "He's being a total jerk about this."

"And so are you," he said, tightening his grip. "Look around. Everyone's watching. Do you really want to continue this conversation? Now walk away, and let me handle this."

Nate and I glared at each other, neither wanting to back down. But I had a lot more to lose. I turned away and made my way through the crowd, hearing people whisper my name. Everyone would be talking about this disaster by the end of the evening. Needing a place to hide, I headed for the bar. The cold granite felt good to my trembling hands. "A chardonnay, please."

A sultry voice beside me said, "Now that was entertaining."

I took a deep breath. "Vivian," I said calmly, turning toward her.

"Quite a performance. If Murphy hadn't stepped in, I think we would have had to call security."

"I was handling it."

"Sure you were." She turned to the bartender. "Gray Goose martini, straight up, with olives." She reached for the bowl of smoked almonds. "I bet you think Murph is trying to calm Nate down right now, to save the account for you. Am I right?"

"Something like that."

She shook her head. "Nope. Nate has been complaining about you for weeks. Shep has promised him a new advisor. Murphy's trying to stake his claim."

"Shep wouldn't do that to me. And neither would Murphy."

"You are so naïve." The bartender brought our drinks. "The firm comes first. Shep would never let you screw up a big account."

"I suppose you're trying to get Nate's account, too."

She picked up the skewer of olives and carefully pulled one off in her mouth. "Of course. I would love to have Nate for a client. He's incredibly sexy. When he smiles, he gets the cutest little crinkly lines around those beautiful green eyes."

"That's my best friend's husband you're talking about," I said, my voice rising.

"Oh, come on, Robbie," Vivian said, her finger circling the rim of her glass. "Don't tell me you never slept with him."

There was a time when I desperately wanted to. When Fontaine and I were both in love with the same tall, handsome medical student. But back then Fontaine's father was a senior executive at a large, prominent company. She had vacation homes and trust funds. My dad died when I was fifteen, leaving behind a large family, a small life insurance policy and a long list of debts. It was no surprise when Nate chose her. "I would never do that to my best friend."

"But you've wanted to. I can see it in your face." She sipped her martini. "He's already slept with half the women in Hastings. What's one more?"

"That's a vicious lie." It was true that Nate always tried to charm the panties off every woman he met, but Fontaine's friends had learned to brush off his teasing advances as just part of his quirky personality.

She chewed another olive. "This is all your fault, you know. You've been hiding out in your office for the past two months. Nate's is probably not the only account you've screwed up."

I wanted to lash out at her, say something absolutely scathing, but I figured I had probably disgraced myself enough for one night. Determined to maintain control, I took a long, slow swallow of wine.

"Get over it, Robbie. You're not the only one with problems. I lost my husband, too."

"You divorced your husband," I said, my voice clipped. "Mine was killed in a car crash."

She shrugged and tipped her glass to her lips. "Same thing. My sheets are just as cold."

"You heartless bitch." I got right in her face, close enough to see tiny pores clogged with makeup. "You'd better stay away from Nate. And I don't believe you about Murphy. He would never steal a client from me."

She set the glass on the bar, then dabbed at her fingers with the cocktail napkin. "You keep telling yourself that. I'm warning you, you can't trust him."

"And I should trust you?"

"No. But at least I never pretended to be your friend." She crumbled the napkin and tossed it carelessly on the bar. "You heard that Shep's announcing the new partner next week?"

I tried to keep my expression blank as I picked up my wine. I hadn't heard about the announcement.

"Oops, looks like someone didn't get the memo," she said. "So sorry. Guess that means you didn't make the cut."

I stood at the bar for a long time after she walked away. No way could I stand Vivian's smug face gloating at me day after day if she got the partnership instead of me. I would have to leave Fairburn, Crandall and start over. I just hoped I would still have some clients left after word got around about my fight with Nate.

The gong sounded for dinner. I headed toward the banquet hall, gleaming like a miniature Versailles, all mirrors and gold trim with elaborate crystal chandeliers hanging high overhead. Arched windows framed the snow that had started to fall outside onto the carefully manicured boxwoods. Round tables covered with heavy white linen tablecloths filled the room, accented with centerpieces of red rosebuds floating in crystal bowls.

Our clients had already gathered around the Fairburn, Crandall tables. I spotted Lydia Kensington, her silver hair glinting in the soft light. She was the second wife and widow of Senator Augustus Kensington, whose family money had been managed for years by Pinkley, Reese. Max Reese expected that situation to continue after the Senator's death, but Lydia complained that he treated her like a feeble old lady who couldn't possibly have any good ideas about how to manage her money. It didn't take a lot of convincing for her to move the account to me. "Lydia, so good to see you. We're still on for lunch on Tuesday, right?"

"Absolutely. It's on my calendar." She turned to the man standing beside her. "Robbie, I'd like you to meet Gus Kensington, the Senator's grandson."

"So glad you could join us," I said, shaking hands. He was tall and thin, about forty, striking rather than handsome, with a long narrow nose and an angular chin. His thick dark hair was tousled about in the carefree, windblown look I knew could only be achieved with a generous application of hair product and a good bit of digital dexterity. "You look so much like your grandfather."

"You knew the Senator?" he asked.

"No, but Lydia has a wonderful portrait of him hanging in her living room. The resemblance is amazing."

I then maneuvered around a very protective Vivian to greet Judge Edmonton and his wife. "Judge, Barbara, so nice to see you."

"Robbie, you're looking wonderful," the judge said. "I've been worried about you." He lowered his voice. "I can't imagine what you've been going through."

"Thank you. It's been a pretty tough time." Vivian's expression was hostile as I put my arm around Barbara. "But your wife has helped to cheer me up."

He nodded. "Yes, she told me the two of you were back to your spa routine. I'm glad to hear it."

Shep motioned for us to take our seats. Hardy and Charlton joined their guests at one table, while Shep, Murphy and I anchored the other. The waiters began to circulate, pouring wine, setting down salads. "Where's Nate?" Shep asked as Fontaine walked up.

"He had to take a call from a patient," she said. "I'm not sure how much longer he'll be. Don't wait for him." She sat beside me and angrily attacked her salad, chopping the leafy green arugula into tiny pieces. "There's no patient," she whispered, leaning toward me. "I told him he couldn't come in here until he sobered up. I heard about what he said to you. We had a huge fight about it. I'm so mad I could spit."

"We probably both said things we regret."

"Maybe. But the good news is that Deidre Chappell wants to talk to you. She said that anyone with the guts to call Nate an asshole at the Winter Ball is exactly the sort of strong-willed person she wants to handle her money."

"Fontaine, I apologize. I never should have said that."

"He deserved it." She stabbed a cherry tomato. "With any luck, he'll choose bourbon over dinner. Which means we probably won't see him for the rest of the evening."

That was good news. The last thing I needed was another confrontation with Nate, especially in front of my boss.

But Fontaine was wrong. Midway through the entrees, Nate ambled up to our table, genially slapping Murphy on the back, shaking hands with Shep.

"Good to see you, Nate," Shep said. "We were afraid you were going to miss dinner. Here, sit down."

Nate eyed the empty chair, reluctant to sit beside me.

"Sit down," Fontaine said in a tight voice. "Don't make a scene."

He reluctantly settled into his seat. The waiter positioned his entrée in front of him, then poured wine. Nate turned toward me. "My wife says I was too rough on you. That I should apologize."

"It's fine, Nate. We'll talk about it another time."

He twisted toward Fontaine. "She's said it's fine. I knew you were making too much out of this."

The waiter reached for his salad plate. "Hey, buddy, I'm not finished with that," Nate said, throwing up his hand. It collided with his wine glass, which wobbled crazily. I reached out to catch it but was too late. The glass fell over. Blood-red liquid splashed onto my plate, the white tablecloth, and into my lap.

"You idiot." Fontaine jumped up and blotted the liquid with her napkin. Lydia and Barbara rushed over to help. Shep signaled for the waiter.

"Sorry," Nate mumbled. "It was an accident."

"Sure it was." Fontaine tossed her wine-stained napkin on the table and reached for a clean one. "You've embarrassed me enough for one night. Get out. I don't want you here."

Nate shrugged, then headed for the lobby. Hardy and Charlton glanced over from the next table, trying to figure out what had caused all the excitement.

"Robbie, I'm so sorry," Fontaine said. "I never thought he'd do anything like this."

"Don't worry about it." I pushed back from the table. "Excuse me, folks," I said with a forced grin. "I need to take care of this."

Fontaine followed me to the ladies room, grabbing some club soda from the waiter as we passed. She wet a napkin and dabbed at the stain.

"Fontaine, stop. It's not doing any good. The dress is ruined." I looked in the mirror at the red splotches across my stomach. "I'm going home. Would you please say my good-byes for me?"

"Don't leave. We haven't even started the live auction."

"I can't stay here like this. I look like I've been in a knife fight."

Her nostrils twitched as she fought back tears. "I swear I'll kill Nate for this."

"It was an accident. You know that. Now come on and walk me out. You need a few minutes to calm down."

We headed for the cloakroom. The coat check girl had disappeared. I walked behind the counter and flipped through the racks of coats until I found mine. "Don't worry about this," I said, giving Fontaine a hug. "Just enjoy the auction and make lots of money for the hospital. I'll call you tomorrow."

Just then we heard a loud thump and a moan. "What was that?" Fontaine asked. "Did somebody fall?"

We walked behind the racks and down the deserted hallway, past file cabinets and cardboard boxes stacked almost to the ceiling, stirring up tiny whirls of dust. I pushed my fingers hard against my nose as I fought back a sneeze. The moaning was louder now, coming from the storage room. Fontaine opened the door and stopped cold. "Un-fucking-believable."

I peered over her shoulder. Vivian was pushed against the back wall, her long copper-colored dress bunched up around her waist, the bodice slipped down to her elbows. Nate, his back to us, was vigorously kneading her breasts, pink nipples peeking out between his fingers. His mouth sucked at hers, swallowing her moans.

I grabbed Fontaine's arm. "Let's get out of here," I whispered.

She pulled away from me. "Give me your phone."

"Why?" I rummaged in my purse. "You calling your divorce lawyer?"

"Even better." She grabbed up the phone and snapped a picture.

Startled by the flash, Nate whirled toward us.

Fontaine's thumbs moved quickly over the screen, then she tossed the phone back to me. "Go home, Robbie. I can take care of this. I'll call you tomorrow."

"Fontaine, let me help."

She shook her head as she pushed me toward the lobby. "I've got to take care of this myself."

§§§

The snow fell harder as I drove home. My hands tight on the wheel, I struggled to see through the blurred windshield. Finally upstairs in my bedroom, I slipped out of my wine-splashed dress and tossed it on a chair. Crawling beneath the covers, I tossed fitfully in the darkness, the image of Vivian and Nate burned on my retinas. I was almost asleep when my ring tone shattered the silence. "Hello?" I said, fumbling for the phone.

"Robbie."

"Fontaine, what's wrong?" I mumbled, my eyes still closed.

"You've got to get back here right away. I need you."

"Back where?" I yawned.

"To the museum."

I peered at the clock, glowing red in the darkness, trying to make my eyes focus. "It's two in the morning. What are you doing at the museum?"

"It's Vivian," she said. "She's dead."

# CHAPTER 5

GRABBING MY COAT AND BOOTS, I headed outside. My BMW was covered with four inches of new snow. I brushed off the windows and climbed inside.

Fontaine had hung up the phone without giving me any details. I prayed she wasn't the one who killed Vivian. She had been so angry when we walked in on them. At least Nate had seemed embarrassed, jerking up his pants once he spotted us. Vivian just stood there, the light from the hallway illuminating her defiant grin.

Mounded snow covered everything as I drove down the deserted streets of my neighborhood, giving new shapes to parked cars and boxwood hedges, making familiar things seem strange, transforming the ordinary into the unrecognizable. The beaming lights of the all-night pharmacy a few blocks ahead were a welcome landmark.

Finally I reached the museum. It looked so different from the sparkling venue of a few hours before, when twinkling strands outlined bare tree branches and low path lights illuminated the front walkway with giant poker-chip rounds of white. Now the front of the building was dark and deserted. Only the security lights were on, casting pale shadows around the entrance.

I circled around to the back. The caterer's van was parked at the loading dock, its rear doors open, boxes of liquor and wine stacked to one side. About fifteen cars were clustered near the museum's rear entrance. I drove toward the far right, where I could see the flashing blue lights of police cars.

A small group of partygoers had gathered, women with coats wrapped around their long dresses, men shivering in tuxedos. I spotted Fontaine standing a bit apart from the crowd, talking to a policeman. Tiny shards of swirling sleet collected on my eye lashes as I walked toward her.

"Thank God you're here," she said, hugging me. "This is just a nightmare."

"Where is she?"

Fontaine took my hand and pulled me through the crowd. Officers had strung up police tape and were setting up a tarp to shield Vivian's body from the snow. It was obviously too late to preserve a pristine crime scene. Footprints and tire tracks went off in all directions.

Vivian was sprawled on her back, one arm flung up into the shrubbery beside her, the other bent at the elbow, fingers tucked behind her ear. The halogen lights of the utility poles gave her lips a bluish cast. Blond curls fell in a wet tangle into the dark puddle around her head. Her eyes were closed, black mascara streaked across a bruised welt on her cheek. A jagged smudge in the center of her forehead, like a smoky Ash Wednesday cross made by the thumb of a zealous priest, marked where a bullet had ripped into her skull.

Around us people were pointing and gesturing at the dead body. Always stylishly dressed and perfectly coiffed, Vivian would have hated being stared at like this, bloody and bruised, so far from perfect. I felt guilty looking at her body in its shroud of snow. Yet I stayed, stuck here with all the others, mesmerized, unable to turn away.

"What happened?" I asked.

"I don't know. I came outside to look for Nate and I found her," she began.

A woman next to us turned and edged in slightly, eager for ghoulish details, tilting her head like a robin listening for a worm deep beneath the earth.

"Let's not talk about this here." I took Fontaine's arm and led her away from the crowd. "Your teeth are chattering. Let's get in my car."

She huddled on the front seat, knees pulled up tight. I started the engine and turned up the heat. "So tell me what happened after I left."

Tears ran down her cheeks. "Nate and I had a terrible fight. We said such horrible things to each other."

I pulled some tissues from the glove compartment and handed them to her. "Where is he now?"

"I don't know." She blotted her eyes. "I kept looking for him, but he disappeared. I guess he went home."

I ran my thumb along the stitching on the leather-covered steering wheel as the question hung heavy between us. There was no gentle way to ask. Finally I just blurted out, "Did you do this, Fontaine? Did you shoot her?"

Her chin dropped in surprise as she twisted toward me. "I can't believe you would ask me that."

A policeman knocked on my window. I lowered the glass a few inches. The wind swirled in, cold enough to make my teeth hurt. "Yes?"

"We're moving everyone into the museum."

I nodded and drove closer to the rear entrance. Fontaine winced as she left the warmth of the car and stepped into the snow, which completely covered her delicate high-heeled evening sandals. I was glad I was wearing my boots and heavy coat.

The policemen herded everyone back to the museum ballroom. The mirrors and gold gilt were still there, but no gleaming silverware, no roses floating in crystal bowls. The white linen tablecloths had been stripped off and tossed in a crumpled heap on the floor. Most of the tables had been broken down and rolled over to a corner, ready for storage. The few that remained looked naked and thin, their particle-board tops stained with years of use. Folding chairs had been stacked on carts and wheeled to the side.

Some men grabbed a few chairs and set them up so we all could sit down. Fontaine and I sat with Leanne Townsend and Annabelle Scotland, both of whom were crying. Leanne's husband patted her halfheartedly on the back. Annabelle's stared stoically at the floor, his legs stretched straight out in front of him.

The catering staff gathered around the bar. I recognized the young bartender who had served me chardonnay. He was in a serious conversation with a young woman whose dark hair was liberally streaked with purple, his hand on her shoulder, shaking his head.

Fontaine pulled out a fresh tissue and blew her nose. "I'm sorry you missed the auction. The Dardishay was a big hit. It went for fifty thousand."

"That's terrific."

"The whole auction was great," she said, sounding more cheerful. "We raised a lot of money tonight, more than I thought we would. The most ever, in fact." She looked out the window toward the flashing lights. "But it's ruined now. All anyone will ever remember is Vivian's murder."

A policeman walked in, a gun strapped to his waist, his heavy black duty belt weighted down with handcuffs, radio, and baton. "Folks, we need to ask all of you a few questions. Several detectives are set up in the next room. We'll move this process along as quickly as we can. Once we've taken your statement, you can leave."

He led a small group of us toward the room that had housed the silent auction. The designer merchandise had been cleared out, the maze of tables dismantled. A few tables and chairs were set up for interviews. "Wait for me," Fontaine said. "Don't leave before I'm done."

"I'll be here."

I headed to the nearest table on the left. The man seated there was built like a football player, with wide shoulders and thick biceps that strained the sleeves of his navy blazer. The wire-rimmed reading glasses balanced low on his nose seemed much too delicate for his rugged bronze face. "Please sit down," he said, his voice deep. "I'm Detective Gutierrez. Your name, please."

"Robbie Bradford."

He flipped to a clean page in his spiral notebook and jotted down my name, then peered at me over the top of his glasses. "You were here at the ball tonight?"

"Yes."

His eyes ran across my jeans, boots, and heavy coat. "You didn't wear that?" he said.

At first I thought he might be joking, but his serious expression convinced me otherwise. "No, of course not. I spilled wine on my dress at dinner and had to leave the ball early."

"What time was that?"

"About nine-thirty, I guess."

"Anyone with you?"

"No. I came alone."

"Can anyone verify what time you got home? Spouse? Neighbors? Friends?"

His staccato questions made me uneasy. My previous experience with policemen had been the few times I'd been pulled over for speeding, when a ready smile and a bit of flirting convinced them to let me off with a warning. Detective Gutierrez seemed resistant to my charms. Folding my hands nervously in my lap, I said, "I doubt it. The roads were horrible. I didn't see anyone else out on my street. And I live alone."

"Why did you come back?"

The folding chair was uncomfortable. I shifted my weight before I answered. "Fontaine Thornton called and asked me to come. She told me Vivian was dead."

"You knew the deceased?"

"We work together. At Fairburn, Crandall. Our firm sponsored tables at dinner tonight for some of our clients." I shuddered as I pictured her lying in the snow, that ragged hole oozing in her forehead.

"I'll need the names and contact information of everyone at the tables."

"Of course."

He made a few more notes, then pulled off his glasses and tossed them carelessly on the table. A puffy pink scar ran from the edge of his dark, close-cropped hair, out toward his eyebrow. It gave him a sinister look, marring an otherwise attractive face. "Tell me about Ms. Sutherland. How did she get along with her co-workers?" He rested his arms on the narrow table and leaned in toward me, his solid body uncomfortably close. If he was trying to intimidate me, it was working.

I settled back into my chair, trying to put more space between us. "Fine."

"No problems? Arguments? Disagreements?"

I thought of Vivian and Murphy arguing at the foot of the spiral staircase. And my own heated discussion with Vivian at the bar. "Our firm is very competitive. There are always disagreements."

"Such as?"

I quickly backtracked. "Nothing specific that I remember. Certainly nothing that could have gotten her killed."

"What about tonight? Did she have any problems with anyone here? Anything unusual happen?"

Across the room Fontaine chatted with another detective. I wondered if she had told him about the storage room. But the odds of her sharing that incredibly embarrassing story seemed pretty slim. "Nope," I said, shaking my head, keeping my tone casual. "I can't think of anything."

"You sure about that?"

My face felt hot. "It sounds like you think someone here tonight had something to do with this, and that's just ridiculous," I said, my voice rising. "She was mugged in the parking lot. This is hardly the safest part of town." Years ago, Hastings had briefly been known as the murder capital of the South, mainly due to its position near Interstate 95, which made it an attractive midpoint for drug traffickers running product up and down the East Coast. An aggressive new police chief had cleaned things up, pushing crime rates down. But a lot of rough neighborhoods still were considered off-limits after dark, including one only a few blocks from the museum.

"Calm down, Ms. Bradford," he said. "We're just trying to get all the facts."

"But you can't possibly think..."

"We don't know what to think," he interrupted me. "Which is why I'm asking these questions." He leaned back in his chair and crossed his arms over his chest. His dark brown eyes bored into mine. "There's nothing else you can tell me?"

I stared back, meeting his gaze, determined not to blink. "No. Nothing."

He frowned, then put his glasses on and scratched something into his notebook. "Thank you, Ms. Bradford. If we have any more questions, we'll contact you later."

"So I can leave?"

He nodded. "Yes."

A middle-aged black man in a heavy overcoat walked up as I reached the doorway. "I'm looking for Mrs. Thornton," he said.

"She's over there." I pointed to the far corner, where Fontaine was still sitting at her interview table.

A policeman stopped him. "You can't go in there. We're talking to witnesses."

He pulled a business card from his pocket and handed it to the officer. "I am Joshua Randolph, Mrs. Thornton's attorney." Pushing past us, he crossed over to Fontaine, bent down and whispered in her ear. She stood up and the two of them headed toward me.

"You called your dad?" I asked.

She nodded. Having a father who was the CEO of a major corporation had its advantages, including being able to get an attorney out of bed in the middle of a snowstorm.

"Do you want me to come home with you?" I asked.

She shook her head. "Mr. Randolph is coming home with me now. My parents are already there. They'll help me sort this whole thing out." She gave me a hug. "I'll talk to you tomorrow."

We walked together to the parking lot, dark except for the bright lights that still illuminated the murder scene. Fontaine and her lawyer drove off. I waited while Vivian, surrounded by strangers, was loaded into an ambulance. Much as I had disliked her, even she deserved a familiar face to keep vigil at a time like this.

A man stepped out of the shadows, bundled up in a heavy jacket, his hood pulled tight around his face. I tensed, suspicious, and glanced toward the few remaining police cars, ready to call out for help. He threw the hood back as he got closer. "Robbie, it's Luddy. Can I ask you a few questions?"

He was thinner than I remembered, his chin jutting out sharply, his cheek bones prominent. Although he was close to my age, his eyes made him look older, dark cynical eyes that had seen a lot of the world and decided it was not an especially good place.

I shook my head. "It's late. I'm going home."

He walked along beside me. "I'm reporting on this murder. You worked with Vivian Sutherland?"

"That's right." I opened my car door.

"Fontaine Thornton found the body?"

"Right again. You have all the answers already. You don't need me." I got in the car and pulled the door toward me.

He grabbed it before it closed. "Robbie, I'm just doing my job. I really want to talk to you."

"That's not going to happen." I started the car and reached for my seatbelt. "Would you please let me shut the door?"

He kept his hand on the door frame and leaned toward me, his eyes plaintive. "Robbie, when will things be all right between us?"

"I don't think they ever will be." I jerked the door from his hand and slammed it shut. My tires crunched through the crusty snow as I drove out of the lot and headed toward home.

# CHAPTER 6

THE POUNDING WAS SHARP AND REPETITIVE, like quick blows of a hammer. I wrapped a pillow over my ears and burrowed deeper into the covers, but I could still hear it. I groaned and opened my eyes a slit. Light seeped in at the edges of the draperies.

A voice called my name, and the pounding on my front door started again. I reluctantly rolled out of bed, peering through the snow-coated waxy leaves of the ancient magnolia tree towering just outside my window. An unfamiliar car was parked at the curb out front.

My jeans and sweatshirt from last night were tossed casually on a chair. I pulled them back on and walked slowly down two flights of stairs to the broad central hallway, blocked with rows of scaffolding and sheets of heavy plastic. Barefooted, I picked my way carefully to the front door, trying to avoid stray nails and loose bits of plaster. "Who is it?" I called.

"Detectives Gutierrez and Caldor," a voice said. "From last night. Can we come in? We need to talk to you."

I was in no mood for company. I had gotten home only a few hours before.

"Ms. Bradford, can we come in?"

I wanted to say no, and hesitated long enough that he said in a loud voice, "Ms. Bradford, are you there?"

"You can't get through this way," I called out. "I'm remodeling. Come around the back."

I moved through the construction toward the kitchen, rising to my tiptoes as the cold tile chilled my feet. The two men rounded the corner of the house as I opened the back door. They stomped vigorously on the back stoop, knocking snow off their shoes. "Ms. Bradford, this is Detective Caldor," Gutierrez said. "We have a few questions about last night."

I moved aside to let them enter, then gestured toward the barstools at the granite island. "You woke me up," I said, reaching for the coffee beans and grinder. "I can't answer any questions without coffee. Want some?"

"Sure," Caldor said, giving me a friendly grin. He pulled off his wool cap, revealing blond hair cropped so short that I could see his scalp. He looked incredibly young, no more than eighteen, although I figured he must be older than that to be a detective. He unbuttoned his heavy jacket and hung it on the back of the barstool.

"Here, let me take that," I said. "Detective Gutierrez, can I take your coat?"

He hesitated, then handed it to me. "Thanks." He was much taller than I had realized, several inches over six feet. He looked tired, the skin under his eyes puffy, making him seem a bit vulnerable, more approachable than when he questioned me so curtly a few hours before. But he still looked very professional, wearing a fresh white shirt and striped tie with his navy blazer. In last night's jeans and sweatshirt, without any makeup and sporting a raging case of bed head, I felt like a slob.

The beans swirled noisily in the grinder. Usually that was a cheerful sound, but today it was the perfect trigger to a headache. I dumped the grounds in the coffee maker and leaned back against the counter. The water bubbled and hissed as the dark brown liquid filled the glass pot.

Gutierrez casually walked across the kitchen to the sunroom, scrutinizing the stone fireplace, the expansive windows, the heavy crown molding at the ceiling, as focused as an interested buyer ready to open closets and ask about storage space. "Nice house."

"Thanks."

He glanced into the backyard at the snow-covered flagstone stacked up for my new patio. "Mighty big house for just one person."

He was right, of course. The house was too big for me -- three floors, five bedrooms, six baths, an enormous dining room, two front parlors. Plus the kitchen and sunroom. "I got a great deal on it. Just couldn't resist. You know how soft the real estate market has been."

Buying the house was probably a mistake. I always tell my clients not to make any big changes when they are going through major life events, things like retirement or the death of a spouse. Take things slowly, I tell them. Let yourself adjust to the changes before you sell the house or move to a different city.

Of course, it's easy to give other people good advice. But when you are the one staring into the abyss of confusion, trying to make sense of the scattered jumble of your former life, it's difficult to be so rational. Every room of my former house had taunted me with memories of Rolfe and Jason, of the happy life that was gone forever. I had to make a fresh start.

"Must be costing you a lot in repairs, though," Gutierrez said. "Looks like water damage. Pipes must have burst."

I followed his glance to the brown stains on the ceiling. "It was an old mansion. Dates back to the 1920's. This was quite a fashionable part of town back then." Over the years, the grand old houses had deteriorated as their residents moved to the suburbs. The area was now in the early stages of gentrification, a mixture of single family homes and duplexes, with a smattering of offices for doctors and lawyers. "It was converted into student housing for City University in the seventies. Unfortunately, they didn't take very good care of it." I knew better than Gutierrez that this house was a wreck. He had not seen the holes in the plaster walls, or the beautiful oak staircase that had been gouged by racing skateboards.

Fontaine had dragged me to it, weeks after the accident, when I was so depressed that I could barely lift my head from the pillow and she was desperate to get me out of the house. Her historical society was thinking of purchasing it, but she quickly reconsidered after a cursory inspection. We had stood in the front hallway, staring up at the beautiful stained glass windows at the top of the landing. "It's too far gone," she said. "The roof leaks. It needs new heating and electrical systems. And half the windows are cracked."

All those things were true. And if I had been my usual analytical, logical, rational self, I would have agreed with her and walked away. The house was terribly damaged. It had had its heart ripped out. But then, so had I. It called out to me, one lost soul to another. I thought maybe we could heal each other. The seller quickly accepted my lowball bid.

I filled three mugs and set them on the island. "Cream or sugar?" I asked.

"Just black," they both said.

I leaned against the counter across from them, my hands curled around the hot mug, one foot tucked behind my leg. The coffee was too hot to drink. I held it close, the comforting steam swirling into my nose and eyes, softening the tight pain in my head.

"I understand you and Ms. Sutherland had an argument last night," Gutierrez said, picking up his mug. "Funny you didn't mention it."

Nothing like getting right to the point. I had given them coffee. There should have been a few niceties first, a little chatting, talking about the weather. Not this straight shot to the details. "Not that I recall."

"We have a witness. Says the two of you were fighting about a client."

I thought about that a minute. Nobody was around when I was talking to Vivian. Except the bartender, eagerly hovering, refilling drinks, bringing us bowls of mixed nuts. He must have been listening to our conversation. "*Fight* is much too strong a word. We had a discussion." I sipped my coffee. It was still too hot, burning my throat as I forced it down.

"About Dr. Thornton, is that right?"

"Among other things."

He pushed aside the heavy plastic hanging from the doorway and peered at the scaffolding in the dining room. "Is Dr. Thornton your largest account?"

I shook my head. "Not the largest, no."

"But a relatively important one?"

"All my clients are important to me."

There was the slightest suggestion of a grin. "Good answer." He then came back toward the island, examining the stainless steel appliances, the decorative ceramic backsplash, the Mexican tile floor. "You get paid on commission, right?"

I shook my head. "Used to be that way, years ago. But too many brokers were tempted to churn accounts, buying and selling just to generate commission income, rather than focusing on the clients' overall financial needs. Now most advisors charge a fee based on assets under management. We benefit from the quality of our decisions, not the quantity. The more I can grow my clients' money, the more I get paid. As they say, win-win."

"Assets under management," he said slowly. "So I guess that means if you lost the doctor's account, you would be managing fewer assets. Is that right?"

"Yes."

"So that would mean lower fee income for you. Which is never good. Especially when you have a lot of expenses. Like this house."

I puzzled over his words. "I don't understand exactly where you're going with..." Then I slammed my mug down so hard that coffee splashed over the sides, onto the black granite. "You think I killed Vivian? To keep her from getting Nate's account?"

He glanced at me, his eyebrows raised. "It's a possibility."

"Seriously?" I stared first at Gutierrez, then at Caldor, who kept his eyes down as he scribbled in his spiral notepad. "That's ridiculous. People in my business lose accounts all the time. We don't kill because of it."

Gutierrez shrugged, setting his mug on the island beside mine. "People kill for all kinds of reasons. You would be surprised at how little it takes to push some folks over the edge."

I grabbed a paper towel to blot up the spilled coffee. "Well, I'm not one of them. And besides, you've got it all wrong. There's no way Vivian was getting that account. I've been friends with the Thorntons since college."

"I see." His tone was skeptical. "Well, you know how it is. We just have to examine all the possibilities. Besides," he said as I tossed the paper towel in the trash, "you did leave the ball early. Probably right around the time Ms. Sutherland was killed."

My headache was getting worse. I poured more coffee in my mug, desperately needing the caffeine to kick in. "As I told you last night, I left the ball because red wine got spilled on my dress. I was a mess. There was no way I could stay there, looking like that."

I refilled his cup. He moved in close to pick it up. "You don't live that far from the museum," he said. "You could have come home, changed clothes, and gone back to the ball. But you didn't. Why was that?"

I tilted my head to look up at him. "You know what the weather was like last night. Nobody was on those roads if they didn't have to be. Once I had gotten out of that dress, I was hardly in the mood to go back."

He sipped his coffee and asked casually, "Do you suppose we could take a look at the dress?"

"Why?" My fingers massaged the throbbing skin above my eyebrows. I had never had much interaction with the police, but I had heard plenty of stories about people who offered up information, trying to be helpful, and then found themselves in difficult situations. There was no way I was handing over that dress without a warrant.

"Just curious," he said, peering over the top of the mug.

"You don't believe me? Ask anyone who was sitting at the Fairburn, Crandall table. They can tell you about the wine."

"We will. But as long we're here…"

"Do you have a warrant?"

He shot a quick glance at Caldor. "Do we need one?"

The acid from the coffee burned in my throat. I turned to pour the contents of my mug in the sink. "Yes. And I don't think I should talk to you without a lawyer."

He poured the rest of his coffee in the sink with mine. "We're just chatting here," he said, setting the mug on the counter. "Trying to figure out what happened. People who bring in lawyers usually have something to hide. And that makes them go straight to the top of the suspect list."

"So I'm a suspect?"

"Early days yet, Ms. Bradford. Most everyone is a suspect right now."

The tension built in my head until I felt it would explode. I needed to talk to Fontaine, to find out what she had told them last night. My minor argument at the bar had made them suspicious. If they knew I walked in on Vivian having sex with Nate, they would probably be pulling out their handcuffs. I had to get them out of my house. Looking pointedly at the clock, I said, "I have a few errands that I really need to take care of this morning. Could we continue this conversation another time?"

Gutierrez hesitated, then motioned to Caldor. "Of course. We have a lot of other people to talk to. We can circle back around to you later."

I handed them their coats, then ran through the house and watched through the front window as they made their way across the yard, their loping strides leaving long narrow tracks in the snow. As they pulled away from the curb, I grabbed my phone to call Fontaine.

# Chapter 7

FONTAINE PICKED UP on the first ring.

"The police think I killed Vivian," I blurted out.

"What are you talking about?"

I could hear noise in the background, people talking, maybe a television. "The police were just here, at my house. They said I'm a suspect." I pressed my aching forehead against the cold glass of the front window. "You didn't tell them we saw Nate and Vivian having sex last night, did you?"

"Of course not. Hold on a minute." I could hear steps and then the closing of a door. The background sounds faded. "Now tell me why the police think you killed Vivian."

I explained about my argument with Vivian at the bar. "The detectives even wanted to see my dress. To make sure it didn't have blood on it."

"Did you show it to them?"

"No. They were so damn pushy, accusing me like that. It really made me mad. I asked if they had a warrant, but they didn't. So I asked them to leave."

"Good. Obviously, they're just fishing. And anyway, I've got bigger problems."

It was difficult to imagine a bigger problem than being a suspect in a murder case. "What's the matter?"

"It's Nate. He never came home last night."

It made sense that Nate would want to lay low for a while, let some time pass before he faced Fontaine's wrath. "He probably stayed with a friend. Have you called him?"

"About a dozen times. He's not answering." I could hear the frustration in her voice. "I've called his friends. The club. Nobody's seen him."

I turned away from the window and headed back toward the kitchen. "Fontaine, I'm sure he's fine. He's just gotten stuck somewhere because of the weather. You'll hear from him soon."

"What if he isn't fine?" she asked, her voice ratcheting up a few octaves. "What if somebody shot him, too? What if he's out there somewhere, hurt, and I'm not doing anything to help him?"

"Slow down, Fontaine," I said, gathering up the coffee mugs and putting them in the dishwasher. "Don't you think you're overreacting just a bit?"

"You sound just like my mother. She and Daddy spent the night with me last night. We are *so* getting on each other's nerves." Her voice sounded more determined. "I can't stay here just doing nothing. I want to go out looking for him. I'll pick you up."

"Are you kidding?" I asked, glancing at the drifts in the backyard. "The roads are horrible. We can't get out in this."

"The roads are fine. And besides, I've got the Range Rover."

The glass door of the microwave reflected my flattened hair. "Give me an hour. I feel grimy. I'm not going anywhere without a shower."

"Fine. I'll see you then."

She pulled into the driveway twenty minutes later, impatiently beeping the horn. Shooting a few final bursts of hot air through my hair, I crossed to the bedroom window and waved. Pulling on my boots and coat, I headed outside and scrambled up beside her. Fontaine looked grim. An unflattering knit stocking cap was pulled down tight over her ears. She obviously had been crying. Her nose was pink and her eyes bloodshot.

As we drove down the street, Geena, the big golden retriever next door, jumped out in front of us. Fontaine slammed on the brakes, fighting to bring the car under control. "I'm so sick of this damn snow," she said.

We all were. Usually Hastings got only a couple of snows a winter, a few inches at a time. This season was different, one of the worst on record. At first it had been fun, the TV news reports full of excited children hurtling down snowy hills, their screams and laughter filling the air. We had our first white Christmas in over twenty years.

But the snow just kept coming. Six inches the first week of January. Another eight inches two weeks later. And not much melting in between. The traffic-blackened residue of one snow had barely shrunk from the curbs before the snow plows were busy piling up the next one. The days were cold, grey and monotonous, a perfect reflection of my own gloomy mood. The nights were full of creaking noises as tree limbs ached to support the heavy snow. Last week a giant poplar had snapped and crashed onto my neighbor's roof.

"The groundhog saw his shadow last week," I said. "We've got six more weeks of winter."

"Six more weeks of this and I'll blow my brains out. Although I suppose that's a pretty insensitive remark considering what happened to Vivian." She waited until Geena was out of sight, then drove slowly down the street. "I can't believe the two of them hooked up last night. Nate and I are supposed to go to the Caribbean this weekend for a second honeymoon."

My mouth twisted in sympathy. "I guess you're cancelling that."

"No." She kept her eyes down, adjusting the climate controls. "It's been really tough between us recently. This trip was meant to give us time alone, to patch things up. And after last night, we need it more than ever."

"Are you crazy? After what he did, you still want to go off on a romantic weekend?"

She took a deep breath. "Yep."

I shook my head. "Then you're a much more forgiving person than I am. I wouldn't go anywhere with someone who pulled a stunt like that." I couldn't understand why Fontaine hadn't kicked Nate out the first time he'd been unfaithful. Or the second. Or the third.

She was silent for a minute. "You know we've been in counseling. And Nate's on medication. To help him control his...urges."

"It doesn't seem to be working," I said dryly, remembering Nate's bare butt as he thrust against Vivian.

"The doc is still tweaking the dosage. And Nate doesn't like to take his meds. They make him moody. Really irritable. Sometimes...well, sometimes he scares me. I'm afraid he's going to hurt me. Or himself."

"That's why he's been so nasty to me over the past few months? Because of the meds?" It was a tough choice. Either he could be the charming, funny guy that Rolfe and I had known for so many years, a good friend whose only flaw was that he couldn't keep his pants zipped. Or he could be the raging bastard who screamed at me at the Winter Ball.

"The meds, and the fact that he lost all that money, which really put him in a tailspin. He's been frantic ever since that happened."

"I tried to persuade him to sell those stocks, Fontaine. I really did. But he wouldn't agree."

"He knows it's his fault. But he's had a tough time dealing with it."

"That doesn't excuse what he did with Vivian. I don't know how you can forgive him for that."

"Now don't go all judgmental on me," Fontaine snapped. "I get enough of that from my parents."

"You're right. I'm sorry." She had been the one person who kept me sane after Rolfe died. I needed to be there for her now. "How can I help?"

"We need to find him."

We pulled onto the entrance ramp of the interstate. "So where are we going?" I asked.

"Gayle's house."

"Nate's nurse?"

She nodded. "I figured we could ride by her house, see if we spot his car."

Traffic was light on the interstate, most people staying off the roads to let the snowplows do their work. Sand crunched under our tires as we steadily moved along the single scraped lane. "It's only two more exits," Fontaine said. "She lives off Hubbard Road."

As we crested the hill, we saw a long line of cars queued up behind a battered pickup truck that was barely moving, its payload stacked high with firewood. "I don't have time for this," Fontaine said, suddenly jerking the wheel to the left, moving into the unplowed lane. "People shouldn't be out here if they don't know how to drive."

I clutched my seat belt and ignored the angry gestures of the other drivers as we sped past, coating their windshields with blinding snow. "Fontaine, be careful."

"I'm not the only one doing this. Another car pulled out behind me. He couldn't stand going five miles an hour, either."

In the side mirror I could see a white SUV following in our tracks, a few car lengths behind. "So there are two idiots on the road today," I said. "That doesn't prove anything. Just try to get us there in one piece, OK?"

"No problem." She passed the pickup and pulled back into the right lane. I gripped the armrest, praying there were no icy spots to send us spinning into a ditch. She eased off the gas as we spotted the green and white Hubbard Road exit sign ahead, then continued to decelerate as we rounded the exit ramp and pulled to a stop. "Better now?"

"Please take it slow," I said. "We've got all day."

She turned left into a neighborhood of cookie-cutter starter homes, churned out years ago by builders more interested in efficiency than aesthetics. Most were painted white or pale gray, blending into the snowy landscape, their dark shutters standing out starkly against the plethora of white. Fontaine drove slowly up one street and down another.

"Do you know where you're going?" I asked.

"Not exactly. Nate and I were here at Christmas, but it was dark and I didn't pay much attention. I know she's on Midland." We circled around a few more streets, then Fontaine pulled to the curb and stopped. "That's it up there."

It was a white frame house much like all the others in the neighborhood, one window on each side of a center door, with dormer windows above. The shutters and door were painted bright red. Tire tracks led to a one-car garage at the end of the driveway. Behind it a thick row of bushy Leyland cypress shielded the back yard from the strip center beyond, where a towering Exxon sign peeked over the tops of the trees.

"I don't see Nate's car," she said. "Although I guess it could be in the garage."

We sat there for a few minutes, our breath fogging up the windshield. "So what's the plan?" I asked. "You going to knock on the door and ask if she's heard from him?"

"I really don't want to do that. If he's not there, I don't want her to know he's missing. She'll tell everyone in the office. And I would rather keep this quiet until I can find him." She started the car and headed out toward the main road. "Let's go check out that garage. We'll come in from the back."

She pulled out of the neighborhood and circled around to the strip center behind Gayle's house. The bakery, nail salon, and dry cleaners were closed, but the grocery store had a few customers parked out front, mostly trucks and SUVs. Fontaine drove back to the loading dock area, deserted on this snowy Sunday. "Gayle's house is on the other side of those trees," she said, pulling up near a rusty red dumpster, overflowing with black garbage bags and crushed cardboard cartons. "We can sneak through here and take a look in the garage."

"What if she sees us? Won't that be just a tiny bit awkward?"

She switched off the car and got out. "If Nate is there, she'll be talking to him, not looking at her garage. And if he's not, then she's probably glued to the TV. She won't notice us."

The sweet smell of rot from the dumpster hit me as I eased out of the car and followed Fontaine. Branches scratched my face as I pushed through the cypress trees. Fontaine paused at the edge of the yard, looked furtively in both directions, then strode quickly to the garage. I ran up beside her and peered in the back window.

A wheel barrow took up most of the floor space, along with a lawn mower and several cans of gasoline. Rakes and shovels hung from a rack on the opposite wall, as well as several coils of rope and a garden hose that curled down toward the floor like a black snake searching for mice. Along the side I could see the rusty metal legs of an old kitchen table, its peeling laminate top cluttered with flower pots, weed killer and bags of mulch. "No car in here," I whispered. "There's no room."

"Let's check out the house." Fontaine had that determined look that I had seen so often in the past when she was set on getting her way, her jaw tight and lips pursed together.

"Not unless you're going to ring the front doorbell. There's no way I'm going to creep around this woman's house, peeking in the windows."

"Nobody will see us. Come on."

As she took a step toward the house, a dog barked. A car door slammed and a woman called out, "Randy, be careful on that ice. The last thing you need is another broken leg."

I grabbed Fontaine's arm. "Let's get out of here."

The dog was barking louder now, coming closer. Fontaine looked around one last time, then reluctantly turned back toward her car, pushing through the trees, retracing our trail through the snow.

Back at the shopping center, Fontaine leaned against the Range Rover as she stared into the trees. "This was my last idea," she said slowly. "I don't know what to do now."

"Just go home and wait for him. He'll show up."

"I'm not so sure about that." She bent down to scoop up a handful of snow. "I mean, we've had fights before," she said, patting the snow into a ball, "but nothing like this." She looked at me, her eyes pained. "I told him I wanted a divorce."

That surprised me. No matter how many times he had cheated on her in the past, Fontaine had always ignored it and soldiered on, hiding the ache of betrayal. "What did he say?"

"About what you'd expect. Got all apologetic. Said he knew he'd been a terrible husband, but he could change. Promised he would take his meds, double down on his counseling sessions. He begged for my forgiveness. Even shed a few tears. It was quite dramatic."

I put my hand on her shoulder. "You forgave him?"

She shook her head. "Not this time. I'd been so convinced that the medication would work, but there he was, screwing Vivian in the museum where anyone could walk in on them. The therapist had told me to be patient, to give him time to work through all his issues, but I just couldn't play that game anymore. I told him I wanted him to move out of the house. That my lawyers would be contacting him. And I reminded him that we had a pre-nup, so he wouldn't be getting any money from me."

"Bet that upset him." Nate would have been desperate to change her mind. His medical practice did not begin to generate the kind of cash flow he was used to. He had always depended on Fontaine's father to fund his investment accounts and underwrite his life style. And now he would lose it all. The big house. The fancy boat. The vacations. And all the money Fontaine would eventually inherit.

"It did. He told me that he would do anything to get rid of Vivian, to make it right."

And then I realized what she was implying. "Fontaine, you don't think…"

"Yes, I do." She hurled the snowball against the dumpster. It smacked hard, leaving a fat white blob which trickled down the red metal. "I knew it as soon as I found her body last night." She turned toward me, her cheeks pink from the cold. "It was Nate. He's the one who killed her."

# CHAPTER 8

"YOU DON'T REALLY BELIEVE Nate killed Vivian?" I said. We were in the Range Rover, headed back toward my house. A few more cars were on the highway now, people eager to check out snow damage, the numerous toppled trees and downed power lines. But this time Fontaine drove slowly, creeping along with the rest of the traffic, concentrating on the road. All of her earlier impatience, that frantic sense of urgency, had completely drained away.

"Yes, I do. And it's all my fault. I shouldn't have threatened him with a divorce. I should have been more understanding." Her chin quivered as a tear slid down her cheek. She brushed it off with a gloved hand.

"This absolutely is not your fault. Nate's a grown man. He's responsible for his own actions." We exited the interstate and drove toward my neighborhood. Snow plows had not yet reached this part of town. People were out at the curbs, sweeping snow off their cars, shoveling the sidewalks. "So what happened after your fight?" I asked. "Did the two of them leave together? Go out into the parking lot?"

Fontaine tightly gripped the wheel as she slowly navigated the icy streets. "Vivian ran out right after you left. I didn't see her the rest of the evening. Until I found her out there in the snow."

"What about Nate?"

"I couldn't stand to look at him anymore. He had lied to me so many times, and there he was, doing it again. I left him in the lobby and went back to the banquet hall."

"We've got to figure out what happened. Was there anyone else in the lobby? Anyone who might have seen them?"

"There were a few people in the lobby, milling around before the auction started. But I didn't pay much attention. I kept my head down, hoping that no one had heard us, that no one would figure out what Nate had been doing."

I was hoping that, too. Otherwise, Fontaine and I would be prime murder suspects. The wronged wife and her best friend, seeking revenge. "Think hard,

Fontaine. This is important. We need to know if they left together. If Nate could have shot her."

She turned down my street. My neighbor Harold was out in his yard tossing a ball to Geena, who wagged her long bushy tail in delight as she scampered through the drifts. Fontaine slowed to curve into the driveway. The dog dashed in front us, with Harold chasing wildly after her.

"That damn dog," Fontaine said, hitting the brakes. "That's the second time today it's run out in front of me. It needs to be on a leash." She glanced in her rearview mirror. "Look back there. I almost got rear-ended by that SUV. And it would have been that dumb dog's fault."

Pulling into the driveway, she threw up a hand in apology as a white SUV rolled slowly by.

Harold grabbed Geena's collar. "Sorry, folks," he called out.

Fontaine turned toward me. "Barbara Edmonton."

"What about her?"

"Barbara was coming out of the ladies room. Vivian probably went in there to straighten herself up. Maybe Barbara saw her."

"Good. Did you see anyone else?"

She shook her head in frustration. "I don't remember anyone. I'm trying to blot all this out, not remember it."

"That's fine. It's a start." I gave her a reassuring smile. "Barbara's a good friend. I'll talk to her. Find out if she saw them leave together." I fished my keys out of my purse. "Do you want to come in?"

"No. I need to get home. My parents will be worried."

I opened the door and stepped out into the snow. "For what it's worth, Fontaine, I don't think Nate did this."

"Then where is he?" she asked, her eyes red. "And who killed Vivian?"

"I guess that's what we've got to figure out."

§§§

A wisp of smoke drifted from one of the many chimneys of the Edmonton house as I rode along the spiked wrought iron fence that marked the edge of their property. Barbara had left the ornate entrance gates open for me. I pulled between the towering stone pillars and drove slowly up the winding cobblestone driveway.

The house was a local landmark, a giant Tudor that dated back to sixteenth century England. The judge's great-grandparents had fallen in love with the house on their honeymoon, a brooding mansion of dark timbering and multiple gables, long deserted and scheduled for demolition. They purchased the crumbling ruin, then had it completely disassembled and shipped it back to Hastings, where the house was put back together beam-by-beam and lovingly restored to its original state. The area around it was eventually developed into an exclusive neighborhood of gently rambling streets and expansive homes on large wooded lots, anchored by the stately Edmonton mansion. King's Village was still considered the most prestigious residential area in the city.

Rolfe had proudly pointed it out to me on my first trip to his hometown, on a crisp autumn day when the acreage was a gorgeous explosion of color: red and gold maple leaves drifting to the yellowing lawn, red berries hanging low on the glossy hollies. "Edmonton ancestors once lived in the house, back when it was still in England," he said. "Henry VIII was a frequent visitor."

"Really? The part about Henry VIII? You think that's true?" I asked, thinking it was just a local legend.

"Absolutely." He grabbed my hand and pulled it to his lips, giving my fingers a gentle kiss. "The past is very important to us. We don't joke about things like that."

That was one of the thing I loved about Hastings, its fascination with the past. Many residents traced their bloodlines back for centuries, some to European royalty, others all the way to Charlemagne. Rolfe was a descendent of John Rolfe, the Jamestown colonist and tobacco planter who married the Indian princess Pocahontas in 1614. Fontaine was a relative of Matthew Fontaine Maury, a nineteenth-century oceanographer and Civil War hero. I envied that sense of connection, of knowing where you fit into the annals of history. In contrast, I felt like an anonymous dust speck that floated in from an alien planet. My grandparents died before I was born. My father died when I was a teenager. Mom never talked about any of them.

Rolfe had kicked at the browning leaves on the sidewalk. "Sometimes I think we're too caught up in the past. We romanticize it, reshape it, make it better than it ever was. Just like this house. The original never had central heat and air. Not to mention indoor plumbing." He put his arm around my shoulder. "It's the future we struggle with. We're not good at managing change. We like everything to stay just the way it is."

Now that I had lost Rolfe and Jason, I understood more clearly what he meant. I would give anything to avoid the changes of the past few months. To have my family still with me, all of us untouched by that horrible accident.

Parking my car now in front of the mansion, I walked up the brick steps past huge copper urns planted with Norfolk pines and cascading ivy. Barbara answered the doorbell, wearing a dark green apron tied over her faded jeans, a smudge of flour on her cheek. "I'm so glad you called," she said, giving me a hug and taking my coat.

"Did I come at a bad time? You look like you're in the middle of something."

She grimaced. "Two detectives were here this morning, asking endless questions, getting me all upset. It seemed a bit early for wine, so I'm making chocolate chip cookies instead, to calm myself down. Come on back."

We walked to the kitchen, bright and airy with white cabinets and silvery granite countertops. Through the large windows which looked out over the back garden, I could see a small lumpy snowman with a carrot nose and a plaid scarf wrapped around his neck. "Somebody's been busy," I said.

"The boys had a great time building that. Running in and out of the snow all morning. Mark finally took them sledding so I could have a few minutes of peace." She motioned toward the oak farm table. "Have a seat. Care for some coffee?"

"That would be great." I pulled back one of the heavy chairs. "So the detectives were here asking questions? Gutierrez and Caldor?"

She filled a bright blue mug and set it in front on me. "Yes. They're interviewing everyone who was at the Fairburn, Crandall table."

Shep wouldn't be happy about that. We were already losing clients due to weak investment performance. Having the firm's name linked to a murder investigation wouldn't do anything to restore confidence in our firm. "So what happened after I left? Did you see Vivian leave the ball?"

She shook her head. "After dinner, I was coming out of the ladies room. It reeked of pot." The timer dinged. Putting on an oven mitt, Barbara pulled two baking sheets of cookies from the oven and set them on the granite counter.

"Who was smoking pot? I thought we all gave that up years ago."

"I don't know. Somebody in one of the stalls. I couldn't see her." She slid a spatula under the cookies and transferred them one by one to a cooling rack. "Anyway, Vivian nearly knocked me over as I came out. Didn't say a word. No apology, no nothing. Just went into a stall and slammed the door. The whole row swayed a little."

If Vivian was slamming doors, she must have felt some guilt over her one-on-one with Nate. Maybe she hadn't been quite as cavalier about it as I thought. "Sounds like she was mad about something. Did you see her arguing with anyone?"

Barbara put several cookies on a small plate and set it in front of me. "Not then. But earlier in the evening she had a pretty heated discussion with that Kensington guy."

"Gus Kensington? The Senator's grandson?

"Yes."

I picked up a cookie. "That's a surprise. As far as I know, they'd never even met before Saturday night. What were they fighting about?"

"Who knows? They were dancing, wrapped up so tight that you couldn't have gotten a piece of dental floss between them. Then right before the music stopped, she gave him a strong push and stormed off. You should have seen his expression. He looked kind of sick, like he'd just gotten a swift kick in the groin."

"Really?"

She scraped the last of the batter out of the bowl and slid the cookie sheet into the oven. "I kind of felt sorry for the guy. All through dinner he kept trying to talk to Vivian, and she totally ignored him. Would only talk with Mark and me. Gus was livid."

"Did you tell the police all this?"

"Yes. They wrote it all down." She set the bowl in the sink and filled it with water, then turned slowly toward me. "I hope you don't think I'm a horrible person when I say this. I mean, I'm really sorry that Vivian's dead. But I'm glad she's not going to be managing Mark's money anymore."

"I don't understand. I thought he was happy with Vivian."

"Oh, I'm sure he was. But I've got to tell you, I didn't trust her." She filled a coffee mug and sat across from me. "We argued about it a lot, right after Rolfe's accident. I wanted to wait until you were back in the office. But Vivian kept calling Mark, telling him he was losing money by not moving the account. Finally she convinced him."

"Do you think she mismanaged the account?"

"It wasn't the money I was worried about. I didn't like what she doing with Mark."

"What do you mean?"

"Vivian was in his office one day when I stopped by unexpectedly. I saw her standing behind him, leaning down, pointing to something on his computer screen. Her hand was on his shoulder, her face really close to his. And Mark had this goofy grin." She wrapped both hands around her mug. "We had a big fight about it. He insisted that nothing was going on, that it was totally innocent. But I'm a trophy wife myself. I know how these things start. And after that, I didn't want her anywhere near us."

I could see why Mark would be attracted to Vivian. She looked a lot like Barbara. The same long blond hair. The same narrow face and high cheekbones. But Barbara had a softness about her, an innocence that made her seem vulnerable, in need of protection. Vivian had been tough, always in control, invincible. Until someone put a bullet in her head.

"Barbara, you know that Mark would never do anything to hurt you or the children."

"Maybe. But if she got cozy with all her clients like she did with Mark, I wouldn't be surprised if an angry wife shot her."

The back door opened and Barbara's two boys tumbled in. "Cookies!" they yelled, catching the scents from the oven, rushing to the table to snatch the treats from the cooling rack. Barbara ran after them, pulling off coats and boots, putting dry socks on tiny toes red from the cold, wiping up lumpy snow puddles from the kitchen floor. It brought back so many memories of last winter with Jason that I could barely breathe.

"Barbara told me you called," the judge said, hanging his coat on a peg beside the back door. "Quite a shock about Vivian, isn't it?"

"Yes, it is." I stood up. "Just horrible."

He pulled off his boots as he looked at the boys, perched on their knees on the heavy chairs, fighting over cookies. "I need to talk to you a minute. Let's get away from all this chaos. It's hard to hear yourself think in here."

I followed him to a large room with dark wood-paneled walls and a timbered ceiling. Dim shards of light filtered through the tiny triangles of the leaded glass windows. It was easy to imagine Henry VIII here, standing in front of the huge stone fireplace during a festive evening, looking over the crowd to pick out his next wife. The judge switched on table lamps and gestured toward a big overstuffed sofa, upholstered in a child-friendly textured tweed. He settled into the wing chair beside me, using his foot to push aside a pile of toy trucks scattered near the hearth.

The sofa cushions were wide and deep. I moved some throw pillows behind my back to keep from sinking. "Judge, you don't need to worry about your account," I reassured him. "I'll make sure nothing slips through the cracks." Vivian had outmaneuvered me once to get his account. Now I was determined to stake my claim early, before anyone else in the firm could step in.

"That's good to know," he said, pushing up the sleeves of his thick wool sweater. "But I don't think there's any sense of urgency. Vivian seemed to have everything pretty well under control. There shouldn't be any need to make any changes, at least not right away."

It would have given me a rush to find that she had totally mismanaged the account, that I needed to swoop in and make wholesale changes to protect his money. But I knew the odds of that were low. Vivian was smart, and she did a good job with her clients' accounts. I would probably dial down the risk a bit, since she was always more aggressive than I was, but most likely there was no need for a major repositioning. "You're probably right, but I'll take a look and give you my recommendations in a few days."

There was loud yelling from the kitchen. "No, that's mine," a high-pitched voice shouted.

"That isn't why I wanted to talk to you." He got up and laid a piece of wood on the fire. Sparks danced up the chimney as he poked at the logs. "Two detectives were here this morning."

"Yes, I know. Barbara told me. They came to my house, too."

"They asked a lot of questions about you. Wanted to know when you left the ball. And why."

"That's an easy one," I said. "I left because Nate spilled wine all over my dress. I couldn't stay there looking like that."

"Yes, that's what I told them." He rested his foot on the hearth. Behind him on the mantle was a silver-framed picture of the four of them at Jackson Hole last winter, bundled up in jackets and scarves, wearing helmets and enormous goggles.

"So what happened after I left? Do you have any idea who killed Vivian?"

He shook his head. "After dinner we all hung around the lobby until the auction started, but I didn't see Vivian. There was a bit of excitement -- I almost had to break up a fight between Nate and one of the waiters."

"You're kidding? What were they fighting about?"

"Who knows? Probably about the wine that got spilled." There was a sudden pop from the fireplace, and he bent down to readjust the logs. "I just hope I didn't do you a disservice, Robbie."

"A disservice?"

"Yes. Leading those detectives down a trail where they really don't need to go."

"What do you mean?" I felt vulnerable, sunken down in the depths of the sofa, and grabbed the arm to pull myself upright.

"They asked how long I had known you. I explained that you were the one that originally solicited my account for Fairburn, Crandall. Even though Vivian ended up as my account manager." He jabbed at the fire again, then put the poker in its rack beside the fire. Sitting back down in the wing chair, he leaned toward me, feet flat on the floor, elbows on his knees. "You know, as a judge, I've seen a lot of criminal cases. Things can get twisted in ways that you never would imagine. Sometimes the most innocent actions can be misinterpreted." His somber expression made me uneasy.

I perched on the very edge of the sofa cushion. "I'm not following you."

His forehead wrinkled. "The police think that there was a certain degree of animosity between you and Vivian, because she ended up with the account."

I could see the dancing flames reflected in his steel-rimmed glasses. "I'll admit I was disappointed when you turned over the account to her. But the important thing is that you moved your money to Fairburn, Crandall. Both Vivian and I benefited from that."

"Of course. Nevertheless..." His dark eyes probed deep into mine, as though as I were a defendant in his courtroom, and he was searching hard for the truth. "You should be careful. And before you talk to the police again..."

"Yes?"

"I really think you should contact your lawyer."

# CHAPTER 9

THE JUDGE'S WORDS frightened me. Until then, I had figured that Gutierrez and Caldor were swinging in the dark, trying to fabricate a motive for me where there wasn't one. But the facts were starting to stack up as solidly as the stone towers I passed at the end of the Edmonton driveway as I headed toward home. I had argued with Vivian at the ball about Nate. She had beaten me out to get the judge as a client. We were competing for the partnership at Fairburn, Crandall. Once the detectives realized I had walked in on her having sex with my best friend's husband, I would be in big trouble.

I worked with lawyers all the time, setting up trusts, handling estates, managing business succession planning. If I had been accused of tax fraud or embezzlement or some other financial crime, I would already be punching speed dial to talk with one of them. But murder was different. None of the lawyers I worked with could handle bullet trajectories and blood spatter patterns.

And then I remembered Ana Rodriguez. A prominent criminal attorney, she was a casual acquaintance, not someone I had ever done business with. And she was not a fixture on the charity fundraiser set, like so many of my friends. But she was known as a fighter, not afraid to get her hands dirty to score a win for her clients. And that was exactly what I needed right now. I pulled out my phone to search for her number, then left a message for her to call me.

My street was quiet when I returned home. The smell of grilling meat from several of the local restaurants hit me as I got out of the car. My stomach rumbled, reminding me that two chocolate chip cookies were all I had eaten all day.

Stuffing my hands deep in my pockets, I slogged two blocks through the snow to the Smokey Dog. The neon cigarette-puffing dachshund above the front door glowed bright blue in the gray afternoon light, a reminder of Hastings' history as a tobacco town. The customers on this snowy Sunday afternoon were an eclectic mix of college students and locals, each hunched over a laptop to take advantage of free WiFi, solitary folks enjoying companionship by being alone together. Most of the tables were already full.

Leon waved me over to the bar. "How's it going?" he said, clearing the counter in front of me, setting down silverware wrapped in a paper napkin.

"Looks like the snow didn't keep anyone away," I said, unbuttoning my coat.

"Not this crowd," he said. "Most of them walk over, just like you. Nothing stops 'em."

I glanced at the chalk menu behind the bar. "How about a Guinness and the Smokey Dog special?"

"You got it." A moment later he set a glass mug in front of me. "Enjoy."

I sipped the Guinness, savoring its rich heaviness. Then I pulled out my phone to check for messages. My thumbs were skimming across the screen when a voice beside me said, "What the hell happened last night?"

I turned to see Everett Sutherland, Vivian's ex-husband, cheeks flushed red from the cold, his close-set eyes flashing angrily.

"Everett, I am so sorry. I should have called you."

"You think? The police were banging on my door first thing this morning. That's a hell of a way to find out your wife is dead."

Vivian and I had taken a stab at friendship when I first joined Fairburn, Crandall, going out with our husbands for dinner or a movie. Rolfe and Everett could have made it work, bonding over sports trivia, speaking their own language about a triple option offense and throwing into double coverage. And at first Vivian and I seemed to get along, sharing stories about whitewater rafting in Costa Rica and parasailing in Mexico. But after a few months our competition for the partnership made us too combative. Our social interactions gradually petered out. I hadn't seen Everett in over a year.

"The police think I shot her," he said.

"Why would the police think that? You weren't even at the ball."

He shrugged. "In a murder they always suspect the spouse. Or in my case, the ex-spouse. Especially since I'm still the beneficiary on her life insurance policy."

Leon set a menu in front of him. "Something to drink?"

"Legend Brown Ale." Everett sat on the barstool beside me as Leon walked away. "They kept asking about my alibi. And unfortunately, I didn't have one. I was at home by myself, watching the game."

"They came to see me this morning, too. I guess they're just covering all their bases." I took another swallow of Guinness. "They can't really believe you had anything to do with this. The two of you haven't even seen each other in months, have you?"

His face softened. "Actually, we have. We've been thinking maybe we could get back together."

"Really?" Their breakup had been loud, long and bitter. It was hard to imagine that the two of them could ever put all that behind them.

He bristled at the doubt in my voice. "It might have happened."

Leon set the Legend in front of him. Everett guzzled his beer, then set the bottle down hard. "Look, I know you two didn't always get along. Vivian could be a real bitch at times. Competitive. Opinionated."

His criticism surprised me. I had learned to keep my distance from her, tired of her cutting sarcasm, but Everett had always seemed so calm and supportive. I had thought he was one of the few men I knew who could bear to be married to her.

"But she had her softer side, too," he said. "She was funny. Had a wicked sense of humor. The most exciting woman I've ever known."

Leon came back with my Smokey Dog special, a foot-long hot dog smothered in chili, with generous amounts of grilled peppers and melted jalapeño cheese on top. "Whatever happened between you two?" I picked up the dog and took a big bite, feeling the sting of the jalapeños, the smoky burn of the chili.

Everett studied my reflection in the mirror behind the bar. "Part of it was Hastings. We moved here because of my job, but it was never a good fit for her. You know she was interviewing with other firms? Planning to go back to New York."

"New York?" I mumbled, my mouth full. "That's crazy. What about the Fairburn, Crandall partnership?"

"She didn't really care about that. Just wanted to prove that she could get it. She never meant to stay here long term."

I forced down that first bite, then took a long swallow of Guinness. We had been in a blood battle for that partnership. Scrambling for clients. Pitching our best investment ideas to Shep. If Everett was telling the truth, it must have been just a game to her, to prove she could get the bigger office, more money, more prestigious clients. To prove she could beat me.

He ran his finger in the wet puddle his beer bottle had left on the bar. "Vivian was incredibly talented at getting whatever she wanted. Only thing was, once she had it, she didn't want it anymore. And that included me."

"I'm sorry."

He signaled for his check. "The police asked if she had any enemies. I told them that one of her clients had been giving her a really rough time. You know anything about that?"

"No, I hadn't heard that. Who was it?"

"I don't know. She never mentioned any clients by name. But this guy kept calling her, saying she had screwed up. That she cost him a lot of money. She told him she would look into it. But that wasn't good enough. He kept complaining. Was really pissed."

I was surprised I hadn't heard anything about it. Bad news usually traveled pretty quickly through the office rumor mill. Of course, Vivian would have wanted to keep this quiet. It wouldn't help her partner prospects to have a client screaming about her mistakes. But still, there had to be someone at work who knew something. "I'll check into this tomorrow. See what I can find out."

He pulled out his wallet and threw some cash on the bar. "You'll call me? If you find out anything?"

"Of course."

"Good." He stood up and zipped up his jacket. "I'll talk to you soon."

I sat there for a long time after he left, slowly chewing my hot dog, not sure if the burn in my gut was from the chili and jalapeños or from realizing just how callous Vivian had been. She wanted the partnership just to prove she could get it. To grind me down with her success, a constant reminder that I had not quite measured up. I was sorry she was dead. Nobody deserved what had happened to her. But I wasn't sorry that I never had to see her again.

# CHAPTER 10

ON MONDAY MORNING the news reports were full of school cancellations and business delays. I wanted to stay inside, curled up by the fire with my coffee. But Fairburn, Crandall marched to the beat of the New York Stock Exchange. Whenever the stock market was open, we all had to be at work. Reluctantly, I got in my car in the early morning darkness and powered through the white mounds that snowplows had pushed in front of my driveway during the night.

Only a handful of cars were in the parking deck. I picked a spot near the stairwell, then headed down toward the street. Downtown was a silent wonderland. Everything was so hushed it seemed that sound itself had been given a holiday. Deserted sidewalks were covered with a thick layer of glistening white, punctured by footprints leading to the corner coffee shop and the few offices already open. Traffic lights provided the only color in this frozen landscape, cycling from red to green as they controlled the mostly empty streets.

Walking across the granite plaza, I pushed through revolving doors into the lobby of the Trust National Bank building. The bank had delayed its opening due to the treacherous roads. The building had that hollow weekend feel, quiet and still, with none of the typical morning crowd balancing coffee and briefcases as they jostled their way onto the elevators. Stomping snow off my boots, I smiled at the security guard. He gave me a curt salute as I punched the button for the eighteenth floor.

Darius was in his usual seat at the front desk when I walked into the Fairburn, Crandall offices. "Meeting in the war room," he said, his face grim. "Right now."

People were crowding in, standing along the wall, squeezing into the corners by the file cabinets. Vivian's was the only available chair. A young staff member sat down, but jumped up quickly, his face flushed, after Hardy mumbled a few words to him. I wondered if we would forever keep the chair empty in her honor, like a retired basketball jersey suspended from a gym ceiling, a lingering reminder of outstanding performance.

Shep stood at the far end of the room, talking quietly with Murphy and Charlton. He looked exhausted, his face pale, dark shadows under his eyes. After we were all quiet, he started to speak. "This is a horrible thing. I know how much Vivian meant to all of us. How much she meant to the firm." His voice trembled a bit, and he cleared his throat as he struggled to maintain control. "We're making funeral arrangements. I'll let you know the details later."

He nodded at Hardy, who opened a file folder and began to pass out papers to the group. "The important thing now is to reassure our clients that everything is business as usual," Shep said. "No one's money is at risk. I don't want them to think we're being distracted by this terrible tragedy." He waited as Hardy worked his way around the room. "This is a script I want you to use in talking with your clients, if they have any questions. Just to make sure we have a consistent message from the firm." He looked around the room. "No gossiping, folks. No speculation about what happened Saturday night. Does everyone understand that?"

We all nodded.

"We'll be getting in touch with Vivian's accounts first thing this morning, to explain what happened and to reassure them that a new account manager will be assigned shortly. I know the competition will be busy trying to steal her accounts. We can't let that happen."

Shep glanced around the room. "On another note, there are some detectives here this morning to talk with all of you. We will be using this conference room for those interviews. They'll call when they're ready for you." He braced his hands on the back of his chair. "Please cooperate as fully as you can. Just be careful not to share any confidential client information." He cleared his throat again and coughed. Then he asked, almost as an afterthought, "Does anyone have any investment issues we need to discuss this morning?"

The group was silent. "All right, then," he said. "Let's get to work."

§§§

I had just gotten coffee and settled down at my desk when Darius walked in and tossed a sheet of paper on my desk. "Here's the list of Vivian's clients that Shep wants you to call."

I nodded. "Thanks. I'll get right on it."

He started to leave, then turned back around, hesitant. His face was an intriguing mix of broad cheekbones, square jaw and mahogany skin. "You were there, weren't you? When they found Vivian's body?"

"I really don't want to discuss this," I said firmly. "It was a very traumatic situation. Not something for office gossip."

"Office gossip?" he said, his eyebrows drawing angrily together. "You think that's why I'm asking?" He stepped closer to my desk. "Look, I know you and Vivian didn't get along very well, but the two of us were friends. She talked to me a lot. Gave me advice about my career. I don't plan to be just the office manager here forever, you know."

Darius was a liberal arts major who had drifted from one low-paying retail job to another until an enthusiastic recommendation from one of our biggest clients convinced Shep to hire him. He was competent, with the computer skills our firm desperately needed, but it was obvious he was unexcited about his job. I was sure he would leave once something more appealing came along.

"Darius, your job is one of the most important ones here. You manage our trades. Keep up with the paperwork. Handle all those countless administrative details that keep us in business." I smiled at him. "I don't know what we'd do without you."

"Then pay me more money. Student loans, the next big bubble. I'm getting pretty tired of living on noodles. Vivian was helping me think through my options."

Money management was very lucrative for those of us at the top of the profession. Staff members like Darius were not nearly as well rewarded. If he knew that my bonus last year was almost twice his annual salary, he'd be even more upset. "Have you talked to Shep about this?"

He shrugged. "Yes. He knows."

"Well, I'm sure he'll figure out some way to work with you."

He didn't seem convinced. "Yeah, right."

"Let me ask you something," I said, as he turned to leave. "Were any of Vivian's clients upset with her? Maybe because of a mistake in an account?"

His shoulders stiffened slightly. "Vivian didn't make mistakes."

"Oh, come on," I said. "Everybody slips up now and again."

"If she had, I would have caught it." He looked at me curiously. "Why do you ask?"

"Someone mentioned to me that a client had been harassing her. That he'd lost a lot of money and blamed it on her. I just wondered if you knew anything about it."

"You think a client killed her? Because of a problem with an account?" His tone was skeptical.

The idea had sounded so promising when Everett and I discussed it at the Smokey Dog last night. In the harsh light of the office, it seemed much less probable. Our clients solved problems through political contributions, under-the-desk payments and on-retainer lawyers. The thought of one of Vivian's wealthy clients attacking her in a dark, snowy parking lot now seemed ludicrous. "Not really. But it doesn't hurt to check out all the possibilities."

"It's not very likely."

"No. Probably not."

I skimmed quickly through the list after Darius left my office, looking for names I recognized, deciding who to call first. And then I realized Judge Edmonton wasn't on the list. I had to fix that.

Several policemen were in Vivian's office as I passed on my way to Shep's office, riffling through her cabinets, packing up her files. Her computer had already been taken away, and her desk was clear except for a few faded pink copies of the *Financial Times*, shoved carelessly aside. The room was fast becoming generic. The only thing that marked it as belonging to Vivian was her glory wall, where rows of tastefully matted photographs, each personalized with a scrawled inscription, showed her confidently huddled with various politicians and celebrities.

Shep was settled back in his black leather desk chair, angled away from the door, the telephone pressed against his ear. I leaned against the doorjamb and waited. "What is it, Robbie?" he asked, annoyed, as he finished his call. "I'm pretty busy here."

I plopped into one of the upholstered chairs facing his desk, ready to do battle, to demand that I be assigned the judge's account. The raw grief in his eyes stopped me. I had seen that aching emptiness countless times in my own mirror, ever since Rolfe's accident.

Whispers of a romantic relationship between Shep and Vivian had long swirled around the office, with guys cracking crude jokes when we gathered for drinks after an especially grueling day. I refused to believe the speculation. In the office their behavior had always been totally professional, beyond reproach. But now, for the first time, I thought the rumors might be true. No one could look as devastated as Shep did right now unless he had lost something he truly loved.

"What is it?" he repeated.

"Judge Edmonton," I said almost apologetically, my anger ratcheted down by the sorrow in his face. "He's not on my list."

"What list?"

I raised the paper in my hand. "The list of Vivian's clients that I'm supposed to call. Judge Edmonton isn't on it. But I've already talked to him. To reassure him that his account is still being carefully managed."

"Is that so?" He closed the fuchsia folder in front of him, the color Vivian always used for her client files, just like the ones that were now being packed up by the policemen in her office. I wondered how he'd been able to hold onto these. He noticed my curious gaze and casually stacked the files at the edge of his desk. "When did you do that?"

"Yesterday. I went over to his house. Talked with him and Barbara."

"On a Sunday?" The corners of his mouth scrunched up into the tightest of smiles. "You didn't waste any time, did you?"

I ignored his sarcastic tone. "It's a lot of money. I thought he deserved some special consideration."

"I agree. He deserves our top attention." He jotted a note on his yellow legal pad. "So I'm going to manage his account myself."

I knew someone would try to screw me out of the account. I figured Hardy or Charlton or maybe even Murphy would lay claim to it, pleading seniority. And I was prepared to rebut any arguments they could offer up. But I never thought Shep would throw me to the mat to grab it for himself. "You can't do that."

"Excuse me?"

I perched on the edge of the chair. "It's my account, Shep. You know that. I brought it in."

He angled his head to the side. "As I recall," he said slowly, "Vivian's the one who closed that deal."

"Only because she stole it from me."

"I don't see it that way. You dropped the ball on that one. She snatched it up just in time."

My face flushed hot with frustration. "I've spent months building that relationship. The judge wants me to manage his money."

"The judge wants Fairburn, Crandall to manage it."

"But…"

He interrupted me. "Remember, Robbie, we're a team here. And you're on the team. But I'm running point on this one."

Most money management firms stressed a team approach, discouraging financial superstars. It was easy to understand why. Superstars could leave the firm and take their clients with them. Superstars could pull in lots of hot money that was chasing performance, only to see it gush back out when they hit a cold spell. Superstars could even get shot dead in a snowy parking lot, leaving clients to wonder if their money was at risk.

The team, on the other hand, always churned carefully in the background, assuring clients of continuity in investment performance. The team focused on attracting "sticky" money, which would stay with the firm no matter what happened to the individual players. But even within the team, some members were more equal than others. The account managers always got the biggest share of fee income. By appointing himself as manager of the judge's account, Shep had just cut me off from one of my biggest potential sources of revenue. And the one that had been my ticket to partnership.

He leaned back in his chair and laced his fingers over his stomach. "Besides, if I were you, I would focus more on holding onto my current accounts, rather than angling for new ones."

"What do you mean?"

"Do you expect me to ignore what happened at the ball? I know Nate threatened to sue us. Until you get that straightened out, there's no way I'm giving you another big account."

I braced my palms against the edge of his desk. "Nate was in a bad mood and had too much to drink. He was just letting off steam. You know he didn't mean any of that."

Shep furrowed his bushy silver eyebrows. "What I know is that he made our clients uncomfortable. And made you look really bad."

"I'll straighten everything out with him. He won't sue us."

"That's good to hear. You know we're not one of those deep-pocket Wall Street firms that can pay out millions in settlements. You remember what happened with Angston Meadors."

Angston had been one of our top grossing financial advisors until a disgruntled client took him to arbitration for putting her into excessively risky investments. The arbitration went against Angston, and Fairburn, Crandall had to pay out large sums in penalties. Shep quickly terminated his position.

"Nate won't sue," I repeated.

"See that he doesn't." He straightened up in his chair and turned toward his computer. "I have a lot to take care of this morning, Robbie. Was there anything else?"

I desperately wanted to know his plans for the partnership, but it seemed pretty callous to ask while we were all still thinking of Vivian sprawled in that snowy parking lot. "Is there anything I can do to help? I know this is a difficult time."

He shook his head. "Nope. Just keep your nose down and stay focused on your clients."

I waited, giving him one last chance to reassure me that I was still in the running for the partnership. But he just clicked on his emails, ignoring me. When his telephone rang, I turned and left his office.

§§§

Fontaine called just as I got back to my desk. "Nate's still missing."

Frustrated over my conversation with Shep, I struggled to focus on what she was saying. "What?"

"Nate didn't go to work. Gayle called here looking for him."

I sat down in my chair and rotated toward the window. "Guess that proves he wasn't at her house yesterday."

"Maybe."

Below me a blue sedan struggled to make its way up the icy hill. Spinning tires threw out salted slush as the rear end slid toward the sidewalk. "Could be he's just gotten held up somewhere because of the weather. The roads are still in pretty rough shape."

"You got to work, didn't you?"

"Yes, but..."

She cut me off. "Look, I know he's a lousy husband, but he really cares about his patients. If he were just delayed on the road somewhere, he would let someone know."

She was right. Nate had disappointed Fontaine many times, skipping her charity fund raisers, cancelling dinners out with friends, leaving symphony performances early. But when a patient called, he always responded. "What did you tell Gayle?"

"That he was ill at home. I apologized profusely for not letting her know. And asked her to reschedule all his patients."

"That's good. You did exactly the right thing."

"But what now?" Her tone was getting more and more frantic. "This just proves he killed Vivian, and he's on the run. He'd never disappoint his patients otherwise."

I was not ready to make that leap. "There must be some other explanation, Fontaine. I'm sure you'll hear from him soon."

"I don't think so. He took his passport. I think he's left the country."

"His passport?"

"I checked last night. Mine is still in the safe, but his is missing."

I tried to reassure her. "Maybe he just put it someplace else. In the nightstand, maybe. Or his dresser."

"Would you stop being so logical?" she said, exasperated. "I've torn the house apart. It's not here anywhere. I'm going to check his office. Can you meet me there?"

I looked at the list of clients I still needed to contact. "Do you really need me? It's pretty hectic here this morning. I'm not sure I can get away."

"Of course, I need you. You have to help me check out Gayle, to see if she's involved in this," she pleaded. "Nate couldn't disappear all on his own."

Fontaine had always been there for me. I couldn't let her down now. "I have to finish up some things here first, but I can be there by one. Will that work?"

"Yes. I'll see you then."

§§§

I spent the morning talking to Vivian's clients, most of whom had already heard of her death on the morning news. They all wanted more details than Shep's script allowed. I gave them as much information as I could, then just listened as they expressed their shock and outrage. That was a primary part of my job, listening to clients, figuring out their greatest concerns. A few people were worried that no one was watching out for their money. I reassured them and promised that someone would follow up shortly to update their financial plans. Shep would need to deal with these right away, before they got picked off by a competitor.

I left voice mails for the few clients who did not answer their telephones, asking them to call me. The last name was Julius Tavenner. The telephone screeched at me before a recording said, "The number you have reached is not in service at this time. Please check the number and dial again." I carefully punched in the numbers again, but got the same result.

I headed out to Darius's desk. "What do you know about Julius Tavenner?" I asked. "He's on my call list for Vivian's clients, but I've got the wrong telephone number. I get a recording telling me it's not in service."

Darius looked up from his computer screen. "Did you check it in our system?"

"Yes. It's the same number as on my sheet."

He shrugged. "I don't have anything different. Maybe you can check Vivian's desk files."

"Too late for that. The police have packed everything up."

"Then I can't help you. Sorry."

"This is a really strange account, Darius. It's five million dollars. All invested in just one thing, Hawthorne Medical. You sure you don't know anything about this?"

"No, I don't." He looked back at his screen. "By the way, those detectives are waiting for you. They're in the war room."

I frowned. I was definitely not in the mood for another round with Gutierrez and Caldor. Plus, I hadn't had a chance to talk with my lawyer yet. "Can you send them somebody else? I have some things to catch up on first."

He shook his head. "You're last on the list," he said. "They've been marching everyone else in and out of there pretty fast all morning."

"Terrific." Just what I needed after my discussion with Shep. I took a deep breath and turned toward the war room.

# CHAPTER 11

"DETECTIVE GUTIERREZ. Detective Caldor," I said as we shook hands. "So nice to see you again." Gutierrez wore his blue blazer, white shirt and royal blue striped tie. I glanced down at my own outfit. Black suit, silk blouse, knee high boots. At least today I was dressed as well as he was.

The flat-screen television, muted, was tuned to Bloomberg. Two talking heads were discussing tax policy, their bullet points posted on the side of the screen.

"How can I help you?" I asked, pulling out a chair at the conference table.

Caldor looked older today and not as friendly. The harsh fluorescent lights hardened his baby blue eyes to a steel gray. He flipped through his notebook, scanning each page. Then he underlined something and slid the notebook across to Gutierrez, who nodded.

"We've been talking to a lot of people," Gutierrez began. "People at the ball. People here at your firm."

"Yes," I said enthusiastically, smacking the table.

"Excuse me?" Gutierrez said.

"Oh, I'm sorry. It's Jallotte Health Care," I said, pointing to the Bloomberg screen behind him. "They had their IPO today, and it's already up twenty percent."

Caldor looked puzzled.

"Initial public offering," I explained. "When a privately held company goes public. We were able to get our clients in on this one. They're going to make a lot of money today."

His smile was unpleasant, his top lip drawn to one side. "You're pretty competitive, aren't you?"

"It's the nature of the beast," I said. "Everyone in this business wants to win."

Gutierrez picked up the remote and switched off the monitor. "At any cost?"

"What do you mean by that?"

"I'm just trying to figure out what you would do to win."

I wrapped my hands around the arms of my chair, my thumbs massaging the coarse fabric. "Excuse me?"

"You have some trouble with your temper, don't you?" Caldor said.

I shrugged. "No more than the next person."

Gutierrez tapped the remote against his hand. "I don't know that I would agree with that. You had a big argument with Ms. Sutherland on Saturday night."

I waved my hand dismissively. "We went through all that yesterday. The bartender made way too much out of it. Vivian and I talked. That's all it was."

Gutierrez shook his head. "I think it was a lot more than that. She had already weaseled Judge Edmonton's account away from you, right? You put in all the time wooing the guy, and she steps up at the last minute and gets all the glory. Takes advantage of you when you're all distraught over your family's death. I know I'd want to get even if something like that happened to me."

The judge had said he might have steered the police in the wrong direction. Now they seemed convinced I had a clear motive for murder. "It's not important who brought him in. What's important is that he's now a client of Fairburn, Crandall. We all benefit from that."

Gutierrez did not look convinced. "Dr. Thornton threatened to sue you. He announced to everyone at the ball that you lost his money. That must have made you really angry."

The detectives had been pretty thorough in tracking my movements Saturday night. "Nate was just blowing off steam. He'd had too much to drink."

Caldor shifted his chair closer to mine. "Ms. Sutherland probably had a good shot at getting his account. Because you had screwed up."

"I did not screw up," I said indignantly, wrapping my arms across my chest. "I tried to get Nate to sell some of his holdings and lock in profits, and he refused. He thought those stocks would go up forever."

Caldor leaned toward me. "How many of your other clients have lost money in the past year because of your screw ups?"

"My clients are doing very well, thank you," I snapped, my voice rising. "At least in my discretionary accounts, where I make all the investment decisions. Nate insisted on calling the shots himself. I'm not responsible for his poor judgment."

Gutierrez laughed. "Shall we talk about your temper again?"

I really wanted to punch him. But that would only prove my temper was out of control. And it seemed they already believed that.

Caldor flipped back a couple of pages in his notebook. "Tell us more about this partnership that you and Ms. Sutherland were fighting over."

"We were both being considered," I said stiffly. "There was no fight."

"Not according to your co-workers."

I wondered who had been so eager to paint me in an unflattering light. Not Murphy, certainly, but maybe Charlton or Hardy. Or even a few of the more junior guys, who would have a better shot at partnership themselves with both Vivian and me out of the way.

"It would mean a lot more money to you, wouldn't it?" Gutierrez tapped his fingers on the table. "What does a partner make at a firm like this? A million? Two million? Maybe more?"

The senior partners probably pulled in that much, but nobody on my level really knew for sure. "It depends," I said. "On a lot of things. New business. Assets under management. Customer retention. Things like that."

"A million dollars. Maybe more. That's a lot of money." He turned to Caldor. "How many years you think we have to work to earn a million dollars?"

Caldor laughed. "I don't think we're gonna live long enough to see that."

I noticed Caldor's eyes on my black Tahitian pearl and diamond necklace. It probably cost more than he made in a year.

"You have a concealed weapons permit, Ms. Bradford," he said. "Tell us about your gun."

I had hoped it would take them a little longer to find out about the gun. Rolfe had bought it for me when I first moved to Hastings, insisting that I have protection when I went out at night. The two of us spent a lot of time at the shooting range as he taught me to use it. "It's in storage. With most of my furniture. You've seen my house. There's hardly anything in it."

"In storage? Really?"

"Yes." I had put my former house up for sale shortly after the accident. There were too many things there that reminded me of the life I had lost forever. Rolfe's dress shoes lined up neatly in the closet. Jason's tricycle tucked in the corner of the garage. Someday I would have the strength to deal with all of that. To decide what I wanted to keep and what I would have to give away. But not yet.

"We need to see that gun."

I glared at Gutierrez. "We're back to that search warrant thing again, aren't we?"

He got out of his chair and moved closer to me, sitting on the edge of the table, one foot on the floor, the other dangling mid-air. He balanced his weight on one hand as he leaned in, so close I could smell the faint citrus of his cologne. "Let's go over the facts. Dr. Thornton threatens to sue you. And then he spills wine on your dress. You're angry. You're frustrated. You stomp away from that table and run into Ms. Sutherland in the parking lot. The woman who stole Judge Edmonton from you. Who is getting ready to steal Dr. Thornton. And who has a much better chance than you at getting the partnership." Gutierrez's eyes dug into mine. "The two of you argue. And you shoot her, out there where nobody can see. Afterwards you go home, change clothes, and come back to the museum when you get the call from Ms. Thornton."

"That's crazy."

Gutierrez pulled a letter-size sheet of paper from his notebook and slid it in front of me. "Look what you did."

It was a photograph of Vivian lying in the snow. I could see the mascara running down her bruised cheek. The dark puddle beside her head. And the bullet wound in the center of her forehead.

"You know," he said, "most people think that a shot to the head will finish you off. Just like that. Bang, you're dead." He drummed his fingers on the edge of the picture. "But it's not always like that. It depends on the bullet, and the distance, and the angle of entry." He pointed with his index finger. "See her hand up there, tucked under the side of her head? She didn't die right away. She lay there, moaning, bleeding out. The pain would have been intense. She put her hand up there, patting the back of her head, trying to get relief. But each time she touched that wound, she pulled away another clump of her brain."

"Please stop," I said.

"She probably tried to call for help. But at that point most likely she couldn't speak. Could only make a few moaning sounds. Not enough for anyone to hear her. Except, of course, for the person who shot her. Who heard those moans. And saw her hand digging out her brains, there in all that cold, wet snow. And then just walked away. That was you, wasn't it, Ms. Bradford? You left her there to die."

I stared at the picture. She must have been so cold. Her coat had fallen open, and snow coated her silk dress. I could feel it. The cold. The wet. And see her hand, reaching for her head, to deal with the pain that would never stop. "I didn't do this."

Gutierrez was so close that the pink scar at his temple was right in front of my eyes. "You were close to losing everything you cared about," he whispered. "Your client. Your promotion. Your house. Everything."

"You had to do something," Caldor said softly, "to protect yourself. You had to get rid of her. To save your career. There was no way out."

"So you got her out in the parking lot, just the two of you, no one else around," Gutierrez said. "And you shot her."

They were so close that I could barely breathe. Their words wrapped around me, hypnotically tying me to the chair. I was falling under their spell. In another few minutes I would confess.

Suddenly I jumped up, shoving back the chair. "That is just absurd. I didn't have anything to do with Vivian's murder. You've got it really wrong."

"I don't think so," Gutierrez said.

I took a step back. "I've already lost everything I care about. My husband and my son. None of the rest of this matters. And as far as the house is concerned, my husband left me a very generous life insurance policy that more than covers any expenses."

Gutierrez kept pushing. "If you tell us the truth, we can help you."

My temper flared, just as bright and scalding as when I was talking with Nate at the ball. "You're making this whole thing up. Trying to get me to confess to something I didn't do. But it won't work." I stepped toward the door. "You need to leave now. I refuse to discuss this with you any more without my attorney."

Caldor came up beside me, his body close to mine. "That's the wrong decision," "We can help you if you cooperate now. You won't get this offer again."

I glared at them, not saying a word. Gutierrez shrugged. Caldor pocketed his notebook. I stood there, feeling my blood pounding in my ears, as they pushed past me into the hall. The two of them just throwing out crazy assumptions in hope that some of them might be true. I had not done anything wrong. There should have been nothing to worry about. And yet, innocent people sometimes got convicted. Our state prison had just released a man who had served twenty-seven years before being exonerated by DNA evidence. My hands shook as I headed back to my office.

# Chapter 12

CONVENTIONAL WISDOM SAYS Southerners do not drive well in the snow. Conventional wisdom is correct. I passed one major pile up, two cars in a ditch, and three fender benders on my way to Hastings Medical Park to meet Fontaine. Most winters it does not snow enough in the South for anyone to get much driving practice. When we get a winter like this one, the snow plows clear the interstates, toss down some sand and salt on the major roadways, and let everyone else play bumper cars until the snow melts. The only people who love this stuff are transplanted Northerners and the body repair shops, which do a booming business until daffodils finally poke through the snow in March. The rest of us just resolutely grind our way through, knuckles clenched, hands tight on the wheel.

Only a few cars were in the parking lot when I pulled in. Most patients had the good sense to reschedule their appointments. I parked beside Fontaine's Range Rover and carefully picked my way through the icy snow to the sidewalk.

Hinton Orthopedic Associates, a practice Nate shared with eight other doctors, was located in Suite 404. The waiting room was deserted except for a young boy scrunched down low in a dark green vinyl chair, his left arm in a cast, playing computer games on his tablet while his mother patiently flipped through magazines.

Fontaine stood at the front desk, bending down to talk through the cut-out in the glass wall separating the offices from the waiting area. I walked up to join her just as a young nurse dressed in pale blue scrubs opened the waiting room door a few inches. Her shoulder length black hair, parted in the center and tucked back behind her ears, framed a pale round face accented with smoky eyelids and glossy red full lips. "Fontaine? What are you doing here?" she asked.

Fontaine flashed a smile. "Hi, Gayle. We've come to pick up a few things for Nate." She turned to me. "This is my friend, Robbie Bradford."

"Nice to meet you," I said, holding out my hand.

Gayle hesitated, looking suspiciously from me to Fontaine and then back to me again. I wondered if she had seen us in her backyard yesterday, peeking into

76

the garage. I tensed, waiting for her angry accusations, trying to put together a reasonable explanation of what we had been doing. But she said nothing, just reluctantly extended her hand, grasping the very tips of my outstretched fingers as though I were a particularly unpleasant specimen of biohazardous waste. Quickly pulling back her hand, she turned to Fontaine. "What do you need? I'll be happy to get it."

"Oh my goodness, I would not *think* of inconveniencing you," Fontaine said, her smile widening as she oozed Southern charm, her drawl even more pronounced than usual. "I'm sure you have enough to do without worrying about us." She took a step closer. "Were you able to reschedule all of Nate's patients?"

Gayle nodded. "All but a few. And Dr. Reynolds was able to squeeze them in, so it's not a problem." She kept the door firmly propped against her hip, blocking the hallway.

Fontaine casually wrapped her fingers around the edge of the door. "That is just wonderful. I know Nate will be so relieved." She tightened her grip and quickly jerked the door open, throwing Gayle off balance, then slipped past her and headed toward Nate's office.

"Wait," Gayle said. Her clogs thumped loudly against the polished floor as she trotted to catch up.

Fontaine had decorated the office much like a gentleman's library in an English manor house. Built-in walnut bookshelves filled an entire wall, stocked with fat reference books and silver-framed photographs. An enormous eighteenth-century mahogany desk was centered between wide windows, whose plaid silk draperies, secured by thick tasseled tiebacks, puddled gracefully on the hardwood floors. Two striped wing chairs faced the desk, flanking a straight-legged Georgian tea table.

Fontaine tossed her coat onto one of the chairs, then switched on the lead crystal Waterford desk lamp. Gayle frowned as she straightened the pleated silk lampshade. "If you'll just tell me what you want..."

Fontaine shook her head. "I don't want to take your time. I know you're busy." She looked pointedly at the door. "We'll let you know when we're done."

"I don't think..." Gayle began, shaking her head, a wave of black hair cascading over her eyes. She carefully eased it back in place with her fingertips. "What I mean is, Nate really doesn't like for anyone to be in his office when he's not here. There's a lot of confidential information in here. Patient files, that sort of thing."

Fontaine nodded. "I certainly understand. And Nate appreciates *so* much your commitment to his patients. I'll be sure to tell him how helpful you've been." She took a step toward Gayle. "But right now I need a few minutes alone. So you get back to whatever you were doing before we got here, and I'll let you know when we're finished."

"But..." Gayle hesitated.

"And would you please close the door after you? Thank you so much."

Gayle stood there a minute, the stiff set of her shoulders and determined angle of her jaw making it clear she was determined to protect Nate, even from his wife. Or perhaps, especially from his wife. But Fontaine was pretty much an unstoppable force. With a frustrated shrug, Gayle backed out into the hallway and gently closed the door. We waited a few moments until we heard her footsteps moving down the hall.

I laid my coat beside Fontaine's. "You think she knows where he is?"

She nodded. "I'd put money on it. Nate couldn't have disappeared all on his own. And from the way she was protecting this office, there must be something in here that tells us where he is. So let's find it." She jerked open the top drawers of the desk, pulling out the contents, piling everything on the desk. "Here, you look through this. I'll check out his computer."

There was a lot of unopened mail -- solicitations from various charities, advertisements from medical supply companies, invitations to financial planning seminars. I flipped through the latter with a heightened sense of professional curiosity, eager to know who was trying to poach my client. There were also a few medical journals and a number of back copies of *Sports Illustrated*. I laid them on the desk in stacks, trying to bring order to the chaos. "Doesn't he ever throw anything away? This is a mess."

"He's quite the pack rat. You should see his desk at home."

I skimmed through crumpled receipts for office supplies, business lunches and car repairs. "His accountant must love working through all this."

"That's what we pay him for." She pulled the keyboard toward her and typed in Nate's password.

I picked up a glossy brochure. "Here's something about Brazil. You think he could have gone there?"

She gave it a quick look. "That's from the medical conference we went to last fall. The one where he met Katarina. The sleazy little waitress that he couldn't keep his hands off of."

"Oh, yes. I remember you telling me." Fontaine had ranted for weeks after that conference, checking Nate's emails, convinced he was still in touch with the woman.

She frowned at the screen. "The password isn't working. Maybe I hit a wrong key." She typed it again, more slowly. "You know," she said, looking up at me, "Nate has been a little bit crazy ever since that trip."

I set the brochure aside. "Because of the waitress?"

"There's that. But he was also incredibly jealous of the keynote speaker, who had started a company that's now worth about a gazillion dollars. The other docs followed him around all weekend, on the golf course, at the pool, during cocktail hour. I think guys were even holed up with him in the john. All trying to figure out how he had done it, to see if they could put together something like that for themselves." She looked back down at the screen and drummed her fingers on the keyboard. "Nate must have changed the password."

"Are you sure? Try it one more time."

She keyed it in again. "The thing is, Nate knew this guy. He said he wasn't all that smart, had barely squeaked through med school, but now he was worth a fortune. It put him in a nasty mood. He was really chapped that this guy had been able to pull off something like this, while Nate was just plodding along in his career."

I glanced at the antique desk, the upholstered chairs, the mahogany bookshelves. "Nate has a very successful practice. I would hardly call this just plodding."

"You know what I mean. Nate can't stand to think that someone else is more clever than he is. Or richer." She smacked the edge of the computer. "Damn it, he's changed the password. If he's hiding something in here, I'm not going to get it today."

She walked toward a dusky oil painting on the opposite wall, a Victorian hunting scene of shotgun-toting gentlemen traipsing through the English moors, taking aim as their dogs flushed up pheasants into a cloud-streaked sky. She grasped the intricately carved gold frame and slowly pulled to the left. The painting rotated out on its hinges, revealing a small gray metal safe flush with the wall. She spun the combination dial, then tugged on the handle. "It won't open."

She went through the process again, rotating the dial to the right, then left, then right again. "Nothing," she said, jiggling the handle. "The combination was the date of our wedding. And now he's changed it. Guess that sends me a pretty clear message."

I struggled to say something reassuring. "There could be a hundred reasons why he changed that combination."

"Yes."

"You know he loves you."

"He loves my daddy's money. I'm not so sure he loves me." She pushed the painting back against the wall. "Let's go. There's nothing for us here."

I pulled open the desk drawer. "Give me a minute to put all this away."

"Leave it. I want him to know I was here checking up on him."

There was a soft knock at the door. Gayle came into the room, tightly gripping a stack of files, her French-manicured fingers splayed out like unsheathed claws. I wondered how long she had stood in the hallway, her ear pressed to the door, listening to us. "I just need to put these files..." She glanced at the haphazard tower of papers on the desk, still a jumble despite my efforts to organize them into manageable stacks. "What have you done?" She stomped toward me, her voice shrill, her eyes hostile under their heavy coat of mascara. "You have no right to go through Nate's things like that."

"We have every right," Fontaine said. "I'm his wife. Or have you forgotten that?"

Gayle whirled around, pumped up for a confrontation. But she quickly deflated when she saw Fontaine's angry expression, her previous Southern charm as cracked as the veneer on a yard-sale nightstand. "Of course not. But still...this is important information."

"Really?" Fontaine crossed to the desk and picked up a handful of *Sports Illustrateds*, then dropped them back on the desk one by one, studying the colorful covers featuring muscular, testosterone-fueled athletes. "Yes, I can see that these are really important. Especially this one." She slammed down the swimsuit edition. A tall brunette, her long curls blown back over her shoulders, smiled seductively as her round breasts bulged out of the tiny triangles of her bikini top. Her thumbs had jerked the bottoms low enough to require major airbrushing.

Gayle kept her eyes down as she set the files in the brass inbox. "Did you find what you needed?" The question was straightforward enough, but there was the slightest undercurrent of triumph in her voice, a little frisson of victory. And I suddenly realized she knew the passwords had been changed, that we would not be able to find any information in his office. She probably had the new ones jotted down somewhere, tucked away in a secret spot, in case Nate needed her to access something while he was out of the office.

Fontaine's quick breathing told me she was thinking the same thing. "We found enough." She grabbed her coat. "Come on, Robbie, let's get out of here."

We probably could have gotten down to the parking lot, or at least out to the elevators, before Fontaine's seething emotions exploded. But then Gayle said in a perky voice, "Be sure to tell Nate that I hope he feels better."

Fontaine stopped abruptly. She turned back around as she slowly wrapped her scarf around her neck and flicked her hair free, sending a thick tangle of dark curls shimmering to her shoulders. She glared at Gayle. "Tell me where he is."

Gayle looked puzzled. "He's at home, sick. That's what you told me when I called this morning."

Fontaine adjusted her coat cuffs, pulling them down over her gloves. "And yet we both know that's not true, don't we?"

"I don't know what you mean."

I gently nudged her elbow. "Fontaine, let's go."

She shook me off. "I know you helped him disappear," she said, her voice louder. "Where is he?"

A nurse looked at us curiously as she passed by the doorway. Behind her trailed the young boy with the cast, followed by his mother.

"Fontaine, calm down," I said. "The whole office can hear you."

"You've got this all wrong," Gayle said, shaking her head, her flat palms raised protectively in front of her. "I don't know where he is."

"Sure you don't."

"Excuse me." We turned to see Dr. Brayton Reynolds standing awkwardly in the doorway, hands stuffed deep into the pockets of his white jacket, his pudgy cheeks flushed with embarrassment. He was the newest hire on staff, charged with managing the office and covering appointments while the more senior doctors took a snow day. Breaking up a fight between his boss's wife and his nurse was probably not something he expected to be on the duty roster. "Is there anything I can help you ladies with?"

There was a moment of silence as Fontaine shot a last venomous look at Gayle. Then she smiled and said, "Why, Brayton, how nice to see you." The lilt was back in her voice, her Southern charm rising once more to the surface. "I hope you didn't have too much trouble getting into the office today?"

"Not too much. The back roads were a bit slippery, but the interstate had been plowed."

"Good to hear." She nodded to me. "I think we're all finished here. Let's go."

# CHAPTER 13

FONTAINE HAD COOLED DOWN a bit by the time we reached the parking lot. Promising to call her later, I got in my car and headed east. Slowed down by icy roads, it took me longer than expected to reach the law offices of Rodriguez and Simpson. But even though I was ten minutes late for my appointment, I still had to wait another twenty minutes before the door of the conference room finally opened. Ana Rodriguez's services were evidently very much in demand.

"So sorry to keep you waiting," she said. "It's just been crazy today."

"Not a problem," I said, standing and shaking hands. "Thanks for squeezing me in."

"Of course." She motioned for me to sit down, then took the chair across from me, opening her leather notebook and shaking back her long dark hair. "What can I help you with?"

I told her about the events of the ball: the wine on my dress, walking in on Vivian and Nate, then being grilled by the two detectives after her murder. "I'm sure they think I had something to do with her death, which is ridiculous. It's true that I didn't like her very much, and we were competitors for the same job, but I would never kill her."

Ana finished jotting down some quick notes, then asked, "Who are the detectives?"

"Gutierrez and Caldor."

"Ah, yes, I know them both," she said, nodding. "Very thorough. Very good at their jobs."

I clenched my palms. "I don't know that I would agree with you. They were pretty abusive to me this morning. I thought they were going to arrest me right then."

She gave me a wry smile. "Detective Gutierrez has a high solve rate. He's found that guilty suspects will quickly confess if his questioning is sufficiently intense. There have been some complaints against him. He's been cautioned a few times. But as long as he gets results, no one is pressuring him too much to change his style." She read over her notes, then glanced back up at me. "This is a high profile case, no? Vivian Sutherland was well known in the community?"

"Yes. So is Nate Thornton. He's the son-in-law of Wallace Baxter, the CEO of Daremaxon Industries."

"So Detective Gutierrez will be especially careful to investigate all possibilities. Of course, he always does. No matter who the victim is. Nonetheless, you were wise to insist on a search warrant before you let the detectives examine any of your things. We must always cooperate with the police, but we are not required to make their jobs easy for them."

"So what should I do now? You'll take my case?"

"Yes. Do not talk with the detectives again unless I am present. And do not discuss the case with anyone else. You never know when someone may repeat to the police anything you have said, even some casual little comment that may be taken totally out of context. In a murder investigation, every action, every statement, gets examined over and over again."

"So I do nothing?"

"Exactly. Give me a call if you hear from the detectives again, or if you want to talk some more. But for right now, I think you should just carry on as usual with your job, your life. You have a family?"

I shook my head. "My husband and son were killed in a car crash a few months ago."

"I am so sorry," she said, her face full of sympathy. "It is difficult to deal with this investigation all alone, is it not?"

"I'm not totally alone," I said, reaching for my coat. "I've got Fontaine."

Her forehead crinkled. "The woman who thinks her husband killed Vivian Sutherland?"

"Yes."

"I do not think you should discuss your situation with her."

"Why not? We've been best friends forever."

"But you say Nate has disappeared?"

"Yes."

"So what if the police suspect both you and Nate of murder? Which will Fontaine protect? Her husband? Or her friend?"

I hesitated. That was a tough call. We were dearest friends, and yet, she had taken Nate back time after time, despite his infidelity. It was obvious that she loved him.

"You see?" Ana said, reading my expression. "These situations are not so easy to predict. It is difficult to know what a person will do when someone they love is threatened."

"Fontaine would never betray me," I said.

She shrugged. "So she would betray her husband?"

"No." I shook my head. "She wouldn't do that either."

Ana took my hands in both of hers. "You say she is your friend. So be a good friend to her. Don't make her choose between the two of you."

§§§

I was halfway back to my office when my cell phone jangled. I pressed the phone icon on my steering wheel. "Hello?"

"Robbie, it's Everett." His excited voice boomed through my speakers. "I know who it was."

"Who what was?"

"The client who was threatening Vivian. I know his name."

"That's fantastic. Who is it?"

"Edgar Nelson. Do you know him?"

"The name sounds familiar. Vivian must have mentioned him." I pulled into the right hand lane to take the downtown expressway. "How did you find him?"

"It was in the safe deposit box. I was pulling out all her trust documents, and there they were. Six months of Fairburn, Crandall statements for this Nelson guy. He has to be the one."

The EZ Pass toll gates were just ahead. I slowed until the arm lifted to let me through. "Six months of statements? Why would she keep that in her safe deposit box?"

"Must have been keeping some kind of evidence against him or something." He paused. "I've told the police, but I thought you would want to know. At least this gives them another suspect besides me."

The downtown streets had been plowed and salted while I had been out. Traffic was getting back to normal, the magical quiet of the morning replaced by the more typical angry horns of impatient drivers. "What did they say about it? Do they have any idea why he was threatening her?"

"You know how the police are. They want to be the ones asking all the questions. They wouldn't tell me anything."

I pulled into the parking deck and started up the ramp, driving slowly up and up until I finally found an open spot on the fourth level. "I'll dig through our records and see what I can find out about this guy. There must be something in there that will tell us what was going on."

"Good. Do you want the statements? I kept copies. I can scan them and email them to you."

"Yes. Send them over. I'll look into it right away."

I locked the car and headed to the Trust National building. Darius frantically signaled as I entered the Fairburn, Crandall offices.

"Emergency meeting of the investment committee in the war room," he said. "Better get in there quick."

"What's going on now?" I asked, pulling off my gloves.

He adjusted the earpiece of his telephone, then held up a finger signaling me to wait. "No, that's not right," he said. "Ten thousand shares of Graveley Industries. Account number 261335827. It should have settled Friday. Yes, I'll hold." He looked up at me. "I don't know, but Shep is in a panic."

I figured it had to be another meeting about Vivian. Shep would want an update on her clients, to make sure no one was planning to leave. "Did you find any better contact info for Julius Tavenner?"

Darius put his hand over the mouthpiece. "I haven't had time to do that. I've been on the phone with these idiots all morning. Another screwed up trade." He turned back to the telephone. "Account 261335827. CUSIP number AJ5624289. Ten thousand shares."

"When you can get to it, I'd appreciate your help," I said, shrugging out of my coat.

He nodded, then turned his attention back to his telephone call. "That's right. Graveley Industries. Now you want to tell me what happened to those ten thousand shares?"

§§§

I heard angry voices as I walked down the hall to the war room. "It can't be that bad," Hardy insisted. "Everybody knew this was coming. It was only a question of when."

I slipped into a chair beside Lyman.

"Thank you for stating the obvious. The problem is that nobody expected the *when* to be *now*." Shep slammed his palm against the table so hard that the coffee cups rattled.

Hardy's face reddened under his winter tan. Shep usually stayed on the sidelines during these meetings. He would let the rest of us fight it out, arguing about earnings growth and market share and barriers to entry, sniping at each other with barbed sarcasm and not-so-subtle insults. He would remain silent, remote and aloof, until a bloodied opponent finally yielded the field in frustration. But today he was right in the middle of it, his carefully tailored suit jacket tossed aside, necktie loosened.

"What's going on?" I asked Lyman, my voice soft.

"One of the Fed governors gave a speech today at a financial conference," Lyman whispered. "Said the Fed would be raising rates soon. Our bond portfolios are taking a hit."

Interest rates had been so low for so long that we all knew the next move had to be up. And that meant bond prices would go down. I always explained to my clients that interest rates and bond prices were like two ends of a seesaw. When rates went up, bond prices went down. When rates came down, bond prices went up. For the past thirty years, interest rates had been coming down, which meant bond prices had been going up. Financial advisors who had stuffed their clients' portfolios years ago with long term bonds looked like geniuses.

"This didn't catch us off guard," Hardy said. "We've been positioning for this. Shortening duration for months. Our average now is what...about three?"

Duration measured the weighted average period of time to receive the interest payments from a bond. By selling our long term bonds and holding ones with short to intermediate maturities, we reduced the duration of our portfolios and made them less vulnerable to a price decline.

Murphy leaned back casually in his chair, shoulders slumped, his right foot resting on the opposite knee. "We've been educating our clients about this, preparing them for a rate increase. It's not going to be a surprise."

"So you think it won't matter to them, when they open their statements and see how much money they've lost?"

"Come on, Shep," Charlton said. "We have most of our clients laddered in individual bonds. As long we hold to maturity, it's only a paper loss."

"Are you all a bunch of idiots?" Shep snapped. "Our customers don't care if it's a paper loss. When they see those negative numbers on their statements, they're going to be voting with their feet."

Murphy pushed his heavy glasses higher on his nose. "I think we've acted very prudently in a challenging situation. The only way we could have avoided this is to not hold any bonds whatsoever."

"He's right," Hardy said. "We can't go naked in bonds. Our clients need the steady income. As well as the diversity that bonds give to their portfolios."

Shep took a deep breath. There was an air of desperation about him, his skin pale, eyes drooping. "We've been lagging our benchmarks on our equity portfolios. And now we're losing money in bonds, even though it is only a paper loss. I'm not sure our clients are going to be as complacent about all this as you think they are. Do you have any idea how many assets have walked out the door in the past two years?"

Of course we did. Darius ran the numbers for us every week. We spent so much time talking about client retention that we hardly had time to talk about investing. We all knew it was a problem. Unfortunately, no one seemed to know how to fix it.

"We're getting to the end of the road, folks," Shep said. "You guys better get your heads out of your asses and figure out what we need to do next. Or else this whole firm is going to disintegrate right in front of our eyes." He grabbed his jacket and flung back his chair so hard that it tipped to the floor, resting on its back, wheels spinning in the air, as he marched out of the conference room.

The rest of us sat there in silence. "What the hell just happened?" Charlton finally said. "Is he on drugs or what?"

Murphy tried to smooth things over. "Come on, guys. You know Shep's having a rough time. This situation with Vivian...the police and news reporters have been relentless."

"If this is like that thing with Vince..." Charlton said.

"This is nothing like Vince," Murphy said quickly. "Shep is fine. He just needs some time to settle down." He gently set Shep's chair back on its feet. "And the rest of us need to get back to work."

§§§

Back in my office, I searched my emails until I found the message from Everett. A number of Edgar Nelson's financial statements were attached. Nothing odd jumped out at me as I glanced through the first few. I would have to study them more carefully to figure out what was going on.

I printed the first one and headed to the copy room to pick it up. Charlton and Hardy were already there, their heads close together, their voices low. "I knew this thing with Vivian would push him over the edge," Hardy said. "There's nothing wrong with our bond portfolios. If we're going to make our move, it has to be now."

Charlton frowned as I walked in. "Not here," he said.

Charlton had never been one of my biggest fans. Office gossip said he voted against hiring me, skeptical that a young woman from the Midwest would be able to grow a book of business in a conservative Southern city like Hastings, where family connections and college affiliations drove so many business relationships. "Men want other men to manage their money," he told me. "And women want men to manage their money. Nobody wants some hysterical female at the controls." He seemed more irritated than relieved when I proved him wrong.

The printers were noisily churning out full-color glossies of client performance, multi-page documents that Darius would compile into booklets for the financial advisors to use in client meetings. My print job had to be far down the queue. I waited, hoping Charlton and Hardy would resume their conversation, wanting to hear their take on Shep's bizarre behavior. But they just stood there, not saying anything, obviously waiting for me to leave. Finally I gave up. "Guess I'll check back later," I muttered, walking out of the room.

Curious, I stood in the hallway, my back pressed against the wall. In a few moments they started to talk again, their voices subdued, the low rumble of frustration in Hardy's voice playing just at the edge of my hearing.

"What are you doing?"

I jumped. "Darius. You startled me. I...ah...I came to pick up something from the printer, but your job has the machines tied up."

He looked puzzled. "So why are you out here hugging the wall?"

"Just admiring that painting right there. Quite striking, don't you think?" It was an impressionist scene of deep purple clouds feathered into a bright yellow sky, above a pink beach daubed with thick black. We always joked that it looked like a Gulf Coast oil spill.

"Damn ugly, if you ask me." He stepped into the copy room. "I'll let you know when I'm done."

Back in my office, I pulled up Edgar Nelson's account in our computer system. Vivian had completed a thorough customer analysis, listing his assets and liabilities, his risk tolerances, and his financial objectives. Shep always said a good financial advisor knew more about a client than anyone except maybe his proctologist. He encouraged us to figure out our clients' hopes and dreams, as well as what kept them up at night. Clients stayed with us not only because of good investment performance, Shep stressed, but because of close relationships that encouraged them to share their deepest secrets, knowing we would never betray a confidence. That we would always help them achieve their financial goals.

Our files indicated that Nelson was in his mid-seventies and had retired about ten years ago from his position as Director of Human Resources for Ellerson Enterprises, a venture capital company. His portfolio was a mix of domestic and international stocks and bonds, along with some alternative assets such as private equity, real estate and commodities. The account was more aggressively postured than I would have recommended for a retiree, but had had very strong returns over the past four years, so it was hard to argue with success.

All that had changed, however, in the last few months. His equity investments had taken a half-million-dollar hit. A number of different stocks had suffered big pullbacks. I could understand why he made those angry telephone calls to Vivian, why he would insist on getting a good explanation.

There was no mention of his calls in Vivian's quarterly file updates, which was not surprising. None of us liked to put any negative information in the computer, where another advisor in the firm could see it and try to solicit an unhappy client for himself. If she had kept records of their conversations, they would be in her personal desk files. But the police had already packed those up and carted them away, which meant I had no chance of checking through them until they were returned. And that would probably be much too late, considering how determined those detectives were to arrest me for Vivian's murder.

I was still mulling this over when Darius stuck his head in my office. "Shep said we can all leave as soon as the markets close. It's started snowing again. The roads are lousy, freezing back up."

"Thanks." I walked to the window. Dark gray clouds were so thick that I could barely make out the giant blue "H" at the top of the Homestead Life office tower across the street. Far below me red tail lights flickered as commuters started their exodus from downtown, snaking their way through the fog.

The office quickly began to empty out. I heard briefcases snap shut and car keys jingle. Charlton and Elena, our new research assistant, passed by my door, her laughter tinkling. Hardy called out, "Hey, remember I'm going to be late tomorrow. I've got that client meeting." The elevator dinged and someone yelled, "Hold it. I'm coming."

Murphy stood at my doorway, wriggling into his overcoat. "Can I walk you out?"

"No, thanks. I'm in no hurry to join that fender-bender traffic. Think I'll try to get some work done while it's quiet."

"How about a beer at Billie's instead?"

"I don't think so. But thanks for asking."

"Sure thing." He picked up his briefcase. "I'll see you tomorrow."

"Hey, Murph?" I called as he stepped into the hallway.

"Yes?" he said, turning back.

"Did you know that one of Vivian's clients had been threatening her?"

"No. She never said anything about it. Who was it?"

"Edgar Nelson. Retired HR guy from a venture capital company. Do you know him?"

Murphy thought for a moment, then shook his head. "The name is vaguely familiar, but I can't say I do."

"There's not much information about him in the system."

"That's not a surprise. Vivian was paranoid that we were all trying to steal her clients. She kept most of her info in her desk files."

"I know. Unfortunately, the police have all of those." I clicked out of our customer database, closing Nelson's file. "I thought I'd give him a call. Check him out."

Murphy frowned. "Robbie, I don't think you should do that."

"But if he's the murderer…"

"Then you definitely shouldn't be anywhere near the guy. It's not safe. If he threatened Vivian, the police need to investigate. Not you."

"But that's just it. You should have heard those two detectives grilling me this morning. They know I left the ball early, which gave me plenty of time to kill her. And my co-workers filled them in about how we were both scrambling for the partnership, which they think gives me a strong motive." I studied his face to see if he had been one of the people who shared that information with Gutierrez and Caldor, but he showed no signs of guilt. "I think I'm at the top of their suspect list."

"Now, Robbie, I'm sure the police don't think you did this." He spoke in that slow, calming tone that he always used with clients who were frantic for him to *do something* in the face of a jumpy market. "Leave Nelson alone. I'll tell Shep what you've heard. Let him take care of it."

"Shep's got enough on his plate right now. All that stuff this morning about bond exposure. He seemed really frazzled."

"Vivian's death has hit him pretty hard," Murph admitted.

"Charlton asked if this was anything like Vince. He meant Vince Crandall, right? Shep's former partner?"

"Charlton was way out of line. Should have kept his mouth shut."

"I heard that Vince left to set up a London office. But now he seems to have just dropped out of sight. What's the story?"

"It was a long time ago, Robbie. There's no point in dredging all that back up now."

Murphy and I had always had a comfortable relationship, celebrating our successes, commiserating when trades went sour. He was the only one from Fairburn, Crandall to visit me at Fontaine's during those devastating weeks after the accident, the only one I would let see me cry. But now his face was stern. It was obvious he wasn't going to tell me anything more.

"Drive safe," he said. "I'll see you tomorrow."

§§§

The quiet gently washed over me after everyone had left. I opened some of the Wall Street research reports that had been clogging my inbox, things I never had time for during the work day. For almost an hour I made myself plod through them, searching for some good ideas to make money for my clients. But it was tough to concentrate. With everything that had happened in the last few days, my brain seemed to be working at half power. The colorful pie charts blurred on the page. I read the same sentence three times without really comprehending it.

Finally I gave up. Massaging my stiff neck, I shut down my computer and locked my desk, stuffing the keys in my pocket. Then I remembered Nelson's financial statements. They had to be ready by now.

It was oppressively quiet as I headed to the copy room. No ringing telephones. No clicking keyboards. No casual banter about weekend games. I passed deserted cubicles and darkened offices. The same spaces that were so familiar during the work day suddenly became full of menacing shadows. I felt like an intruder as I walked down the hallway.

The financial statements weren't in the printer. I searched the work tables along the wall, even the trash cans, but didn't see them anywhere. They must have gotten mixed up in someone else's job. I would have to print them again.

I passed Shep's office on the way back to my own. He had been reading Vivian's fuchsia files this morning. Maybe one of them was Edgar Nelson's. It might explain why Nelson had been threatening her.

Snooping through my boss's office was not something I normally would have even considered. It was a huge violation of trust and privacy. Plus, if I got caught, I could get fired. But these were far from normal times. Vivian had been murdered, and the detectives thought I did it. I needed answers about Nelson, and I was willing to do what it took to get them.

I eased Shep's office door open. The room was dark, the ceiling lights turned off. I activated the flashlight app on my phone. His desktop was surprisingly neat, the usual clutter cleared off. No day-old *Wall Street Journals*. No back issues of business magazines. Even his inbox had been straightened up. And the pile of fuchsia files on his desk had disappeared. I ran my light over his credenza and bookcases, to see if he had moved them. There were none in sight.

I crouched down and tugged at a desk drawer. It was locked. But I knew our office furniture was built more for show than security. With enough patience and a bit of luck, we could open many of the desks in our offices. I had done it often enough for Murphy when he had forgotten his keys. Pulling my desk key from my pocket, I gently edged it into the lock, jiggling it slowly back and forth, up and down. Then I put one hand on the bottom of the drawer and pushed up. The lock clicked open. I slowly pulled out the drawer.

None of the files were fuchsia. But then, he might have transferred Vivian's information to plain files, to make them less obvious. I pulled out a handful and set them on the floor, flipping them open one by one, hoping to find something about Edgar Nelson.

Suddenly I heard a door close. If somebody caught me in here, I would have a lot of explaining to do. I quickly gathered up the scattered files and stuffed them back in the drawer. My hands trembled as I wiggled the key out of the lock. I heard voices. Someone was walking down the hall, getting closer. I scrambled to the far end of the desk and squatted down, contorted into a tight ball, arms squeezed around my knees, head bowed, barely daring to breathe. The footsteps stopped just outside the door. My mind raced as I struggled to come up with a reasonable explanation for why I was in Shep's office.

But then the footsteps started up again, moving on down the hall. I let out a long, slow breath of relief as I scrambled to my feet and moved toward the door. A quick look showed the corridor was deserted. I quickly tiptoed to my own office. Another door closed somewhere. I pulled on my coat, grabbed my purse and briefcase, and stepped into the hall.

"Stop right there."

I froze. It had to be someone from security. I bit my lip, trying to calm my pounding heart. There was no reason that someone should challenge me. I worked late all the time. But guilt is a funny thing. It can turn a perfectly normal situation into something much more threatening. I glanced toward the voice, trying to look casual, even though my stomach was knotting up inside.

A husky man was standing in the reception area, dressed in dark pants and a striped shirt, his name embroidered on the pocket. "Don't miss that office back there," he said, wiping his hands on a cloth. "It got skipped last week, and the tenant complained. The boss gave me hell."

"Got it," said a voice behind me. I turned to see a thin woman enter the office several doors down from mine, coming out with a trash can in her hand. Relieved, I headed toward the exit. The woman followed me and emptied the can into a large black plastic trash barrel. I nodded to them as I pushed through the glass doors. The whine of a vacuum cleaner followed me as I waited for the elevator. Only when the doors slid shut behind me did I realize that I was still holding my breath.

Down at street level, cold wind slapped me in the face as I pushed through the revolving doors to the sidewalk. Tightening my scarf, I put my head down and strode across the icy street to the parking deck, ten depressing floors of dim lights and crumbling concrete. I punched the button for the elevator and waited. It was slow, as usual, grinding down from a higher floor, then stopping, then grinding again. When the doors finally opened, I stepped in and punched the button for the fourth floor. The elevator shuddered as it labored to lift me up.

The landing was in shadows when I stepped out. The new owner of the deck had finally started badly need repairs. Dangling wires indicated where new fixtures would be installed. Irregular chalk outlines on the pitted concrete floor, looking like ghoulish body sketches from a crime scene, marked rough areas that needed to be patched. Shivering, I rushed toward my car, the only one left on this level. Gritty, gray powder from jack-hammered concrete had settled on it like a shroud.

The workmen's equipment was stored against the far wall, protected by a hanging wall of heavy plastic sheeting. A whoosh of cold wind suddenly whipped back the plastic, revealing pale brown bags of cement and faded orange jackhammers. Something clattered to the floor, and I froze in place. There had been several attacks in various parking decks throughout the city over the past few weeks. The last victim had been beaten pretty badly, even lost a few teeth. The same mugger could be back there, hiding behind the bags of cement. I listened carefully, but heard only the gentle sighing of the plastic as it settled back into place.

I started again toward my car. And then I heard footsteps.

# Chapter 14

MY GLOVED HANDS DUG into my purse as I raced to the car. I couldn't find my keys, and frantically tossed out sunglasses, a brush and a lipstick as I ran. Ripping off my gloves, I jammed my hand back into the purse again, pushing aside my wallet and cell phone. Finally my trembling fingers tightened around the keys. The footsteps were closer now, and fast.

I punched the remote to start the engine. Wrenching the car door open, I caught my thumb in the handle, sending a wave of pain shooting up my arm. Ignoring it, I jumped into the driver's seat. Before I could shift into reverse, a man flung open the door and grabbed me, pulling me out and throwing me back against the car.

He was a big guy, with short cropped hair, hooded eyes, and a nose that had seen the wrong side of a fist in too many barroom brawls. I lunged at him, thrusting my knee toward his crotch, but he angled sideways, deflecting my shot. His hands dug into my shoulders, pressing back hard, leaving me little room to maneuver. I pounded my fists into his chest, trying to push him back, to twist away from him, but he was too strong for me. He caught my wrists and wrenched them up above my head as I screamed.

"Shut up." He clamped a hand over my mouth, his face so close to mine that his whiskers scratched against my cheek and the earthy smell of his leather jacket filled my nose. "I've got a message for you."

He leaned in close, his raspy voice whispering in my ear, but I was too frantic to listen. Desperate to escape, I chomped down on his fingers. Surprised, he jerked his hand back, then quickly grabbed my chin, hooked his thumb under my jaw and pushed up hard, jamming my teeth into my tongue. Blood squirted hot and salty into my mouth.

My booted foot stomped down on his toes. "Get away from me," I screamed. Jerking my hands free, I scraped my fingernails across his cheek.

"You stupid bitch." He pressed his hand against his bloody face. "You'll pay for that." He grabbed my scarf and pulled it tight. I wrenched at it with frantic fingers as the fabric cut into my neck, digging deep into my throat, making me gag.

Then I heard squealing tires and a blaring horn. "Let her go," someone shouted.

My attacker tightened his grip on the scarf. Blood pounded in my ears. Sparks of light flashed at the edges of my eyes.

An enormous explosion reverberated through the deck as someone fired a gun. Bits of concrete chipped from the column only a few feet from my head. "Let her go," the voice said again.

My attacker pulled me tight against him. "I'm not finished with you," he said, his mouth close to mine. Then he slammed me against the car and ran off down the ramp.

I dropped to the concrete, yanking desperately at the scarf, gasping for air.

A hand grabbed my shoulder. "Are you all right?"

A car was stopped at a crazy angle only a few feet from me, its headlights piercing the gloom, the driver's door thrown open. A man put his hand under my elbow and helped me to my feet. "Oh, my God, Robbie, it's you," he said, his voice warming with recognition. "Are you hurt?"

I clutched my neck, trembling, gulping air in short, shallow wheezes.

"Robbie, it's Murphy," he said, pulling the scarf loose. "You're safe now."

Sharp pains gripped my chest as my lungs fought for oxygen.

"You're hyperventilating. Try to relax. Breathe slow."

I shuddered, my throat making desperate squeaks.

"Look at me, Robbie. Look at me. You're safe now. Relax."

I heard sirens in the distance, then closer and louder. Suddenly a police car roared up the narrow ramp toward us, lights flashing, blocking the exit. Two uniformed officers jumped out, guns drawn. "Drop the gun," one of them yelled as he rushed toward Murphy. "Get on the ground. Now."

Murphy sank to his knees and laid the gun down beside him.

The second officer ran toward me, her blond hair pulled into a tight bun at the back of her head. "Ma'am, are you all right?" she asked.

I nodded, coughing, my throat tight.

Footsteps pounded toward us from a car stopped farther up the ramp. "You've got the wrong guy," a man yelled, running toward the policeman who was patting down Murphy. "He saved her. Scared the other guy away. I saw the whole thing. I'm the one who called 911."

More police cars screeched into the deck. Suddenly uniforms were everywhere, searching the dark corners, poking behind the plastic sheeting that covered the construction equipment. Flashes of light bit into the darkness as someone snapped pictures of the scene. Murphy and the other man were huddled together with the policemen. My eyes blurred as I raised my head and looked around.

"Don't worry about all that," the officer said, her eyes kind. "Just talk to me. I'm Officer Brady. Can you tell me what happened?"

"He came out of nowhere. I was terrified."

"Did he hurt you?"

"He tried to choke me," I whispered, patting my neck.

Brady gestured toward my hand. "You scratched him?"

I nodded, staring at my bloody fingertips.

"We'll get DNA from this," the officer said. She eased my hands into paper bags and fastened them with tape. "Did you get a good look at him?"

I nodded. "Big guy. Crooked nose."

Behind me a patrolman dug a bullet out of the concrete column. "You could have killed that guy," he said to Murphy.

Murphy shook his head. "If I wanted him dead, he'd be lying on that ramp right now."

Brady put her hand on my shoulder. "We're going to take you to the hospital. A forensic nurse will check you out, make sure you're all right. She'll get DNA samples from your nails, then see if there's any other evidence, strands of hair, anything like that."

I shook my head. "I don't want to go to the hospital."

Her eyes flickered over my face. "There's blood on your mouth. And it looks like your jaw is bruised. The nurse really should take a look at you. Plus, this may be the same guy who's attacked all those other women over the past month. Any evidence we can collect can help us catch him before he does this to anyone else."

I nodded. "All right. I'll go. But what about my car? And all my stuff?" I gestured toward my sunglasses and lipstick, all the items I had tossed out of my purse while I was hunting for my keys. Everything was scattered across the concrete.

"We'll gather it up for you. And we can bring you back here afterwards, to pick up your car."

Murphy put his arm around me. "That scared me, Robbie. I'm glad you're okay."

"Thanks, Murph."

"You need me to come with you?"

I shook my head. "No. I'll be fine. I'll see you tomorrow."

The officer helped me into the police car and we started down the ramp. My hands trembled inside the paper bags. I peered into the darkness, convinced my attacker was still hiding there somewhere in the shadowy corners of the deck. But all I could see were the flashing blue lights of the police cars as we drove off.

§§§

The forensic nurse was gentle, swabbing blood from beneath my nails, manipulating my jaw, shining a light into my mouth. "Your tongue will be sore," she said, "but you don't need stitches." She took pictures of my injuries. "You've got some bruising on your neck. It'll probably get worse over the next day or so."

When she had finished, Officer Brady led me into another room. "We'd like to get a description of your assailant. Do you feel well enough to talk about this right now? We can wait until tomorrow if you'd rather."

My tongue felt enormous, making it difficult to talk, but I wanted to get this over with. "Yes. Let's do this now."

She opened her laptop and pulled up facial composite software. I sat beside her, choosing from numerous images of eyebrows, noses, and lips until she came up with a reasonable image of my attacker. The cropped hair. The square face. The hooded eyes. And that unforgettable nose, angled off to the right. "That's him," I said.

"Good. We'll get this picture out right away. Hopefully we can track him down soon." Her fingers clicked on the keyboard, then she shut her laptop. "Are you ready to leave now? I'll take you back to your car."

Seeing that face again made my heart race and my throat spasm. "I'd like to just sit here for a few minutes by myself," I said. "If that's all right with you."

Her expression was sympathetic. "Of course. Let me bring you some water. And then when you're ready, we'll have someone waiting for you in the lobby to take you to your car."

"Thanks." I sat there a long time after she brought the water, my arms clenched around my waist, trying to slow down my breathing and get my emotions under control. I kept replaying the scene over and over in my head. The deserted parking deck, his body pressed hard against mine, his whiskers scratching against my cheek. If Murphy hadn't turned up when he did, that monster would have killed me.

Finally I mustered the courage to head for the lobby. Luddy Driscoll was standing by the reception desk, talking on his cell phone, as I pushed open the swinging doors. I ignored him and glanced around the waiting room, looking for my ride.

He ended his call and walked up to me. "Ready to go?" he asked.

I shook my head. "A policeman is taking me to my car."

"Afraid not." He smiled sheepishly. "Officer Brady and I go way back. I told her I would give you a ride. That we were old friends."

I grimaced. "I made it clear Saturday night that we're not friends. I'm not going anywhere with you."

He shrugged. "You're out of luck, then. Officer Brady already headed back out on patrol. Looks like I'm your only choice."

Not believing that Brady had left me stranded, I looked around the waiting room. I saw a teenager whose right hand was wrapped in bloody gauze. A middle-aged man hunched in his chair, eyes closed, face twisted in pain. But no policeman. "I can't believe you did this."

"Just trying to be helpful," he said. "Thought you'd be happy to see a familiar face."

"Sure you did." I thought of calling a car service, but figured drivers would be in short supply on a snowy Monday night. Besides, I was tired and shaky, my throat hurt, and I really wanted to get home as fast as possible. "Fine," I said. "Where's your car?"

"Right out front." He pushed open the door for me.

"What are you doing out on a night like this, anyway?" I asked as we walked outside.

"Tracking down the mugger who's been hitting downtown parking decks. Thought yours might be the same guy."

"You think it was?"

He shook his head. "No. Your guy wasn't wearing a mask. And he didn't beat you up."

"So sorry to disappoint you. Maybe Murphy just got there too soon." I followed Luddy toward a faded green Toyota, parked near a pole light that beamed down on its rusted hood. The right back fender was bashed in, and a long streak of black ran from the fender to the wheel well. "New car?" I asked as Luddy unlocked the passenger door.

He laughed. "The places I park, I need something that nobody wants to steal." He gestured toward the front seat. "Just move that stuff out of your way."

I picked up a jacket and binoculars from the seat and tossed them into the back, already crowded with paperback books, several folded dress shirts, and a muddy pair of rubber boots. "Do you carry all your worldly goods in this car?" I asked as he slipped behind the wheel.

"Pretty much. It's kind of an office. I've even got a suit and tie in the trunk, for special occasions."

My foot crunched against a large soft drink cup with an attached top. "Trash?" I asked, picking it up.

"Not exactly." He grinned. "It's for when I'm on stakeout. Sometimes the facilities are in short supply."

"Yuck," I said, hurling it behind me.

He started the engine, buckled his seat belt and turned down the radio. "So tell me about your attacker. What do you remember?"

I sniffed. "Working on your story already? And here I thought you were worried about me."

"I *was* worried about you. If anything had happened…" His hands tightened on the steering wheel. "But you're safe now," he said after a few moments, turning toward me. "So we can talk about the story."

I ran my fingers down my sore jaw. "Let me guess. You want to know how I felt when that man jammed my teeth into my tongue. What went through my mind when he pulled my scarf so tight I thought I would pass out."

He backed out of the parking space and headed for the exit. "If that's what you'd like to tell me."

I twisted angrily on the seat to face him. "I don't want to tell you anything."

His jaw muscles tightened. "Listen, Robbie…"

"You enjoy this, don't you?" I interrupted him. "Getting people to relive the most horrible things in their lives."

"Of course not."

"Yes, you do. The more emotions you can wring out of your readers, the more newspapers they'll buy."

He glanced at me. "That's harsh."

"You think? What about your series on the Allista gang? You wrote about how that little girl felt when her big brother got shot right in front of her."

He pulled into the street, then stopped at the intersection as he waited to turn. We sat quietly, the only sounds my own ragged breathing and the click of his signal light. The big yellow M of the fast food place on the corner reflected into the windshield, turning his face sallow. "I like to find the truth," he said finally. "If it takes tough questions, that's what I'll do."

"Is that how you justify it? You wrote that she crouched over her brother as he died, her tiny hands pressed against his chest to stop the blood. You took a very private moment and exposed it to the whole world."

He pulled onto the interstate and headed for downtown. "She was scared to death when he was shot," he said, his voice quiet. "Wouldn't talk to the police. So I sat there with her, holding her hand until her mom got there. And she told me some details that helped put Jaral Allista behind bars."

"Don't try to make yourself sound like the good guy," I snapped. "You revel in other people's pain." We were close to the financial district now. The red glow of the Trust National logo marked the top floor of my building.

"If that's the way you prefer to see it, then I don't guess I can change your mind. But I can tell you that she loved that story. She was proud that people knew she had stayed with her brother to the end and hadn't run away. Not everyone would have done that."

We pulled onto Main Street. The parking deck was at the next corner. He stopped at the light, then made a right on red.

"You said horrible things about Rolfe," I said. "You made people think he was a careless drunk who killed his son."

He pulled into the alley entrance for my deck and stopped. "Firemen told me the accident scene reeked of alcohol. Bourbon and vodka were splashed all over the back seat. There was a trash bag full of empty beer cans."

"It was a tailgate, Luddy. We always brought the liquor. Rolfe didn't even drink beer. He was bringing home the empties to recycle." I opened the passenger door. "You played poker with the guy every Friday night for three years. You knew he only drank bourbon. And when he had Jason in the car, he never drank at all."

He grabbed my arm. "I admit I made some mistakes in that story. And I printed a retraction."

I jerked my arm free, then stepped to the pavement. "Big deal. Nobody ever saw it."

He shut off the ignition. "Let me walk you to your car."

"No need. I'm fine," I said.

"I'm coming with you. To make sure it's safe."

I walked briskly up the middle of the ramp, Luddy trailing behind me. The police cars were gone. The deck was deserted except for my car, sitting all by itself on the fourth level. This time I was ready, with keys in hand, and punched the remote to start the engine.

"Robbie, let me make it up to you."

I opened the car door. "What can you possibly do?"

"Find the guy that attacked you tonight, for one. Maybe it *is* the same guy that has attacked all those other women. Or maybe it's somehow tied in to Vivian's murder."

"Why would you think that?"

"Two women who work for the same firm attacked within a few days of each other? Doesn't that sound suspicious to you? Please, Robbie, let me help you."

"I don't want your help. Every time I look at you, I see Rolfe. And I just can't deal with that right now." I got in the car and slammed the door. Luddy jumped back as I threw the car into reverse.

I could see him in the rear view mirror as I squealed toward the exit, his hands stuffed deep in his jacket pockets as he plodded slowly down the ramp. Maybe he was right. Maybe this attack did have something to do with Vivian. And maybe I did need some help in figuring this all out. But not from Luddy.

He had betrayed Rolfe. I couldn't trust him.

# CHAPTER 15

DARIUS POUNCED ON ME when I entered the office the next morning, rushing out from behind his desk, arms spread wide. "Robbie, I'm so happy to see you. That attack was terrifying."

I stiffened at his unexpected hug. "Murphy told you?" He had promised to keep it quiet. The last thing I needed was negative headlines that might make my clients nervous. Especially so soon after the devastating news about Vivian.

"Not Murphy. Somebody put a video on the internet. We could see that guy attacking you. Word is all over the building."

"The internet? How did that happen?" And then I remembered the driver who had called 911, who had been so brave once the attacker had run out of the deck. He must have been recording the entire time, calmly watching while I fought for my life.

Gradually people started to gather around me, two of the research assistants, our new intern, a few folks from accounting, then the analysts and portfolio managers as word spread that I was in the office. Charlton and Lyman came out into the hallway. Everyone was asking questions, reaching out to pat my shoulder, grab my hand. It amused me that people who barely said two sentences to me in a normal workweek were suddenly so concerned for my well being.

Someone called out, "Here comes the hero," as Murphy walked up and put his arm around me.

"So tell us about it," Darius said.

I took a deep breath and looked out over the group. "There's not a lot to tell. That guy came out of nowhere. If Murphy hadn't shown up when he did..."

Murphy shrugged. "Glad I was in the right place at the right time."

"You should have shot the bastard," Charlton said.

"I just wanted to scare him off. I didn't want to kill the guy."

"Not sure why not. This guy's been attacking women all over town."

"We need to have more security around here," one of the research assistants said. "It's just not safe. First Vivian gets gunned down. Now this. The police have to do something."

"I'm not working late anymore," the woman standing next to her said. "I can guarantee you that. They don't pay me enough to take that kind of risk."

"Since when did you ever work late?"

"Well, I'm sure not doing it now."

"Folks, I really appreciate your concern," I said. "It was really scary. I'm just glad that Murphy was there. And now I need to get to work."

There was a jumble of conversation as everyone offered an opinion. "We need to organize something." "Some kind of buddy system." "Maybe a sign up sheet, or a schedule." The crowd broke off into groups of two and three, mumbling as they filtered back to their desks.

"Guess that was my fifteen minutes of fame," I said, walking with Murphy toward his office. "Thanks again for saving my life."

"Glad to be of help. But I didn't do anything anyone else wouldn't have done."

"Oh, I don't know about that. You could have just sat in your car and filmed a video to post on the internet."

He grimaced as he hung his suit jacket on the back of his door. "I know that guy. Works on the eighth floor. At least he called 911, but he was pretty much of a jerk for filming the whole thing instead of getting out to help. I'm going to have a few words with him later this morning."

"You won't shoot him, will you?"

"No, but I might threaten to. Just to keep him in line." He studied my face. "You still pretty shook up?"

"More than I want to admit." I ran my fingers along my jawbone and neck, still bruised and tender from last night. "I really thought he was going to kill me. I can't remember when I've been so scared."

Murphy moved behind his desk. "Next time you're working late, I'm going to stay and walk out with you."

I sat in the chair across from him. "You don't need to do that."

"But I want to." He sat down and booted up his computer. "I don't want anything like that to happen again."

"That makes two of us." I glanced down at the broken fingernails on my right hand. Even though the nurse had cleaned them thoroughly when she swabbed for DNA, and I had scrubbed them again when I got home, I still felt like there were traces of my attacker lingering on my fingers. "By the way, did you happen to see my briefcase last night?"

"Your briefcase?"

"Yes. I dropped it when that guy started after me. I can't figure out what happened to it. The police didn't pick it up when they gathered the rest of my things. I thought you might have seen it."

"No, I didn't." He glanced down at his computer screen. "Did you check the deck?"

"Yes." I had walked through every level of the deck this morning, squatting down to look under all the cars, pulling back the plastic sheeting that protected the construction materials. "But it's not there. I just can't figure out what happened to it."

"Was there anything really important in there?"

"Not really. Just some research. Thankfully, I didn't have my laptop in there. That's tonight's project. I've got a couple of stock ideas I'm trying to flesh out."

"Good. We could use some fresh ideas."

I picked up the leather-framed photograph at the edge of his desk. "How's Thad these days?"

In the photo Thad floated incredibly high off the floor, several feet behind the three point line, legs dangling, arms flexed. The basketball he had just released angled upward, high over the fingertips of the opposing player who had stretched up to block the shot. It had been the winning shot of Thad's high school championship tournament.

Murphy crinkled his forehead. "The ankle's still giving him trouble. Doc said it's not healing like it should."

I rubbed some dust from the top of the frame. "He's young. Give it time."

"I guess. But it's really messed him up for this season. He's had to spend most of his freshman year sitting on the bench. And it doesn't look like that's going to change anytime soon."

"There's always next year." I sat the frame back on his desk. "He'll be back, stronger than ever."

"I hope so." He angled the photo toward him. "You know, the only thing Thad has ever wanted to do is play basketball. During high school he was always outside, first thing in the morning, last thing at night, shooting baskets. Drove his mother crazy, that ball pounding in the driveway at all hours. When he got that college basketball scholarship, it was the answer to all his dreams." He pushed out his lower lip. "And now this."

I stood up and moved to the door. "Thad's a good kid. He's got plenty of playing time ahead of him. Just be patient."

He nodded. "I guess you're right. It's just been a really tough year."

"For all of us," I agreed.

§§§

I left Murphy's office, got coffee and settled down at my computer, checking the opening indicators for the market, skimming through the day's headlines, reading my emails. Trying to focus on work, on anything to keep my mind off last night's scene in the parking deck. Which was really difficult since my co-workers kept stopping by all morning, some expressing concern, others wanting more lurid details about what that man had done to me. All of them telling me how lucky I was that Murphy drove by at just the right moment.

I agreed with them, laughing as I described how surprised my attacker was when Murphy took a shot at him. But I didn't feel lucky. All the details of that man were deep inside my head: his smoke-scarred voice, his earthy smell, the weight of him as he pressed me back against the car. His cropped hair marked him as ex-military, or maybe an ex-cop. Someone who had been trained to hurt people. Someone who was ready to hurt me.

Financial advisors are supposed to be rock solid in a crisis. To stay calm and composed during the most unsettling gyrations in the market, even when clients are screaming at us. To push through the hype and the headlines and the chatter in order to ferret out the very best investment opportunities. We're trained to be never rattled, never emotional, never frightened.

But I had been terrified. I called Fontaine as soon as I got home, needing to hear a friendly voice. But she never picked up. Her phone went to voice mail, over and over again. I spent the entire night huddled up under the covers, staring into menacing shadows, afraid to sleep. I kept twisting my charm bracelet round and round my wrist, massaging those tiny icons from Paris and London and Venice, seeking strength from good memories of traveling with my family, trying to push the demons away.

But it wasn't enough. "I'm not finished with you," he had said. It was not over. He would be back.

# CHAPTER 16

MY SCHEDULED LUNCH with Lydia Kensington was a welcome excuse to get out of the office. Traffic was light as I drove to the Raleigh House, formerly the elegant home of a nineteenth-century tobacco merchant, now a private club that was a favorite for galas and wedding receptions.

The house had been rescued from ruin in the early 1920's by a determined group of well-connected women, dismayed to find its roof leaking and squirrels racing around the ballroom where handsome couples had once waltzed. They organized innumerable dances, auctions and raffles to raise funds to renovate the building, refinishing the oak floors, patching cracks in the twelve-foot ceilings, repainting the heavy crown molding.

Lydia was leaning back in a large rattan chair in the solarium, eyes closed, head bouncing slowly. A giant fern tapped gently against her cloud of short silver hair. My boots clicked loudly on the black and white marble floor as I walked toward her. Her eyes fluttered open. "So glad you could make it," she said, pulling out her ear buds and wrapping them around her phone. "I thought we might have to reschedule because of the snow."

"The roads are still a mess, but as long as you drive slowly, it's not so bad."

A waiter in black pants and a starched white shirt set a champagne flute in front of Lydia as I sat down across from her. "Something to drink?" he asked, handing me a menu.

"I need something hot. It's freezing outside. Do you have Earl Grey?"

"Yes."

"I'd like that, please." I glanced at Lydia's champagne as the waiter walked away. "Are you celebrating something?"

She chuckled. "At my age, I am constantly celebrating making it through another day. You never know when it will be your last." She angled her head, her lips turned down at the corners. "Just like that poor woman from Saturday night. I can't believe we were all sitting together at dinner, and now she's dead." She stretched out her fingers to touch mine. "Was she a close friend?"

108

I shook my head. "Not really. You know how it is in a big office." Murphy was the closest thing to a friend I had at Fairburn, Crandall. The rest of us were fierce competitors, always driven to outdo the guy in the next office. To bring in more money. To make better stock picks. To fine tune our portfolio allocations. It was all about sales goals and performance and those really big cash bonuses at the end of the year.

"Everyone is talking about it. Such a terrible thing to have happened. I know this is very upsetting to all of you." Her eyes were sympathetic as she sipped her champagne. "Any suspects yet?"

Her compassion would probably cool pretty quickly if she knew I was at the top of the list. I cringed at the memory of Gutierrez and Caldor cornering me in the conference room. "I'm sure the police are working on it."

"Well, hopefully this will all be cleared up soon. It's just dreadful. She was such a charming woman. My step-grandson was quite taken with her."

"Oh, really?"

"Yes. Gus said she was a marvelous dancer."

I shook out the linen napkin and smoothed it on my lap. "I'm sorry I didn't have more time to talk with him at dinner."

Her eyebrows shot up. "Consider yourself lucky. I wish I had never mentioned the ball to him. He insisted on coming as soon as he knew you would be there."

"Why's that?"

She tapped her fingernails on the edge of her champagne flute. "It's all my fault. It's just that I was so tired of having him constantly pester me for money. So I told him that you had total control over my finances. If he needed anything, he would have to go through you."

I pulled my notebook from my purse. "Do you want me to set something up for him? Some kind of distribution?"

"Absolutely not," she said, setting the flute down with such force that I thought the delicate stemware would break. The two men at the next table looked over at us curiously.

Lydia lowered her voice as she leaned closer to me. "Gus was very adequately provided for in Augustus's will. But he's squandered it all away in one scheme after another. Real estate. Alternative energy. A social media startup. Each time he runs out of cash, he comes back to me for more. I've helped him out numerous times over the years, but I've had enough. It's time he learned to get along on his own." She slowly twisted her wedding rings, multiple bands of diamonds reaching to her knuckle. "Besides, I want Augustus's money to go toward an endowed chair at his law school. You said you would help me with that."

I nodded. "It's well under way. All the details should be finalized in the next few weeks."

"Good."

The waiter returned with a delicately flowered china pot and a small plate of tea bags. I opened one and dipped it down into the hot water. "So tell me more about Gus."

She sighed. "He's a smart young man. Has doctorates in philosophy and Eastern religions. But he hasn't done anything with all that education. Has never been a college professor or researcher or writer or anything like that. I don't think he's held a steady job his entire life."

"So what does he do?"

"At the moment he's into commodities. I think that means he travels around the country buying and selling gold out of the back of his car." Her fingers beat out a restless staccato on the starched tablecloth. "I'm quite put out with him. He left me stranded there at the ball. Went out to the lobby looking for you after dinner, and then just disappeared. I had to get a ride home with a neighbor."

"Disappeared?" I wondered if he had seen Vivian as she left the cloakroom, easing that copper dress back over her shoulders, straightening her hair. Barbara Edmonton had said Vivian ignored Gus at dinner. Maybe he had followed her out to the parking lot, demanding an explanation. "Where did he go?"

Lydia gave a dismissive wave of her hand. "I don't know. He called yesterday. Just said something came up. And then he wanted me to set up a meeting with you. I refused, of course. Told him to call your office and take care of it himself."

"I haven't heard from him."

"I'm sure you will soon. Be sure to give my best regards. But just none of my money."

My charm bracelet jingled as I poured tea into my cup.

"What a charming bracelet," Lydia said. She pointed to the enameled black hat with big round ears. "Is that Mickey Mouse?"

"Yes. We took Jason to Disney World last year." I could still remember his delighted screams as we soared skyward on the elephant ride. "Rolfe always bought me a charm from each of our vacations. This is a gondola from Venice. Here's Big Ben, in London. And the Eiffel Tower from our honeymoon in Paris."

"It's comforting to have good memories, isn't it?" Lydia said. "I have a lot of mementoes from my travels with the Senator. They help me get through the long nights." She glanced at my wrist as I set down the teapot. "Gracious, Robbie, what happened to your arm?"

Even after all these weeks, the scar was still red and puckered. "Kitchen accident. I got a little careless." At least that was the story I had told everyone at work. And I didn't see any reason to change it now. I pulled my hand back into my lap, feeling my face flush.

"Does it hurt?"

"No. It's nothing." I pulled a glossy packet from my briefcase. "Let's talk about your portfolio. Everything is performing quite well. I think you'll be pleased."

# CHAPTER 17

I HEARD THE CHEERS as soon as I got back to Fairburn, Crandall after my lunch with Lydia, loud low whoops of victory coming from the far end of the hall. The last time we had that much excitement in our office was when City University's basketball team made it to the Final Four in the NCAA tournament. That had been a real long shot, with odds of about 87,000 to one, and had turned the CU team into a national sensation. We were so thrilled at their victory that none of us minded that the unexpected win totally busted all our brackets, and that Hardy's eight-year-old daughter, who had made her picks based solely on the names of the mascots, won the office pool.

I followed the noise to Charlton's office, where he was staring at his computer, with Hardy and Dennis Freeman, another portfolio manager, leaning down to get a better view of the screen. "What's going on, guys?" I asked. "Good news?"

Charlton grinned. "I'll say. Word on the street is that Hawthorne Medical is getting taken over. The stock's up 30% in the last hour."

"That's fantastic." We had added Hawthorne to our portfolios in January, despite Murphy's protests that a small pharmaceutical company with no approved products and a steady bleed of cash was too risky.

"I told you guys this would work," Dennis said, pounding his fist into his palm. He took a step back and went into his batter's stance, feet apart, knees slightly bent, hands wrapped around an imaginary bat. "I could feel it. Just like when you're up at bat and it's all tied up, bottom of the ninth, two outs and bases loaded." Dennis had been a star player in college and had even been picked up by the majors for a season or two before a torn ACL got him sidelined. "That ball whizzes in, straight and sweet, right up the middle." He swung at an invisible ball. "And then it's just an easy trot around the bases as you watch that baby sail right out of the park."

Hardy laughed. "Hold on, Derek Jeter. You're full of it. Hawthorne wasn't your idea. Vivian came up with it."

"Well, yeah, but I did my own research," Dennis said, his voice defensive. "I knew it would work."

"Oh really? You're that good, huh?"

"Absolutely."

Hardy straightened up. "So what's your next hot idea?"

Dennis hesitated.

"Come on, man. I got some cash all queued up. What's your call?"

"Still working on that one."

"I bet you are." Hardy laughed.

"Vivian had the touch, didn't she?" Dennis said. "She could just see things. Remember she got us into Triad? We made a killing."

"And Dandridge Oil," Hardy said. "My clients are still thanking me for that one."

"And she got us out of Bovender." Charlton glanced at the computer screen. "Which is down another three percent today."

Vivian was turning into myth right before my eyes, the golden girl who could do no wrong, her magical powers of prediction raking in millions of dollars for our clients. Obviously, she had made a good call on Hawthorne. But she had made a lot of bad calls, too. There was the time we bought Alden Industries and it just stalled for over a year, badly underperforming its peer group. Or the time she convinced us to double down on Sylvan Products when it missed earnings and the stock price took a dive. It just kept going down and down until we finally couldn't take it anymore and pulled the plug. But Hawthorne was her last call, and it was a big winner. It was the one that everyone would remember. "Who's the buyer?" I asked.

"Still under wraps," Hardy said. "Lots of speculation. I'm hearing Merck."

"I heard Sanofi," Dennis said.

"So it's not a done deal?"

"Not yet."

"Anybody here ready to take profits?" I asked. "Buy the rumor, sell the news? With it up 30% today, we may have already seen the biggest gains."

"Are you kidding?" Hardy said. "It's way too early to bail on this one. We're probably looking at a bidding war."

It was certainly possible. Bovender wasn't the only pharma company facing patent expirations, which meant declining sales and profits. Buying an early-stage blockbuster drug could be much faster and cheaper than developing one in-house. There were probably a lot of companies out there salivating over

Hawthorne's pipeline. If we waited for multiple bidders to jump in, the stock could go up a lot more.

On the other hand, this could be just wishful speculation on the part of a Wall Street analyst, or the musings of an eager blogger who had sent his thoughts flying into cyberspace. If no viable buyer surfaced within the next few weeks, then the stock could roll over. And it was tough to explain to clients why you let all that upside just slip through your fingers. "I'm going to take a little off the top," I said. "Lock in a gain."

"Too soon, Robbie," Charlton said. "This one has room to run."

"Maybe. I'll give it some thought."

The three of them continued to celebrate Hawthorne's move as I headed back to my desk. Murphy called out to me as I passed his office. "What's going on? Someone win the lottery?"

I stopped in his doorway. "Even better. Rumor is that Hawthorne Medical's being bought. Stock's up huge."

He winced, then pulled off his glasses and massaged the bridge of his nose. "That's terrific," he said, his voice flat.

He had fought hard against Vivian as she laid out a compelling argument for Hawthorne, aggressively challenging each point she offered up, long after the rest of us had been convinced it was worth a shot. We had all grown tired of his rants. "Come on, Murph, I know you weren't exactly on board with this, but we're going to make a lot of money. Cheer up."

He squinted at me with blurry eyes. "You know this was just luck. That company is hemorrhaging cash. The stock could just have easily have gone in the other direction." His argument with Vivian had progressed from moderate disagreement to personal vendetta as she continued to push Hawthorne.

"Luck or not, my clients will be really happy when they hear about this. And so will yours."

His mouth contorted in a grimace. "I never bought any Hawthorne for my clients.

"Why not?" I asked, slipping into the chair across from his desk. "We all agreed to add it to the buy list."

He lifted his chin stubbornly. "I didn't agree. Hawthorne was too speculative. I kept my clients in Bovender. And they'll thank me in the long run."

Assuming they stick around that long, I thought. Even though we preached to our clients that investing was for the long term, that they should not chase short term volatility, it was tough for them to ignore headline news about big stock movements, especially when it seemed we were caught on the wrong side of a trade. Clients were quick to remind us they were not happy to lose money. "Murph, I can't understand why you've fought so hard against Hawthorne. This isn't the first time we've stepped into a stock long before the market thought it was a sure thing. That's how we make money, acting on a good idea before everyone else sees it."

"Please, Robbie," he said, polishing the lenses with his tie and settling his glasses back on his face. "There's a difference between prudent investing and rampant speculation. Surely you know that."

"Oh, come on, Murph," I said, irritated by his condescending tone. "Wasn't Bovender considered a speculative stock when you first bought it years ago?"

He shrugged. "That was different. We were at the start of a big bull market. Clients were banging down the door to give us their money. Everything we touched turned to gold." He straightened some papers on his desk. "I'm a lot older now, Robbie. And a lot more cautious. And so are my clients. The return *of* their money is just as important as the return *on* their money. I can't just rely on luck."

"Luck?" I slapped my hands against the arms of the chair. "You know we work our asses off to make good calls for our clients. Do the research. Run the projections. It's not just a shot in the dark."

"Isn't it?" He leaned back in his chair and laced his fingers over his beach-ball belly. "Picking good stocks is tough, Robbie. We try to convince ourselves that we know what we're doing. That we can look at a whole universe of stocks and pick the winners." His eyes looked huge through his thick lenses, the whites marked with crooked lines of red. "But it's like trying to predict the exact path of those hurricanes that barrel up the East Coast each year. You hold your breath hoping that your beach house will be the one still standing after the winds die down and the flood waters recede. But sometimes it's the house next door that survives. All that's left of yours is some crooked pilings poking out from the sand."

"So what are you saying? That we can't make a difference for our clients? We should just give their money back and tell them to invest in index funds? Or those computer-driven robo funds?"

"Sometimes it feels that way. You know, this business used to be so much easier. Company managements gave information to their favorite Wall Street analysts, and those guys passed it on to us. And during earnings season, the analysts would write up their reports and snail-mail them to us. We could take our time studying the results. But now a bunch of idiots blast their opinions all over the internet before the market opens. A stock can tank before I've even turned on my computer." He lowered his chin, his fleshy neck spilling over his collar. "I don't like all these changes, this brave new world of investing. I want it to be like it used to be. Everything was so much better then."

"You can't stop change, Murph. Either you roll with it, or it'll leave you all by yourself on the side of the highway without a ride home." I stood up. "And you're making too much of this whole situation. So you made one bad call. Stuck with Bovender even when the danger signals were flashing. It's not the end of the world."

"I'm not sure about that. Shep's been rumbling about early retirement."

"His? Or yours?"

He glanced up. "Are you kidding? He's not leaving until they take him out on a stretcher." His expression was grim. "It's mine he's pushing for. And maybe he's right. Maybe it's time for me to walk away."

§§§

I felt very unsettled as I headed back to my office. A year ago our firm had been at the top of our game. Now Fairburn, Crandall seemed ready to implode. Shep was ranting about interest rates and bond prices. Murphy doubted we could pick outperforming stocks for our clients. Hardy and Charlton were obviously plotting something. And I was a murder suspect.

Vivian's death had shaken up our entire group. Until her murderer was caught, nothing could go back to normal. Fairburn, Crandall was the most important thing in my life right now. If it fell apart, I would too.

Edgar Nelson had threatened Vivian. I needed to find out more about him, to figure out if he could have killed her. I pulled up Everett's email again, looked through the financial statements that he had sent. There was so much data in the reports, it would take me days to go through it all. It would be quicker if I just contacted Nelson myself.

Murphy had warned me to stay away from him. Shep would probably go ballistic when he found out I was interfering with a client. But Everett had said the police didn't seem very interested in questioning Nelson. *Somebody* had to figure out if he killed Vivian. Maybe that somebody was me.

# CHAPTER 18

EDGAR NELSON LIVED south of the river in an expensive gated neighborhood named Royal Bounty. Five years ago the area had been vast acres of sleepy farmland, too far away from downtown Hastings to be valuable to anyone except tomato farmers and grizzled guys driving dusty pickups.

Once the circumferential highway was completed, however, the entire area was quickly developed into high-end subdivisions. Now self-made overachievers lived in sprawling houses with their trophy wives, near trendy mini-malls of designer shoppes, artistically landscaped with brick walkways and sparkling fountains.

The entrance to Royal Bounty was protected by a tiny guardhouse, a neat brick building with white trimmed windows and a shiny black door. I quickly worked up a cover story to convince the guard to let me in. But the gate opened automatically as I pulled up. The guardhouse was empty and looked like it had been for a long time. There were no work schedules posted on the walls. No papers on the desk. No telephone. Maybe the plan had once been to have someone standing guard to protect the residents, but now it was just an elaborate speed bump.

The central road led straight to a massive two-story brick clubhouse, with a wing on each end and a white columned portico leading to the front entrance. Individual neighborhoods, each marked with antique brass carriage lanterns positioned on ivy-covered brick entryways, curled out on the sides. Nelson's house was located on Queen Anne's Trail, which my GPS indicated was two streets up and to the right. I followed the gently curving road past sprawling three-story brick Georgians and Colonials. Whoever had the brick concession for this neighborhood must be worth a fortune. I needed to track him down and add him to my client pipeline.

The computerized voice directing me said, "You have arrived at your destination, on the right." I parked the car, then walked up to the house and rang the doorbell. There seemed to be no activity inside the house, no footsteps, no music or sounds of a television. Just when I had decided that no one was at home, the door opened a few inches. A tall, dark haired woman peered out, dressed in a pale yellow tee shirt and black yoga pants that hugged her slim hips. "Yes? What is it?"

"Mrs. Nelson?"

"Yes. Who are you?"

I knew from the file that Nelson's wife had recently turned fifty, but this woman looked at least ten years younger, with smooth flawless skin, contoured cheeks and a firm chin. Amazing what a gifted plastic surgeon and a few shots of Botox could do. "I'm Robbie Bradford. From the investment firm Fairburn, Crandall. I'd like to speak to your husband. Is he available?"

She wrapped her arms around her body as cold air flooded inside the house. "Is he expecting you? He didn't say anything about it."

"No. I'm sorry. I know I should have called first, and I apologize for that. But it will only take a few minutes."

She skeptically studied my face as I gave her my most reassuring smile. "This isn't a good time. We're really busy. Why don't you call him and set up something up for another day?" She started to close the door.

I grabbed the edge with my gloved hand. "Please, Mrs. Nelson. It's about your investment account. We think there might be some irregularities. Your money may be at risk."

The mention of money caused her to open the door open a few inches. "Who did you say you were with?"

"Fairburn, Crandall."

"Fairburn, Crandall," she repeated. Then her eyes widened. "This is about that woman, isn't it? The one who was murdered."

I nodded. "Yes."

She glanced back into the house, then said, "Wait here. I'll go check."

I hoped she would invite me inside, out of the frigid wind, but no such luck. I stood on the porch, shivering in front of the closed door, while I waited for her to return. Finally the door opened. "Come on back," she said. "He wants to talk to you."

I got a quick glimpse of taupe walls and a broad curving staircase as I followed her across the two-story foyer, through the dining room and into the kitchen, decorated in pale citrus tones of lime and tangerine. A tall deeply tanned man, his white hair cut in a buzz cut, stood ramrod straight behind the counter. His haircut and posture signaled retired military, which reminded me all too much of my attacker from last night. It would take me a while to push that incident to the back of my mind.

"Mr. Nelson?" I said.

"Yes." He scraped something from a cutting board into a blender, then pulled a towel off his shoulder to wipe his hands.

"So nice to meet you," I said, walking toward him. "I'm Robbie Bradford, with Fairburn, Crandall. Thank you so much for seeing me."

"Call me Edgar," he said, coming around the counter and giving my outstretched hand a firm shake. "Sybil says you're here about the money."

"Yes."

He motioned toward a round glass-topped table, surrounded by four brightly patterned upholstered chairs. "Have a seat."

He settled across from me while Sybil walked back to the counter. Soon I heard the quick pulse of the blender. She poured the contents into two glasses and set one in front of him. "Energy drink," he said. "Full of vitamins and antioxidants. Would you like one?"

"Looks delicious," I said, eyeing the lumpy green sludge, "but I had a late lunch."

"Suit yourself." He took a big gulp, leaving a greenish mustache on his top lip. "Someone from your office called me yesterday, to tell me about Vivian. Terrible business. Any idea who did it?"

Sybil dabbed at his lip with a napkin, then sat down beside him, edging closer, putting her hand on his arm.

"The police are investigating, but I don't know that they have any firm suspects yet," I said.

"That woman was a crook," Sybil spat out. "She deserved to get shot." There was a weird disconnect between the passion in her voice and the blandness of her expression. She had slightly overdone it on the plastic surgery, her skin stretched so tightly that her face could no longer reflect her emotions. Only her eyes, darting quickly between Edgar and me, showed any energy.

"Now, hon, that's unkind," he said, frowning.

"But it's true. She kept promising to make it right. But she never did. Just kept giving us the run-around."

I pulled a notepad from my purse. "I'm so sorry to hear that. And we're going to do everything we can to fix things. But I need a few details. Can you tell me what the problem was?"

He wrapped both hands around his glass. "Vivian did a good job for me for quite a while. I'm retired, and Sybil and I travel quite a bit, so I needed someone I could count on to handle my money. To make decisions for me when I wasn't around."

"So overall, you were pleased with her work?"

"Absolutely. We met quite frequently at first, and she always asked all the right questions. My risk tolerance. My tax situation. Beneficiaries. Charitable donations. All that sort of thing."

I turned toward Sybil. "Were you in these meetings also?"

Sybil shot a quick look at Edgar. "Only a few."

Edgar patted her hand. "I wanted to spare her from all that. Sybil's not really interested in managing money, just spending it. The thought of investing bores her silly."

Sybil's right eyebrow moved up a fraction of an inch. Considering the lack of movement in the rest of her face, that much body language seemed the equivalent of a vicious snarl. I figured maybe she was more interested in investing than Edgar gave her credit for. Or maybe she didn't like all those tête-à-têtes between her husband and an attractive blonde. I waited for her to comment, but she kept her eyes down and reached for her energy drink.

"Our meetings tapered off after a while. The account was doing so well that I didn't check it as carefully as I should have. But then, that's what I was paying her for, right? To be the watchdog for my money? Make sure I don't have any big losses?"

I gave him what I hoped was a sympathetic smile. Watching Sybil's immobile face was making mine do strange things. The corner of my mouth was developing an uncontrollable twitch, hopefully very tiny and unnoticeable. "So what changed?"

"We got together a few months ago to go over the account. Update some things. Discuss some investment ideas. And I told her to start ratcheting down the risk. I felt the market was overvalued, and I wanted to take some chips off the table." He took several swallows of his beverage, then wiped his mouth on his sleeve. "Anyway, she said she'd take care of it. And I assumed she would. But then I got my last statement. Instead of dialing down risk, she went in the other direction, dumping more stocks in my account. And suddenly I had a half-million-dollar loss. I wasn't too happy about that."

"I can imagine. That's a lot of money."

He brushed his hand over the top of his buzz cut. "Well, it wasn't even the money so much. It was the fact that she told me it had been taken care of. So either she lied to me, or she was just careless with my account. In any event, I told her I was planning to move my money."

"What did she say?"

"She asked me to be patient. Said it was a big mix up, and she would get it sorted out. So I promised to hold on for another few weeks. And now she's dead. And I don't know what's going to happen with my half million. Can you get it back for me?"

The chances of that seemed fairly remote, but I tried to be reassuring. "I will certainly check into it and try to figure out what happened." I tapped my pen against the table. "So you called her a number of times over the last several months to demand your money back?"

He looked surprised. "No. I talked to her once or twice after I discovered the losses. As I said, she promised to fix things."

"Vivian told her ex-husband that one of her clients was threatening her. Do you think she could have been talking about you?"

"Me threaten her?" His eyebrows shot up in surprise. "Hell, no. We were always very friendly." He relaxed against the back of the chair. If he had threatened her, he was hiding it well. "I liked Vivian a lot. She was incredibly smart. Had a really good feel for the market. I always enjoyed talking with her." He grinned. "Plus, she was really easy on the eyes."

Sybil blinked rapidly at this comment, then stood up and walked toward the counter.

"Hey, honey, how about a refill?" Edgar asked, holding out his glass. Then he turned to me. "I was very fond of her. That's why I didn't rush to move the account. I kept hoping we could work everything out."

I flipped through my notes. "You said you had been traveling. Were you in town on Saturday night?"

He nodded. "Yes, we came home for a family wedding. My cousin's child. It was a big shindig at First Landing. You know, that colonial plantation out on Route 5, by the river?"

"Yes, I've been there. Very impressive."

He draped one arm over the back of his chair. "My cousin pulled out all the stops. Champagne. Caviar. Dinner and dancing. Even planned for fireworks afterwards, but the snow put the kibosh on that."

First Landing was about an hour's drive from the museum. Depending on what time they left the wedding, it was possible that they could have gotten there in time to shoot Vivian. Somehow I had to check that out.

Edgar was pretty low key. It was hard to imagine him pulling the trigger. Sybil, on the other hand, seemed perfect for it. I could see her frozen face in that frozen landscape, expressionless as Vivian pleaded for her life.

Edgar twisted his wedding ring on his left hand. "I'd really appreciate it if you could get this cleared up in the next couple of days. We head to Argentina next week. Going to spend some time at Iguazu Falls. Ever been there?"

"No, I haven't."

"It's gorgeous. Right on the border of Argentina and Brazil. Second biggest falls in the world after Victoria. Much bigger than Niagara. Water rushes down so hard that you can't even hear yourself think."

"Sounds delightful."

"Anyway, if I could get all this straightened out before we leave, it would make me feel a lot better. I always like to take care of business in person, rather than having to do things long distance."

"I understand. I'll be back in touch as soon as I know something."

§§§

My thoughts raced as I got back in the car. The Nelsons definitely had a motive to kill Vivian. A half-million-dollar loss could be tough on retirees. Might crimp their luxurious lifestyle, make them pare back on international travel. Sybil might even have to postpone that next cosmetic procedure. But my suspicions were not enough. I needed to know if they had really gone to that wedding. And more importantly, what time they had left.

I didn't have the faintest idea how to go about finding out something like that. It wasn't like I could just call up the bride and ask her. My fingers drummed impatiently on the steering wheel. There had be a way to find out. Maybe I could pretend to be someone connected with the wedding. A musician. Or a caterer. Calling to find out something about the guests. Maybe I had found something that had been left behind, and I was trying to track down the owner.

But I wasn't convinced I could pull it off. There had to be an easier way. A way to get perfect strangers to talk to me. To just call up, and ask my questions, and find out exactly what I wanted. And then I thought of someone who was really good at doing just that.

He picked up on the first ring. "Driscoll," he said in his dry, fact-focused reporter's voice.

"You said you wanted to help. Did you mean it?"

"Robbie?" he asked, his voice warming.

"Yes."

"Of course, I meant it. What can I do?"

He sounded so eager that for a moment I felt guilty. He would think that my call meant I had forgiven him, that we could have something close to a normal relationship. There was no way that was happening. But I needed him, needed his contacts, his ability to ferret out information. "How good are you at checking out alibis?"

"I have my sources. What do you need?"

"A couple named Edgar and Sybil Nelson. They said they were at a wedding Saturday night, down at First Landing on Route 5. I'd like to know if they were really there. And how long they stayed."

"Saturday night?" He hesitated. For a moment I thought he was going to turn me down. "You want to know whether they had enough time to get back to the museum parking lot and shoot Vivian?"

"Something like that." He caught on fast. No wonder he was such a good reporter.

"So these guys are suspects." His interest level shot up. "Can you tell me a little about them? Who are they?"

"Clients of Vivian. Unhappy clients, I might add. Especially the wife. She seemed much angrier at Vivian than her husband was."

"Anything else?"

"Can you check their phone records? Vivian had been getting threatening phone calls. Can you see if the Nelsons were behind it?"

He whistled softly. "You expect a lot, don't you? I'll admit I can pretty much work miracles when it comes to tracking down information, but I'm not a cop. Checking phone records is not something I routinely do."

"Oh, come on, Luddy. You said you were buddies with Gutierrez and Caldor. Get them to check the records for you. I'll bet anything that Sybil Nelson made those threatening calls to Vivian."

"I'll see what I can find out."

"Thanks. Let me know when you have something. And please keep this confidential. My boss wouldn't be pleased to know I had asked you to investigate our clients."

I was ready to hang up when he said, "Wait. I do have some information I need to share with you."

"What is it?"

"I need to show you something. How about dinner tonight?"

"Sorry. I'm spending the night with a friend."

He hesitated. "Guy friend? Or lady friend?"

"Not that it's any of your business, but lady friend." Fontaine had been horrified when she heard about the parking lot attack. She insisted that I not stay alone in my house, that I spend the night with her. "I'm on my way to her house right now."

"Then how about lunch tomorrow?"

Calling him had obviously been a bad idea. Now he was hopeful that I would forget the horrible things he had written about Rolfe. "Tomorrow is absolutely packed. I'll be lucky if I can wolf down a sandwich at my desk."

"Breakfast then."

"I don't eat breakfast out. Takes too much time."

"I'll bring it to you. At your house. Those big sticky cinnamon buns from Maxine's. I know they're your favorite."

His persistence was starting to wear me down. "And just how do you know that?"

"I have my sources. Tomorrow, 7 am, your place. You'll be back home by then, right? I'll even throw in a caramel macchiato. I know you never turn those down."

"Have you been stalking me?"

"I'm a reporter, Robbie. I stalk everybody."

"Somehow that's not very comforting."

"We can discuss it tomorrow. See you then."

# CHAPTER 19

IT WAS GETTING DARK as I reached Fontaine's house, a large contemporary, all glass and stained wood, set on a bluff high above the river. In warmer months a plethora of leafy oaks, maples and birches camouflaged the house, making it almost invisible from the road. Now the tree limbs were bare against the hazy winter dusk, their fallen leaves hidden under drifts of snow. Only the towering pines and red-berried hollies broke the stark black and white of the landscape.

I pulled off the main road onto her winding graveled driveway. Someone had taken a stab at clearing it, mounding up snow haphazardly along the edges, but it was still challenging to make out the path in the fading light. On my right, the terrain dropped off sharply into a deep ravine full of huge rocks and fallen branches, its treacherous contours blurred by the snow. A thin line of pine trees was the only border between me and the frozen creek far below.

I followed the tracks of Fontaine's Range Rover as I crept slowly along, hugging the left side of the hill. My tires dug steadily through the icy crust as I steered around the last curve and up the hill to the house.

Fontaine threw open the door as soon as I pulled in front. "Robbie, I've been so worried about you," she said, coming out onto the porch. "I feel terrible that I didn't get your messages last night. I would have come over right away. But the phone just would not stop ringing. Reporters. Friends. Everyone wanted to know more about what happened at the ball. I finally just turned it off. Didn't check it again until this morning."

I yanked my overnight bag from the trunk and slammed it shut. "There was no reason for you to come out in the middle of the night. I was fine."

"Are you sure? Did he hurt you?"

I walked resolutely up the steps. "Please, Fontaine, I've been trying my best all day to forget about that guy. I really don't want to talk about it."

Her forehead crinkled in sympathy. "I understand. Not another word." She took my bag and set it inside the foyer. "But I'm so glad you came. My parents have been here ever since Nate disappeared, and we all really needed a break. They only agreed to go home because you were coming over."

We walked into the kitchen, fragrant with smells of spices and roasting meat. She grabbed a tray of fruit and cheese from the refrigerator and set it on the counter. "Shut up, Webster," she called to the yapping puppy in the corner. "We've heard enough from you."

I kneeled down to peer inside the crate. A fuzzy German Shepherd jumped up against the wire door. "So this is Nate's new guard dog. He's adorable. Can I take him out?"

"Only if you promise to clean up after him if he pees on the floor. I've already done my quota for the day."

He playfully nipped my fingers and wriggled against me as I pulled him from the crate. "Aren't you the cutest thing?"

"Just keep an eye on him. He keeps finding another piece of furniture to chew on. We're not exactly on the best of terms right now." She pulled a bottle from the wine rack. "Grab some glasses while I open this."

We headed into the den, a dramatic room with a soaring ceiling and a full wall of windows which looked out over the terraced stone deck and the pool below. Rolfe and I had been here for Fontaine and Nate's annual July 4th bash. Crowds of adults mingled as they sipped beers and frosty margaritas. Children shrieked as they dove into the swimming pool. Jason had jumped off the side again and again, splashing into Rolfe's waiting arms. After dark, fireworks screamed into the heavens from a barge on the river, then exploded in a waterfall of colors that filled the night sky.

It was all so different now. The pool was covered, its tarp weighted down with snow. The fat pots that had overflowed with red and white geraniums were empty. The massive blue hydrangeas at the end of the pool had shriveled to bare sticks. I snuggled the puppy close to my chest and shivered.

"Are you cold?" Fontaine pointed the remote at the fireplace and the fire crackled to life, its flames flickering up over the ceramic logs. "I hate this house in the winter. It's always freezing in here." She tossed me a soft throw, which I wrapped around my shoulders as I settled onto the leather sofa. "I keep trying to talk Nate into moving, but he likes it out here. It's as far away from my parents as he could get and still be in range of the hospital. Which is probably a good thing, considering that he and Daddy have hardly spoken since that medical conference we went to last fall."

"The one in Rio?"

"Yes." She handed me a glass of wine. "Tell me what you think of this chardonnay."

I sipped the wine. "It's good. Very crisp. I taste apple. And maybe some pear?"

"Right." She spread goat cheese on a cracker, then popped it into her mouth as she sat down beside me.

"So what happened between your dad and Nate?"

"Money, of course." She swirled her wine, took a big swallow, then held the stem loosely in her fingers. "When we got home, Nate was all hot to invest in that company I told you about. Only he didn't have any cash."

Webster curled into a contented ball as I rubbed behind his ears.

"He tried to convince my dad to invest, but that was a total nonstarter. Daddy's funded too many of Nate's crazy schemes in the past. He wouldn't go anywhere near the deal. And my money's all tied up in trusts, so I couldn't do anything for him. And I wouldn't have, anyway, after he spent the whole weekend flirting with that waitress." She pulled a few grapes from the tray in front of her. "But the clincher was when he tried to draw down a couple of million dollars under the credit line Daddy had set up for his real estate business. The bank guy called my dad, to make sure it was OK, and he said absolutely not. Then he and Nate got in a huge fight."

I slowly ran my hand down Webster's back. "Why didn't Nate talk to me? I could have helped him get the money."

"I told him to call you, but he said you wouldn't be any help. He said..." She stopped, an embarrassed look on her face.

"What did he say?"

"He said..." She stared down at her wine glass. "That you were still in a fog from the accident."

"He was probably right about that."

"And that you would just tell him to sell some of the stocks he already owned. But he didn't want to do that."

I set my wine glass on the ottoman. "Considering how much his stocks have pulled back since then, that wasn't his best call."

"Tell me about it. Anyway, he finally stopped talking about it. But then he started on all these home improvement projects. New outdoor lighting. A new security system. And the dog." She looked toward Webster, sleeping contently in my lap. "Of course Nate's at work all day, which means I get stuck with the damn dog, who does nothing but pee on the floor every time I take him out of his crate. The vet checked him out to see if he had a bladder infection or something, but he couldn't find anything. He said it's my fault. Evidently, I make the dog nervous."

Webster suddenly squirmed in my lap and jumped to the floor, barking loudly as he raced to the door. We heard the slam of car doors out front. "Are you expecting somebody?" I asked.

"No."

I followed behind as she walked toward the foyer. "It's my parents," she said as she peered through the glass panel at the side of the front door. "I can't believe they're back here again."

"I didn't think they were coming over here tonight."

"They weren't." She opened the door as the Baxters rushed in, setting their suitcases down in the foyer. One look at her mother made it easy to see what Fontaine would look like in thirty years. Dark hair streaked with gray. Still attractive but a little heavier, with a softening chin and wrinkles around her eyes when she smiled.

"Mom, Daddy, you don't need to be here," Fontaine said. "I told you that Robbie was staying with me tonight."

"You know how your mother is," Wallace Baxter said, putting his arm around his wife. "She just wanted to make sure her little girl was all right." He was a big man, tall with broad shoulders, and the unshakeable confidence of someone who was used to telling other people what to do.

"Robbie and I were planning a quiet dinner. Just a girls' night," Fontaine said. "You shouldn't have come."

"So you want us to leave now?" her father asked. "With the roads as bad as they are? I could barely navigate through that driveway of yours. Looks like somebody almost slid into the ravine."

"That would be me," I said. "Took the curve a little too tight."

Her mom came over and gave me a hug. "I'm glad you're here with Fontaine," she said. "You're always such a steady influence on her."

"So what's it going to be?" her father asked. "You want us to leave?"

Fontaine sighed. "Of course not. Come on back. I'll fix you some wine, and we can start on dinner." She walked into the kitchen and pulled another bottle from the wine rack. She had just handed her father the corkscrew when the doorbell rang. "Now what?"

"I'll get it," her father said. He was gone for a few minutes, and then he called, "Fontaine, can you come out here?"

She headed toward the door as her mother and I lagged behind. Two uniformed police officers stood in the doorway. "Mrs. Thornton?" one of them said as she approached.

"Yes?" She stared from one to the other. "Is this about my husband? You've found him? Is he all right?"

"We've found his car. And we'd like for you to come with us, to answer a few questions."

# CHAPTER 20

WE FORMED A SOLEMN CARAVAN, Fontaine riding with her mom and dad, me in my car behind them, following the red tail lights of the police car back through Fontaine's winding driveway and out to the main road. No one said the words aloud as we put away the wine and cheese, turned off the oven, and locked Webster in his crate, but I was pretty sure we were all convinced that Nate was dead.

I wanted to go with her to the police station, to hold her hand, to be strong for her when she cried, all those things she had done for me a few months ago after Rolfe and Jason's accident. But her father insisted that I go home, that he and her mother were the ones that needed to be with Fontaine right now. She wilted in front of me, her strength melting away, too shell-shocked to put up much resistance to her dad's strong personality. I watched them bundle her into their car, checking her seat belt, making sure her arms and legs were inside the car before they shut the door, much as they would have done when she was a small girl.

Salt-streaked asphalt glimmered in my headlights as I drove down my street. Unwilling to do battle with the snow still piled in my driveway, I parked at the curb, pulled my things from the car, then trudged through the snow to the back door, looking around carefully to make sure no one was hiding in the shrubbery ready to jump out at me. Once inside, I tossed my purse on the counter, then slipped my keys into my coat pocket before hanging it on the peg by the door.

There was nothing much in the refrigerator for dinner. I held the door open, the light bright on the empty shelves, my mouth salivating just a bit as I remembered the fragrant smell of Fontaine's kitchen. The best I could come up with was a tired-looking package of ravioli, crystal-covered and months past its sell-by date, which I pulled from the freezer and slid into the microwave.

I poured a glass of chardonnay and flipped through the mail while I waited for my meal to heat. Since the accident my nightly glass of wine with dinner had gradually become two, and sometimes even three. I liked the way it rounded out the hard edges, helped me ignore the dull ache I felt each night as I crawled into my empty bed. Tonight it did not seem to be working. My head hurt and my stomach churned. All I could think about was Fontaine, standing in the police station ready to identify Nate's body, her dad on one side and her mom on the other, holding her up as she slipped limply to the floor.

The microwave dinged. I pulled out the plastic tray, peeled off the cover and transferred my dinner onto a plate. The first bite stuck in my throat, hard bits of flavorless noodles and over-salted nuggets of tomato and beef long past their prime. I washed it down with big gulps of wine, which immediately collided with the roiling acid in my stomach, making me gag. I tossed the rest of my dinner into the trash, then refilled my wine glass and headed upstairs.

The air grew hotter with each step. My antiquated heating system struggled to regulate the temperature, defying the earnest workmen who kept adjusting knobs and replacing pipes. Even when I kept the thermostat low enough downstairs to make sweat pants and a heavy sweater my required wardrobe, my third floor bedroom verged on the tropical. At the doorway I flicked on the ceiling fan, its gentle rotation sending down sultry air to caress my face.

Setting my wine on the nightstand, I took off my necklace and earrings. Then I unhooked my bracelet and gently polished each charm with jewelry cloth, a nightly ritual that was my oblation to the gods of memory. Laying the jewelry in the velvet-lined squares of my top dresser drawer, I stripped off my clothes, pulled on a tee shirt and climbed into bed.

I grabbed a book but my mind refused to focus on the story. Instead I kept seeing Fontaine's expression when she saw those patrolmen at her door. Above me the fan vibrated hypnotically, sending shadows stumbling across the ceiling. Gradually my eyelids drooped and the words blurred on the page. The book slid to the floor as I stretched to turn off the lamp.

I slept fitfully, my dreams as usual full of crashing trees and swirling blackness. Suddenly I was standing on the highway, beside a car smashed against a tree, propped up on its side, wheels still spinning. The windshield was cracked, with fissures veering off crazily in all directions. Putting my face tight against it, I could see Rolfe trapped inside, his head bent at an awkward angle. Desperate to save him, I slammed my hand through the glass, causing brittle fragments to bounce loudly against the hot hood.

My heart pounded as I struggled to wake up. The duvet had wrapped tightly around me as I thrashed through my dream, the sheets hot with sweat. My parched tongue stuck to the roof of my mouth. I slowly worked it loose bit by bit, like easing an old bandage from a scab. Untangling the covers, I was just about to get up for some water when I heard a noise.

I lay there a moment trying to figure out what it was. Squirrels scampering across the roof. The giant magnolia tree in the front yard scratching the window. The normal settling of an old house. The creaky ceiling fan. I held my breath and listened again, attacking the silence so hard that my ears started to ring. But there was nothing. Just the wind, sighing in the trees. I pounded my pillows into a more comfortable shape and rolled over. Closed my eyes and tried to quiet down my racing brain.

And then I heard it again. The sound of breaking glass, just like in my dream. I sat up and threw back the covers. Someone was in the house. I reached for my cell phone to call for help, then remembered it was in my purse, downstairs in the kitchen. I perched on the edge of the mattress, trying to figure out what to do. If Rolfe had been here, he would have pulled his gun from the top shelf in the closet and boldly confronted the intruder. But my Glock was packed away. And I didn't feel very bold.

My mind rapidly ran through alternatives. I could pretend to be asleep. I could hide, perhaps under the bed or in the closet. I could stay and fight, defend what was mine. I looked around the room for a weapon. A lamp. The vanity stool. The hair dryer in the bathroom. Nothing seemed adequate.

A floorboard creaked as a foot neared the first landing. I knew exactly where that board was, had stepped on it a thousand times myself when running up the stairs. The intruder was softly making his way upward, no doubt clinging to the carved mahogany railing as he put down each foot carefully to minimize the noise. He was on the second floor now, moving quickly through the empty rooms.

I clutched the duvet around me, paralyzed with fear. Maybe I could slip down the stairs and get past him while he was wandering through the second floor.

Slipping noiselessly out of bed, I headed for the door. But I was too late. He was on the stairs again, faster now, more confident, heading for the third floor. A small light danced in the hallway, coming closer and closer. My heart was beating so hard I was sure he could hear it.

Time was running out. Whatever I was going to do, I had to do it now.

I quickly padded toward the window. Fontaine had been furious with me when I had replaced the drafty hand-blown windows with new double-paned ones, but I had been tired of the cold wind that whistled across my bed each night. As the new window slid quietly open, I gave a prayer of thanks to my contractor. Leaning down, I grabbed the sill and stepped gingerly out onto the balcony, trying not to slip on the ice. Tightly gripping the frame for balance, I pulled the window down behind me, leaving it open an inch so I could get back in.

Staying as flat as I could against the house, I twisted just enough to peer back into my bedroom. The light was at the doorway now. It moved around the room, shining in the corners, bouncing off the blades of the ceiling fan. Then it focused on the bed, hesitating as it moved slowly over the rumpled covers. The light swept across the edge of the dust ruffle. I could see a hand pull back the fabric and shine the light under the bed.

The cold wind whipped across my bare legs. My feet ached from the ice. My fingers were numb from their death grip on the window frame. I could not stay here much longer. But there was no one on the street I could call for help. The college students had stopped partying for the evening, their dorm windows firmly shut, blinds pulled down against the darkness. It was just me, the stars and the crusty snow.

I looked back through the window. The light was stationary now. The burglar must have set it on the dresser, because it reflected against the mirror, casting an eerie glow. He opened the dresser drawers, one by one.

I had to get off the balcony, down to the ground to call for help. Moving to the railing would be easy. The tin floor of the balcony angled down slightly to guide rainwater to the gutters below. I could just sit down and slide to the edge if I had to.

But from there it got tougher. A wide band of dentil molding separated the third floor balcony from the stocky Corinthian columns that ran down to the front porch, putting them far out of my reach. Even if I could figure out a way to shimmy down, the fluted columns were so ice-slicked that I would never get a good grip.

Desperately I looked around, trying to figure out an alternative plan. The ancient magnolia in the front yard grew almost to the roof of my house. The branches were about four feet from the edge of the balcony. I sat there trying to think it through, analyzing it step by step, working it all out carefully in my mind. I would silently edge my way down toward the railing, throw my leg over, and stretch way out until I could grab a strong tree branch. It had to work. There was no other choice.

Trying to move quietly, I took the first step and slipped, landing hard on my butt, sliding toward the railing. The burglar heard me. The flashlight beam raced back and forth across the windowsill. A hand reached out to pull the window open. He was coming after me.

My careful plans were out. I had to escape.

I threw myself over the railing and dove wildly for the tree.

# CHAPTER 21

FOR A FEW TERRIFYING MOMENTS, I sailed through bare air. Then my flailing arms and legs skimmed the top of the magnolia tree. I grabbed handfuls of hard waxy leaves and wrapped my legs around the branches.

A sudden crack warned me that the thinner outer branches could not support my weight. Burrowing through the thick leaves, I found the stronger core and held on tight, pressing my head against the trunk, breathing hard, spitting out bits of seed pod. A light flashed against the thick outer leaves, probing the darkness. The burglar was at the window, searching for me. I had to get down.

I stretched out a cautious leg. My toes found a branch and I gently lowered my weight to it, praying it would hold. A bushy tail swept across my leg. I had woken a nest of squirrels, and they scampered angrily along the branches as their noisy chatter warned me to get out of their territory. I lost my grip and started to slide.

Digging my fingernails into the bark, I stopped my downward momentum and clung to the tree, panting. Mustering up my courage, I stuck out a foot and slowly began to ladder my way down the trunk, one branch, and then another, my feet so cold that I could barely feel the limbs as I stepped on them, focusing straight ahead, afraid to look down.

I stretched my foot out again, searching for the next branch, but felt only air. The bottom of the tree had been trimmed up to allow a lawn mower to run underneath. I had reached the last branch and would have to drop down the last eight feet or so to the ground.

Suddenly I heard a dog barking ferociously right below me, and something furry brushed against my dangling leg. The squirrels had come back. I screamed and thudded to the ground.

§§§

"Robbie. Robbie, can you wake up?" A sandy loofah rubbed against my face, hot and wet. It felt marvelous.

135

"Robbie, are you all right?"

How could I not be, with that rough heat caressing me? I could lie here forever.

"Robbie, open your eyes. Please open your eyes."

The loofah moved away. I put my hands up to my face, searching for it. And felt fur. Lots and lots of fur. I screamed as I opened my eyes and frantically tried to flick the squirrels away.

"Take it easy, Robbie. I've called 911. Help will be here in a minute." Harold Finley, my next door neighbor, kneeled beside me. Geena, his golden retriever, nuzzled me, that steaming loofah tongue stroking once more across my face. A fog of hot dog breath filled my nose as her saliva dripped onto my cheek. I relaxed as I realized it was Geena, and not the squirrels, that had brushed against my face.

I pushed myself up on my elbows. I was lying on the ground in the snow, at the base of the magnolia tree. My tee shirt had twisted itself up around my ribs, giving Harold an unforgettable view of my bare midriff, bare legs, and pink polka-dotted thong.

He realized I had caught him staring. Embarrassed, he quickly pulled off his coat and draped it over me. "Here, put this on. What are you doing out here, anyway?"

"Somebody broke into my house. I was trying to get away from him."

Noisy sirens raked the silence as a rescue squad van and several police cars jerked to a stop in front of my house. Harold told them about the burglar, and several uniformed men ran toward the house.

I was quickly surrounded by people who poked, prodded and asked lots of questions. A medical technician flashed a small light in my eyes. "No concussion. And nothing seems to be broken. Can you sit up?"

I nodded.

"I'm Steve," he said as he wrapped a blanket around me. "The police are checking out your house. Let's get you in the van until they give us the all clear. It's warmer there."

Harold and Geena stood beside me as I waited with Steve. Lights flashed on and off throughout my house as the police moved from room to room, floor to floor. I wished I had been neater. Dinner dishes were still in the kitchen sink. The wine bottle on the counter. Newspapers and mail strewn across the island.

The police were going through every detail of my home, lights blazing, every nook explored, every secret exposed.

A policeman walked around from the back of the house and motioned to us. "Can you walk?" Steve asked.

"Do you have a spare pair of shoes?"

He looked down at my bare feet. "Hold on." He came back with a pair of sneakers dangling from his fingers. "These should be good enough."

The shoes were tight. I hobbled toward the back of the house, holding Steve's arm. Cameras flashed as we neared the back door, highlighting the missing panes of the sidelights. Jagged shards of glass crunched under my feet, the same brittle sound as in my dream.

A policeman approached me. "I'm Officer Ingram. Can you tell us if anything is missing?"

Aside from the number of people milling around my kitchen, taking pictures and spreading fingerprint dust, at first everything looked the same. My coat on the peg by the door. The mail scattered across the island. The small TV above the refrigerator. Then I realized what was different. "My purse is gone," I said. "And my laptop. They were on the counter."

Ingram made notes as he asked more questions. "Can you walk upstairs and take a look?"

I clung tight to the banister as I climbed the steps. Even though the policemen had checked the house, even though one of them was right beside me, I still felt uneasy, as though someone were still hiding there, waiting for me. We reached the second floor. "This level is empty," I said.

"That's good to hear. We were a little worried when we checked all the rooms and didn't find any furniture."

We walked up to the third floor. I stopped at the entrance to my bedroom. It had been beautiful, copied from a page ripped from *Architectural Digest* and handed to my decorator when I first moved in. The queen-sized bed was covered with a heavy bedspread embroidered in shades of dark peach, pale green and gold. A pale green silk bed skirt hung down to the floor, with a matching canopy gathered above the bed. Tasseled valances topped long silk draperies that puddled on the floor.

It did not look beautiful now. The draperies were pulled back and black fingerprint dust was everywhere. On the windowsill. The dresser. Spilling out onto the clothes and the carpet.

The contents of my dresser drawers had been dumped on the floor. Lingerie. Shirts. Sweaters. A stranger's hands had touched all my clothes. I could imagine him fondling the soft cashmere, holding it to his face, smiling.

"My jewelry." I jerked open the top drawer of the dresser, hoping it would all still be there, somehow undisturbed in the middle of all this chaos. But the velvet-lined dividers were empty. I shoved my fingers to the back, hoping to find something. "Oh, my God, it's all gone." My black Tahitian pearls were missing. The sapphire necklace I had worn to the ball. The heavy gold-link necklace we had bought in the Caribbean. All the pieces that Rolfe had picked out for me, special gifts for my birthday, our anniversary. And my charm bracelet.

I felt light-headed, and grabbed the edge of the dresser for support. Insurance would cover the most expensive pieces. But the charm bracelet. Those little chunks of gold, the memories of all the adventures we had shared. There was no way I could replace that.

"Are you all right?" Ingram said, putting his hand under my elbow.

"Yes. It's just such a shock. To see everything like this."

"I understand. And we'll do everything we can to find the guy that did this and get your things back. Can you give me a list of your missing jewelry?"

I nodded. "I can get the details from my insurance policy."

"Good. That will help a lot."

I tugged at the blanket around my shoulders. "Can I get dressed now?"

"Of course."

I changed in the closet and came out in jeans and a sweater, the blanket and shoes under my arm. "Could you see that these get back to the rescue squad folks?"

"Sure."

He led me back down to the kitchen. Harold was down there chatting with the police officers, fixing coffee. "Do you know of anyone who might want to break into your house?" Ingram asked. "Maybe someone who knew about your jewelry?"

I thought of the impatient look that Gutierrez and Caldor had given me when they eyed my pearl necklace. "I wear my jewelry all the time. Anyone who sees me knows I have a lot of it."

"Any arguments with anyone recently? Someone who might want to hurt you?"

I crossed my arms over my chest, remembering the parking deck. "Someone attacked me last night at work. There should be a police report on file." I rubbed my arms where that man had grabbed me. He told me he was not finished with me. And now he had been here, in my house, in my bedroom.

Ingram pointed to the back yard. "There are a lot of footprints out there in the snow, but they're all pretty jumbled. I don't know if they'll tell us anything."

"It's the workmen. I'm having a lot of repairs done on the house."

"Do you think one of them could have robbed you?"

"I doubt it. They've been working here for weeks. If they had wanted to steal anything, they could have done it before now."

There were heavy footsteps as the crew from upstairs came down to the kitchen.

"Looks like we're finishing up," Ingram said. "Is there someone I can call for you? A relative? A friend?"

I immediately thought of Fontaine, but she had her own issues tonight. "No, my neighbor is here." I gave Harold a weak wave. "He can give me a hand if I need anything."

Ingram walked to the back door. "We can rig up some cardboard and duct tape to cover the hole in this door. At least it will keep the cold wind out until you can get someone over here to replace the glass. And we'll keep a patrol car circulating in the neighborhood, to make sure the guy doesn't come back."

"Thanks. That would be very helpful."

The house echoed ominously around me once everyone had finally left. The police had checked it thoroughly. Every closet. The attic. The basement. Even the washer and dryer. No one was here but me.

And yet I was sure I heard creaking floorboards upstairs. I forced myself to go up there, to look around. Finally satisfied that I was alone, I pulled some blankets from the linen closet and headed back downstairs.

I didn't plan to sleep. I was pumped so full of adrenaline that I didn't think I would ever sleep again. That thin square of cardboard taped to my door was the only thing between me and all the evil swirling outside.

Turning on the gas fireplace logs, I sat on the sofa swaddled in blankets, a big carving knife clutched in my hand. I missed Rolfe so desperately that I could hardly breathe. He would have fixed all this, chased off the burglar, made sure I was safe. But he was gone. And so was the bracelet. I didn't even have those tiny charms to give me strength. I was totally on my own.

The blade of the knife flashed in the firelight. I had been such a coward, sneaking out of my own window, letting some intruder take everything that was dear to me. That would not happen again. Next time, I wouldn't run away.

# Chapter 22

BY SIX THE NEXT MORNING, I had filled one black plastic trash bag and started on the second when there was a knock on the kitchen door. Luddy Driscoll peered in the window, his breath making foggy circles on the glass. "What?" I said in an annoyed tone, opening the door a few inches.

"I brought breakfast." He held a cardboard tray with two coffees.

I stared blankly at him, then groaned as I recalled our conversation from yesterday. "I'm sorry, Luddy. I forgot."

He lifted up a bulging bag. "I've got cinnamon buns here, too. Extra gooey."

I shook my head. "This isn't a good time. It's been a pretty rough night. I'm not ready for company quite yet."

He looked down at my rubber gloves, and then at the cardboard taped to the broken glass panel at the side of the door. "What happened here?"

"Someone broke in last night. I was robbed."

He set down the food and grabbed my shoulder. "Oh, my God, Robbie, were you hurt?"

I shrugged. "Just some scratches and a few bruises."

"Bruises? What did he do to you?"

"Nothing." I gave him a quick summary of last night, including my slide down the magnolia tree.

He pulled me closer. "If anything had happened to you…"

Rolfe had always teased me about Luddy. "He skips half our poker nights, out chasing some story. Except when it's at our house. Then he never misses. He's hot for you, babe."

"That's ridiculous," I had said. But I knew he was right. Luddy would fold his hand early in the game and follow me into the kitchen, telling me funny stories as I pulled out chips and salsa.

Now I pushed away, uncomfortable at his touch. "I'm fine, really."

"Of course." His face colored in embarrassment. "Is there anything I can do for you? Fix the door? Call anyone? Drive you anywhere?"

I shook my head. "The workmen will be here soon. They'll take care of the glass. And my neighbor loaned me his phone last night, so I've already called the credit card companies. When I get to work, I'll take care of everything else."

He carried the coffee and buns to the island. "Caramel macchiato, as promised."

"Thanks." I pulled off my gloves and reached for the coffee. "So what did you find out about the Nelsons? Have you checked into their alibi for Saturday night?"

"Boy, you expect quick service, don't you?"

"Patience has never been my strong suit."

"I've left messages with some of my contacts. I should have something by the end of the day." He unwrapped the pastries. The smell of warm cinnamon drifted toward me, making my stomach gurgle. "Tell me more about the robbery," he said.

I eased the lid off the coffee and sipped the hot liquid as I filled him in on the details from last night.

"So you didn't get a good look at him?"

"No. I went out the window before he got into my room."

He stirred sugar into his coffee. "But you think it was the guy from the parking deck?"

I nodded. "The police are looking into it. Checking fingerprints. I just don't know why he would keep coming after me."

He tapped the wooden stirrer against the edge of his cup. "You think anyone in your firm could be behind all this? Someone who would want to get rid of both you and Vivian?"

"I've been up all night thinking about that. Trying to figure out if there's some connection. But it doesn't make any sense." I swirled the foam around in my macchiato. "We've both brought in a lot of new business to the firm. Even more than some of the guys who have been there for a long time."

"So was there anyone who wasn't too happy about all this business you were bringing in? Anybody see you as a threat?"

"I can't see it. The more money we bring in, the stronger the firm is. And that benefits everybody. Except..."

"Except what?"

"It's just...well, Charlton is so old school. He doesn't approve of women as financial advisors. Doesn't think we have the temperament for it. He never wanted Shep to hire either one of us." I popped the last bite of cinnamon bun into my mouth. "And I know he was against either of us making partner."

"Sounds like quite a charmer."

"It gets worse. When Vivian and I were first hired, he started an office pool to bet on who would get pregnant first. He figured we would quit and stay home with the baby, wasting all the time and money that the firm had spent on us."

"Let me guess. You won?"

"Yes." I grimaced. "It wasn't the plan, but sometimes these things happen. Jason was born my first year there. But I didn't quit. I just worked harder than ever."

Jason had been a fussy baby, waking up all during the night, his hungry mouth latching onto my aching breasts, that tiny tongue scraping like fine sandpaper on my raw nipples. I would rock him to sleep, humming softly, my heart almost bursting with love for this tiny creature that Rolfe and I had created.

But I was exhausted each morning when I handed Jason off to the nanny and headed for work, struggling to stay awake during staff meetings. Shep would come into my office for sales updates and find me completely zoned out, my eyes glazed over as I stared at my computer, my chin propped up in my palm. He made it quite clear that I needed to step up my game and get my personal life under control.

As a result, for Jason's first few months I added a night nanny. And a weekend nanny. And a housekeeper. My own private staff, all to help me get some much-needed sleep and stay focused on the job. So that all those times when I was out entertaining clients and prospects, when Rolfe was working days, nights and weekends at his family's law practice, when Jason was up half the night crying, I could still hold onto some semblance of sanity, could convince myself that my life was not slowly, irrevocably, spinning out of control.

Luddy sipped his coffee. "Was Charlton at the ball Saturday night?"

"Yes. But I can't see him being involved in something like this. Although I know he and Hardy are planning something. Hardy's next in line to take over after Shep retires, and he's getting impatient."

Hardy had good performance numbers. A great book of business. High client retention rates. Certainly not as charismatic as Shep, much more of a numbers guy, but generally steady and focused, unflappable while the markets were zigging and zagging around him.

"Would killing Vivian make it easier for him to get the top job?"

I hesitated. "I don't see how. But I did hear Hardy talking to Charlton the other day. Hardy said he knew the thing with Vivian would drive Shep over the edge. And they needed to make their move now."

"So maybe they killed Vivian, and now they're coming after you? To put the firm in chaos? So Shep will step aside, and they can take over?"

"I guess that's possible. But I just can't believe they'd do something like that."

He thought for a minute. "Then how about a competitor? Anybody think you're stealing their clients?"

"We all steal each other's clients. I mean, there are only so many high net worth individuals out there. So everybody is scrambling to get them. But we don't kill each other because of it."

He leaned in to dab the edge of my mouth with a napkin. "Hold on. You've got some foam there."

His closeness made me uncomfortable. I jerked back and rubbed my face with the back of my hand. Eager for our breakfast to end, I gathered up all the pastry wrappers and stuffed them in the trash.

He tossed back the last of his coffee as I headed back to the sofa. "So what are you doing over there? With all those clothes?"

I pulled on my rubber gloves. "That jerk last night handled everything in my dresser. Dumped it all over the floor. And then the police dusted for fingerprints. Everything is coated with black powder. So I'm tossing all of it."

"Couldn't you just send it to the dry cleaners?"

"Wouldn't work. Every time I wore any of these things, a sweater, a pair of jeans, it would just remind me of last night. Of how scared I was when I heard that guy creeping up my stairs. Watching that flashlight come down the hall, getting closer and closer. Trapped. Not knowing what to do." Tension ratcheted up my neck. I twisted my head from side to side to relieve the stiffness.

"Well, when you put it like that..."

"Besides, I always run away from unhappy memories." I stuffed a blouse into the plastic bag, tightened a twist tie around the top, and set it beside the door. "I burned them, you know."

"Burned what?"

"My clothes. From the accident. The night Rolfe and Jason were killed."

He walked toward me, his head angled, eyes puzzled. "Your clothes?"

"The ones you talked about in your article. Don't you remember?" I turned toward him, arms crossed defiantly against my chest. "You described my silk dress. My cashmere coat. Said I had been out to a big dinner at a fancy restaurant. You made me sound like some heartless society bitch who partied while her family was dying."

"I didn't mean..." he began.

"Of course you did. Sensationalism sells a lot of papers, doesn't it? Too bad you didn't know the whole story. You probably would have sold more."

"The whole story?"

"You know, how the grieving widow felt when she came home to an empty house. Isn't that the kind of thing you love to write about?" All the anger I had felt toward him after the accident flared back, hot and vicious. I was ashamed that I had chatted with him over breakfast as though we were old buddies. It was a betrayal of the ones I loved most.

He took a step toward me. "Robbie, don't. I feel terrible about that article."

I grabbed another trash bag. "When I came home that night, I just sat in the car for a long time. I couldn't go in the house, knowing that Rolfe and Jason weren't there. Would never be there again." I picked up a pair of yoga pants. "The smell of their blood was everywhere. On my hands. In my hair. On my clothes. I stripped off everything and piled it in the fire pit on the patio. My neighbor found me naked in the freezing rain, screaming in front of the fire." I balled up the pants and threw them into the bag. "Now there's a bit of drama for your readers, right?"

"I'm so sorry, Robbie."

"Sorry doesn't really change anything, does it?" I pulled off my rubber gloves and tossed them on the end table. "I think you'd better go."

He took a step toward me but I backed up, maintaining the distance between us.

"OK, I'm going," he said, holding up his hands. "But first I need to show you this." He pulled an envelope from his jacket. "I told you I had information for you." He opened the envelope and pulled out a stack of pictures. "A witness saw Vivian leaving the ball with someone. I think he's a good suspect." He fanned them out on the coffee table. "Our photographer took a bunch of pictures for the society page. Luckily, we've got a shot of the guy."

I squatted down to get a better view. I recognized Annabelle Scotland dancing with her husband. The Townsends checking out some of the items in the silent auction. Gus Kensington, sitting at the Fairburn, Crandall table, chatting with Barbara Edmonton. "It was this guy," he said. "You know him?"

"That's Gus Kensington. The grandson of the late Senator. You think he killed Vivian?"

"Maybe. He's wanted by the police in Colorado. A fraudulent land deal. Stole a lot of money from some very angry investors."

I ran my finger along the edge of the picture. "Lydia told me he left her stranded Saturday night. Just disappeared, and she had to find a ride home with a neighbor."

"Definitely sounds like he might be our guy. And there's something else."

"What?"

"Neighbors saw a man coming out of Vivian's house early Sunday morning."

"You think it was Gus?"

He shrugged. "Don't know. He was all bundled up, hat, gloves, scarf. Got into a silver car and drove off."

"Fifty percent of the cars on the road are silver. They couldn't narrow it down for you?"

"I'm lucky I got that much. It was still snowing. Nobody would have seen anything if some guy hadn't gone outside to get his newspaper. I'm checking back in her neighborhood today to try to get a better description of the car. Maybe a license plate." He started to gather up the pictures.

"Wait a minute. Let me see that again." I held up the picture of Gus and Barbara. "Look. There in the background."

"What is it?"

I pointed to the waiter in his black jacket and white shirt, holding a tray of drinks at shoulder height. His face was partially obscured, but I could see enough. The short dark hair. The square chin. And that nose, skewed slightly to the right. "That's him." I shivered as it all flooded back, the smell of his jacket, the feel of his lips as he whispered in my ear.

"Who?"

"That man. The waiter. He's the one who attacked me in the parking deck."

# CHAPTER 23

LUDDY QUICKLY LEFT to take the picture to the police. I headed to my office. Without my phone I felt completely cut off from the world. I needed to get to my desk, to call Lydia and warn her about Gus. And I was desperate to reach Fontaine, to find out about her meeting at police headquarters, what they had told her about Nate.

But Darius grabbed me as soon as I walked in the door. "Where have you been? The investment meeting has already started. Everyone's been looking for you."

"I've got stuff to do first. It's important."

"Not as important as this," he said. "Shep said to send you in there as soon as you got here. There's some kind of emergency."

"It's not the Fed again, is it?"

"I don't know, but he looked pretty damned serious."

I debated whether to make my phone calls first and make Shep wait. But Darius stayed on my heels as I walked down the hall to my office. "I'm going, I'm going," I said, tossing my coat in my office. I grabbed a legal pad and pen, then walked into the war room.

Everyone was focused on Shep, sitting at the end of the table, papers spread out in front of him. "So we've locked down Travis Dalton," he said. "You're sure he's sticking with us?"

Lyman nodded. "Absolutely. He's just waiting to be assigned a new financial advisor to replace Vivian. Said he was completely comfortable with our firm."

"Thank God someone is," Shep said. He turned to me and frowned. "So glad you could join us, Robbie. Hope we didn't interfere with your leisurely morning routine."

"Sorry," I said, tossing the pad on the table. "My house was broken into last night. It slowed me down a bit this morning."

His dour expression turned to surprise. "What? Are you serious?"

"Quite serious. The thief stole my cash, credit cards, phone, laptop, jewelry...pretty much everything."

147

I looked around at the group, expecting a bit of compassion, a few inquiries about my well-being, some words of reassurance. I had worked with these people for five years. I knew about their families. That Hardy had a teenage son determined to get into Harvard. That Lyman's granddaughter was a top swimmer and hoped to make the Olympic team next time around. And they knew about mine -- that Rolfe and Jason had been killed just three months ago. And now I had been knocked down yet again, by having someone break into my home. But no one seemed concerned. Both Hardy and Charlton stayed focused on the papers in front of them, not looking up at me. Maybe Luddy was right. Maybe they did have something to do with the break in. Had set in motion some kind of conspiracy to get rid of Vivian, to get rid of me, to completely unnerve Shep so he would step aside.

"You need to get in touch with our tech support guys immediately," Shep said. "Get them to kill your phone and computer. We can't risk having any of our client information get out."

So much for compassion. I was ready to blast back until I took a good look at him. Usually so immaculate, this morning he looked haggard, the skin below his eyes smudged and fragile. There was a small cut on his chin where he must have nicked himself while shaving. It looked like his day was off to as rough a start as mine. I toned down my anger and said simply, "I already did. Last night, right after the police left."

"Good."

"Are you all right?" Murphy asked. "He didn't hurt you?"

"I'm fine. Thanks for asking." I pulled out the chair beside him and sat down.

"I guess insurance will take care of everything?" Lyman asked.

"Pretty much."

"Good. Well, let's get back on point here," Shep said, looking down at the papers in front of him. "Vivian's next client is Steven Hershrod. What do we know about him?"

Charlton leaned back in his chair. "Hershrod's a problem. Said Wadsworth Capital's been dancing around him for months, trying to get him to move his account. He only stayed with us because he was loyal to Vivian. But now that she's gone, he's ready to pull the plug."

"That's a ten-million-dollar account," Shep said, his voice pained. "No chance of talking him out of it?"

Charlton shook his head. "I tossed up every argument I could think of. Talked myself blue. Couldn't convince him."

"I'll call him myself," Shep said, circling the name on his list. "See if I can change his mind. Now what can we do about Julius Tavenner?"

My stomach tightened. "He's on my list," I said, waving my hand. "But I haven't been able to get in touch with him. His telephone number is out of service. And he hasn't responded to my emails."

Shep threw down his pen and glared at me in angry disappointment. "That's all you've got?"

"What do you mean?"

"I mean, the rest of us have gotten in touch with everyone on our list. What's your problem?"

"Shep, I…" My face flushed hot.

He interrupted me. "Tavenner moved everything out of his account yesterday. We wired it to a bank in the Caymans."

"You're kidding."

"I never kid about money." He circled the name on his list. "I want you to stay on this guy and get that account back. Five million dollars is not something we want to just slip through our fingers."

"What am I supposed to do? You want me to fly to the Caymans and track him down?"

His shoulders stiffened. "I expect you to do whatever it takes to get that account back." The veins in his neck bulged as he reached up a hand to loosen his tie. "Vivian found this guy, brought him in as a customer, and got him to hand over five million dollars for us to manage."

"Yes, but…"

He held up a hand to stop me. "Now, I know that she was an exceptionally talented and persuasive woman. She always had her sales hat on, every day, everywhere she went. Found clients in places where the rest of us never even thought to look. So maybe this one is too difficult for you. Maybe there's nothing you can do to get him to move his money back to us. But the least you can do is figure out how to get in touch with the guy."

It had been tough enough to compete against Vivian when we sat together in the same room. Now that Shep was elevating her to sainthood, there was little chance that I could measure up. "Fine. I'll take care of it."

"See that you do."

He continued to go down the list of Vivian's accounts, getting each portfolio manager to report on his progress. When we had finished, he carefully studied the list. "Looks like we have six accounts at high risk of leaving us, and another four that are questionable. That's about a hundred million dollars ready to go out the door. So what are we going to do about this?"

Charlton shrugged. "We're not going to lose all those accounts. A few of them, sure, but not all hundred million."

"You think not? Every firm out there is targeting high net worth individuals, and Vivian's accounts are at the top of everyone's list. We've got to play better offense here. If not, we'll be out of business in a few years."

"Oh, come on, Shep, don't you think you're overstating it just a bit?" Charlton said.

"Overstating it? Are you kidding me? We're bleeding assets, and not a single person in this room is on target to hit their sales goals this year. If anything, I'm not coming down on you guys hard enough."

Lyman twisted uneasily in his chair. "In the first place, Shep, it's only February, so it may be a bit premature so say none of us will hit our sales goals." He frowned. "But we all know that the business has changed. It's not as easy as it used to be. Nobody wants to pay for financial advice anymore. Clients these days are convinced they can handle their own money, get all the information they need from the internet. They just set up an online account, throw in a few index funds or exchange traded funds, and they're good to go. Or they turn their money over to one of those robo advisors who charge rock-bottom fees and manage money based on computer algorithms."

Shep sat up very straight. "If it were easy, we wouldn't pull in such big bonuses each year. Remember, you've got to sell our value proposition. We bring a lot to the table. Risk management, portfolio diversification, alternative assets, tax strategies, estate planning. Things investors can't get from an online account or with ETFs. Or from a robo advisor. Clients with the kind of money we're targeting need those services. And they're willing to pay for them."

Hardy looked up from his laptop. "We've been sucking wind on stock performance ever since Vince left. That's a tough sell."

Shep glared at him, his face flushed. "I don't want to talk about Vince. This firm has an excellent long term performance record. I'll admit we've been a bit weak lately, but we can fix that."

Lyman shook his head. "I don't know, Shep. Just seems we can't get back on track. We held onto gold too long and watched it roll over. Cut exposure to emerging markets right before they bounced back. Got too conservative last year when the market was strong. Now we've added on risk, and suddenly the market is cautious. No matter what we do, we're late to the party. Our numbers show it."

"And whose fault is that?" Shep asked. "All of you are on the investment team. If you think we're picking the wrong stuff, speak up and recommend something else. Vivian was never afraid to pound the table on a stock she thought was a winner."

"Can we stop talking about Vivian?" Hardy said. "She didn't walk on water like you think she did. She had a few good stock picks, sure, but a couple of dogs, too. Remember Inversion Therapeutics? Dillard Eateries? Or how about Sylvan Products? We lost a shitload on all three of those."

"Nobody bats a thousand on stock picking. You know that," Shep said. "But let me remind you that Vivian brought more assets into this firm last year than anyone else."

Of course she did. She scooped up Judge Edmonton after I had done all the heavy lifting, wining and dining him for months, convincing him that Fairburn, Crandall was the very best firm to manage his money.

"And how many clients did she have to sleep with to make that happen?" Hardy said.

I whirled to face him. Did he know about Nate and Vivian at the museum? Had he murdered her to stop her outrageous behavior?

Hardy had taunted Vivian a few months ago about sleeping with clients, after she had bragged about bringing in a new account. It was during one of our late night drinking bouts, all of us crowded elbow-to-elbow in a dark bar, tossing off insults from liquor-loosened tongues.

"You really think that's the only way I can attract new business?" Vivian asked.

"Pretty much," he answered.

"Up yours, Hardy," she said, accenting her words with an explicit hand gesture.

We had all shrugged it off. Money management was a stressful business, a high testosterone environment. It took guts to plunk down big money day after day. A few wrong decisions could torpedo a career. Crude comments and abusive language were accepted after-hours ways of blowing off steam.

But nobody talked like that in the Fairburn, Crandall war room. Across from me I could see Murphy's eyes widen, his irises becoming tiny specks of blue in a sea of white.

Shep blanched, the dark smudges under his eyes standing out sharply. His jaw muscles tightened. "Vivian was an invaluable member of our firm. Her memorial service is today. Why don't you show a little respect?"

Hardy snorted. "Like she respected the rest of us?" His lips curled back to show perfectly aligned, brilliantly white teeth. "Give me a break. We're better off without her."

Shep jumped to his feet and rounded the table. "Get up."

Hardy stayed in his chair, a mocking grin on his face.

Shep yanked him to his feet and shoved him back against the metal bookcase, sending thick black binders of research reports cascading to the floor.

"What the fuck, man," Hardy said. "Are you crazy?"

Our team was used to trading insults, but body blows were a whole new ball game. Lyman and Charlton pushed back their chairs and moved toward the two men.

Shep grabbed the lapels of Hardy's jacket and pressed him against the wall. Hardy was twenty years younger, but Shep was five inches taller and at least fifty pounds heavier. "Nobody in my firm talks like that," he said.

"It won't be your firm much longer," Hardy said. "Not unless we get things turned around. Maybe it's time somebody else was in charge."

"Like you? I know you've been scheming behind my back to take over. You really think you could manage this firm better than me?"

Hardy snorted. "A trained monkey could do a better job."

"Listen, you asshole." Shep's nose was only inches from Hardy's. "I've spent my entire life building this firm. And there is no...fucking...way," he said, jabbing his finger into Hardy's shoulder with each word, "that you or anyone else is going to take it away from me."

"Get your hands off me, old man." Hardy sprang away from the wall and stiff-armed Shep hard in the chest. Shep staggered backwards, off balance, and grabbed the edge of the table for support.

"You idiots," Murphy yelled. "Stop this."

Lyman and Charlton each grabbed Hardy by an arm. Shep angrily straightened his jacket and tugged at his cuffs. "Enough," he said. "I have to get ready for Vivian's memorial. We'll discuss this later."

He left the room, Murphy trailing behind him.

Hardy took a few deep breaths, his nostrils flared. "We need to talk," he said to Charlton. "My office."

They headed down the hallway, heads close together, voices low. Whatever they were planning, I was sure the timetable had just been accelerated.

§§§

Back at my desk, I called Fontaine.

"Where have you been?" she said. "I've been calling you all morning."

"My phone was stolen." I gave her a quick summary of the robbery.

"I can't believe someone broke into your house. Especially right after this parking deck thing."

"Yeah. Kind of sounds like somebody has it out for me, doesn't it? But what about you? Did the police find Nate?"

Her voice sounded tense. "No. Just his car."

"Where was it?"

"Down by the river. At the old tobacco warehouses."

"That doesn't make any sense." Pallatere Cigarette Company, once a major employer in Hastings, used to run three manufacturing shifts per day at its plants near the river, transforming giant hogsheads of dry brown tobacco leaves into slender white rods of pure golden cash flow. But health-related lawsuits and government regulation pressured the industry, causing Pallatere to shutter much of its local production and move its facilities offshore. The once bustling manufacturing district had gradually disintegrated into a dangerous mire of broken windows and abandoned buildings. "That's a really rough part of town. Nate would never go down there."

"Oh, Robbie, you wouldn't believe the pictures they showed me. The windows of the car were shattered. And there was blood everywhere. A big puddle in the driver's seat. Splatters all over the console and the dash. It was like a war zone. I've never seen anything like that."

"But they didn't find Nate?"

"No. But the police are pretty sure he's dead. They think the murderer dumped his body in the river. If he doesn't surface soon, they'll send down divers."

"Oh, Fontaine, I'm so sorry."

"I feel so guilty." Her voice cracked as she fought back tears. "I convinced myself that he killed Vivian and was hiding out somewhere. And all this time he's been at the bottom of the river."

"You had no way of knowing." I knew how guilt could poison every minute of your life, making you blame yourself long after the tragedy had passed and everyone else had moved on. "This is not your fault."

"Isn't it? What if I had called the police Sunday morning, when I first realized he was missing? Maybe they could have found him before this happened."

"Stop beating yourself up. The police don't even start looking for someone until they're been gone a day or so."

"No," she insisted. "I should have done something. Not just sat around waiting for him to show up."

It was pointless to try to change her mind now, while the tragedy was still so fresh. Eventually she would realize it wasn't her fault and would stop blaming herself. But not yet. "Do the police have any idea who did this?"

"No. They're still processing the crime scene. And they went through our house. Searched everything. Took his computer. Even took a glass of water beside the bed, to get fingerprints and DNA." She started to cry. "They're checking his office this morning. Maybe they can get some information out of that bitch Gayle."

"What can I do? Do you want me to come over?"

"Not now. Maybe later." She sighed. "I'm staying with my parents for a few days, just until things get sorted out. And it's pretty crazy around here. Dad thinks the police are too slow. He's pulling in his own private investigators."

"That's not a bad idea. I need to do more digging myself, since it looks like I'm the next target. I can't wait for someone else to figure this out." I thought for a moment. "How about the coat check girl who was supposed to be on duty Saturday night? Can you get her contact info for me? I'd like to talk to her. She must know something about what happened."

"Probably. I'm sure one of my committee chairs has it."

"Text me her address and I'll check her out." I glanced at the clock. "I've got to go. I'm heading out for Vivian's memorial service. I'll call you later."

# CHAPTER 24

I THOUGHT I HAD ALLOWED enough time to get to Vivian's service, but the towering steeple of St. Timothy's Episcopal was still three blocks away when the cars ahead of me came to a dead stop. I sat motionless as the minutes ticked by, debating whether to stay in the parking deck line or to take my chances finding a spot on the downtown streets.

A quick glance at the dashboard clock told me I was running out of time. Pulling out of the queue, I made a quick right on Third, then another right on Stuart, rolling slowly down the street. But each time I started to pull into a spot, I noticed a street sign with another creative way to just say no. No parking bus stop. No parking loading zone. No parking four to six p.m.

I circled around, down one street, up another, getting farther and farther away from the church. Another few blocks and I might as well drive all the way home and just walk the two miles to St. Timothy's. Finally I backed into a too-small space beside an alley, nudging up tight against the car behind me, hoping to be back before its driver returned.

Buttoning my coat against the cold, I walked quickly to the church. People were crammed shoulder-to-shoulder in the polished wooden pews, a crowd rivaling Easter Sunday or the midnight service on Christmas Eve. Nothing brought out mourners like the grisly murder of a beautiful young woman.

"We have a few seats left in the balcony," an usher said. "Otherwise, we've set up an overflow room in the downstairs fellowship hall."

"I'm with Fairburn, Crandall."

He looked at me blankly.

"Mrs. Sutherland's firm. We have reserved seating at the front." I pointed to the front pews where my co-workers were crowded together. Only a few spaces remained. He nodded and let me enter.

The sanctuary, dim and cool, resembled a medieval cathedral, with gray stone columns, pointed arches, and a towering vaulted ceiling. Outside light struggled to penetrate the ornate stained glass windows. It was one of the oldest and biggest churches in Hastings. Rolfe's family had worshipped at St. Timothy's for generations. Jason had been baptized here.

Candles flickered on the altar as I walked down the center aisle. Classical Bach swelled from the organ, flowing up to the ceiling, then down to wrap around the whispering crowd. Vivian had no religious affiliation, so Shep had chosen his own church for the memorial service. She would have been pleased that her final send-off was from such a majestic setting.

Murphy nodded in greeting as I squeezed in between Charlton and Lyman. Shep and his wife Eloise were in the pew in front of us. Everett Sutherland, Vivian's ex-husband, sat beside them, his head bowed and eyes closed. I took a deep breath to steady myself. The funeral for Rolfe and Jason had been like this, the pews packed with relatives and friends, business associates, parents from nursery school. Even well-meaning strangers. Fontaine had sat beside me, holding tightly to my hand, as a drug-induced haze allowed me to sit calmly through the service.

The organ music built to a dramatic crescendo, the final chords reverberating into the far rows of the balcony before gradually flickering into silence. A female priest stepped up to the pulpit, not much older than Vivian, with the same long golden hair. I could see Shep's shoulder muscles tighten. He must have noticed the resemblance also.

The priest started with the familiar words of the liturgy. "I am the resurrection and the life," she said.

The congregation soon joined in with the appropriate responses. I found solace in the ritual, dragging out the red velvet prayer cushion from under the seat in front of me, kneeling as I rested my arms on the back of the pew. Many of these same words had no doubt been spoken at Rolfe and Jason's funeral. This time I could listen.

After the homily, the priest asked for comments from Vivian's loved ones. Everett sobbed as he said how much he would miss her. Another man, thin and balding man, his eyes red-rimmed, praised her generosity to the Hastings Symphony.

Several clients stepped up to describe her as not just a financial advisor, but a family friend. One told of how she visited his cancer-stricken son when he was in the hospital. Another described how she had comforted his grandmother on her deathbed. I could hear sniffles behind me. It felt like I had wandered into the memorial service of a stranger. Was I the only one who thought she was a ruthless manipulator who would do anything to get what she wanted?

When all the others were finished, Shep slowly walked to the front. "She was a brilliant, ambitious woman," he said, his hands grasping the edges of the wooden pulpit. "She had an uncanny ability to see things that other people didn't, to put facts together in a special way, what we in the industry call a *mosaic*. She was incredibly important to..." he hesitated, biting his lip as he struggled for control. I watched him, wondering again if he had been having an affair with Vivian. "To the firm," he finished, taking a deep breath. "She will be missed. By all of us."

There were a few more prayers, another hymn, and then we were slowly filing out. Shep's wife Eloise grabbed my arm. "You're coming to the reception, aren't you?" she asked. She looked very different from the last time I had seen her. Her graying hair had been dyed an intense shade of matte black, a dense nimbus packed tightly around her face.

"I don't think so. I really need to get back to work."

Her grip tightened. "Please. I need to talk to you." The dark hair made her pale skin appear even more pallid than usual, accentuating the hollows in her cheeks. If the new look was supposed to make her look younger, her hairdresser owed her a refund.

Eloise had always ignored me at company functions, directing all her attention toward the partners and their wives. I couldn't figure out why she wanted to talk to me now. But it seemed a good idea to humor the boss's wife. "Sure. I'll see you there."

She slipped down the aisle ahead of me. I followed the crowd down the granite steps and across the cobblestone courtyard toward the large three-story building next door. Once a majestic city town home, with ornate brickwork and an imposing columned entry, it had been bequeathed to the church after its elderly owners found it impossible to sell, suffering from too few modern amenities and too much deferred maintenance. St. Timothy's had done an extensive renovation to convert the building into classrooms and meeting space.

I entered the broad central hallway with its twelve foot ceiling. To the right, three connecting parlors ran the depth of the house, each arranged into an attractive seating area of stylish upholstered sofas and wing chairs. The lilies sent by Fairburn, Crandall sat on a polished antique chest. Red roses in a crystal vase graced a mahogany end table. The middle parlor sported an arrangement of white tulips, their bending stems reflected in an enormous gold-framed beveled mirror. Baskets of leafy ferns were massed in front of the marble fireplaces, shielding their blackened interiors. The space looked like a designer home during Garden Week.

Sounds of laughter came from the social hall to the left, where free food and alcohol had quickly transformed the solemn mood of the memorial service into a convivial atmosphere of handshakes and hugs. The noisy crowd lined up on each side of the long serving table, filled with heaping platters of grilled tenderloin, ham biscuits and chicken puffs. I circled around the room, greeting clients and friends, then joined the line at the bar.

The two men in front of me were discussing basketball. "That game last night was a disaster," the taller one said. "Their offense just isn't working." He turned to the bartender. "A Stella, please."

The second man nodded. "And it won't until Thad Greeley gets back in the game. They're fourth in the conference right now. I doubt they get a tournament bid."

I realized they were talking about Murphy's son. I leaned in closer.

"I've heard Thad isn't coming back," the first one said. "His ankle injury is a lot worse than everyone thought. This is his last season."

"That's too bad," the second man said as he ordered a Heineken. "The kid is good. Even had the pros sniffing around. Guess that won't happen now."

"Nope. Tough break, huh?"

I hoped they were wrong. Thad had dreamed his whole life of making it to the pros, following Jordan and Magic and LeBron, all those legendary players he had worshipped ever since he was a little boy. It would kill him -- and Murphy -- if all that got snatched away now.

The bartender had just handed me a glass of chardonnay when Gibson Tyler touched my shoulder. "My condolences, Robbie. This is such a tragedy," he said, giving me a hug.

"Yes," I said. "It's quite a shock to all of us."

Gibson was a managing director at Wadsworth Capital, one of our biggest competitors. We had served together on the board of a local finance group. He had been programming chair, tasked with finding speakers dynamic enough to discuss derivatives, statistical correlations and Fed policy without putting to sleep all the guys who had come to meetings primarily for a hearty lunch and a chance to network. "Shep holding up?" he asked. "He looked pretty rough during the service."

I could see Shep working the room, moving slowly from group to group, accepting murmured words of sympathy. This was where he was at his best, not at his computer reading research reports and examining stock charts, not chairing our dysfunctional team meetings, but here with the crowd, always seeking out customers and prospects, gaining energy from every person he touched.

"He's managing," I said. "We're all pulling together to get through this."

Gibson sipped his wine. "It's hard to believe that anything like this could happen in Hastings. No one will relax until that guy is behind bars."

I thought of Gutierrez and Caldor grilling me in the conference room, almost wrangling a confession to a crime I did not commit. "I'm sure the police will find him soon."

Gibson hesitated. "Look, I know this isn't the best time, but there's something really important I really need to run by you."

"What's up?"

He shook his head. "Not here. How about breakfast tomorrow morning? Old Point Restaurant at eight?"

I grimaced. "Sorry, Gibson, but if you've got me in mind for some major fundraiser, I'll have to pass." We had worked together on a number of community projects, everything from auctions and antique shows to duck races and marathons. I had spent long hours on the telephone to solicit volunteers. "Right now I have neither the patience nor the energy to handle anything like that."

"It's not a fundraiser," he assured me, smiling. "And I think you'll be interested."

The same enthusiasm that made him so successful in recruiting speakers also worked on me. It was impossible to say no. "Breakfast is fine. Just don't be disappointed if I turn you down."

"I don't think you will. See you tomorrow."

As he walked away, I turned toward the buffet table and had just reached for a ham biscuit when Eloise grabbed my elbow. "I've been looking for you," she said, tightening her grip. "Can we go somewhere quiet?"

"Of course." I followed her across the broad hallway to the front parlor, the air thick with the scent of lilies.

She perched on the wing chair closest to the fireplace, over which hung an oil painting of a thin, white-haired man dressed in a black jacket and priest's collar. "Robbie, I know the last few months have been very difficult for you. What happened to your family...it was just horrible. I'm so very sorry."

I sat down on the sofa and balanced my plate on my knees. "Thank you. You're very kind."

"Shep thinks so highly of you. He is very pleased with what you've been doing for the firm."

But not enough to make me a partner. "He's been very supportive." I bit into the flaky biscuit, filled with thinly sliced layers of Smithfield ham.

"Good to hear." Eloise hesitated as a small group left the reception and gathered in the foyer, pulling on coats, saying goodbyes. She nervously twisted her hands together as she waited for them to leave. "As you know," she said, when the door finally closed behind them, "Shep and I have been married for a long time. And sometimes, when you've been married a long time...well, people change. People's needs change. Do you understand what I am saying?"

Of all the topics that I had thought Eloise might want to discuss with me, Shep's marital needs were not even on the list. The salty ham stuck in my throat as I looked back toward the social hall, hoping more people would filter out in our direction, giving me an excuse to end this very uncomfortable conversation. "Not really."

She stood up and walked to the fireplace, her back to me. "Don't toy with me, Robbie. You know what I'm talking about."

"No, Eloise, I don't. If you have something to ask me, could you please just ask it?"

She turned slightly, her profile accentuating the sagging skin of her neck. "Shep is a virile, handsome man. Women have always chased after him. In the past, he's always been faithful. But now..."

I grabbed my glass and took several deep swallows of wine, fighting off a very disturbing vision of a flabby, naked Shep crouched at the foot of my bed. "Eloise, you don't think that Shep and I..."

She whirled around. "Of course not," she said. "Not you. I would never think he would sleep with you."

I mulled that one over for a moment, uncertain whether it was a compliment or an insult. "Then what are you asking?"

"You heard him, during the service. Making that speech about how much Vivian meant to her clients. How important she was to him."

I guess that explained her new hairdo. She thought Shep was having an affair, and she was fighting back. "Eloise, that's not exactly what he said."

"It was obvious what he meant." She crossed over and sat down close beside me on the sofa. Her dark red lipstick had bled into the little cracks below her mouth. "You would tell me the truth, wouldn't you? Was he having an affair with her?"

I slowly set down my wine glass as I debated what to tell her. Everyone in the office seemed to think Shep and Vivian had slept together. He certainly acted like a man who had just lost someone he loved, out of focus, distracted, irritable. But there was no point in sharing any of that with Eloise. "I have never seen any behavior between Shep and Vivian that was not totally professional."

Her fingers dug into my arm. "Are you sure?" There was a vulnerability in her eyes that I had never seen before. It was obvious she wanted desperately to believe me.

"I'm sure."

"It's just that...I've been so worried. He just hasn't been himself since Saturday night. He can't sleep more than a few hours at a time. He has horrible dreams, and wakes up screaming."

I knew all too well the demons that haunted the dreams of the grieving. But there nothing to be gained by confirming her suspicions. "Shep is worried that we may lose a few of Vivian's accounts. And it's been a tough time for the business, with the markets so crazy. He's just got a lot on his mind."

"That's all it is?"

I nodded. "Yes."

She sniffed as she blotted her eyes with the side of her finger. "Thank God. I was so afraid that the two of them were having an affair. You don't know what a relief it is to find out the truth."

I put my arm around her shoulders in a friendly hug. "Shep would never do anything to hurt you."

She stiffened at my touch, making it clear that I had greatly overstepped my boundaries. She shook off my arm and stood up. "I'm sure I can count on you to keep this conversation private," she said, her voice as brittle as antique crystal.

Sufficiently chastised, I nodded. "Of course."

She patted my hand, gave me a stiff smile and then walked quickly from the room.

§§§

I waited a few minutes to make sure she had plenty of time to blend back into the crowd, then grabbed my wine glass and headed to the bar for a much-needed refill. Everett stopped me just inside the arched entrance of the social hall. "Have you talked to that client yet? The one who was threatening Vivian?" He looked about three caffeine fixes over the line. His left eyelid quivered, an irregular twitch like a cat poking at a doomed mouse.

"Yes, I have."

"So what do you think? Is he guilty?"

"He's angry, I can tell you that. And so is his wife. They've lost a lot of money."

"But did they kill her?" he said, loud enough that several people nearby looked at us curiously.

"Everett, we can't discuss this here," I said.

He glanced at the crowd milling around us. "Let's go outside."

We walked quickly down the hall to the back exit, onto a small porch that overlooked a playground. A scramble of tiny footprints led through the snow from the gate to the swings. Everett leaned back against the wooden railing and pulled out a cigarette, then patted his pockets to find a match. "Did they kill her?" he asked again.

"I thought you stopped smoking."

He drew in a deep lungful of smoke. "I did."

I stepped back as he exhaled a thick cloud. "I don't know. They said they were at a wedding on Saturday night. I've got someone checking their alibis."

The corner of his mouth twisted. "What about the financial statements I sent over? Did they prove anything?"

"I'm still working through them."

His face flushed a bright red. "What's taking so long?"

"I'm sorry, Everett. There's a lot of data there. And I've had a lot of things going on."

"Well, I've had some pretty heavy stuff going on, too. The police have questioned me non-stop all week. I'm their prime suspect." He jammed his fist into the snow piled on the railing.

I thought I had that honor. It was comforting to know there was another contender. "Because of the life insurance?" I asked, remembering our conversation on Sunday night.

"Because of the insurance. And because we had a huge blowup. In front of dozens of witnesses."

"When? I thought you guys hadn't seen each other recently."

He took another pull on his cigarette. "Last month she asked me to meet her for drinks. At Salazar's. It was our favorite restaurant, and I was crazy enough to think it meant she wanted to give us another try." He flicked some ash into the shrubbery. "Instead, she told me she had changed her will and was leaving pretty much everything to charity. And I guess I just lost it."

"But you said you didn't want her money."

"It wasn't the money. It was knowing that this time it was really final. That we weren't ever getting back together."

I would have thought the divorce would have clued him in on that one. Vivian had made it painfully clear that their relationship was over.

"I pleaded with her, trying to convince her to give us another try," he said. "She kept telling me to shut up and leave her alone. I guess I got a little out of control. My hand hit my drink, and suddenly there was broken glass everywhere. Everybody around us jumped up from their tables. And then two big guys dragged my ass out the door."

"Oh, Everett..."

"Someone even took a video. And now the police have it." His face was gray in the fading light. "I've told them about Edgar Nelson, but they just ignore me. I need some proof of what was going on with that account, to show them someone else had a motive to kill her." He tossed his cigarette into the snow. "And you're the only one who can get that for me."

"I'm still following up. I'll let you know what I find out."

He pulled out another cigarette. "You're my last hope, Robbie. No one else believes me. I can't eat. I can't sleep. My stomach is shot. I don't know how much longer I can take this."

"Believe me, I understand how you feel. There's nothing I want more than to catch Vivian's murderer."

§§§

The flashing lights on the tow truck were visible as soon as I turned the corner. Two men crouched by my car, chains in hand. "Hey, wait," I called out, waving my hands and running toward them. "That's my car."

"Sorry, lady," the driver said. He was dressed in a grease-stained gray jacket, his nose red from the cold. "The cops called us. We've got to tow it."

"Please don't do this," I said, panting, trying to catch my breath. "This has been a horrible day. I've just come from a funeral."

He looked at me suspiciously. I was dressed all in black and certainly looked upset. But he wasn't buying it. "We've been towing cars all day," he said, pointing to his partner, who was crawling underneath my car to attach the chains. "Snow makes people crazy. They leave their cars anywhere. Blocking alleys. Just like this one."

"Please," I said again. "I can't have my car towed." I fumbled in my purse, pulled out a fifty dollar bill and held it out to him. "If you could just give me a break this one time."

He shook his head. "I don't know..."

I pulled out another fifty and shoved them both into his hand. "Please. I beg you. Please don't tow my car."

He looked down at the cash, then called to his partner. The two of them squatted by the back tire, heads together, whispering. Then he stood up and walked back to me. "Sorry for your loss," he said, as his partner unhooked the chains.

As they pulled off, I angrily ripped the parking ticket off my windshield. Vivian could have talked her way out of this, swishing that long blond hair, seducing them with her smile. I had to fork over cold hard cash.

Grumbling, I got in the car and checked my messages. There were several voice mails, including three from Lydia Kensington. Her voice was faint and wobbly, and I had to replay them several times before I could figure out what she said. "Robbie, please come to my home as soon as you get this message. I've been robbed."

# CHAPTER 25

I HIT REDIAL OVER AND OVER as I drove toward Lydia's house. Each call went directly to voicemail. She was fine, I told myself. She had probably gone over to a neighbor's house. Or maybe the police were there, interviewing her, and she was just ignoring her telephone.

But I had visions of her sprawled somewhere in her house, unconscious, bleeding.

The house was quiet when I drove up. No police cars. No neighbors standing around trying to be helpful. A silver car was parked at the curb. I pulled up in her driveway and raced to the front steps.

Chimes reverberated through the house as I impatiently jabbed at the doorbell. Through the sidelights I could see the silk-shaded Chinese porcelain lamp sitting on the gate-leg table in the foyer, illuminating the oil painting hanging above. The polished wood steps leading to the second floor. A corner of the Chippendale table in the dining room. Nothing looked out of place.

Pounding my fist on the door, I called out, "Lydia, are you there? It's Robbie."

After a few minutes, Lydia slowly opened the door.

"I got your message," I said. "Are you hurt?"

She held out her hands. "Robbie, I'm such a coward. Please forgive me."

"Forgive you for what?" I asked, taking her hands in mine. She winced as I rubbed my thumbs gently across her knuckles. The fourth finger of her left hand was red and raw, the knuckle swollen. "What happened to your hand?" I noticed the deep groove embedded in her finger. "Lydia, where are your wedding rings?"

She pulled her hands away from mine and ran her right thumb slowly back and forth over her left knuckle. "I hadn't taken my rings off since my wedding day. Not since Augustus first put them on my hand all those years ago."

"The thief took them?"

She nodded. "I pulled and pulled, but couldn't get them off. I tried everything. Soap. Olive oil. Even Windex. But the rings wouldn't budge. He was so impatient. Kept yelling at me, threatening to cut off my finger. Finally I got them off. But it hurt so much."

I hugged her. "Lydia, I'm so sorry. Have you called the police?"

"No. There was no time." She looked so frail that I was afraid she would collapse. I put my arm under her elbow for support.

"Let's sit down," I said, nudging her into the living room. "And then we'll call the police."

"I don't think so," said a deep voice.

I whirled around to see Gus Kensington leaning against the walnut highboy. He looked so different from the tuxedoed sophisticate I had met at the ball. Now he was dressed in ripped jeans and a faded jacket. Scruffy brown whiskers covered his jaw. His hair, minus styling product, fell limply onto his forehead.

Lydia tightened her grip on my arm. "He made me call you, Robbie. He said he would kill me. He's taken everything. My jewelry. My cash. All the silver."

I looked quickly toward the dining room. The door to the china cupboard was open. Her china was still there, those beautiful translucent dishes with their rose and gold borders, but the silver trays and goblets were missing. The silver tea service and candlesticks had disappeared from the sideboard.

I thought back to the quiet steps edging up my staircase. The empty drawer where my jewelry had been. "It was you last night," I said, twisting around to confront him. "You're the one who robbed me."

"What the hell are you talking about?"

"Someone robbed my house last night. Took my jewelry. It was you."

He shook his head, sending greasy strands of dark hair into his eyes. "Nope. Wasn't me."

"I don't believe you."

He snorted. "Like I care."

Lydia trembled beside me. I needed to protect her, to convince Gus to leave before anyone got hurt. "Gus, you don't want to do this," I said.

"What the hell do you know about what I want?" he asked.

"These things mean a lot to her. The silver. Her jewelry. Her wedding rings." I held out my hands in supplication. "There are a lot of memories tied up in them. Don't take that away from her."

"*Her* memories?" He sniffed and rubbed his jacket sleeve across his face. The edges of his nose were red. I wondered if he was on drugs. "What about my memories? That stuff was here my entire childhood. It all belonged to my grandmother."

Lydia bristled. "My wedding rings never belonged to your grandmother. Augustus bought them just for me."

"Shut up," he snapped, taking a step toward us. "And sit down."

Afraid that he would harm Lydia, I figured our best chance was to get out now, while we were still close to the front door. I rushed toward him and jabbed my fists into his chest. He staggered backwards. "Lydia, go," I yelled, turning toward her.

But Gus was too quick for me. He grabbed my arms and whirled me around. My shoulder slammed hard into the highboy and I lost my balance. I stumbled forward and fell against an end table, causing the delicate Murano glass sculptures it was holding to crash to the floor.

"Robbie," Lydia screamed as she rushed toward me.

"Get on the sofa, both of you," Gus said, rocking back and forth on the balls of his feet, moving to some odd internal syncopation. "That was pretty stupid. Don't try it again."

"You've got what you wanted," I said as Lydia helped me to the sofa. "Take it and leave."

He shook his head. "Those trinkets aren't enough. I've got to get out of the country for a while. And I need some real money to do it." He paced nervously in front of us. "Lydia tells me you control her finances. That she can't make a move without you. That true?"

Clients often used me as a scapegoat in family arguments. It was easier to say that I thought they shouldn't buy their son that expensive sports car, or let their daughter take a six-month sabbatical backpacking through the Andes, than to admit it was their own idea. I didn't mind. I even encouraged them to do it. Better to have a disgruntled relative angry at me than at my client. Made for much more amiable family holidays, with no one tempted to poison the cranberry sauce or spit into the gravy. "I'm her financial advisor, yes."

"Then I want a wire transfer, from her account to mine." He dropped a scrap of paper in my lap. "Ten million dollars. There's the account number."

"I won't do it." If Lydia gave that much money to Gus, she would have to cancel the endowment to the Senator's law school. And that would break her heart.

"Yes, you will." He pulled a gun from his pocket and pointed it at my chest.

"Robbie, please," Lydia said, grabbing my arm. "I don't want anyone to get hurt."

He took a step closer, his hand wobbling slightly as his finger wrapped around the trigger. It would be impossible to miss at this range. It was too late to hide, too late to jump out of the way. I thought of Vivian, with gunpowder burned into her forehead. Soon that would be me.

"Last chance," he said. His pupils were widely dilated, enormous black holes that his soul had crawled out of years ago. He pointed the gun at me, at Lydia, at me again, and then, at the last minute, he angled the gun upwards. The bullet exploded into the ceiling. Chunks of plaster rained down on us. "You ready to transfer that money now?"

I brushed plaster dust from my eyes. "You can't get away with this. The police know you're in town. And they know all about Colorado."

"They do, huh?" He turned the gun back toward me. "Well, there's lots more than Colorado."

"Like Vivian Sutherland?" I asked.

He frowned. "Who's Vivian Sutherland?"

"Come on, Gus. You sat at the same table with her on Saturday night. Witnesses saw the two of you leave the ball together. You killed her, didn't you?"

"Killed her? No way."

"The police think otherwise."

"They're wrong. We just went out for a cigarette. Talked a bit."

"Sure you did."

He shook his head. "I've done a lot of things, but I haven't killed anyone. Not yet, anyway." He walked around the sofa and stood behind us. Lydia yelped as the gun pressed against her head. "But I will if you don't get my money."

I couldn't stall him any longer. But at least I could try to minimize the damage. "Fine. I'll do it. But we can't do ten million. She doesn't have nearly that much in her account."

He moved over to me, so close that I could smell his sour breath. "Of course she does," he said. "The Senator made a fortune during his lifetime."

"But he's been gone a long time. And Lydia has made some generous charitable contributions over the years."

He poked the muzzle into the soft flesh of my neck, digging in hard just under my jawbone. "So how much does she have?"

I was afraid to move, convinced the gun would go off, the bullet spewing gray matter out of the top of my head. Teeth clenched, I held my jaw as steady as a ventriloquist, my lips barely moving. "Three million."

"That's all?"

"That's it."

Lydia's hand, cold as death, quivered in mine.

He chewed the inside of his cheek as he thought this over. "Make it happen."

"I need to get my phone," I mumbled. "To call the office."

He pulled the gun out of my neck and aimed it once more at Lydia. "Fine. But put it on speaker. And be careful what you say."

I punched in the number and laid the phone on the coffee table in front of us. Darius answered on the second ring. "Fairburn, Crandall. Darius speaking. How may I help you?"

I leaned forward. "Darius, it's Robbie."

"Funeral over?" he asked.

"Yes. Listen, I need you to help me with something. And I've got you on speaker."

"What's up?"

"I'm over at Lydia Kensington's," I said, "and I need to make a wire transfer from her account tonight. Can you pull it up for me?"

We could hear computer keys clicking. "I got it. How much do you want to transfer?"

"Three million."

"She doesn't have nearly that much cash."

"I know. We'll have to sell something."

"The market's closed. We won't get a decent price if we sell now."

"That can't be helped." I needed to somehow alert Darius that we were in trouble. "Let's start with Bovender."

"Robbie, what are you talking about? You know there's no Bovender in this account. You sold all that last month."

"Oh, right. Sorry. I don't have the account information in front of me. Let me think a minute." I paused, absently reaching for my charm bracelet, seeking Rolfe's support as I worked through the problem. My thumb touched only the ragged scar on my left wrist. The bracelet had probably already been melted down for its gold content. "How much do we have in Bakken Petroleum?"

"About a hundred thousand."

"And Ferdmont?"

"Three hundred thousand."

"Let's sell both of those."

"Are you sure?" Darius asked. "Ferdmont's got that really nice dividend."

"I know, but it's a bit of an emergency. Mrs. Kensington needs the cash." I drummed my fingers on the table. "How much General Machine do we have?"

"Let's see." I could hear the computer keys again. "Two hundred thousand. But you haven't held it a year yet. She'll get killed on the short term capital gains."

"Can't help it."

"Robbie, are you all right?" Darius asked. "You don't sound like yourself."

Gus wrapped his arm around Lydia's neck. "Don't make me hurt her," he whispered. "You try anything, she's dead."

Lydia's face was a stark white, totally drained of color. Odds were neither of us was getting out of this alive. Once Gus had his money, he wouldn't want any witnesses.

"No, I'm fine," I said to Darius. "Just a bit irritated. You know how small the parking lot is at Holy Trinity Baptist. So I had to park on the street. Turned out it was a no parking zone. I got a ticket." I hoped that Darius would remember that the funeral had been at St. Timothy's.

"This is taking too long," Gus hissed. "Finish it."

I curled around to face him. "I don't have the account information in front of me," I said softly. "It's not like I carry it all around in my head."

"My latest statement is in the secretary," Lydia said in a hoarse whisper. "Back there, against the far wall. Would that help?"

"Yes. Definitely," I said.

"Then let's go get it." Gus released his grip on her neck and pushed her to her feet. "You keep working those sales," he said to me.

"How much Dayton Technologies do we have?" I asked Darius, only half listening. Gus pushed Lydia toward the antique mahogany secretary, its upper shelves crowded with mementos of her many travels with the Senator. Through the wavy hand-blown glass I could see the carved jade dragon from their last trip to China, the red and gold nesting dolls from Russia, and the brightly painted ceramic platter from Costa Rica.

Lydia pulled open the drop-front desk and sat down. The many cubbyholes were stuffed with envelopes and scraps of paper. "Just give me a minute. I know that statement is here somewhere."

"Do you have it or not?" Gus said, impatiently waving the gun.

"I remember now. It's in the top drawer." The drop-front clicked as she pushed it shut and pulled open the long center drawer. "There's just so much stuff in here. It's almost impossible to find anything." She pulled out papers, one by one, balancing them in her lap. "Here it is. I've got it."

She tossed a large manila envelope high above his head, then stood up and lunged toward him as he stretched up to grab it. He grunted and staggered back, clutching at his stomach. Blood oozed between his fingers as he gripped the silver letter opener she had shoved into his gut.

He grabbed at her, but she jerked free and ran toward me. "Robbie, run," she screamed.

# CHAPTER 26

BULLETS PINGED AROUND US as we raced out the front door.

Lydia screamed and grabbed her shoulder. I threw my arm around her waist as we stumbled down the steps. "Come on, Lydia, we've got to get out of here." I pulled her toward her neighbor's house, heading toward the bright lights of their front porch.

"No," she said, "Not the Smithsons. They have two little children. If anything happened to them..."

"Lydia, you've been shot. We can't outrun him. We have to hide."

"The alley," she said.

We hurried across her yard to the back gate. My fingers fumbled with the iron latch, crusted with ice. It finally opened and we rushed into the alley. The snow here had been packed down by traffic, rocks poking through the dirty gray. We ran along the tall privacy fences that marked the backyards of Lydia's neighbors. I pounded on the gates, trying to open them, but they were all locked tight. The frigid air tore at our lungs. After half a block, we were both gasping for air.

"Robbie, I can't do this," Lydia said, bending down, putting her hands on her knees.

"We can't stop." I glanced behind us. Lydia's back gate had disappeared into dusky shadow.

"Maybe he's hurt too bad. He'll just give up."

"I don't think so." Gus was back there somewhere in that dark alley, tracking us. "If he can still walk, he's following us. He won't give up until he gets his money."

A shot rang out, chipping the bark of a giant oak tree just behind us, causing a slab of snow to crash down. Across from us two dogs threw themselves against the fence, barking furiously. A third dog barked, and then another, joining in a cacophonous chorus that spread down the alley. A porch light flipped on, and then several back floodlights, illuminating the ground around us. We made an easy target.

I grabbed Lydia and ducked behind a row of black plastic trash cans. The left sleeve of her yellow silk blouse was sticky with blood. I wrapped my scarf around her arm, tying it tight.

"I can't run anymore, Robbie." She clutched her arm, her face contorted with pain. "You go. Find someone to help us."

"I'm not leaving you, Lydia."

"You have to. Otherwise, he'll kill us both."

Beside the trash cans were scattered household castoffs. A mangled aluminum snow shovel. A rusted basketball hoop. A pair of roller blades, missing a wheel. I picked up one of the roller blades. It wasn't the most effective weapon I could wish for, but was still heavy enough to do some damage. "Not if I can slow him down a bit."

I peered around the trash cans. Gus was about ten feet behind us, one hand pressed against his wounded belly, the other holding the gun. He walked slowly, peering carefully from side to side, searching for us. I aimed for his stomach and hurled the skate into the darkness. It went wide, missing him altogether, and thudded against the far fence.

He pivoted around to track the noise. I grabbed the second skate and slung it sideways like a Frisbee, putting more torque into my throw. It hit the side of his knee and he went down with a groan.

"Get up, Lydia. Let's go." We dodged around trashcans as we hugged the shadows. I could hear a low rumbling ahead of us. As we turned the sharp twist in the alley, we saw a big green garbage truck, its engine idling. I opened the cab door. "Get in, quick."

It was a tight fit, the two of us squeezed together on the gritty floor, our arms wrapped around our knees. The smell of diesel fuel was so strong I could taste it. Behind us we heard the trash men noisily roll cans to the back of the truck.

Lydia's head lolled back on the cracked vinyl cushions. She was shivering, her face very pale, the skin around her lips gray. I wrapped my coat around her and pulled out my phone to call 911. "Hang on. We'll get out of this soon."

She winced as I adjusted the scarf around her arm. "I should have stabbed him harder."

"You were brave to stab him at all. I'm not sure I could have done it." Melted snow on the floorboards soaked through my wool skirt. I pulled down a faded red cushion from the driver's seat. "Here, Lydia. Sit on this."

She shifted wearily onto the cushion. "You think he's still out there?"

"Only one way to find out." I eased up to peer out. Gus was peering down the fence line, looking for us. He whirled the gun up as he spotted me. I ducked down just as a bullet tore through the windshield.

Heavy footsteps raced up from behind the truck, two men dressed in heavy coats and stocking caps.

"What the hell?" the man on the driver's side said, peering at his windshield. The damage looked like a bloodshot eye, a small round hole with ragged cracks running in all directions.

He took a step toward Gus, whose hand shook as he held up his gun.

The driver ripped off his heavy gloves and pulled out a gun of his own. "You crazy, man? You're gonna pay for that."

Gus hesitated, staring at the two men as if weighing his odds. Then he spun around and took off down the alley back toward Lydia's house.

"Teddy, get in the truck," the driver said. "We gotta catch this guy." He opened the cab door. "Hey, what you two doing in there?" he asked, spotting us. "Get out of my truck."

Lydia reached out her hand. "Jerome, I need your help. I've been shot."

He peered into the shadows. "Ms. Kensington, is that you?"

She nodded. "Yes. That man shot me. Please help us."

"You need a doctor."

"I've already called 911," I said. "An ambulance is on the way."

"Then let's get this guy," Jerome said.

The two of them squeezed in with us. Jerome shifted into gear, carefully negotiating the sharp turn in the alley, then picking up speed. Gus had gotten a head start, but we were quickly gaining on him. He struggled with the latch at Lydia's back gate, twisting toward us for a moment, eyes squinting in the glare of the headlights. Then he flung open the gate and disappeared from view.

"He's getting away," I cried.

"No, he ain't." Jerome threw the gearshift into park. He and Teddy leaped from the truck.

There was the sound of a car engine starting. I remembered the silver car at the curb in front of Lydia's house. It must be Gus's. I wondered if it was the same silver car that had been parked at Vivian's overnight.

A few minutes later I heard the wail of sirens. I jumped from the truck and reached the front yard just as two police cars and an ambulance jerked to a stop in the street. "Get on the ground, get on the ground," the officers screamed, their guns pointed at Jerome and Teddy.

They slowly knelt down in the snow.

"Back here," I yelled, running toward them. "A woman's been shot."

The rescue workers followed me to the garbage truck. Lydia was slumped in the seat, her hand gripping my blood-soaked scarf. They loaded her onto a stretcher and carried her through the front yard. I walked beside her to the ambulance.

"Take care of Jerome," she said, her voice faint. "Tell him I'll pay for the windshield."

"I will. And I'll meet you at the hospital as soon as I've finished with the police."

A crowd of curious neighbors had gathered in front of her house, gawking at the police cars, pointing at Jerome and Teddy. "Did they shoot her?" someone asked.

"No," I said. "They saved her life."

# CHAPTER 27

AT THE HOSPITAL Lydia's blood pressure crashed while they stitched up her bullet wound. Doctors rushed in as I stood in the hallway, helplessly pacing back and forth, struggling with the very real possibility that she might die. It seemed like hours before they told me she was stabilized. When I finally got to see her she was sedated, her face no longer that deathly grayish-white, relaxed and gently snoring while the private nurse I hired watched over her.

I, on the other hand, could not stop shaking. Everything about me was cold. My hands. My feet. A lump deep inside my stomach. When I got home, I climbed into a scalding shower and fought the images that swirled in my head. Lydia's blood-soaked sleeve. The hard metal of Gus's gun jammed into my jaw. The bullet hole in the windshield of the garbage truck. I stayed in the shower until the hot water gave out, then pulled on jeans and a baggy sweater and headed downstairs.

The kitchen was dark, lit only by the pendant lights above the island. I crossed to the fireplace and switched on the gas logs. Their graceful flames added a comforting glow to the room. Pulling a bottle of my usual chardonnay from the wine fridge, I ripped off the foil wrapper and reached for the corkscrew before I realized that chardonnay was not nearly strong enough to settle my nerves.

Setting it back in the fridge, I looked over the other selections on the bar. Gray Goose vodka. Famous Grouse scotch. And Maker's Mark, Rolfe's favorite. I grabbed the square bottle and twisted off the red wax cap. The sweet smell of it conjured up pleasant memories: crisp autumn afternoons of football tailgates with Fontaine and Nate; summer nights anchored in the bay, the boat rocking gently as the dark sky glittered above us; neighborhood cookouts with burgers and dogs sizzling on the grill while children ran barefoot in the soft grass.

I poured four fingers of bourbon into a glass. Curling up on the sofa, I gulped down several swallows, then coughed as the liquor burned its way down my throat.

A loud pounding startled me. Luddy Driscoll stood at my back door.

I jumped up, then clutched the sofa arm until the bourbon-buzzed room steadied itself around me. "Luddy, not now," I said, opening the door a few inches. "I've had a really rough day."

"I know. I heard about Gus Kensington."

The cold air swirled around my bare feet. "Don't tell me you're here to interview me? To find out how I felt while Gus was chasing us down that alley?"

Two deep lines formed between his eyebrows. "Come on, Robbie. I thought we'd gotten beyond that." He put his hand on the edge of the door. "Look, I've already filed my story. I came to make sure you're all right. Can I come in?"

I shook my head. "Sorry, Luddy. I'm just not up for company right now."

"You shouldn't be alone. Not after what you just went through."

"So now you're an expert on trauma victims?"

The muscles in his jaw twitched. "I've seen my share."

I shivered in the frigid air. "It's not a good time. It's late. I'm cold. I'm hungry."

"I'll order dinner." He pulled out his cell phone. "Chinese OK?"

Maybe a little companionship was not the worst thing right now. "Fine. Come in."

He followed me into the kitchen, then pulled off his jacket and tossed it on a chair. The bourbon had made my face hot and my stomach queasy. I gestured toward the bar. "Help yourself to a drink. I'll be back in a minute."

My reflection in the bathroom mirror was red and splotchy. I blotted my face and neck with a wet towel, then ran cold water over my wrists until I felt more like myself.

He was sitting at the island when I returned, a pale gold drink in front of him, more water than bourbon. "How's Lydia?"

"She's stable." The remaining two fingers of my drink were dark and potent. I added water and ice to my glass, then stirred it with my finger. "But she lost a lot of blood. She could have died."

"I'm glad she's okay. And that you weren't hurt."

"Just bruised a bit." I rubbed my shoulder where Gus had slammed me into the highboy. "Nothing serious."

"Are you sure?"

I set my glass on the island. "I'm fine. Or at least I will be, once they catch him. I think he's the one who robbed my house last night. He's desperate for money."

"They'll find him. He'll need medical attention for that stab wound. The police are checking with all the hospitals." He sipped his drink. "They pulled bullets out of the woodwork at Lydia's. We should know soon if that's the gun that killed Vivian."

"I'm pretty sure he did it. If you could have seen him, swinging that gun around, ready to shoot us both." I shuddered. "He took a big chunk out of the ceiling."

"I know. I saw it."

I leaned back against the sink, my arms crossed over my chest. "He denied shooting Vivian, of course. Admitted they left the ball together, but said they just went outside to smoke."

He set down his glass. "I don't remember that they found any cigarette butts near the body. I'll check with Gutierrez." He pulled out his notebook. "I've got news about that couple you asked me to check out. The Nelsons."

"Yes?"

"They were both at that wedding, just like they said."

A wave of disappointment washed over me. "So they couldn't have killed Vivian."

"I didn't say that. The husband was there for the duration. Several folks remember seeing him dance with the bride. Turns out he's quite an expert at the tango."

"And his wife?"

"That's where it gets interesting. Evidently she didn't like where they were seated for dinner. Too far in the back...too close to the kitchen...she felt they weren't getting the respect they deserved. So she got into it with Helena, the mother of the bride. Who, as you can imagine, was not willing to rearrange her seating chart just to accommodate the third wife of a distant cousin."

"Let me guess. The claws came out?"

"You could say that. Someone described her as 'that crazy bitch who got into a pissing match with Helena.'" He snapped the notebook shut. "Helena's husband and the groom had to break them up. Sybil left in the middle of dinner. Which meant she had plenty of time to get to the museum and shoot Vivian."

"This means we have another suspect." I swirled the ice in my glass. "That's good news."

"There's something else. I took that picture from the ball to the police. They identified the man who attacked you in the parking deck. His name is Dominic

Syska." He frowned. "This guy is dangerous. He's been in and out of jail a number of times for burglary and assault. Seems he's something of a gun for hire."

"You mean someone hired him to attack me?"

"Looks that way."

I jumped as a knock at the door interrupted us.

"Relax," Luddy said. "It's dinner. I'll get it." He crossed to the door, then came back to the island carrying a bulging bag.

"What in the world did you order?" I asked as he pulled out numerous waxed cardboard boxes.

"Szechuan beef. Cashew chicken. Kung pao shrimp. A couple of spring rolls. Fried rice. Steamed rice." He grinned. "I wasn't sure what you liked, so I ordered a little bit of everything."

I pulled two plates from the cabinet. "There's no way we're eating all this." I put a spring roll and a few spoonfuls of rice and cashew chicken on my plate.

"I thought you were hungry. That's all you're eating? No wonder you're so thin."

I pulled the neckline of my sweater up over my protruding collarbones, then tugged self-consciously at my loose jeans, sagging low on my hips. "Don't have much of appetite these days."

"We'll have to work on that." He filled his plate, piling on a little bit of each selection. "How about we eat by the fire?"

"Sure."

We sat together on the sofa, plates in our hands, using chopsticks to shovel the food into our mouths. It was delicious, but I wasn't in the mood to eat. After a few bites, the rice was sticking in my throat. "I was such a coward today," I said, setting down my plate. "I should have done more to protect Lydia."

"What are you talking about?" He pushed another piece of beef into his mouth. "You got her out of the house and down that alley. Sounds pretty brave to me."

I shook my head. "She's the one who grabbed the letter opener and stabbed Gus. I just sat there and did what he told me to, making the telephone call to pull cash out of her account."

"I think you're being too hard on yourself. The guy had a gun."

I ran my hands through my hair and stared into the fire. "There was a time when I would have wrestled him to the ground and fought for that gun."

"And gotten yourself killed. And probably Lydia, too."

I shifted restlessly on the sofa, tucking my feet underneath me. "It's just that since Rolfe's accident, I've been so...muddled. I'm constantly second-guessing myself, not sure I'm making the right decisions." I reached for my glass. "Nate accused me of mismanaging his account. Maybe he was right."

"You just need time. It's only been a few months."

"Time won't bring back what I've lost. God knows, Luddy, I've tried. I go to work every day, smile at my clients, pretend I care about their money. But it's all an act. I feel so empty."

"You've had a huge loss. It's going to take a long time to come to terms with everything."

"I don't want to come to terms with it. I just want my life back, the way it was before. And no amount of time is going to make that happen."

"Robbie..."

"How did my life get so screwed up?" I could feel my chin quivering as I fought back tears. "I lost my husband. I lost my son. And now two men are trying to kill me. I just want to wake up and find out it's all been some horrible dream." I bit hard on my lip, trying to hold onto some bit of composure. "Please leave," I said as salty tears ran down my cheeks. "This is so embarrassing. I really need to be alone right now."

"That's the last thing you need." He wrapped his arms around me and pulled me close, not saying anything, as grief and fear and heartbreak gushed out of me. He didn't try to stop my tears. Didn't offer any words of consolation. Just waited until I was completely hollowed out, until my noisy blubbering had finally slowed to a gasping whimper. I remembered his story about the little girl cradling her dying brother. This is what he does, I thought. He just holds on tight and lets the pain flow out. This is why people trust him, why they share the agonizing details of their loss.

He rubbed his cheek against my hair. I could smell his cologne. It was the same fragrance that Rolfe always wore.

I sat very still as he gently kissed my forehead. I missed Rolfe so much. Desperately wanted him. Needed him to touch me after so many weeks alone. I knew this wasn't Rolfe. But if I kept my eyes shut tight, if I pushed away time and space and reason, I could pretend.

Through my closed eyelids I could sense the firelight dancing in the windows around us. Luddy ran his hands under my sweater and stroked my skin. I didn't resist as he pulled the sweater over my head and gently pushed me down on the sofa, the cushions scratchy against my back.

Moaning, I ripped at his clothes, running my hands along his body. We caressed in the darkness, his skin against mine, his chest hair soft against my breasts. He moved his fingers gently down my ribs. We started tenderly, but soon there was a frenzy to our love making, a madness beyond longing as I locked my legs around his hips and we thrashed in the firelight.

Afterwards, when we were both exhausted, I snuggled up to him, my eyes still closed. Putting my mouth close to his ear, I whispered, "Rolfe, I love you so." He tensed slightly beside me as I drifted off to sleep.

# CHAPTER 28

SUNLIGHT LASERED THROUGH my closed eyelids the next morning. I turned away from the light, throwing my arm over my eyes as I tried to figure out why my down featherbed felt so scratchy. Or why my head felt so thick and my mouth woolly.

Groaning, I sat up and looked around. The woolen throw that covered me fell to my waist, exposing my breasts. My clothes were heaped haphazardly on the floor beside me. I remembered the dinner, the chopsticks, the fire. And then the rest of it. "Stupid, stupid, stupid," I said as I wrapped the throw around me and walked into the kitchen.

The plates and glasses from last night's dinner were washed and neatly stacked. The island was wiped clean. I peeked in the garbage can beneath the sink. The bottle of Maker's Mark rested on a nest of crushed Chinese takeout containers.

There was no sign of Luddy. I wasn't sure if I was disappointed or relieved. Last night had been a big mistake, brought on by too much bourbon and too much adrenaline. It wouldn't happen again.

I glanced at the clock on the microwave. It was after seven. There was something I needed to do this morning, but I couldn't remember what it was. I thought back over the events of yesterday. Gus Kensington terrifying us with that gun. Shep's wife asking me if he had been having an affair with Vivian. Everett Sutherland begging me to check out the Nelsons.

And then I remembered my conversation with Gibson Tyler. We were supposed to meet for breakfast this morning at Old Point Restaurant. I took a quick shower, then dressed and rushed to my car.

When I got there, Gibson was already seated by one of the broad windows that provided marvelous views of the river. In the summer it was almost impossible to get a table at Old Point, with impatient diners crowded four-deep around the bar as they waited. Now, on a cold winter morning, most of the tables were unoccupied.

He stood as the waiter led me to him, grabbing my hand in a firm shake. "Good morning. Thanks for joining me so early."

"I hope you haven't been waiting long," I said, shrugging out of my coat. "I'm running a little late this morning."

"Not at all. I've only been here a few minutes myself."

The waiter handed me a menu. "Something to drink?" he asked.

"Coffee, thanks."

I glanced out the window at the river below. My last visit to Old Point had been during the May regatta. Rolfe, Jason and I had been among the thousands of sun-seekers who rushed out to celebrate spring under an achingly clear blue sky, feathered with tiny puffs of white clouds. Jason cheered as teams in brightly colored shirts pulled smoothly at the muddy brown water. Then, mesmerized by the tangy smell of grilling meat, he pulled us toward the food tents.

Jason's hot dog slid off his plate as we searched for somewhere to sit. He screamed when I wouldn't let him eat it, his face flushed, snot running down to his chin. Rolfe's beer was warm and his burger cold by the time he fought the lines and got back to us with a clean hot dog and a fresh puddle of ketchup. But by then Jason, a typical three-year-old, had filled up on chips and cookies and no longer wanted it. Rolfe just laughed and swung Jason up on his shoulders as we walked along the river path to watch the rowers below.

This morning that path was covered with snow, only a few footprints marking the trail, the river deserted. An osprey circled high in the steely sky, searching for breakfast.

"So, Gibson, what's been going on with you?" I asked as the waiter returned with my coffee. We both ordered and handed him our menus.

He shrugged. "Not a whole lot. Mostly work. Doing some traveling with the wife."

"Hope you went someplace fun."

"Switzerland. A ski trip."

I tore open a sugar packet. "That sounds exciting."

He gave a wry grin. "A little chilly for me, but Janice loved it. And as long as the wife is happy, I'm happy." He stirred his coffee. "I'm so glad I ran into you yesterday. I've been planning to call you for the past few weeks."

On the drive to the restaurant, I had thought through various scenarios of what Gibson might want to talk to me about. I had narrowed it down to the upcoming United Way campaign or the October marathon supporting cancer research. Both were huge projects requiring thousands of man-hours and an army of volunteers to pull off. I had practiced my refusal speech during the drive to the restaurant. "Oh, really? Why's that?"

"I have a proposition for you."

Gibson was a friend. I was reluctant to turn him down. But I was still struggling to get through each day. There was no way I could take on anything new. "Come on, Gibson, I told you. No fundraisers. No big projects. All I'm focused on right now is my job."

He nodded in approval, his gray eyes magnified by his glasses. "Good to hear. That's what I wanted to talk to you about."

"My job?"

He tilted his head slightly, giving me that persuasive smile that had convinced so many clients to let him manage their money. "Yes. I want you to come work for me. At Wadsworth."

I set down my coffee. "That's a surprise."

"It shouldn't be. You have great performance numbers. A great book of business. And your clients are annoyingly loyal. I've been trying to peel Lydia Kensington away from you for years. She won't hear of it. So I figure the only way I can get them is to hire you."

"Gibson, I'm flattered. I just…"

He sipped his coffee. "We've had an eye on you for quite a while. We can offer you a pretty handsome signing bonus. A good payout based on client retention and performance. Your take would be significantly higher than what you're getting now."

"That sounds tempting, but…"

His eyebrows lifted skeptically. "Don't tell me you've never thought of moving to another firm?"

A few months ago my answer would definitely have been no. Now, with Shep squelching my partnership hopes, I wasn't so sure. "Everyone is always thinking about future opportunities, I guess. But so far, I've been pretty content at Fairburn, Crandall."

The corners of his mouth turned down. "You shouldn't be."

"And why is that?"

Gibson leaned back in his chair. "Because word on the street is that Shep's shopping the firm."

Acquisitions were disruptive enough when your firm was the buyer, in control of the process to work out differences in people and products and computer systems. When you were the one being bought, it was easy to get pushed out if the new owner decided you weren't a good fit.

"That can't be right," I said, smoothing the linen napkin in my lap. Shep's passion when he threw Hardy against the wall at our meeting yesterday did not match up with someone ready to sell out. "Shep has spent his entire life building Fairburn, Crandall. His name and reputation are all wrapped up in it. Why would he sell?"

"Because he wants to go out on top. And the longer he waits, the less likely that is to happen."

The waiter came with our meals, scrambled eggs and bacon for Gibson, an English muffin and fried apples for me. I waited until the waiter had refilled our cups. "Why do you say that?"

Gibson glanced at me, one eyebrow raised. "Because his performance is slipping and he's losing clients. But then, I'm not telling you anything you don't already know."

I tore off a bit of English muffin. "I can't comment on that."

"I admire your loyalty, Robbie. But it's hard to keep these things quiet. Other people in the business know what's going on." He loaded a generous amount of eggs onto his fork. "Shep's a great guy, and a super salesman, but he's no stock picker."

"That's not true." I speared an apple slice. "Everybody knows he's got great long term numbers." That was always a major selling point with our clients. Anyone could have a good year. Make a few lucky stock picks, sidestep a few land mines. But it took real skill to do it year after year, to constantly outperform your benchmarks. And Shep had proven he could do it.

He shook his head. "Vince Crandall was the stock picker. The quant guy. Shep was just the public face of the firm. Once Vince left, everything started to fall apart."

"Vince went to London, right? To open an office?"

"That's the story they put out. But it's not true." Gibson shifted in his chair. "It's pretty sad. The guy had a complete mental breakdown."

My fork stopped halfway to my mouth. "You're kidding."

"Afraid not. All those models that had always worked so well for him in the past just fell apart during the financial crisis back in 2008. Vince couldn't take the pressure. They found him one morning, curled up under his desk, drooling onto the carpet. He was talking gibberish. Didn't even know his own name."

"That's terrible."

He nodded as he bit off a piece of toast. "It was a huge loss. One minute the guy was a genius. The next he couldn't tie his own shoes."

I had known several guys just like Vince in New York, quant jocks who got paid big bucks to correctly predict the future. But of course, nobody could. No matter how many variables they used, how many sensitivities they ran, there was always some low-probability, black-swan event that would eventually pop up and screw the model. And when it happened, clients lost big money.

The constant pressure to always be right eventually caused many of them to turn to alcohol. Or drugs. Or sex. Or a combination of all three. Or like Vince, they had a breakdown.

Gibson mixed bits of bacon into his eggs. "At first Shep refused to believe that anything was wrong with Vince. He figured he just needed a day or two of rest, and he would snap out of it. But finally he had to accept that Vince wasn't coming back. Shep shut himself up in his office, refused to talk to anyone. For a while it looked like he was going to have to check in at the psych ward himself."

"But he pulled himself together?"

"Not at first. Nobody knew what to do. Without Vince, they really struggled. Made some bad investments, lost a lot of money. A couple of guys left and took all their clients with them. There was a real danger that the firm would go under."

I could understand now why Hardy didn't want to go through that again.

"But then Murphy stepped up. Talked Shep down from the ledge. Got him focused on investing again. And convinced the group to bring in some new talent. Including you and Vivian. And gradually things got better. But not good enough. So that's why he's trying to sell out now, while he still can."

I slowly chewed my final bite of muffin. "That's quite a story."

Gibson drummed his fingers on the edge of the table. "So what do you think? Are you interested in working for me?"

"Give me some time to think about it." Murphy would know if Shep was planning to sell the firm. I needed to talk to him before I made a final decision.

Gibson laid his fork across his plate. "Just don't take too long. You're the one I want, but there are several other good people at Fairburn, Crandall. If they become available, I'll need to act quickly."

"I understand. I'll get back to you soon."

§§§

Mulling over Gibson's offer, I got back in my car and pulled out my phone to check for messages. Fontaine had texted me the address for Laney Alton, the coat check girl from Saturday night. A college student, she lived in a high-rise about six blocks from the City University campus. Hoping to catch her at home, I pulled out of the parking lot and headed for her apartment.

The elevator smelled of pizza and stale beer. I knocked on the door of 5C.

"Who is it?" a woman called out.

"Robbie Bradford. Can I talk to you for a few minutes?"

"Whatever you're selling, I don't want it."

"I'm not selling anything. Please, it's about Saturday night. The murder of Vivian Sutherland. I really need to talk to you. It will just take a minute."

The young woman who opened the door had long, dark hair liberally streaked with an intense shade of purple. I recognized her at once. She had been talking with the bartender after the police had herded us all back into the ball room. "It's not a good time for me," she said. "I have class in a few minutes."

"Please. The police think I killed Vivian. I've got to find out what happened Saturday night, so I can convince them I'm innocent."

She reluctantly waved me into the room. "Five minutes. No more."

We sat on a lumpy, stained sofa that looked like a cast off from a homeless shelter. "I know you were working the cloakroom Saturday night. Did you see her?"

She nodded. "She came up to the counter and said she'd give me a hundred bucks to get lost for half an hour."

"Was she with anyone?" I wondered if Laney had witnessed Nate and Vivian's rendezvous.

"Nope. I took the money and went outside to smoke. Only it was like zero degrees out there. So after about five minutes I went back in, to the ladies room."

Barbara Edmonton had told me someone was smoking pot when Vivian charged into the ladies room. That had to be Laney. "Did you see Vivian again?"

"Yeah. She stomped in the ladies room, like really pissed, slamming doors and everything."

So Vivian wasn't quite as cool and calculating as I had first thought. She probably didn't regret her dalliance with Nate. But she had been angry that she got caught. Or at least annoyed that she had been interrupted. "Did you talk to her?"

"Are you kidding me? No way. Just stayed in the end stall, waiting for her to leave."

"And then what?"

"And then some guy came in." She picked purple polish from her thumbnail as I waited for her to continue.

"And?" I said finally.

"And they got in a huge fight. He slapped her. And then they left."

"Slapped her?" I guess that explained the bruise on her cheek.

"Yes. She was laughing, this really grating, obnoxious laugh. He told her to shut up. And when she didn't, he slapped her."

That man had to be the murderer. I put my money on Gus Kensington. He must have seen her coming out of the coatroom, her dress askew, her hair tangled, and realized what she had done. And then he went into the ladies room to confront her. "Could you describe the man?"

"Nope. Didn't see him."

"Maybe a tall, thin guy? Dark hair?"

"I told you, I didn't see him." She stood up and reached for her backpack. "I've got class."

I was so close to finding out who had killed Vivian. I wanted to stay, ask more questions, see if I could somehow prod her memory. But it was obvious our conversation was over. "Thanks for your help." I fished a business card from my purse. "If you think of anything else, please call me."

She shoved it in her jeans pocket. "Sure."

I took the elevator back down and had just gotten into my car when the phone rang. "Hello?"

"Robbie, it's Ana Rodriguez."

"What's up, Ana?" I backed out of the parking space and headed for the exit.

"You need to meet me at the police station right now. Gutierrez has more questions for you."

Gutierrez had already chewed up big chunks of my time this week. I wasn't in an accommodating mood. "Can't do it right now. I've got to meet with a client. Tell him I'll come by this afternoon."

"I think you should reschedule that client meeting," she said. "He wants to talk to you right away. But don't say anything until I get there."

I looked in both directions, then pulled onto Maple Street. "What's going on, Ana?"

"It's not good, Robbie," she said. "You and Fontaine had a fight with Nate's nurse on Monday, right? Gayle Watling?"

I laughed, remembering the look on Dr. Reynolds's face as he stepped in to separate the two of them. "Well, yeah. I guess Fontaine came down pretty hard on her."

"This isn't funny. Gutierrez wants to talk with both of you. Gayle has been murdered."

# CHAPTER 29

AT THE POLICE STATION, a uniformed officer directed me to a small interior conference room. It was fairly spartan, containing only a table and four wooden chairs, with a large mirror on one wall. I had watched enough crime shows to realize that there was probably someone on the other side of that mirror watching everything I did.

So for the first ten minutes or so I tried to look relaxed, sitting down in one of those very uncomfortable chairs, casually pulling out my cell phone to check email, like anybody else waiting for a meeting to start. I wanted to send a strong message to the guy behind the mirror that I wasn't worried about a thing. But it was getting tougher and tougher to sit still. I had talked to Gayle two days ago, and now she was dead. Gutierrez wouldn't have summoned me here for another grilling unless he thought I had something to do with her murder.

I was ready to start pacing the floor when Ana finally came in, looking very professional in a black suit and white blouse, her long hair pulled back in a sleek bun.

"This is all just so crazy," I said, jumping up. "They can't believe that I..."

"Stop." She quickly rolled her eyes toward the large mirror behind us, a silent reminder that we were being observed. "Relax," she whispered, twisting me away from the mirror.

"But I didn't..."

"Get yourself under control, Robbie. You can't get emotional. Gutierrez just feeds on that."

"He can't think..."

She shook her head to cut me off. "You know how he works. He'll try to browbeat you, hit you hard with questions. Annoying as hell, but it's just his way. If I don't like the way the questioning is going, I'll jump in. Otherwise, we'll just let him play his game. Understand?"

I took a deep breath and nodded.

"In the meantime, let's see if we can shake him up a bit." She grabbed a chair. "I'll sit here at the head of the table, and you sit here," she said, indicating the chair on her right. "Gives me a little more control. And I won't be staring into that stupid mirror."

We looked up as the doorknob clicked open. Gutierrez came in first, coffee in hand, wearing that same blue blazer that apparently was his work uniform, paired this morning with a pale yellow shirt and a blue paisley tie. Caldor followed behind, the loyal acolyte, several manila envelopes and file folders tucked under his arm.

"Javier," Ana said, her hand outstretched in easy greeting, "so nice to see you again."

Gutierrez smiled appreciatively as he took in her short skirt and long, muscular legs. He set down his coffee and wrapped her hand in both of his. "Ana, it's been a while. How have you been?"

"Very well, thank you. And you?"

"Fine." He held her hands just long enough for me to wonder exactly what the history was between the two of them. Hopefully, it was a relationship that would work in my favor. "You've met Detective Caldor?"

"Yes. Good to see you."

Caldor nodded. "Likewise."

"Before we get started," Gutierrez said, "can I get you ladies anything? Water? Some coffee?" He was being much more solicitous than at our earlier meetings. Maybe with Ana running interference, he wouldn't be quite so rough on me.

Ana shook her head. "No, thanks."

"How about you, Ms. Bradford?"

"No, I'm fine, thanks."

"Well, then, let's all take a seat." Gutierrez glanced at the table, noticing the rearranged chairs. A tiny grin played at the corners of his mouth as he grabbed a chair and very deliberately moved it to the opposite end of the table from Ana, claiming his own position of power. Caldor set down his envelopes and folders in a neat stack, then settled across from me.

On the surface it seemed so normal. The four of us could have been business associates, getting together to discuss strategy. Or maybe two couples sitting down for a friendly card game. But there was nothing normal about this. We were here to talk about a murder.

"We're recording this interview," Gutierrez said. "Standard procedure. That all right with everyone?"

He glanced at Ana, who nodded.

"Good." He flipped through his legal pad until he got to a clean page. "We have a few questions about Gayle Watling," he said, turning to me. "Can you tell me when you last saw her?"

At least he was starting with something easy. "Monday afternoon. Fontaine Thornton and I went to Dr. Thornton's office."

"Why was that?"

"Nate Thornton hadn't been home since the ball Saturday night. Fontaine was worried. She hoped something in his office might indicate where he was."

His left eyebrow shot up. "And did it?"

I shook my head. "No." Nate had changed his computer passwords and the combination to his safe, which meant there were things he didn't want Fontaine to know. But unless Gutierrez specifically asked, I wasn't sharing that. "No, it didn't."

"That must have been frustrating for her." His eyes were bloodshot. I wasn't the only one not getting much sleep these days. "I understand she and Ms. Watling had a big argument."

I glanced at Ana, but her neutral expression gave me no guidance. "An argument?"

"The nurses told us they could hear the two of them all over the office. Did you somehow miss that?"

"Fontaine was upset because she didn't know where Nate was," I said. "And Gayle was being very protective of Nate, not sharing information. So the two of them clashed a bit. But I wouldn't call it a big argument."

"Ms. Thornton thought Gayle Watling knew where the doctor was?"

"She thought it was a possibility."

His eyes lit up, as though he had finally gotten the answer he wanted. "So the two of you went to her house Monday night, to get the truth out of her."

"No." I shook my head. "On Monday I was attacked in my parking deck at work."

He flipped back through the legal pad. "Ah, yes. You went to Mercy General to be checked by the forensic nurse. And what time was that?"

"Around eight-thirty, I guess."

"Eight-thirty?"

"That's right."

He glanced at Caldor and nodded. "Watling was killed in her home sometime between ten p.m. and three a.m. We found your fingerprints in her house."

"That's impossible. I've never been inside."

"But you know where her house is?"

Our visit to Gayle's had seemed pretty harmless at the time. Now I wasn't so sure. "Fontaine and I drove by on Sunday. When we were looking for Nate. But Gayle's car wasn't there, so we figured nobody was at home."

"Just drove on by, huh?" Caldor asked. "Didn't stop?"

"That's right." It was close to the truth. We had stopped in the parking lot of the Food Lion, not at Gayle's house.

Gutierrez ran a hand across his closely cropped hair. "Then the two women a neighbor spotted sneaking up through the woods behind the house. The two women peeking into the garage. That wasn't you and Ms. Thornton?"

I remembered the woman calling for her dog. She must have spotted us. I should have told him the truth when he first asked. Rather than change my story, I tried to finesse. "I don't know what a neighbor saw."

Gutierrez shifted his coffee cup a few millimeters to the right. "Did you see any rope in that garage? The one you didn't look into?"

"Where are you going with this, Javier?" Ana asked.

Gutierrez took a long, slow breath as he glanced over at Ana. Then he pulled a pack of cigarettes from his pocket and offered me one.

"No, thanks. I don't smoke." I was surprised that the police department allowed smoking inside the building. Most companies now made their employees go outside to satisfy their addiction.

He flicked his lighter and held it to the end of his cigarette. "No? How about Ms. Thornton?"

"Not for years."

Gutierrez took a long drag on the cigarette, then leaned back in his chair and blew the smoke toward the ceiling. "But she used to smoke?"

"For a year maybe. When we in college. But she quit a long time ago."

"You think maybe she picked it up again? You know, it's a really tough habit to break. I've quit four or five times myself."

"Not that I'm aware."

He drew another long puff, pulling the smoke into his lungs, his eyes closed. Then he quickly exhaled and tossed the cigarette into his coffee cup, where it landed with a gurgling sizzle. He nodded at Caldor, who pulled a photograph from his file folder and slid in front of me. "You're absolutely positive?"

The picture was of a woman seated in a kitchen chair, her arms twisted behind her. A rope through her mouth forced her jaws open and her head back, so that her chin pointed toward the ceiling and her long black hair hung down toward the floor. The grayish skin of her face and neck was liberally pocked with what appeared to be cigarette burns.

Fontaine didn't smoke. But Gus Kensington did. And so did Everett Sutherland.

"That's Gayle?" I felt queasy.

"What's the matter? You don't recognize her?"

"No."

"You sure? Take another look. People don't look quite themselves when they've been dead a few days."

"Javier, put that picture away," Ana said.

Gutierrez ignored her. "She didn't want to tell you where the doctor was, did she? After all, she loved him. All the nurses in the office knew that." He fingered the picture. "You probably started on her neck. Her head jerked back so that tender flesh was all stretched out and vulnerable. She couldn't move. Couldn't twist away. Just had to sit there and take the pain."

I shrank down in my chair.

"There's nothing quite like the hot sizzle of burning flesh. The sound of it. The smell."

"Javier, that's enough," Ana snapped.

"How loud did she scream while you were burning off her eyelids?"

Ana grabbed the picture and flipped it face down. "Stop it. You have no right to treat my client like this."

My eyes were wet as I turned toward him. "You really believe I could do something like this? That any woman could?"

He sucked in his cheeks as though he had bitten into something sour. "You would be amazed at the things I've seen women do."

Caldor rotated his pen back and forth between his palms, clicking it against his wedding ring. "When she finally told you where to find the doctor, you lured him to the warehouse district, didn't you? You knew nobody else would be there that time of night. We found his silver car there."

"Fontaine told me about the car," I said.

"There was a lot of blood in it. And fingerprints. The doctor's, of course. Ms. Thornton's. And several prints we haven't identified yet. I'm betting some of them are yours."

"I'm sure they are," I said. "I've ridden in that car plenty of times." Ana put her hand on mine, a caution that I shouldn't admit to anything,

"There were drag marks from the car down to the river," Caldor said. "The doctor's body was heavier than you expected, right?"

Gutierrez leaned forward. "And then you pushed him in the water. Watched him sink. Did you weight him down with something, so he wouldn't pop right back up again? Did you think of that?"

Ana jumped in. "Javier, stop this. You haven't found the doctor's body. You can't even be sure he's dead. Why would you think Robbie had anything to do with this?"

"We searched the doctor's house to get his DNA, to test against the blood in his car. Also checked out his cell phone and computer." He nodded at Caldor, who rummaged through the envelope and pulled out another photograph. "The lighting in this photo isn't so good. And the angle's bad," Gutierrez said, holding it up, turning it from side to side. "But it didn't take us long to figure out what these folks were doing. Although it did take a while to figure out who it was. Well, at least a few minutes, anyway." He tossed it on the table in front of me. "Look familiar?"

I glanced down at the picture. The scene was just as I remembered it. Vivian's face in her moment of passion, mouth twisted, chin slack. Nate's bare butt facing the camera.

"According to the doctor's phone records, this picture was sent to him a little after 9 p.m. on Saturday night."

When we walked in on the two of them, Fontaine had borrowed my phone and snapped the shot, her fingers racing over the keys before she tossed it back to me. I figured she was emailing the picture to herself, so she would have proof to confront Nate later. But she must have sent it to him also. And now the police had a copy. I felt my face getting hot, my cheeks reddening.

"It was sent from your cell phone," Caldor said.

I hadn't shared this with Ana. Never even thought about it. Ana reached out her hand for the picture. I ran my tongue over dry lips as she studied it, pushing her glasses higher on her nose, holding the photo up close, then laying it back down in front of me.

"We can even determine the location," he continued. "See the corner of the file cabinet? And those boxes stacked up against the far wall? All that stuff is still there. In the storage room behind the coat closet at the museum. Must have been quite a shock to see Ms. Sutherland and Dr. Thornton there doing the deed, right? So you took the picture."

I wanted to shout out that I hadn't taken it. But that would have put all the blame on Fontaine, which would not have helped anything. It would just prove that both of us were there, both witnesses to Nate's indiscretion.

"You showed the picture to Ms. Thornton. There was no way she was going to let the two of them get away with that. She wanted justice right away. To get even."

"You've got this all wrong," I said.

Ana nudged me with her foot. She had told me to stay calm, but it was difficult to sit there passively and let them accuse me of murder.

Caldor brought his fingertips to his chin, rubbed them back and forth, deep in thought. "The problem is, how to kill Ms. Sutherland and not get caught. Ms. Thornton is chairman of the ball. The live auction is getting ready to start. If she's not there, if she rushes out to shoot Ms. Sutherland, everyone will notice." Then he smiled as if he had just figured out a vexing puzzle. "But you. Everyone knew you had wine spilled all over your dress. No one would be surprised if you disappeared for the rest of the evening."

"No," I said.

"You're the logical shooter anyway. You have experience with guns. A concealed weapons permit. Bet you keep your gun in your car, for when you're out late at night calling on clients. Just in case you run into trouble."

Gutierrez and Caldor had used this technique before, when they interviewed me in my office, the two of them going back and forth, trying to confuse me, make me admit guilt. I refused to fall for it again.

Caldor pulled out the picture of Vivian lying in the snow, the same one he had shown me when they questioned me at work. One hand in the shrubbery. The other at her head, pulling out brain matter with each painful touch. "See that black residue there on her forehead?" he asked, pointing with his finger. "That's powder burns. The shooter was right in her face."

The photograph had lost its shock value. I barely glanced at it. "I'm a much better shot than that. If I had done it, I wouldn't need to get that close."

Gutierrez's voice was soft. "Maybe. But I figure you would want to. When you screamed at her about having sex with your best friend's husband." He was almost whispering now, his voice raspy. "When you're that close, stuff gets on your clothes. Blood. Brains. On your hands. On your face. That's why you went home, right? So you could clean off all that mess? Wash the smell of her out of your hair?"

My heart pounded in my chest, my neck, the back of my head, the beats growing louder and faster. It seemed that all the oxygen was being sucked out of the room. I took shallow, rapid breaths.

"Javier, could you tone down the theatrics just a bit?" Ana said, her eyes flashing. "My client came in willingly today to answer your questions. This abuse isn't necessary."

Caldor took up the questioning, his steely blue eyes glaring into mine. "Ms. Thornton stayed at the ball, front and center at the live auction, to establish her alibi. Later she slipped out, to see if anyone had discovered the body. But Ms. Sutherland was still out there, all alone in the cold. Ms. Thornton needed the body to be found, to establish time of death, to prove her own innocence. So she ran back to the museum, screaming, and got everyone to come out to the parking lot. To kneel down beside the victim, touch her, try to help. Someone even tried CPR. Much too late for that, of course."

He glanced at the picture. "You'd think they'd know better. Especially with a bullet wound right in the middle of her forehead. Kind of obvious to anyone that she was dead. But then, most folks aren't around murder victims too often. It's tough to remember exactly what you're supposed to do."

My hands were cold and clammy. I rubbed them against my skirt.

Ana's gold bangles clinked as she fingered a diamond earring. "Is there a question there, detective?"

"Maybe Ms. Thornton couldn't be sure that the snow had completely covered your footprints," Caldor continued. "It was really dark out there, at the edge of the parking lot. So she got her buddies to trample all over the scene, to make sure we couldn't tie it back to you."

"Why are you so anxious to pin this on me?" I asked. "I'm not the bad guy here. I've been a victim, too." I looked from Gutierrez to Caldor, trying to convince them. "Didn't Luddy Driscoll give you that picture of the waiter from the ball, Dominic Syska? The man who attacked me in the parking deck?"

Caldor nodded. "Yep, we've got it."

"So maybe he killed Vivian," I said. "Or what about Gus Kensington? He left the ball with Vivian." Ana pushed her knee hard against mine. I knew she wanted me to keep quiet, but I couldn't stop myself. I had to persuade them that I wasn't guilty. "The coat check girl told me Vivian was arguing with some man in the ladies room. It was probably Gus. Why aren't you questioning him?"

"We're questioning a number of suspects," Gutierrez said.

That didn't seem very reassuring. I chewed my lower lip, trying to slow down my breathing.

Caldor drummed his fingers on the table. "You know, maybe this isn't your fault. Maybe Ms. Thornton came up with the whole plan, and talked you into going along. She convinced you to shoot Ms. Sutherland. It was her idea to get the information out of Gayle Watling and then persuade the doctor to meet the two of you at the warehouse so you could kill him. If you tell us what happened, we can reduce the charges against you. Go after her instead."

"There's nothing to tell," I said. "We're both innocent."

Ana closed her notebook. "I think it's time we wrapped this up, gentlemen. Your story is pure speculation. Anyone could have borrowed Robbie's phone to take that picture. It doesn't prove anything."

"Then why has your client refused to give us her dress?" Gutierrez said. "And the gun? We've asked for both of them."

"I don't have the dress," I said. "It's at the cleaners."

"The cleaners can't fix this for you," Caldor said. "Bloodstains always show up, no matter how many times you wash something. Nothing gets them out of fabric, not even bleach."

"I doubt my cleaners would use bleach on a silk evening gown," I snapped.

He shrugged. "We can get a warrant if you want. Of course, if you're innocent, I don't understand why you're not willing to make those items available to us."

Ana stood up. "I would like to speak privately with my client. Please turn off the recording."

"Of course." Gutierrez and Caldor gathered up their files and left the room.

"I didn't do it, Ana," I said, as soon as the door closed. "Not any of this."

She shifted so we both had our backs to the mirror. "Who took that picture?" she whispered.

"Fontaine. But we didn't kill anyone."

"Gutierrez is looking for some hard evidence to tie you to the crime. He thinks your dress and gun will do it. If there is any chance, any chance whatsoever, that he's right, then we need to hold onto the dress until he gets a search warrant. Keep it out of his hands as long as we can."

"I'm not guilty," I said.

"But if he's wrong…if you're absolutely positive that there's no blood on that dress, that your gun wasn't used in this crime, then the best thing to do is turn them over. Once he sees there's no evidence linking you to Vivian's murder, he'll have to back off."

"I didn't do any of this. I didn't kill Vivian. Or Nate. Or Gayle."

"If you have any doubts about the evidence…"

I shook my head. "There are no doubts."

"Then let's do this." Ana opened the door.

Gutierrez was waiting in the hall.

"My client is willing to turn over the dress she wore Saturday evening," she said, "as well as her gun. We'll get them to you today."

He looked a little disappointed. No doubt he had been convinced that those items would prove my guilt. "Thank you for your cooperation."

"Of course." She picked up her briefcase. "And now we're leaving."

"But I have more questions."

"She doesn't have time to listen to you spin these ridiculous fantasies." Ana put her hand on my shoulder and gave me a slight push toward the door. "Show me the proof, Javier. Until then, leave her alone."

# Chapter 30

MY HANDS WERE STILL SHAKING as I left the police station and called Fontaine from the car. "You've heard the news about Gayle?"

"The whole world knows about it," she said. "It's on television. Radio. The internet. Everybody's speculating on whether it's some kind of murder-suicide pact or whether some stalker killed both Nate and Gayle."

"Gutierrez just had me in his office, grilling me. He thinks we were involved."

"I know. They called me first thing this morning."

"Ana kept saying they don't have any proof, but I've got to tell you, Fontaine, I'm worried. Those detectives are relentless."

"I'm not worried about the detectives," she said. "My lawyer can handle them. "But I am worried about Syska or Kensington or whoever the hell is behind all this. They've already come after you. I know I'm next. And I'm not just going to sit around and wait for somebody to put a bullet in my head."

"What are you going to do?"

"You know Nate and I were supposed to go to St. Martin this weekend. I never got around to cancelling our reservations. So I'm headed there, and I want you to come with me."

"Can we do that? Will the police let us leave the country?"

"My attorney says it's fine, as long as we stay in touch. We're not under arrest. We haven't been charged with anything. What do you say?"

"I don't know. I've been out of the office so much the last few days. I've got a lot of catching up to do."

"Don't tell me you're not scared, knowing Gus and Syska are both out there looking for you?"

"Of course I'm scared. I keep looking over my shoulder to make sure no one is sneaking up on me."

"Then come with me. A few days in the Caribbean sun, away from all this freezing snow. Not having to watch our backs. Tell me that's not just what we need."

"Let me run it by Shep. See if I can get someone to handle my clients. And I'll call Ana. If she says it's OK, then I'll go."

"That's the spirit. The flight leaves first thing tomorrow. Don't be late."

§§§

My telephone rang just I walked in my office. "Fairburn, Crandall. Robbie Bradford speaking," I said, grabbing the receiver as I set down my coffee.

"Finally," a deep voice snapped. "I've been calling you for two days. Why haven't you called me back?"

Only one client used that exasperated tone with me. "Gordon Pashman," I said. "How are you?"

"Not good. Why haven't you called? I've left a dozen messages with that assistant of yours. He didn't tell you?"

"Darius?"

"I don't know his name. But I told him it was really important. That there was a huge mistake in my account. He said I would have to talk to you about it. And you've never called me back."

"Gordon, this is the first I've heard of this. What's the mistake?"

"I'm losing a hell of a lot of money, that's the mistake. Three hundred thousand dollars. You want to explain that?"

"Three hundred thousand? Let me pull up your account and see what's going on." The screen showed his holdings, the usual list of solid, dividend-paying stocks I liked to use for all my clients, then a smattering of more aggressive stocks that we had added for additional growth. "I don't see anything unusual so far."

"Keep looking," he said. "And tell me why you put Trexler Dynamics and Stoner Holdings in my account. And that Jaylord Limited thing. What the hell is that, anyway? I've never even heard of it."

I scrolled down the page. He was right. All three stocks were in his account. And all showed big losses. But I hadn't purchased any of them. "I see what you're talking about, Gordon. And obviously it's a mistake." Little glitches in our computer system were not that uncommon. Every now and again I had to get Darius to reverse some rogue trade that just showed up in a client's account. But I had never run across anything as severe as this.

"At least you admit it. You'd better fix it, right away. I've already talked to my lawyer. There's no way I'm eating this."

"Of course not," I reassured him. "Must be a computer glitch."

"So you'll take care of it?"

"Absolutely. We'll reverse these trades right away. And I am so sorry for all the concern this must have caused you." I paused. "Is there anything else I can help you with?"

"Take care of this first. Then we'll see if anything else needs to change."

Shep came into my office just as I hung up the telephone. "Robbie, we need to talk," he said, closing the door behind him.

My stomach tensed. Shep was not the kind of boss who circulated among the troops, asking about everyone's weekend, talking about the latest game. Except for our staff meetings, he generally stayed in his office all day, chatting on the telephone with clients. When there was something he wanted to communicate with the rest of us, he would shoot out a quick email. "Of course," I said. "What can I do for you?"

He settled heavily into the chair facing my desk. "Edgar Nelson called me."

"Oh?" There was always the off chance that Nelson had called just to check on his investments, but from the angry expression on Shep's face, that didn't seem likely.

"You went to his house. Talked to him and his wife."

"Yes...but..." I could feel my face heating up.

"After Murphy told you not to do that. To let me handle it." The muscles in his jaw twitched as he waited for my explanation.

My mind swirled as I tried to come up with a reasonable excuse for what I had done. It seemed best just to confess and hope for forgiveness. "You're right. I should have checked with you first. It's just that you've seemed so distracted lately. I knew you had a lot on your mind, and I didn't want to make things worse."

He rubbed his hand against his forehead. "Well, you have made things worse. A lot worse. Detectives have been questioning him and Sybil about Vivian's murder. And he thinks you put them up to it." He shifted uncomfortably in the chair. "Did you?"

"Not exactly." Luddy had told Gutierrez about the Nelsons. But I had set him on that path.

"Which means yes. Damn it, Robbie, why would you do something so stupid?"

I picked up my mug and took a long, slow swallow of coffee, stalling while I waited for inspiration. Finally I decided to just tell the truth. "Everett Sutherland told me a client had been harassing Vivian. Then he found copies of Nelson's statements in her safe deposit box, so he figured Nelson was the one. I wanted to talk to him myself, to see if it was true."

"Everett Sutherland? That nutcase?" He smacked his palm against the arm of the chair. "You know Vivian took out a restraining order against him?"

"No. Why did she do that?"

"He threw a drink at her, right in the middle of dinner. Security had to haul him out of the restaurant."

"Oh." That wasn't the way Everett had told me the story. "But Shep, there definitely was something bad going on between Vivian and the Nelsons. Sybil was pretty hostile when I talked with them. Said Vivian deserved what she got."

"So maybe Sybil was jealous of Vivian. Thought Edgar was paying too much attention to her. But they were at a wedding Saturday night. About forty miles out of town. They couldn't have shot her."

"Sybil left the wedding early," I said quickly. "She could have done it."

He leaned back in the chair and studied me over tented fingertips. "Do you have any idea how ridiculous that sounds? To think that some woman drove forty miles, in the snow, to an event that I don't even think she knew was happening, to kill someone who conveniently happened to be in the parking lot when she drove up?"

"Well, when you put it like that…"

"You'd be a better suspect than Sybil. You know, I didn't realize until the last couple of days how contentious the relationship was between you and Vivian. You had as much motive as Sybil to shoot her. And a lot easier access." He dropped his hands to his lap. "You showed incredibly poor judgment in contacting the Nelsons."

"I'm sorry. It won't happen again."

"No, it won't." He cleared his throat. "I want you to take some time off."

"Time off?"

"A few days at least. Probably longer. Until we have more visibility on the whole situation."

I felt the floor dropping out from under me. Not only were my partnership hopes squelched, now he seemed on the verge of firing me. "Shep, don't do that. I'll call the Nelsons and apologize. Whatever you want me to do."

"It's not just the Nelsons, Robbie. You seem to be at the center of a lot of bad news. Darius told us about Lydia Kensington. How is she?"

"She should get out of the hospital in a few days."

"Good. Darius caught your tip about Holy Trinity Baptist. Knew something was wrong. Then called 911 when he heard gunshots."

"I'll have to thank him for that." I had been terrified as we ran down that alley, Lydia stumbling as blood seeped from her body. "I've hired a private nurse to take care of her."

"I'm sure Lydia appreciates your taking care of things."

"She does. And so do my other clients. Shep, I can't take time off right now. Just this morning I got a call from a client with some really weird trades in his account, stocks I never bought for him. I need to follow up on that."

"Murphy can take care of that for you. And handle your other accounts while you're gone."

"But I don't want…"

"It's not a matter of what *you* want, Robbie. It's what best for the firm. Somehow you've become a target. The attack in the parking deck. Breaking into your house. What if you were with a client, and whoever is doing this decided to strike again? We can't take that kind of risk."

"You sound just like Fontaine."

"What do you mean?"

"You heard about Gayle Watling, Nate's nurse?"

"It was on the news this morning."

"Fontaine thinks the same person killed Nate and Gayle. And he'll come after her next. She wants me to go to St. Martin with her, until the police find out who's behind all this."

"That's perfect, then." He nodded, as though everything were totally resolved. "The two of you go for a little R&R, and by the time you get back, maybe everything will be cleared up." He stood up and walked toward the door.

"And if it isn't?"

He hesitated, his hand on the knob. "Then we'll have to talk again."

I called Ana right after Shep left my office. She was not enthusiastic about my travel plans. "It sends the wrong message, Robbie. Right in the middle of a murder investigation, the victim's wife and her best friend take off for a Caribbean holiday. A bit unfeeling, don't you think?"

"It's more like self-preservation. Vivian, Nate and Gayle are all dead. Fontaine and I think we're next. So can I go? I don't want to get pulled off a plane in handcuffs."

"The police haven't charged you with anything, so you can go," she said reluctantly. "I'll let Gutierrez know your plans, just in case he needs to get in touch with you."

"Good."

"But are you sure you want to do this?"

"Trade twenty-degree temperatures for a few days of basking on the beach? Yes, I'm sure."

Her tone was cautious. "This trip was Fontaine's idea?

"Yes."

"Gutierrez thinks Fontaine is behind the murders. She was jealous, and killed her husband and his girlfriends."

"That's ridiculous."

"The police found Fontaine's fingerprints inside Gayle's house."

"That's not surprising. She told me she and Nate went there for a Christmas party."

"How do you know she wasn't at Gayle's Monday night? Or at the warehouse with Nate? You said you couldn't get in touch with her. That her phone kept going to voicemail."

"She was with her parents Monday night. Had her phone turned off. She told me."

"I'm just saying, it would be pretty convenient for her if something happened to you while the two of you were alone on St. Martin. Then she could claim you were behind all these murders."

"I can't believe you said that. Fontaine's been my best friend since college. She would never kill her husband. Or anyone else. And she would never do anything to hurt me."

"You sure about that?"

"You've been spending too much time with Gutierrez. By the way, I wasn't too happy about the grilling he gave me this morning. I thought you were supposed to run interference. Keep him from beating up on me like that."

"I know that was a bit uncomfortable. We had words about it after you left. But I warned you that's how he operates. Likes to put pressure on suspects, hoping they'll confess. And we got a lot of good information from that interview."

"Seems to me that he was the only one getting information."

"Not true. It's obvious he doesn't have a positive ID on the women at the garage. He was hoping you would clear that up for him. Thankfully, you didn't.

And you gave him a very plausible reason for why your fingerprints might be in Nate's car. Unless he finds your prints in Gayle's house..."

"He won't. I've never been inside."

"Or he finds any evidence on your dress and gun..."

"There's nothing to find."

"Then I'm feeling really good about this whole investigation. He's long on speculation but very short on hard evidence. Which means he has to keep looking for another suspect."

§§§

I stopped by Murphy's office right after I finished my conversation with Ana. "Have you seen Darius? I can't find him anywhere, and I've got a problem with a client's account."

"He had to take his car to the shop. Got involved in a fender-bender yesterday."

"Sorry to hear that." I leaned against the door frame. "Shep is putting me on leave. For at least a few days. Or until these murders are solved."

Murphy looked up from his computer screen. "I told you not to talk to the Nelsons. Edgar gave Shep hell this morning. Threatened to move the account."

"I'm sorry. But those detectives had me right in the crosshairs. I had to do something to find another suspect." I plopped down in the chair across from his desk. "Shep said you would look out for my clients while I'm gone."

"Of course."

"Most of them probably won't need anything much. Assuming that it's only a few days, and not forever. But I need you to check on Gordon Pashman. He called this morning. He's losing money on stocks I never bought for him. I wanted to talk with Darius about it, see if he could figure out what happened."

"Gordon Pashman," he said, slowly writing the name on his legal pad. "I don't remember you ever mentioning him."

"I never needed to. We had his investment plan all set up, and the account's been pretty much on auto-pilot for the last few years. He made regular contributions and I invested them, just rebalancing every few quarters or so. No sweat."

"So what changed?"

"His company went through some downsizing. He got pushed out. Hasn't been able to find another job. And now he's terrified that he's going to run out of money."

"You think he will?"

"Of course not. Even if he never works another day in his life, he'll have plenty to last him in retirement. But I haven't been able to convince him of that."

He frowned. "Probably something just got coded wrong. I'm sure Darius can fix it."

"That's what I figured." I stood up. "I'll check back with you later to make sure everything got taken care of. And please take good care of my clients while I'm gone."

"We've got it under control. Don't worry about a thing."

# Chapter 31

THE ALARM BLASTED ME AWAKE at 4 a.m. Groaning, I smacked it silent, then collapsed back on my pillow. I had slept fitfully the entire night, nodding off for an hour or so, then jumping awake to check the clock, afraid I would oversleep and miss my flight to the Caribbean. Snuggling under the covers, I was almost asleep when the snooze alarm buzzed. Smacking the clock a second time, I pushed myself out of bed and headed for the shower, hoping the hot water would clear my foggy head.

It was still dark outside when I wrestled my suitcase down the steps and out to my car. Clouds overhead obscured the moon and stars, the only light coming from scattered street lamps. There were few other cars on the interstate. Rush hour traffic wouldn't start for at least another hour.

At the airport, the parking deck was nearly full. I circled up several levels, searching for a space, and finally squeezed between two SUVs on the top level. My wheeled suitcase thumped noisily on the textured concrete as I crossed over the transit bridge and entered the terminal.

Two policemen stood off to my left, scanning the crowd. I froze, thinking they were there for me, ready to arrest me after all to prevent me from leaving the country. But after a few minutes they wandered down to the other end of the terminal. Relieved, I rolled up to the international counter and handed the clerk my passport. He checked my luggage and handed me a boarding pass.

Fontaine was waiting for me at the security gate. She evidently had not slept well either. Her eyes were puffy and her cheeks gaunt.

We threaded our way through the black tapes of the security line. Ahead of us a passenger, arms held aloft, was being patted down by a security guard. I loaded my belongings into a rectangular rubber bucket and pushed it onto the inspection conveyor belt. The attendant waived me through the screening portal. I slipped on my shoes, gathered my things and headed to a nearby bench to put myself back together.

Fontaine was still making her way through security, waiting for her hand luggage to pass inspection. Finally she was through the line, and we walked toward our gate. Once there, Fontaine flopped wearily into one of the hard plastic seats, dumping her possessions in the chair beside her.

I set my bag on the other side of the small built-in table. "If you'll stay here and watch our stuff, I'll get us some coffee," I said. "And maybe a sausage biscuit or something?"

"Whatever," she said.

I wandered down the terminal. There were not a lot of breakfast choices in the early-morning Hastings airport. Most of the restaurants were still closed. I was almost back at security when I finally spotted a coffee kiosk. I ordered two large coffees and bagels, then grabbed several sugars and containers of cream as I headed back toward our gate. "Here you go," I said, handing Fontaine her coffee and a bagel.

"We'll have plenty of time to enjoy breakfast," she said, pointing to the message board above our gate. "Our flight is delayed two hours. Thunderstorms in Atlanta. I bet we miss our connecting flight." She emptied a container of cream into her coffee and took a sip. "This stuff is ghastly," she said, curling her lip. She tossed the coffee in the trash, then moved toward the wide windows overlooking the runways.

I walked up beside her. "We'll get through this, Fontaine."

"I'm not so sure." She crossed her arms over her chest and stared out at the tarmac.

"Did something happen last night? You seem upset."

"It's those reporters," she said. "They won't leave me alone. They followed me to my parents' house. All night there were news trucks parked out front, enormous lights pointed at the windows, the telephone ringing nonstop." She pulled her scarf from her neck, twisting the fringe around her fingers. "Dad finally brought in his own security detail to handle the crowd outside."

"That's terrible." So far no reporters were hassling me. I wondered if Luddy had anything to do with that.

"Dad's investigative team was at the house all last night, huddled around the dining room table, going over and over everything connected with the case, testing alternative theories of what happened. They kept asking me questions. About Nate and Vivian at the ball. You and me at Gayle's house. About Nate and Gayle. You and Vivian. It just wouldn't stop."

"I know it's hard, but the more people that are working on this, the quicker we'll find out the truth," I said.

"I can't take much more. Not knowing if Nate killed Vivian. Or who killed Nate." She wound the scarf fringe so tightly that her fingertips turned white. "You know, at first I thought maybe he wasn't dead. That he faked his death and skipped the country. But then the police found his passport in his office safe. And there's been no activity on his credit cards. So I guess it's time to stop kidding myself." She unwound the scarf and balled it up in her fist. "My mother can't stop crying. She's driving me crazy, treating me like a little kid who's had a bad day at school, bringing me hot cocoa and cookies, as though that could somehow make all these horrible things go away."

"Your parents love you, Fontaine. They'd do anything to protect you."

"I know that." Her fingers nervously kneaded the scarf. "But when I look at Dad's eyes, I see something that scares me."

"What's that?"

She knotted the scarf once more around her neck. "He knows how much Nate's infidelity has tortured me over the years. How I've been pushed to the limit time and time again. He's trying to figure out how to resolve this case without hurting me." She pulled her hair free and shook it loose over her shoulders. "Because deep down, so deep that he doesn't even want to admit it to himself, my own father thinks I might be guilty."

§§§

The rain delay almost caused us to miss our connection in Atlanta. We jumped on the shuttle to the international terminal, then raced toward our gate, arriving just as the flight attendants were ready to close the doors. Once on board, Fontaine quickly drank two glasses of cabernet and then fell asleep, her head wedged against my shoulder.

I was too nervous to sleep. We flew through rain and thunder most of the way, the pilot warning of turbulence, reminding us to keep our seat belts buckled. The plane took a few ominous dips mid-flight, causing my stomach to jump up toward my throat. Fontaine just readjusted her position and kept right on sleeping. I figured it was her escape strategy, to avoid thinking about her father, and Nate, and this ungodly mess that we had gotten swept up into.

The skies cleared as we approached St Martin. Peering through the rain-spotted windows, I could see that incredibly beautiful turquoise water, shimmering in the hot Caribbean sun. The plane, so small while we were fighting thunderstorms, seemed gigantic as its shadow lowered over the ocean and we swooped down toward the tiny island. All I could see was water, water, water rushing past me as we screamed toward the runway.

With a sudden bump we touched land. The screeching brakes fought to slow the speeding plane, but we kept moving, past the palm trees, past the squat buildings. I stiffened and clutched the seat arms, sure we would overshoot the runway and plunge nose first into the ocean. But the plane finally came to a shuddering halt. Fontaine stretched beside me as we taxied to the terminal.

There was a familiar ding as the captain turned off the seat belt sign, then a collective click as we all snapped open our seat belts. I jerked my carry-on from the overhead bin and followed Fontaine as she made her way down the jet bridge.

We waited at the baggage carousel for our luggage, then lined up to clear immigration. As we exited the terminal, I stepped into humidity that surpassed the soggiest dog days of a Hastings summer. Compared to the snow I had left in Hastings, it felt marvelous. I breathed in deeply, exhaling the stale airplane air from my lungs.

The taxi driver loaded our luggage in the trunk. "Where are you headed?" he asked.

"Maison La Plage," Fontaine said. "It's on the French side of the island, in Anse Marcel. Do you know it?"

"Of course. Lovely spot. Top of the mountain."

The taxi crossed the bridge then turned right, passing through Philipsburg and heading north. The barren hills were covered mostly with scrub, small plants struggling to survive in the baking sun. High above us a goat perched on a giant rock, surveying his fiefdom. "This is one dry island," I said.

"Parts of it. Especially the Dutch side, which they call St. Maarten. But don't worry," Fontaine said. "Maison La Plage, the Beach House, is beautiful. Very green, with the most gorgeous bougainvillea and fragrant frangipani you can find anywhere.

The winding road hugged the coastline. Off to the right, sailboats bobbed in the blue water as we passed Oyster Pond. "That's the nudist beach," Fontaine said, pointing to a sign for Orient Beach.

"You're kidding." I peered through the window, looking for naked sunbathers. If they were down there, they were well hidden from the road. "Please don't tell me we're staying here."

"Of course not," she said, rolling down the window to let the warm breeze caress her face. "Our resort is much prettier than this."

The road turned away from the coast and into a dense stand of trees. The taxi's engine strained as we edged up the steep grade. I could no longer see the water as the road, narrower now, continued to curve inland. We were the only car in sight as we kept climbing upward. Finally we reached the crest of the mountain. Fontaine tapped the driver on the shoulder. "Can you stop here for a moment, please?"

He nodded. We climbed out of the taxi and stood in the weeds at the side of the road, the sun beating down on us, hot breezes ruffling my hair. Looking down through the trees, I could see a collection of four-story red roofed white buildings nestled at the bottom of the hill, surrounded by colorful flowers and lush swathes of green. To the far right was a marina, with a large number of boats tied up at the slips. Curved arms of extinct volcanoes stretched out into the Caribbean, encircling our own private harbor of shimmering turquoise water.

"This is it. Isn't it beautiful?"

"Yes. Pretty amazing."

We got back into the taxi and wound down tortuous curves, through the entrance gate to the hotel. The cab driver unloaded our bags, and a smiling bellman stacked them onto a wheeled brass cart. "This way, ladies," he said, leading us inside to the registration desk.

The lobby was big and airy, with polished marble floors and casual groupings of white wicker furniture fitted with overstuffed tropical-print cushions. Ceiling fans rotated high above us, stirring the humid air. At the back of the lobby, sheer white curtains billowed lazily in the breeze, framing the sparkling sea beyond. I was eager to fling off my shoes and dig my toes into the white sand. "This place is gorgeous," I said.

"I knew you would love it."

We registered and the bellman led us through a side exit down a long stone pathway that curled through the gardens. We reached our building and rode the elevator to the fourth floor. Our adjoining rooms were light and cheerful, with queen-sized beds topped with white coverlets. We tipped the bellman as he deposited our suitcases on the luggage racks.

Fontaine pulled open the glass door to the balcony. We walked out, staring at the waves. "Nate always loved St. Martin," she said. She reached back and twisted her long hair into a tangled braid, then piled it on top of her head.

"I can see why. It's lovely."

"Yes, it is. Just as I remembered it." She leaned forward, resting her elbows against the railing. "This is so wrong, Robbie," she said, just above a whisper. "I shouldn't have come here. Not without him."

"Fontaine, you can't keep…"

"Do you think he was already dead when they tossed him in the river? Or was he still fighting, gasping for air, trying to spit out water the whole time he was sinking?"

I put my hand on her arm. "Don't think about that. It will drive you crazy. Believe me, I know." In my nightmares I still saw Rolfe and Jason in that mangled car.

She turned toward me. "How do you bear it? Knowing you've lost them forever?"

"It's not easy. There are days when I miss them so much I can barely breathe." The nights were worse, endless hours of unrelenting longing, when I would give anything to feel Rolfe's arms around me. My thoughts drifted back to the flickering firelight of a few nights ago, when I pushed back reality and made myself believe that the man touching me with such tenderness, making my body respond to his, was Rolfe.

Fontaine caught the pain in my voice. "Oh, Robbie, I'm so sorry, bringing all this up. That's so unfair to you."

"It's fine. You need to talk about it. I understand."

"No, I don't. I'll ruin the weekend for both of us." She shook out her hair and flipped it back behind her shoulders. "What I need is an attitude adjustment," she said, her voice artificially bright. "Some sunshine and a couple of those umbrella drinks. Let's get changed and go down to the pool."

§§§

We walked between tall palm trees toward the wide oval pool edged with decorative blue tiles. At the far end, a small waterfall noisily splashed through lichen-covered rocks. An attendant led us through the crowd to two empty lounge chairs, quickly snapping down a towel on each, then fashioning a second towel into a headrest. "Can I bring you anything?" he asked.

"A piña colada for me," Fontaine said. "And something to munch on. Maybe some fruit? Cheese? Something like that?"

"Of course. And for you?" he asked me.

"I'll have the same." I settled into my chair, enjoying the marvelous heat baking into my skin, thinking of those poor souls back in Hastings still shoveling snow from their sidewalks.

Fontaine sprayed herself with suntan lotion. "There's nothing quite like the feel of that warm Caribbean sun," she said. "Just be sure to use plenty of sunscreen. With that pasty white skin of yours, you'll crisp up just like fried butter at the state fair."

"I've got an SPF 45 here," I said, obediently spraying my body. "That should do it." I leaned back and closed my eyes. It was so relaxing. Scents of coconut, mango and pineapple wafted on the breeze. Even the sounds were seductive, multiple languages swirling around my head -- French, Spanish, others I couldn't identify. All around me beautiful bodies were splayed out on their lounge chairs, oiled sacrifices to the sun god.

In a few minutes the attendant handed us each a piña colada, then set a tray of fruit and cheese down on the table between us. "Ladies, enjoy," he said, then walked away.

The drink was thick, sweet and potent. I let my mind drift, thinking of nothing, listening to the muted sounds around me. Couples chatting. Caribbean music streaming out from the beach bar.

The gentle sighing of distant waves reminded me of the Venice trip that Rolfe and I had taken with Nate and Fontaine a year ago. It had been October, cold and so rainy that the canals had overflowed their banks, with waves of dirty water slapping into St. Mark's Square, flooding the beautiful mosaic floors of the cathedral. Businesses set up pathways of low metal tables so the tourists could walk around the square without sloshing through foot-deep water.

The four of us took a gondola ride, bundled up in rain slickers, laughing as we maneuvered down narrow canals, between ancient buildings coated at the waterline with slimy moss. Afterwards Rolfe bought me a gondola charm for my bracelet.

Only I didn't have the bracelet anymore. All I had was the memories, gradually becoming more faded and brittle as the months went by, like old photographs stuffed in a shoebox. Already I was struggling to hold onto the details of our trip, the name of our hotel, the restaurant that served such marvelous wine. "Fontaine," I said. "What was the name of that restaurant in Venice? The one that served the pinot noir we all loved so much?"

"Venice?" She propped herself up on her elbows and looked at me. "That was over a year ago. What made you think of that?"

"I don't know. I guess just being around all this water. Remember how the city was flooded?"

"I remember. It took my shoes three days to dry out. What a mess."

"The restaurant," I said again. "What was the name of it?"

"I don't remember. But I've made reservations for tonight at Chez Pierre. It's the best seafood restaurant on the island. You'll love it."

"Thanks." I kept trying to think of the Venetian restaurant, with those funny cushioned chairs and the chandeliers hanging from thick chains, and Rolfe pouring me another glass of pinot noir.

But then I remembered it had been the waiter, not Rolfe, who poured the wine. And we had sat on wooden benches at that restaurant, not cushioned chairs. The cushions had been at another restaurant. Maybe in Paris?

This is the way it will be, I thought, without my bracelet to help trigger memories of my past. All the vivid details, all the memories I was sure were unforgettable, will gradually dim, pushed into some remote corner of my brain. Someday, all I will remember is that Venice was cold and raining and gray. That is, if I even think of that trip at all.

# CHAPTER 32

CHEZ PIERRE SPRAWLED AT the top of a cliff, a low-slung wood building stained gray by the sea air. Our taxi maneuvered through a full parking lot to drop us off at the entrance. Customers were gathered on loveseats and lounge chairs on the big front porch, nursing their drinks as they waited for a table.

"Reservation for Thornton," Fontaine said as we reached the top step.

The maitre d' ran his finger down the page until he found her name. "Of course." He signaled to a server. "Table six, please."

The server led us through a crowded dining room to the deck outside. "Here you are," he said, pulling out our chairs and setting down menus. "Welcome to Chez Pierre. Could I get you something to drink? Something from the bar, perhaps? Or a bottle of wine?"

"Let's get something light," Fontaine said, taking a quick look at the wine list. "How about sauvignon blanc?"

"Fine with me," I said.

"We'll take this one." She pointed to a name on the list. "And a bottle of sparkling water."

Our table was set against the deck railing, near a cliff which angled down sharply to the water below. "Isn't this gorgeous?" Fontaine gushed, settling into her chair. "This is one of the best views on the island."

The sea was flat, foaming gently back and forth on the shoreline like little crabs scuttling after their dinner. The setting sun burned a path through the dark water, bruising the waves with flickers of gold.

Our server returned with our water, then set down a basket of bread and some herb-infused oil.

"So who do you think killed Gayle?" I asked as he walked away.

Fontaine rummaged through the bread basket and selected a tiny baguette. "Rule for the evening," she said, as she broke off a piece and swirled it in the oil. "No conversations about dead people, or police, or anything remotely depressing. We're here to get away from all that."

"But we need to figure out who did all this," I said. "The coat check girl said Vivian fought with some man in the ladies room. He had to be the one who killed her. And I bet it was Gus Kensington."

Fontaine shook her head. "I don't care. I don't want to think about all that right now." She popped the bread into her mouth. "Tell me something fun."

I thought for a moment as I reached for the bread basket. "I slept with Luddy Driscoll."

"What?" She started to cough, choking on her bread.

"Are you all right?" I asked.

She patted her chest, then took several swallows of water. "Luddy Driscoll? You're kidding me. You hate that guy. You've told me a dozen times. How insensitive and callous he was about Rolfe's death."

"Well, maybe I was wrong about some of that. He's been helping me investigate Vivian's murder. So we've been spending more time together. And I realized he's not really such a bad guy. When he wrote those articles, he was just doing his job."

She smirked. "The classic excuse people use when they want to be forgiven for doing something unforgivable."

The waiter returned with our wine, uncorking the bottle and pouring a small amount into Fontaine's glass. She sipped it, rolling the wine around her tongue. "This is fine," she said.

He poured more into her glass, then filled mine and set the bottle in an ice bucket beside our table.

"So when did this happen?" Fontaine asked.

"The night Lydia Kensington was robbed," I said.

"Details, please."

"There's not a lot to say. It had something to do with bourbon, and a flickering fire, and being terrified after Gus Kensington took a shot at me. And then...well, then it was the next morning."

Her eyes widened. "Was it great sex? Bodice ripping, buttons all over the floor, underwear on the ceiling fan?"

"You've been reading too many romance novels."

"Well?"

I grinned. "Something like that."

She fell back in her chair. "I'm so jealous. Nate and I haven't had sex like that for years. Even before this thing with Vivian, he barely talked to me except to ask if I'd picked up the dry cleaning. Or gotten the oil changed in the car. Or paid the insurance bill."

"Don't get so excited, Fontaine. It was just a one-time thing. It won't happen again."

"Why the hell not?" she asked. "Sounds like you two are great together."

"No. I've felt guilty ever since it happened. It's not fair to Rolfe."

"Rolfe would want you to be happy. And when we finally get ourselves out of this mess, when we go home and you claim that partnership that is much overdue…"

I dipped my bread in the oil. "I'm not sure I want to go back to Fairburn, Crandall."

"Why's that?"

"Because Shep is being so nasty about all this. Putting me on leave just because I talked to the Nelsons. I worked so hard to make partner, and now that's not going to happen."

"You don't know that," she said, trying to reassure me. "Shep is just upset about Vivian. Worried about losing another client. Let a little time go by, and then bring up the partnership again."

I shook my head. "I heard Shep is trying to sell the firm. I'd like to get out before that happens."

"Oh." She sipped her wine. "Do you have any plans?"

"As a matter of fact, I got a job offer yesterday," I said.

"From whom?"

"Gibson Tyler. With Wadsworth Capital."

She nodded. "That's a good firm. You going to take it?"

"I don't know. I'm not sure the guys at Wadsworth would be any more supportive than those at Fairburn, Crandall. It's just so tough for a woman in this business. Murphy is about the only friend I have at work. And even he's been acting weird recently."

She picked up the menu. "There's another choice, of course."

"What's that?"

"You could start your own firm."

I laughed. "I don't think so."

"Why not? Isn't that what you always wanted? It's all you talked about in college. Going into business for yourself? Just like your dad?"

When I was a child, my father's hardware stores had seemed magical places, full of towering shelves crowded with all the merchandise any homeowner could ever want. Dad was at the center of everything, patiently giving advice, knowing all the answers to his customers' many questions. I wanted to be just like him. I spent summers unloading delivery trucks and stocking inventory, trying to learn every facet of the business, to be ready when it was my turn to take over.

But Dad died of a heart attack when I was fifteen, right after he helped a customer load a new lawn tractor into the back of his pickup. I lost the father I idolized. And I also lost the company that I had always thought would be mine. Mom quickly found a buyer for the stores, saying they were too much for her to handle. I never quite forgave her.

"It's not as easy as you might think, to be in business for yourself," I said.

"What would it take?"

I broke off another piece of bread. "A lot of assets, for one thing. I would need to persuade my current clients to come with me. Plus find lots of new ones."

She nodded. "I could help you with that. I know plenty of people with money to invest. So does my dad."

"It takes a lot of convincing to get people to move to a new advisor."

She thrust up her palms. "So tell me anyone who is better than me at asking people for money?"

"This isn't the same thing, Fontaine," I said, dipping the bread in the oil. "It's not like a one-time donation to a charity."

"You don't think I could do it?"

"I think you can do pretty much anything you set your mind to," I said. "But this is something really different. You would be asking for a lot of money. And a long term commitment." I chewed slowly. "Besides, you're not a professional investor."

"You're the professional investor," she said. "What you need is a salesman. Someone to bring in the money. And I can do that."

"It's not that easy."

"Of course it is. I've been around you long enough to talk the talk. Asset allocation. Dividend streams. Risk management. Alternative investments." She grinned. "How am I doing? All I have to do is get the clients in the door. Then you do the heavy lifting."

"You would have to get licensed. Pass a lot of really hard tests."

"Not a problem. You know I've always been an over-achiever."

I appreciated her enthusiasm, but starting a business was tough. Starting with a total novice meant almost certain disaster. "Why would you even want to?"

She looked out toward the sea, darker now that the sun had gone down. "Because I don't want to think that all the good things in my life are behind me."

"What does that mean?"

She frowned. "Nate is dead. That part of my life is over. I've already raised money for every charity in town. I've been on the board of a dozen non-profits. I look into the future, and there's no new challenge. I need something to give me purpose."

"Starting a business has to be much more than just some kind of personal therapy. It's a lot of long hours. A lot of stress. You have to work your ass off." I thought of my dad, struggling to expand his hardware chain. How he worked nights and weekends. Never took a vacation.

"Oh, come on, Robbie. You know you will work your ass off no matter where you are. So why should all that effort benefit Shep Fairburn or Gibson Tyler or anyone else? It's time you were in charge."

She had a point. I had been relentless in getting the judge's account, and then Shep turned it over to Vivian. It was tempting to think I could be the one in control. But I was still hesitant. "It's too much for one person. Compliance. Trading. Research."

"So you outsource. Daddy does it all the time with his company."

"What about all the services Fairburn, Crandall offers? Estate planning? Tax advice? I couldn't do all that."

"You wouldn't need to. Just set up a good referral network. Make alliances."

"I just don't know." As a fifteen year old, I had no fear at the prospect of managing my dad's chain of hardware stores. At thirty-five I was much more cautious, afraid to take the chance. "What if I make the wrong decisions? Lose all my clients' money?"

She slapped the menu against the table. "You're not going to lose your clients' money. You're the best investor I know."

"You're saying that because you're my friend."

"I'm saying it because I believe in you. Why can't you believe in yourself?"

I could feel the tug of that old longing, wanting to run my own company, to be the one my clients depended on to grow their investments and keep them safe. "I'll think about it."

"Think about this," she said impatiently. "Shep Fairburn was about the same age you are now when he started his company. He had nothing but ambition and a dream. If he could do it, why can't you?"

Shep had been tired of other people telling him what to do. He saw opportunity and reached out to grab it. Why couldn't I do the same? The entrepreneurial streak was in my blood, inherited from my father who spent his whole life building a business he loved. Fontaine's enthusiasm was contagious. I began to think it just might be possible to do this on my own, without Shep, without Gibson Tyler. I could make this work.

"You really think we could this?" I asked.

"Absolutely. It's time for both of us to make a new start."

We both talked at once, thinking of our new firm, throwing out lots of ideas about what we needed to do, how to get started. The waiter came to take our orders. "We need a few more minutes," Fontaine said.

My eyes followed the waiter as he crossed to the bar. The glass shelves holding bottles of alcohol were illuminated by colored lights which slowly turned everything blue, then orange, then yellow, then green, one color building up and then fading into the next. A man was seated there, wearing a flowered shirt and a baseball cap. He looked vaguely familiar. I was trying to figure out how I knew him when he suddenly turned and I saw the familiar twisted angle of his nose.

"He's here," I said, my throat tight.

Fontaine sipped her wine. "Who?"

"That man at the bar. Standing up, ready to leave."

She twisted around at the urgency in my voice. "Is it Gus Kensington? Where is he?"

"No, it's not Gus." I stood up. "It's Dominic Syska."

# CHAPTER 33

HE WAS TOO QUICK for me, in his car and rolling out of the parking lot just as I got to the front porch of the restaurant. I ran back to Fontaine and threw some cash on the table. "I was too late. He got away. But I saw which way he was headed. Come on. We've got to follow him."

We jumped in the backseat of a waiting taxi and pulled into the roadway. "Where is he?" Fontaine asked.

I pointed to a blue car ahead of us, disappearing into the darkness as it made its way around the curve of the mountain. "He's headed toward Philipsburg."

"Robbie, we can't follow this guy. He's dangerous. He tried to kill you."

"I'm tired of running away from everything, Fontaine," I said, trying to make her understand. "I need to know why he's after me." I leaned toward the driver, a twenty-dollar bill folded longwise between my fingers. "This is yours if you catch him."

The driver grabbed the bill, stuffed it in his shirt pocket, and stomped on the gas. Suddenly we were flying up and down the curves around the mountain, windows down, the wind whipping short strands of hair across my cheeks and into my eyes, stinging like shards of glass. Above us were the dark night sky and glittering stars. Beside us the narrow shoulder of the road dropped off treacherously into hazy patches of dry rock. I felt suspended in air, unable to get my bearings, not knowing if the next curve was solid roadway or a straight shot into the abyss.

We passed one car. Then another. Speeding up, getting closer to the blue car. "Robbie, this is crazy," Fontaine said. "We've got to slow down."

"We're fine," I said. We passed the next car and slid in behind a lumbering truck, its gears grinding as it struggled to pull the hill. Impatient, I tossed another twenty to our driver. He pushed hard on the gas and pulled beside the truck.

"Robbie, stop this," Fontaine screamed. "You'll get us killed."

Headlights suddenly blinded me, an oncoming car headed straight for us. There was nowhere to go. Mountain on one side. Sheer drop on the other. Our driver swerved back into our lane and slammed on the brakes. I smelled rubber as our tires grabbed the roadbed. We slid toward the truck's red tail lights, getting closer and closer to the rusted silver of its drooping rear bumper. Our driver lifted up in his seat, neck tendons bulging, fingers gripping the wheel as he pressed hard on the brakes.

Suddenly he wrenched the steering wheel to the left. The torque threw me against the door as we strained sideways, tires screaming for purchase. We spun around, headlights coming at us from all directions, horns blaring. My body tensed as we skidded toward the mountain. I closed my eyes and waited for the crash.

The seatbelt dug deeply into my shoulders as we thumped to a stop. I sat there, not moving, waiting for all the spinning molecules of my body to settle back down where they belonged. "Fontaine, are you all right?"

"I think so. How about you?"

I clicked open my seatbelt. "I'm good."

As we got out of the taxi, people poured out of the cars around us, asking if we were hurt. The drivers stood in a little knot in the roadway, arguing with each other, gesticulating, shouting, trying to assign blame. Our driver jumped around excitedly, pointing at his dented fender, bent down tight against the tire. The truck driver helped him pull it free, then headed back to his vehicle.

Traffic was backed up in both directions, headlights winding around the curves. Our driver walked toward us, frowning at me. His driving had been reckless, but I had pushed him to it. The twenty-dollar bills were still peeking from his shirt pocket. "You two okay?" he asked.

We both nodded.

Horns beeped behind us. "Then let's go," he said.

Fontaine grabbed my arm. "We've had enough for tonight. We almost got ourselves killed. Let's go back to the resort."

"No. I have to find Syska."

"We'll never find him now. He's too far ahead. Let's go back."

I opened the back door of the taxi. "He followed us here. We need to know why."

She hesitated, then climbed in beside me and slammed the door. The driver maneuvered the taxi back and forth, inches at a time, until he had turned it around and was headed once more toward Philipsburg. The blue car was nowhere in sight.

"One condition," Fontaine said. "We drive slower this time. And we don't pass anybody."

"Agreed," I said.

§§§

Philipsburg was an explosion of light after our drive through the countryside, aglow with neon signs and street lamps. Brightly lit cruise ships towered over the distant docks. Our driver rolled slowly up and down the few streets of the town, passing storefronts painted peach, blue, and yellow. We got out on Front Street and stepped into the jostling shorts-and-sandals crowd, sweaty bodies pushed together, smelling faintly of suntan lotion.

"Robbie, we'll never find him in all this," Fontaine said as we threaded our way through palm trees lining the sidewalks.

"We've got to try. You take this side of the street. I'll do that one. Take a quick peek in all the shops and casinos. Then let's meet at The Spiny Lobster." I pointed to the casino in the next block, with a huge neon lobster sitting on its roof.

Fontaine nodded and walked off with long purposeful strides, like an eager tourist determined to check off three cathedrals and two museums by lunch time. I passed shops selling tablecloths, clothing and souvenirs, taking a quick look inside of each. I spotted a man wearing a flowered shirt in a crowded jewelry store and threaded my way through glass display cases of glittering emeralds and sapphires, a treasure surely sufficient to pay off the national debt of several emerging-market countries.

A smiling sales assistant, dressed in a dark skirt and white blouse, approached me. "Can I help you?" she asked.

"I'm looking for someone." The man in the flowered shirt turned toward me. It wasn't Syska.

"Are you interested in emeralds?" She directed me to one of the cases behind her. "We have some lovely pieces that would look very nice with your coloring."

"I'm really not..." I began.

"Perhaps you prefer gold?" she said, anxious to make a sale. "We have several designer pieces that are quite outstanding. Let me show you." She held up a ring of keys and started to unlock a glass case.

"Sorry. I have to go," I said, ignoring her frown as I turned back to the street.

I moved down the block, checking out all the retail stores and casinos, the humid night air assaulting me each time I left the air-conditioning and returned to the sidewalk. By the time I finally reached The Spiny Lobster, sweat was running down the back of my shirt and my linen pants were sticking to my thighs.

I pushed through the revolving glass doors into the dimly lighted vestibule of the casino. The noise hit me first -- bells, loud clanking, repetitive riffs of music, all coming from rows of back-to-back slot machines that snaked through the main room, their colored lights flashing bright against the darkness. A bosomy blonde in tight Capri pants and a sequined tank top was seated near the entrance, her glittered nails flashing as she fished quarters from an enormous paper bucket and fed them into the slot machine. One diamond, then two, and then three, slipped into place. She stiffened her shoulders, excited, anticipating a win. But then a yellow duck quivered into the fourth spot. Smacking the machine in frustration, she reached into the bucket to fish out more quarters.

I circled through the crowd, past roulette wheels and blackjack tables, then spotted Fontaine standing by the craps table. "I didn't find Syska," I yelled in her ear.

A woman scooped up the dice and clutched them in her fist, eyes closed, lips silently moving. Then she opened her eyes and slammed the dice hard down the length of the table, shrieking with excitement.

"Me either." Fontaine reached for her purse. "Let's get some chips and try this game. It looks like fun."

I shook my head. "I gamble every single day when I pick out stocks. It's not something I want to do for fun."

"You sure?"

I could tell she was disappointed. "I'll wait at the bar for you if you want to play."

She took one last glance at the table, then shook her head. "Nope. It's been a long day. Let's head back."

# CHAPTER 34

THE TAXI DRIVER DROPPED US off in front of our hotel. As Fontaine and I stepped out of the elevator, I said, "You want to come over?"

"Sure. I'll be there in a minute."

I went in my room and pulled off my sweaty clothes, slipping into a terry cloth robe. There was a faint knocking at the door.

"Party time," Fontaine said as I opened it, holding up a bottle of wine.

"I'm not sure how much partying I can do. You wouldn't believe how bad my sunburn is," I groaned. "Every inch of me is bright red."

"I told you to use sunscreen."

"I did. But obviously, not enough."

She set the wine on the counter. "You really are an alarming shade of red," she said, examining my face.

"Tell me about it. It's like my whole body is one big open wound. My skin is on fire." I rummaged through the bar for a corkscrew.

"You know, what you need is an ice bath," Fontaine said.

"An ice bath?" I pulled the foil off the wine.

"Yes. It will cool your skin right down. And take out the pain."

"That's a crazy idea." I eased out the cork and reached for a glass.

"It's not crazy at all. I've done it before when I've had a bad sunburn." She walked into the bathroom and turned on the faucet. "I'm running you a cold bath. And I'll get some ice. You just relax."

"I don't want to do this, Fontaine," I said, sipping my wine.

"You'll thank me tomorrow. When you're feeling a lot better."

I perched on the edge of the bed, eyes closed, listening to the water gush into the tub. The door opened and shut as Fontaine went back and forth down the hall to the ice dispenser. An ice bath was about the last thing I wanted right now, but I knew that once Fontaine set her mind on something, she was pretty determined to get her way. And I didn't have the energy to fight her.

"I think it's ready now," she said. "Come on in here."

The tub was full of water, with cubes of ice floating on the surface. "This is one of your stupidest ideas ever," I said.

"Everybody knows ice is good for burns. Hop in."

I gingerly stepped into the tub. The water was bitingly cold, sending shock waves soaring up my legs. It felt like the first pool day of the summer, when I would ease into the cold water inch by jarring inch, up my thighs, to my waist, gritting my teeth the entire time, until finally in desperation I would force myself to dive under the water, trembling with cold. "I hate this," I said.

"Just lie back. I'll be out here just in case you need me."

My heart did strange little stutter-steps as I laid back in the water and the cold worked itself into all my tender spaces. Pain radiated through all my nerve endings, up under my arms, into my neck. I took quick shallow breaths. I felt as though I had been stabbed. Or shot. I hurt everywhere.

"Everything all right in there?" Fontaine called from the next room.

"Yes," I managed to choke out.

Gradually my body started to numb. I could hear a burst of music from the television in the next room. A few drips from the leaky tap. It was peaceful. I thought of Vivian, sprawled in the snow as the unrelenting cold gradually seeped up legs, her arms, throughout her body. Was she afraid while she slowly bled out, alone in the dark? Or did she just relax and let it happen?

I slipped lower in the tub, putting my head under the water, feeling the cold liquid rush into my ears and nose. Ice cubes floated aimlessly above me. I blew bubbles toward the surface.

Suddenly I was jerked upward. "What the hell are you doing?" Fontaine said, grabbing me by the arms.

I coughed, spitting out water, gasping for air.

"Stand up. Get out of that tub." She pulled me to my feet and wrapped me in a thick white towel. I leaned heavily on her as I stepped onto the tile floor. "What were you thinking?" she said, her eyes intense, her face flushed red. "I thought we were beyond all this. I can't believe you would try it again."

"Try what?"

"Don't play the innocent with me. You promised you would never do that again," she said, grabbing my wrist, running her fingers over the scar. "You promised," she repeated, her voice breaking.

I jerked my wrist away from her as I thought back to that horrible Christmas Eve. Fontaine had insisted that I spend the night at her house, not wanting me to be alone so soon after the accident. Nate had been in a foul mood at dinner, sniping at both of us, complaining about his stock market losses. Late that night I stared at my reflection in the bathroom mirror, the pale skin, the long dark hair that Rolfe had always loved. But Rolfe was gone. And the hair was a painful reminder of everything I had lost.

Aching from the loss of my family, my mind fuzzy from too much wine and a solid dose of antidepressants, I found scissors in the cabinet and started to cut out huge clumps of my hair. Then I dug the sharp tip deep into my wrist, getting perverse pleasure from the pain. Fontaine found me sprawled on the floor and held me while Nate stitched me up. On Christmas morning I sat obediently while her hairdresser struggled to transform my ravaged hairdo into something more presentable, the pixie style I'd sported ever since.

"Fontaine, no, it wasn't like that," I said, walking away from the tub. "I wasn't trying to kill myself."

"Then what the hell were you doing?"

"I don't know. I just…" I shivered in the wet towel. "Fontaine, I'm freezing."

She led me into the bedroom and pulled a nightgown from my suitcase, then pulled back the covers, plumped my pillows and settled me in bed. I was still shivering, and she got an extra blanket from the closet. At the bar she fixed a mug of hot tea. "Here," she said, wrapping my fingers around it. "It's chamomile. It will help you sleep."

I forced down several swallows of the hot liquid.

Fontaine sat in the chair beside the bed. "I'm staying here with you tonight."

"No, Fontaine, there's no need for that."

"I think there is."

"I'm sorry I scared you."

"If anything happened to you…." she said.

"Nothing is going to happen. I'm just really tired. But I can't go to sleep with you sitting there watching me."

"You shouldn't be alone."

"Fontaine, I'm fine, really. Please go. I'll call you if I need anything."

Her eyes flitted over my face, as if trying to decide whether to believe me. With a sigh, she picked up the wet towel and took it into the bathroom. I heard it slap against the tiles as she mopped up the liquid I had dripped on the floor. There was a low gurgle of draining water as she pulled the plug in the tub. She stayed in there a few more minutes, straightening up. When she came back her face was more resolute than angry, the expression of someone who has averted disaster yet again, but was not convinced the danger was over. "I'm going to call Daddy and tell him about Syska," she said. "You won't do anything crazy if I leave you?"

"Of course not."

She walked toward the door. "I'll see you tomorrow, then. Sleep well."

I stayed curled up in bed after she left but was too restless to sleep, thinking about Syska, why he had followed me to St. Martin. My mind swirled, trying to make sense of the puzzle in my head, to make a pattern from unrelated dots. Vivian was dead. Nate was dead. Gayle was dead. There had to be a connection, but I couldn't see it. I would call Ana tomorrow. Maybe she could help me figure this out.

# Chapter 33

THE RINGING TELEPHONE roused me from a deep sleep. I slapped at the nightstand as I searched for the phone. "Hello?"

"How's the sunburn?"

Hazy gray light was peeking in at the edge of the draperies. "Fontaine, it's the middle of the night. Why are you calling me?"

"Because we need to catch the ferry."

"What ferry?" I yawned. "What are you talking about?"

"The ferry to St. Bart's."

"Why do I want to go to St. Bart's?"

"Because it has terrific stores there. Lots of designer stuff. You'll love it."

"It's too early."

"The ferry leaves in fifteen minutes. Now get your ass out of bed and meet me at the dock."

I pulled on a sundress and walked outside. Fontaine stood in the middle of a long line which snaked along the dock and back toward the grassy area that bordered the beach. Anchored in the crystal blue water behind her was a wide double-decker boat, painted white with blue trim.

Fontaine saw me and waved furiously as the line started to move. "I was afraid you weren't going to make it," she said, handing me a coffee. "How are you feeling?"

"Much better, thanks. I guess the ice bath did the trick."

"I knew it would."

I pulled back the tab on the coffee lid. "Listen, I'm sorry I scared you last night."

She shrugged. "It's fine. I probably overreacted. But when I saw you under the water..."

"It was a stupid thing to do. I promise it won't happen again." The line moved a few steps and then stopped. "Do you think we're even going to be able to get on this thing? It looks pretty crowded."

"Don't worry, they'll squeeze everyone on."

I turned to look at the crowd waiting behind us. "I'm not sure that makes me feel better. If all these people get on, the boat will probably sink before we get out of the harbor."

"Relax. That ferry is pretty tough. We'll be fine."

We finally got up to the gangplank, handed over our tickets, and squeezed our way onto the deck. The few benches fore and aft were already full. For the rest of us, it was standing room only. Passengers were pressed shoulder to shoulder, looking up, down, or sideways, anywhere but directly into the eyes of the people melded against them.

The crew bustled around, untying lines and pulling up the gangplank. Once everything was locked into place, we puttered slowly away from the dock, out of the harbor and into open water. The beach became a thin line behind us as the ferry picked up speed, riding up and down on the swells, thumping hard against the waves. The pounding shook my teeth and ground down my spine. "I'm going to be two inches shorter by the time we get there," I said, holding tight to the railing.

"Quit complaining. It's a beautiful day. Imagine if we were coming through this in a storm."

I glanced up at the clear blue sky, threaded with a few wisps of delicate white clouds. "If there's a single black cloud in the sky when we head back, I'm spending the night in St. Bart's."

"Just relax and enjoy. We've been in worse than this in Hastings Bay."

"And I didn't like it then, either." I flexed my knees to get in sync with the rhythm of the boat. Gradually I got used to the movement and loosened my death grip on the railing.

Fontaine pointed toward the metal ladder attached to the back of the cabin. "Let's try the upper deck. We'll have a better view from there."

I followed behind her, holding tightly to the ladder as the boat dipped. The wind was stronger on the upper level, whipping the colorful flags on the mast above us. There were several middle-aged couples gathered on the port side, the men in khakis and golf shirts, the women in Capri pants and brightly flowered tops. A few feet beyond them a woman stood by herself, long dark hair hanging down her back, one hand on the rail, the other anchoring her pale blue sun hat as she stared at the wide white wake that gushed out behind the boat.

"That woman looks familiar," Fontaine said. "I feel like I've seen her before, but I can't figure out where."

"You want to go talk to her?"

"No. I'll just mull it over for a while. It'll come to me." She shrugged. "I called Daddy last night. He's sending his guys here to look for Syska. And he wants me to come home. Would you be okay if we cut our vacation short?"

I nodded. "Yes. We came here because we thought we'd be safe. But I guess that's not happening. So we should probably go back home."

We stayed on the top level of the ferry for the rest of the trip, each lost in our own thoughts. Finally we could see the red tiled roofs of St. Bart's. The harbor was crowded with tiny sailboats that bobbed in the turquoise water, their sails furled around the masts. Our ferry chugged slowly toward the dock. A few crew members jumped out to cleat us off, while others positioned the gangplank. The passengers gathered their belongings and lined up to exit the ferry.

Fontaine and I hung back as the other passengers went down the ladder. The young woman Fontaine had spotted maneuvered to the front of the line, waving enthusiastically to someone on shore. We watched as she stepped across the gangplank and then ran down the boardwalk. A man grabbed her up and swung her around.

Fontaine dug her fingernails into my arm. "Oh, my God. Do you see that?"

The sun reflected harshly on the water, casting a glare that made it difficult to see much of anything. I fumbled with my sunglasses, pushing them up higher on my nose. "See what?"

"That man. With the woman from the ferry."

"Is it Syska?" The man was tall and broad shouldered, like Syska, but the hair was all wrong. Not the buzz cut that I remembered when Syska had pressed me back against the car, his face so close to mine. This man had dark blond hair that he shook back off his forehead as he set the woman down and leaned over to kiss her.

"No. Not Syska," Fontaine said.

I cupped my hands around my sunglasses to cut the glare, then watched in disbelief as the woman walked into the main street of Gustavia, hand-in-hand with Dr. Nate Thornton.

# CHAPTER 36

"HE'S NOT DEAD, he's not dead, he's not dead, he's not dead," Fontaine said over and over again, fast and loud at first, then slower and softer, like a child's wind-up toy running out of momentum. She grabbed the railing of the ferry, swaying slightly.

Somehow Nate had managed to resurrect himself, escaping from his watery grave in the icy mud of the Hastings River, to a new life in the warm, sunny Caribbean. A new life which obviously did not include Fontaine.

"I don't understand. The car. The blood." She pounded the railing. "I thought he was dead. The police think he's dead."

"He fooled all of us," I said.

"I can't believe he would do that to me. He's done some pretty bad things over the years. But never...never did I think he would do anything like this. Fake his own death, and run off with another woman. Even I didn't realize he was quite that much of a bastard." She put her hand over her mouth. "I think I'm going to be sick."

A crew member walked past us, collecting leftover coffee cups, newspapers, all the casual detritus left by the passengers, readying the ferry for the return trip. He looked at us curiously.

"Let's get off the boat," I said, taking her arm and leading her off the ferry. "Sit down here a minute. I'll get you some water." I eased her onto a wooden bench in the shade of a towering palm tree. She leaned over, burying her face in her hands.

By the time I returned she was sitting up, chewing on her lower lip, a determined look on her face. She twisted the top off the water and took a long drink. "They were headed this way," she said, pointing down the street. "We have to catch them."

"You sure you want to do that?"

"Oh, yes. I'm very sure. He needs to know that we've found him."

We walked toward a row of elegant boutiques, their windows filled with artfully arranged designer clothing and sparkling jewelry. We checked out the stores one by one, moving quickly up and down the aisles of brightly colored skirts and patterned tops, past counters of fragrant soaps and delicate perfumes. "They're not here," Fontaine said.

"Maybe they've gone to one of the beaches," I said.

"There are a lot of beaches on this island. It won't be easy to find them, unless we're incredibly lucky. And I'm not feeling very lucky right now." Fontaine pointed toward a restaurant near the end of the street. "Why don't you wait for me there? I'll go back to the tourist office and get a map of the island. Then we can sit down and figure out our next move."

The restaurant was dark and cool, a pleasant relief from the bright sun outside. It was fairly empty this early in the day, only a few people lingering at the umbrella-sheltered tables outside. A young couple laughed as they dipped their spoons into a shared dessert. An older couple farther beyond them was angled toward the water, their shoulders pressed affectionately together. I noticed a man alone, off to the right, leaning back in his chair, one leg crossed casually over the opposite knee.

I had expected something different. That Nate would look haggard, or haunted, or at least a little fatigued, after killing Vivian and then faking his own death. But he looked very much the same, well rested, relaxed, just a little redder from the Caribbean sun. He was dressed in khaki shorts and his favorite golf shirt, the pale green and white striped one with the Hastings Yacht Club logo.

I walked out on the patio and stood behind him. "Nate."

He turned, surprised that someone in St. Bart's knew him. The sun was in his eyes, and he squinted and shifted in his chair to get a better angle. When he saw me, his mouth fell open. "What are you doing here?"

"I'm here with Fontaine. So she can get away from all the reporters and camera crews who've been hounding her ever since the police found your car. Full of blood, shot up with bullets. Everyone thinks you're dead. That your body is at the bottom of the river."

I anticipated guilt, or denial, or maybe even a little shame as he thought about what he had done. Instead, he looked relieved. "Thank God. Maybe I can get out of this mess after all."

"You want to explain that?"

He picked up his beer. "This is nothing you need to get involved in. Just walk away and forget you ever saw me."

"Walk away? Are you kidding me? The police think Fontaine and I killed you in a jealous rage. After we killed Vivian." I held my thumb and forefinger close together and jabbed them in front of his eyes. "We're this close to being arrested. You have to go back to Hastings and explain what happened."

He rested the beer on his knee, casually brushing away the little drops of condensation that slid down the bottle and onto his skin. "I'm not going back."

"You would let your wife be arrested for murder, and not do anything to help her?"

He snorted. "Fontaine always lands on her feet. If there's any problem, her daddy will be there to fix everything for her. Like he always does." He set down his beer and stood up. "Now I've got to go."

Fontaine came out of the restaurant just then, blinking a bit in the bright sunlight, rushing across the patio as she spotted me. She pulled up short when she saw Nate, hesitating, a tiny smile fluttering at the edges of her lips. It was obvious that she still loved him, that she wanted to forgive him, even now. That if he took her in his arms and explained everything away as a horrible mistake, she would believe him and give him another chance, just as she had so many times before.

But he didn't say anything. Didn't move toward her. He just stood there, wilting under her stare, his eyes dropping to the table.

Her smile disappeared as she stepped closer and slapped him hard in the face. "How could you do this to me? I've been frantic for days. The police found your bloody car near the river. I thought you were dead."

Nate winced and slowly rubbed the rough whiskers on his face, flexing his jaw muscles. "And yet, the grieving widow still found time to squeeze in a Caribbean vacation. How charming."

I clenched my fingers, fighting the urge to strangle him.

"You brought another woman here," Fontaine said, her voice quivering. "This was supposed to be our second honeymoon. Our chance to make everything right between us. How could you do that?"

He smiled, that long, slow smile that always started deep in his blue eyes, the smile that had captured Fontaine's heart from the moment she met him all those years ago. "To tell you the truth, I really didn't expect you'd still come out here. I figured a dead husband might make you cancel your trip." He shrugged, twisting his palms upward. "But obviously, I was wrong."

Her face reddened. "You contemptible prick. Who is she?"

"Her name's Katarina."

"Katarina?" Fontaine paused. "Oh, my God, she's that trashy waitress from Brazil. No wonder she looked so familiar."

The other couples on the patio turned toward us, mumbling among themselves, uncertain whether to stick around for the fight or to leave now before the cutlery started flying. The waiter noticed the disturbance and started toward us, but I shook my head, warning him away.

"How did you do it?" I asked. "The car? The blood?"

Nate sat down and calmly reached for his beer. "It's not hard for a doctor to get his hands on some blood. And Gayle helped me with the rest."

"Gayle?" Fontaine took a short, sharp breath as she sat beside him and grabbed his arm. "Did you kill her, too?"

"Gayle's dead?" His forehead wrinkled in confusion.

"The police found her a few days ago," I said. "Tortured. Cigarette burns all over her face."

"Oh, God, that had to be Syska," he said, his face suddenly white beneath his tan. "She probably told him where I am. I've got to get out of here. If he finds me, he'll kill me."

He tried to stand up, but I was too quick for him, leaning my full weight on his shoulders, knocking him off balance. "You're not going anywhere until we get some answers. Tell me about your buddy Syska. He attacked me in the parking deck after work. Were you behind that?"

A few drops of sweat formed at his temples. "No. I don't know anything about that."

"Somehow I don't believe you. What the hell have you gotten yourself mixed up in?"

He shrugged. "I borrowed a lot of money. From the kind of folks who break your legs if you don't pay it back. They sent Syska to collect. He's been threatening me for weeks."

Fontaine's eyes widened. "So that's why you got that stupid dog. And put in the security system."

He nodded. "I gave him some of it. Drew down the equity line on the house. Borrowed from my retirement plan. But it wasn't enough." He rotated his beer bottle back and forth between his palms. "One night after work he waited for me in the parking lot, sitting there in that big white SUV, this crazy grin on his face while he told me what would happen if I didn't pay up. The next night I had four flat tires on my car. A few days later he smashed the windshield. I knew he wouldn't give up."

My skin prickled. "A white SUV?" I remembered the car behind us on the way to Gayle's, the one that almost rear-ended us at my house when Geena ran in front of Fontaine's Range Rover. "He followed us to Gayle's house Sunday morning. We led him right to her."

Nate angrily slammed the beer bottle on the table. "Why would you do that?"

"I was looking for you," Fontaine said. "Vivian was dead. You were missing. I thought Gayle might know where you were."

He looked out at the water, avoiding her eyes. "I was at Vivian's."

"Vivian's? Why would you go there?"

"Well, I didn't think I would be very welcome at home after you walked in on the two of us at the ball. Vivian told me I could stay with her until you cooled down. Told me where she hid the key."

"So it was your silver car the neighbors saw." I had been sure it was Gus's rental.

"She was supposed to meet me there," Nate said, "but she never showed up. Then the next morning, when I heard about Vivian, I panicked. A bullet in the head, for Christ's sake. Execution style. Quick and neat. No chance of escape. It had to be Syska. I knew I was next."

"You didn't kill her?" Fontaine said.

"Kill her? Of course not. Why the hell would you think that?"

Fontaine's eyes studied his. "Because you told me…after I caught you with Vivian…you told me that you would do anything to make it up to me, to make things right between us."

He let out a slow laugh. "Oh, my God. You thought I would kill somebody for you? Seriously?"

Her voice trembled. "I found her in lying in the snow. There were footprints leading away from her body. I thought they were yours. I got all my friends out there, to trample through the snow, to give Vivian CPR, all to protect you."

"Looks like all you did was destroy evidence. No wonder the police think you were involved."

"Why would Syska kill Vivian?" I asked. "And why would he come after me?"

Nate picked up his beer and began to nervously pick off the label. "Syska was at the ball, working as a waiter so he could track me down. Caught up with me in the lobby, right after the two of you walked in on Vivian and me. He told me I was out of time, that I had to pay. The guy terrified me. I mean, you've seen him. He's built like a pro wrestler. I wouldn't have stood a chance against him. So I said the first thing I could think of to get him off my back. I told him you and Vivian controlled my money. He could get it from the two of you. And luckily, Judge Edmonton walked up right then, so Syska decided to back off."

"Vivian was managing your money?" I asked.

He nodded. "Some of it. She'd been after me for a long time. Said she could do better for me than you could. And then I heard about this terrific investment, so I figured, why not? Let her check it out, see if there was anything to it. She came back with a big thumbs up. Found out the guy already had a few offers to sell the company. Told me she could set it up in a temporary account, to keep it under the radar, and then we could sort it all out later."

"Under the radar? You mean so I wouldn't find out about it?"

"I knew you'd raise holy shit," he said. "And you'd go straight to Fontaine and tell her. I didn't want to deal with all that. At least not until Vivian proved she could make money for me."

"So what was this terrific investment?" I asked.

"Hawthorne Medical. It's a biotech company that's figured out how to regenerate cartilage. I found out about it at that conference last fall in Brazil. A guy I knew in med school is the CEO."

"Hawthorne Medical?" Vivian had been so excited about its prospects when she pitched it to our investment committee. I thought she had discovered the company herself. Instead, Nate had pointed her to it, the hot new idea that she claimed as her own. "But why didn't you just bring it to me? I could have handled it for you."

"Right." He snorted. "You were so confused after the accident you barely knew what day it was. And you would have given me endless crap about investing in such a speculative stock. Besides, if you had done your job, everything would have worked out just fine. The plan was to cash out my winning stocks and repay the loan. But you let them all blow up. So I couldn't pay off Syska. You're the one who screwed up the whole deal."

"I screwed it up? Why didn't you just sell the Hawthorne and repay your loan?"

"Are you kidding? Hawthorne's going to make me a fortune. Cartilage is just the beginning. Hawthorne's targeting nerve cells next. Can you imagine? People who've been injured, confined to wheelchairs, suddenly able to walk?"

He set his bottle on the table. "It nearly killed me when I had to sell some of it, just to get away. A new identity is expensive, if you do it right. Passport. Credit history."

"New identity?" I thought of the five-million-dollar account invested in Hawthorne Medical, the one whose owner I could never locate. The account that had suddenly been transferred out of Fairburn, Crandall. "You're Julius Tavenner."

He nodded. "You guessed it."

"So what now? How do you figure to get yourself out of this mess?" I asked.

"All I need is a little time. Once Hawthorne makes it big, I'll have plenty of money to pay everyone back."

"You really think Syska will wait that long?"

"He won't have any choice. I'm taking off on my new boat. Gonna see the world." He gestured toward a forty-foot sailboat in the harbor, with the name *Wave Chaser* painted on in bright red letters. "Syska will never find me."

"You idiot," Fontaine said, "he's already found you. We saw him last night in St. Martin."

His face went pale and he stood up quickly, pushing back his chair. "Then I've got to get out of here."

"It's too late for that, Nate," I said. "You're screwed. Syska will find you. You'll never get away."

# CHAPTER 37

FONTAINE WAS STARING at the sea the next morning when I joined her on the terrace for breakfast, oblivious to the little yellow bird perched on the edge of her plate pecking at leftover chunks of pineapple and mango. I shooed the bird away, then sat down and signaled to the waiter. He set a fat blue mug in front of me and filled it with steaming coffee, then topped off Fontaine's. Her hand wobbled as she lifted the mug to her mouth.

"Rough night?" I asked.

"You could say that." She seemed faded despite her Caribbean tan, her features drawn and pinched. "Nate called me last night. We met for drinks."

"Drinks?" Fontaine had been devastated yesterday after her confrontation with Nate. On the ferry ride back from St. Bart's, we had discussed divorce lawyers and debated whether Nate would contest the terms of their pre-nup. Fontaine had called her dad as soon as we got back to the resort, to fill him in on what had happened. I figured Nate would sail off on the *Wave Chaser* and we'd never see him again. I was surprised that he had called her. And even more surprised that she had agreed to meet him. "Where?"

"Here." She set down the mug and reached for the sugar. "Down at the bar."

"What did he want?"

Her lips wrinkled in an exasperated pout. "What he's always wanted. Money."

"You're kidding. He had the nerve to ask you for money? After everything he's done?"

"Oh, yes. He wanted to borrow money from my dad. It seems Syska has run out of patience." Her eyelids drooped wearily as she stirred her coffee.

"So Syska caught up with him. I figured it wouldn't take long." The islands weren't that big. A couple of nights of barhopping, trading rounds with the locals, was probably all it took to find out everything he needed. "What did you tell Nate?"

"I didn't tell him anything. Just got Daddy on the phone and let Nate plead his case."

"Bet that went well." Fontaine's dad had the natural bluster of someone used to being in charge, a bit intimidating under the best of circumstances. Nate had to be desperate to bait that bear. "What did your father tell him?"

"That there's nowhere he can hide. If he doesn't come home and tell his story to the police, my dad will hunt him down."

The waiter brought me a menu and cleared Fontaine's plate.

"Nate turned quite pale," she said. "He hung up the phone and left immediately. I'm surprised his boat is still here. I thought he'd be long gone by now." She pointed toward the end of the marina, where the *Wave Chaser* was tied up, gently riding the swells.

"Have you seen him this morning?"

"No. And I don't want to." She nervously twisted her napkin around her fingers. "I've been such an idiot about this whole thing. I really believed Nate had killed Vivian to make things right with me. And when I thought he was dead...when I saw the pictures of his bloody car...it was as though someone had ripped out my soul. And the whole time he was here in the Caribbean, with Katarina."

I reached out to grab her hand. "He's the idiot, not you. To throw away everything he had. A loving wife. A successful career. All for some stupid money grab. There's no way he can get away with this."

"I guess you're right." She clutched my fingers and looked up with pleading eyes. "Would you mind if we caught a flight out this afternoon? I'd really like to go home."

"Sounds good to me." I grabbed at my menu as a sudden gust lifted it. Looking up, I could see that gray clouds had drifted over the sun, striping the terrace with shadows. A storm was moving in. "I talked to Ana last night and told her Nate was here, alive and well. She's passing the info along to Gutierrez. He'll get the local police here to pick up Syska for questioning."

"Good. Maybe then I'll feel safe. I keep thinking he's right behind me somewhere, ready to grab me if Nate doesn't pay up."

A man in a dripping bathing suit suddenly darted past, his bare feet slapping against the terrace tiles, sprinkling us with drops of water and bits of sand. In a moment he raced back, followed by the reception desk clerk, his burgundy coat flapping behind him as he ran. We heard shouts coming from the beach, far off to our left. "What's going on?" Fontaine asked.

"I don't know." I leaned over the railing to get a better look. "There's a crowd gathering down there. Let's check it out."

"You go. I've had enough excitement for one vacation. I just want to sit in peace."

I rushed down the terrace steps. A woman pushed past me, a small child dangling under each arm, running back toward the hotel. "What is it?" I asked her. "What's going on?"

"It's bad," she said, and kept running.

I worked my way into the crowd gathered at the shoreline, women in bikinis, men with towels draped around their necks. A teenager was kneeling at the water's edge, flakes of skin peeling off his sunburned shoulders. "Looks like a shark attack," he said.

"Must have taken a night swim," said a heavyset man beside me, tattoos running down both arms. "Damn fool thing to do."

I balanced on my toes to see over the crowd. A man lay on his back in the sand, his blond hair washing back and forth as the waves gently massaged his face, distorted and pock-marked where something had nibbled at his flesh. One eyelid had been torn off. Tiny fish swarmed around his left temple, pecking away at the grayish skin. His right arm had been chewed off just above the elbow, leaving a few inches of exposed bone.

"God, what a mess. It's gonna take dental records to figure out who this is," the tattooed man said.

I had to agree. Whatever he had looked like before, he certainly did not look like that now, sprawled awkwardly in the surf, one pulpy eye staring skyward. And then I noticed his clothes. Khaki shorts, sodden and coated with sand. A green and white striped golf shirt, with that familiar HBYC logo on the breast pocket, a sailboat heeling into the wind. My heart started to pound. I looked at the face again, at the scraggly blond beard that barely covered his once-firm jaw line, now soft and sagging. And I started to scream.

# CHAPTER 38

SIRENS ELECTRIFIED THE AIR as police descended upon the scene, cordoning off the area, trying to keep the crowd back. Tourists ignored them and pushed in to get a better angle, clicking the cameras on their smart phones, sending that horrific image of Nate out into the internet, a viral sensation that would get millions of hits before the day was over. No doubt for many it was the highlight of their vacation, an exciting story to be repeated countless times in the future, at cocktail parties over very dry martinis, at backyard cookouts over spicy nachos and ice cold beer.

A police officer walked Fontaine and me toward a quiet corner of the terrace and signaled for the waiter to bring us coffee. "Was he alone?" she whispered as the officer walked away.

Fontaine had rushed toward the beach when I told her about the body. "I have to make sure it's him," she said "That this isn't just another stunt. Something he's staged to fool us all. So we'll think he's dead, while really he's sailed off somewhere with Katarina." But I had held her back, blockading the steps down from the terrace, not wanting her last memories of him to be that gray face and mangled arm.

"Yes. He was alone."

"Too bad. We can only hope the sharks got Katarina, too."

We could see several officers squatting in the sand at the water's edge, their heads close together, talking among themselves. A stocky middle-aged man stepped away from the others and headed for the terrace. "Mrs. Thornton?" he said with a slight French accent as he approached our table. "I am Detective Vouray. I am very sorry for your loss."

Fontaine gave a tiny nod, her lips pressed tightly together.

Vouray pulled out a chair and sat across from us. "And you are?"

"Robbie Bradford. A family friend."

"Good. I am glad that Mrs. Thornton has someone with her at a difficult time like this." His dark brown eyes were sympathetic. "You are in St. Martin for a holiday, yes?"

"Yes," she said. "It's been snowing back home all winter. We needed some sunshine."

"Of course." He pulled out a notebook. "Now Mrs. Thornton, I need to ask you a few questions. First of all, do you know of anyone who would want to hurt your husband?"

"Hurt him? I thought this was a shark attack."

Vouray rubbed a hand through his graying hair. "That's certainly possible. It looks like a shark attacked the body once it was in the water. But there is also a head wound that looks suspicious."

"So you don't think this was an accident?"

"It doesn't look that way. But we can't be totally sure until our doctors have had a chance to examine him. At this point we are still gathering information. Can you tell me what Dr. Thornton did while he was in St. Martin? Where he went? Who he talked to?"

Fontaine sat up straighter in her chair, her shoulders back. "He was on St. Bart's yesterday. With his boat, the *Wave Chaser*. It's tied up at the end of dock." She pointed toward the marina.

"You sailed with him?"

"No. Robbie and I took the ferry to St. Bart's yesterday for some shopping. Nate was off doing his own thing."

An ambulance stopped at the edge of the parking lot. Several young men jumped out and unloaded a stretcher, then trudged through the soft sand down to the shoreline. Leaning down low, they covered Nate's body with a sheet, then carried him back to the ambulance.

"I need to make arrangements," Fontaine said. "To take him home."

"We can help you with that," Vouray said. "One of my men can bring you to the station. And I still have some questions for you."

"Of course."

I waited until Vouray left the terrace. "Why didn't you tell him about Syska?"

"There's no point in going into all of that. We just need to get out of here as quickly as we can."

"But why? Syska's the guilty one."

"I'm not so sure about that."

"What do you mean?"

"All those things my father said last night. He was so angry." She gripped the arms of her chair. "I think my father might have had him killed."

§§§

After Fontaine left for the police station, I went back to my room to pack, setting the luggage by my door, ready for check out. Then I went out on the balcony, focusing on the churning waves, the swooping gulls, the pulsing rhythms of the steel band playing down by the pool, anything to push the vision of Nate's sprawling body out of my head.

Over at the marina I could see several policemen standing on the gunwale of the *Wave Chaser*. I wondered if Syska had followed Nate to the boat last night after he left Fontaine. If there was any evidence in the cabin of a struggle -- dishes broken in the galley, bloodstains on the sofa cushions.

The policemen finally finished their inspection. They jumped down to the dock and exited the marina, veering off to the parking lot and out of sight. They weren't carrying any bulging evidence bags, so I figured the boat wasn't the crime scene. Syska must have jumped Nate on the beach, then pushed him out into the water, hoping the sharks would finish him off. No doubt he had left the island by now. The police would have a tough time finding him.

The wind picked up as the storm moved closer, fluttering the edges of the pool umbrellas, sending plastic drink cups skittering along the concrete. Sunbathers slipped into shoes and cover ups, gathering tote bags and paperback books, heading for the canopy of the pool bar.

A lone man trudged down the pathway toward the marina as the first raindrops hit, a baseball cap pulled low over his forehead.

A sudden flash of lightning splintered the sky. The man twisted around, tilting his head to study the approaching storm. I recognized the thick neck, the angled nose. It was Syska. I hunched down low on the balcony before he could spot me. If he was still here on the island, that meant he would be coming after Fontaine and me, to try to get back some of the money Nate had borrowed.

He started back toward the marina. I watched as he passed the general store and continued past the tied-up yachts toward the end of the dock. He had to be heading for the *Wave Chaser*. I knew it would satisfy a portion of the debt if he could get it out of St. Martin and hand it over to Nate's creditors.

I pulled out my phone and texted Fontaine, telling her that Syska was stealing the boat, that the police needed to get back to the marina.

But I knew it was a long shot. Assuming she got my message, it would take time for the police to arrive. Much more time than it would for him to power up the engine and get away. I couldn't take that chance. Syska had killed Vivian. And Gayle. And Nate. And he had tried to kill me. I had to stop him.

I raced down four floors to the lobby, then ran out of the building and cut across to the marina. The rain was coming down hard now. The metal fittings of the halyards clanked noisily against the masts of the swaying boats.

No one was in sight as I walked cautiously toward the *Wave Chaser*. But as I got closer, Syska suddenly came out of the cabin and started to unwrap the lines securing the boat. He spotted me and I pulled up short, ready to run. But instead of coming after me, he threw off the lines, settled into the captain's chair and started the engine. It sputtered, and for a hopeful moment I thought it would flood. If it wouldn't start, if he had to get off the boat, then the police just might get here in time. But after a few more tries, the motor caught.

He slowly backed out of the slip, then shifted into forward and opened the throttle, clipping the boat tied up next to him. It was obvious he didn't know much about handling boats. I understood why he had waited until daylight to steal it. It would be tough enough for him to get the boat out of the harbor and into a friendly port while there was still reasonable visibility. Trying to manage that in the dark would have been suicide.

I whirled around, desperately trying to figure out what to do. There was a power boat tied up near me, a 22-footer similar to the one Rolfe and I kept at Hastings Bay, with the key still in the ignition. The owners must have gone into the general store for some quick shopping. I quickly untied the lines and jumped in. I had to cut Syska off before he got out of the harbor. Once he hit open water, it would be impossible for me to stop him.

Roiling black clouds dumped down stinging rain, blinding me. I breathed in water as my wet hands struggled to grip the wheel, slamming hard against Syska's wake as I raced toward him.

To my left was a rocky cliff where waves pounded against tumbled boulders, falling back in spewing foam. We had come through here yesterday on the ferry. Boats had to turn sharply to the right as they left the harbor, following the channel markers to pick up deep water. I knew that Syska was unfamiliar with the harbor. Unfamiliar with his boat. All I needed to do was keep him out of the deep channel, steer him toward the cliff, and he would run aground.

He was just ahead of me. In a few minutes he would be in open water. I couldn't let him escape.

I pushed the boat to its full speed and pulled up beside him. I was close enough to see his hunched shoulders, the determined set of his jaw.

I angled my boat toward his.

His boat was a lot bigger than mine. I knew a collision between the two of us would destroy my boat but probably do only minimal damage to his. But I was hoping he didn't realize that. And that he would be willing to veer away from me to protect the collateral that he was returning to Nate's creditors.

The red *Wave Chaser* letters were just above my head. I was inches from him, bracing myself against the collision. I wouldn't pull away. I would hold my course.

He stayed in the middle of the channel. In another moment he would be beyond that rocks and into open water.

If I didn't stop him now, it would be too late.

Closer. Closer.

In another second my boat would crash against his.

At the last moment he jerked the wheel to port.

There was an explosive crunch as the *Wave Chaser* hit the rocks.

# CHAPTER 39

I IMMEDIATELY CUT BACK my speed, maintaining just enough power to keep the boat steady in the strong current. Syska pushed his engine hard, trying to work free, but just churned up lots of sand and silt. He was hard aground and wasn't going anywhere without a tow.

Several other boats quickly surrounded us. I shouted out to them, explaining what had happened. We all waited until the police arrived and took Syska into custody.

Detective Vouray grilled Fontaine and me for hours, demanding to know why we hadn't told him about Syska, trying to trip us up, to find holes in our story, as we explained what had happened. Vouray let us each make one call. I checked in with Ana. Fontaine, as usual, called her dad. Both of them had long conversations with Vouray, and he finally was convinced we were not involved in Nate's murder.

We caught a flight home the next day. I went straight to Ana's office from the airport.

"I can't believe you did that," she said, leading me back to her office as I explained what had happened. "You could have been killed."

"Maybe. But I had to make sure Syska couldn't escape. Not after all the horrible things he had done. And I was really tired of being the victim. Syska and Gus Kensington both tried to kill me. It was time to fight back." I sat down across from her desk. "So what about everything here? Have you convinced your buddy Gutierrez that I didn't kill anybody?"

She shrugged. "Syska's gotten a lawyer and clammed up. No surprise there. He's not admitting anything. But the police found his fingerprints at Gayle's house. So Gutierrez is comfortable going after him for that one. And the St. Martin police have charged him with Nate's murder."

"Nate seemed pretty convinced that Syska killed Vivian."

"We're still waiting for DNA results. So there's nothing yet to definitely tie him to her murder."

"How about Gus Kensington? Does Gutierrez think he killed Vivian?"

248

She shook her head. "His gun wasn't the murder weapon. But he has been apprehended. He faces charges for shooting Lydia. And he'll be sent back to Colorado to stand trial for that real estate scam he was involved in."

"That's good news. Should keep him out of circulation for a while." I took a long, slow breath. "So I'm still a suspect in Vivian's murder?"

"Gutierrez hasn't totally ruled you out, but there's no hard evidence tying you to Vivian's death. There was no blood spatter on your dress, and your gun wasn't the murder weapon." Ana walked to her closet and pulled out the dress and gun. "I have both of these here for you."

"So who killed her?"

She sat on the edge of her desk. "To tell you the truth, Gutierrez is stumped. He has a whole list of suspects, including you, that had motive and opportunity. But he hasn't found the murder weapon. Until DNA results come in, everything is still on the table. He's not ready to rule anyone out."

"That's just terrific. So we're right where we were before. Fontaine and I are still on his short list."

"You're still on the list, but a lot closer to the bottom. And the police will keep searching for evidence. They'll figure out who did it."

"But in the meantime, the killer is still out there. So I have to keep looking over my shoulder to make sure I'm not the next victim?"

"I guess so."

"That's not very comforting." I put the gun in my purse. "I have to do something to protect myself. Until we find Vivian's murderer, I won't feel safe."

§§§

I hadn't been to the shooting range since Jason was a baby, but it hadn't changed all that much. It was still a nondescript cinderblock building on the outskirts of town, not so busy on a weekday afternoon, with only a handful of determined men and women standing in the stalls, repeatedly firing at the paper targets positioned against the far wall. The noise level was deafening, and I picked up some safety headphones along with my ammunition.

I spent some time cleaning my Glock, reacquainting myself with the feel of it, the weight, how to load the magazine. I was definitely out of practice, and my first shots went wild, scoring only a few hits on my paper target, most of them missing altogether. But gradually my eyes and my hands and my body remembered how to hold the gun, how to line up the sight, how to rack the slide. After a while I got my rhythm back, mostly hitting my paper target dead center, with only a few shots straying off to the sides.

It was late afternoon when I finally got to Fairburn, Crandall. Considering that I was no longer a suspect in Nate and Gayle's murders, and that Gus Kensington had been arrested, I was hopeful that Shep would be ready to take me back. Edgar Nelson was probably still furious with me for involving him with the police. But if I could figure out what had happened with his account, fix it so he didn't have those large losses, both Nelson and Shep might be willing to overlook what I had done.

Darius wasn't at his desk, so I was able to slip through the reception area and into my office without being spotted. Spreading out my copies of Nelson's financial statements, I started up my computer and began the tedious process of comparing the paper reports to his online history, month by month, starting with September of last year. The discrepancies were small at first. The online records showed him paying more for various stock purchases and receiving less for his sales than the paper records indicated. Someone had backdated our computer records, changing them after the paper statements had already been mailed to the client.

The October statements had more conspicuous changes. Discrepancies in the number of shares bought and sold. Discrepancies in transaction prices. And by November and December, there were discrepancies in the stock holdings themselves, companies showing up in the online account that had never been purchased, according to the paper statements. Or, like Bovender, remaining in his account after it had been sold.

In effect, cash was being siphoned out of Nelson's account while losing trades were being dumped into it. Small amounts at first, which he probably never even noticed. Our clients were fairly cavalier about checking their monthly statements. As long as the outstanding balance looked reasonable, very few of them scrutinized the transaction history to track exactly what was bought and sold and at what price. And why should they? They paid us, their financial advisors, to do that due diligence for them.

By the end of the year, the losses in Nelson's account were large enough that even the casual observer would notice. He had a huge loss in Bovender, which I knew Vivian had sold months before. Whoever had been manipulating Nelson's account had gotten greedy, or sloppy, or both.

Next I pulled up Gordon Pashman's account. The changes that Murphy had promised to fix while I was out of town had all been taken care of. But I looked back through the transaction history to the last quarter of the year, comparing it to the paper statements I always held onto for backup. The discrepancies were similar to those in Nelson's account. Incorrect transaction prices. Incorrect numbers of shares held. Stocks added that I had never purchased. Some kept that I had already sold, all showing a loss.

I quickly checked the accounts of several more of my clients. They all showed the same pattern, although the dollar amounts were much smaller. Losing trades in the past few months for stocks I never purchased. Cash being sucked out. Shares of Bovender sitting in each account, all showing a loss. I had been too absorbed in my own grief to notice that my clients were being cheated. This was my fault, and I had to fix it.

Darius had to be involved in this. He was the only one with the technical skills to pull it off. But he would never have done it by himself. Someone much higher up had to have authorized it. I printed out the online reports, then scooped them up and headed for Murphy's office.

"Robbie. You're back," he said, glancing up from his computer screen. "I didn't expect to see you so soon."

"We came back from St. Martin a little earlier than we expected."

"Yes, I heard all about that. I can't believe you rammed that boat to keep Syska from getting away."

"I didn't have much choice. It was the only way I could stop him."

"This whole situation has been so horrible. He killed those people, and it was all tied to Vivian? To that account she set up for Julius Tavenner? I just don't understand why she would do something like that."

"People do funny things for money. Things they probably regret, and wish they could unwind. But sometimes, it's just too late for that, isn't it?"

"Too late for Vivian, that's for sure." He picked up some files from his desk and put them in his out-basket. "So, have you talked to Shep? Gotten everything straightened out?"

"I wanted to talk to you first," I said, sitting down across from him. "Thanks for fixing Gordon Pashman's account."

"Happy to do it. These damn computer systems. We keep getting these rogue trades showing up. I guess Shep will eventually have to bite the bullet and spend some big bucks to get our systems updated."

"You really think that will take care of it?"

He leaned back in his chair. "Of course."

I shook my head. "There's a lot more than rogue trades going on, Murph. But you already knew that, didn't you?"

"What do you mean?"

I tossed the printouts on his desk. "You want to tell me why all these losing trades have been dumped into my clients' accounts? Trades that I never authorized?"

"I don't know..."

"Somebody's been backdating the records. Changing transaction histories. Putting losing trades in Bovender in every account. And I figure nobody would do that but you."

His face flushed. "It's not what you think."

"It's exactly what I think. Fraud. Account manipulation. Darius had to be in on this. He's the only one with the computer skills to pull this off. Did you promise him you'd pay off his student loans if he helped you out?"

"I never meant..." he stammered.

"How could you do this, Murphy? How could you betray everyone?" I stood and gathered up the stack of printouts. "It's all right here. The proof of what you did."

"What are you going to do with that?"

"I haven't decided. Turn it over to Shep, I guess. But I wanted to give you a chance to tell him first." I turned toward the door.

"Wait." He jumped up and grabbed my arm. "Let me explain."

"Go ahead."

He shook his head. "Not here. Too many people listening in. How about we go to Lynley's for a drink?"

"I'm not really in the mood for a drink."

"Please, Robbie." He gestured toward his cluttered desk. "I need to wrap up a few things here. But I'll meet you there in fifteen minutes. To tell you the whole story."

# Chapter 40

THE HAPPY HOUR CROWD had already gathered when I walked into Lynley's, a restaurant known for its specialty burgers and extensive selection of craft beer. I grabbed a table in the far corner and sat down to wait for Murphy.

After a few minutes, a waitress approached. "What can I get you?"

"Do you have Devil's Backbone Striped Bass?

"Yep."

"I'd like that. In a mug."

"You got it."

Murphy showed up just as the waitress returned with my beer. She popped open the turquoise can and tilted the frosted mug as she poured in the golden ale.

"I'll have a Sam Adams," he said, sitting down in the chair across from me, pulling off his gloves and stuffing them in his pocket.

I sipped my beer, then licked a bit of foam off my top lip. "So Murph," I said as the waitress walked away, "you want to tell me what you did with the money you stole from my clients?"

His face reddened as the corners of his mouth twisted down. "I never considered it stealing. It was just..." He drummed his fingers on the table. "Just a temporary reallocation of assets."

"Yeah, right. Those losses didn't look very temporary to me. And they didn't look that way to Edgar Nelson or Gordon Pashman, either."

He shook his head. "Robbie, you're misinterpreting this whole thing. I never intended to cheat anyone."

"You mean you never intended to get caught." I set my mug on the table. "So how did it work? You backdated all those losing trades, pulled the cash out of the accounts, and then what? You bought a new boat? Another condo in New York?"

"Not a penny of that money went to me personally. It's all still in the firm."

"Where?"

"In my clients' accounts."

I mulled that one over for a moment. "Let me get this straight. You stole money from *my* clients, then gave it to *yours*? In what universe did that seem like a good thing?"

He took off his glasses and held them up to the light, checking for smudges. It was a typical stalling technique I'd seen him use a thousand times in meetings, when he needed time to pull his thoughts together. "You know how lousy our performance has been. How we've been losing assets?"

"So?"

He huffed very deliberately on each lens, then slowly polished them with his handkerchief. "So I had some big losses in major accounts. I knew they would pull their money away from me once they saw the numbers. You saw what happened with the Drakes." He put his glasses back on and blinked rapidly. "And I couldn't afford to lose any more clients. Shep's been on my back for months. So I just rearranged things a little bit. To give me some breathing room."

"So you cheated everyone else to save your own ass." I slowly ran my finger around the rim of the mug. "How long has this been going on?"

"It started just before year end."

"Before year end? Right after Rolfe died, when I was out of the office?"

He nodded.

"Let me guess. You figured that when I got back, I would be too grief stricken to notice." I waited for him to deny it, but he was silent. "Damn it, Murphy, how could you take advantage of me like that? I thought we were friends."

"You're making this sound much worse..."

I interrupted him. "How can it possibly sound any better?"

"It was just a short term thing, Robbie." He stopped as the waitress came with his beer. "I knew the market would rally eventually. It always does. And then I would put everything back the way it was supposed to be. I was just protecting my clients."

"And you were cheating mine. And Vivian's. And who knows how many others in the firm. How widespread is this? How many accounts have you screwed up?"

He raised the bottle to his lips. "I don't know. I started small. Picking accounts without much client contact. Like Edgar Nelson. The guy was always traveling. Vivian complained that she could never get him to focus on his account. That he wouldn't return her calls."

"And Gordon Pashman?"

"You never mentioned the guy. I thought by the time you noticed, I would have fixed everything."

"So why didn't you?"

"The markets didn't cooperate. You know the kind of volatility we've had. The S&P is up 1% one day, down 2% the next. Interest rates up, then down. Oil prices down, then up. Everything bouncing all over the place. I couldn't get enough of a trend going to unwind all those positions. I just kept losing money. And then Bovender went into freefall when the FDA delayed approval of their new drug. My clients already had so much exposure to it, I had to put the new purchases in other accounts. But there really wasn't any risk there. The stock had gotten so cheap, I figured it couldn't go much lower."

"Oh, come on, Murph, we both know that once a stock blows up, valuation doesn't matter. It can always go lower." We had seen this play out so many times before. A broken growth stock fell into uncharted territory. Growth investors weren't interested. And value investors wouldn't step up until everyone who wanted to sell had finally gotten out. Until the stock stopped going down on bad news. Until the bar of expectations had been lowered so far that a grandma on roller skates could glide right over it. "You knew it wasn't safe to get anywhere near Bovender. So why did you keep buying it?"

He signaled to the waitress for another beer. "Because of Thad."

"Your son?" I thought of the picture on Murphy's desk, of Thad floating high above the court, shooting that game-winning three pointer.

"They were going to kick him off the basketball team, Robbie. His ankle's not healing right, and the docs aren't sure when he can play again, if ever." His forehead wrinkled, a deep crease forming at the inner edge of each eyebrow. "It would have killed him."

"What's that got to do with Bovender?"

"Mitch Harton, Bovender's CEO, told me he could keep Thad on the team. Mitch is a big contributor to the school, has a lot of pull. All I had to do was keep buying Bovender. Since Fairburn, Crandall was one of the biggest institutional holders of Bovender, Mitch thought it would send a positive signal to the market. Help put a floor under the stock."

"So you put Bovender in my accounts. And Vivian's. And countless others. You cheated our clients because of *basketball*?"

"I did what any father would do to protect his son," he said defensively. "Basketball was his dream."

I pounded my fist on the arm of the chair. "Don't try to make yourself sound so noble, Murph. Like you're some kind of hero for protecting your son. What about our clients' dreams? Of paying for their kids' college educations? Or a secure retirement? Don't those dreams count?"

He grunted. "Our clients have so much money, they'll never miss it."

I couldn't believe he was being so cavalier. "Edgar Nelson missed it. So did Gordon Pashman. And I'm sure they're not the only ones." I drew a quick breath. "That's what you and Vivian were arguing about the night of the ball, wasn't it? She figured it out and was going to tell Shep. Then it would all be over. No seven figure job for you. No basketball scholarship for Thad."

He grimaced. "Vivian was a real pain in the ass. I told her the stock would bounce back once Bovender got FDA approval of that drug. I'd trim back our positions at a huge profit, and the cash would go back into the accounts we borrowed it from. Nobody needed to know. And nobody would get hurt. But she wouldn't listen."

"Who are you kidding, Murph? Of course we'll get hurt. Once the regulators find out what you did, they'll shut us down."

"There's no reason for them to find out. I've been very careful."

"*I* figured it out."

"But you wouldn't have if Sutherland hadn't sent you the financial statements..."

"How did you know about those?"

He slumped down into his chair. "Darius gave them to me. He found them in the printer."

"I knew he was in on this. You could never have done it without his help. So when you told me you didn't know Edgar Nelson, that was a lie, wasn't it?"

The waitress brought his beer and picked up the empty bottle.

"I'm not proud of what we did," Murphy said. He pulled something from his pocket and tossed it casually on the table. "Here. You probably want this."

It was my bracelet, all the charms tangled together. I had thought I would never see it again. "Where did you get this?"

"From Darius."

"Darius? I don't understand. How did he get it?"

"We had to find out what you knew about Edgar Nelson. And there wasn't anything in your briefcase..."

"My briefcase?" I clutched the bracelet so hard that the charms dug into my palms. "You took my briefcase from the parking deck after Syska attacked me?"

"I had to, Robbie. But it didn't tell me anything. So Darius figured if we got hold of your laptop and phone, we could see what information you had about Nelson."

"My laptop and phone?" I was so confused by all this. The bracelet. The briefcase. The laptop. And then it all began to fall into place. "Are you shitting me? You're the one who robbed my house?"

"Robbie, please keep your voice down," he said. "It wasn't me. It was Darius."

"Darius?" I repeated. I thought back to that night, hearing the glass break in the kitchen door, and then the footsteps slowly coming up the stairs. "My laptop and phone were in the kitchen. Darius could have gotten those and been out before I even woke up. But he didn't. He searched my whole house. Came upstairs. Into my bedroom."

Murphy took a long swallow of beer. "Yeah, well, that wasn't supposed to happen."

"So just what did he plan to do when he got up there?"

"He just wasn't thinking straight. Thought he could grab some jewelry before you woke up. Use it to pay off his student loans."

"And what was the plan if I woke up? Was he going to kill me?"

"Of course not. He never planned anything like that. He just got carried away, in the heat of the moment. We never meant for anything bad to happen to you."

"And I guess you never planned for anything bad to happen to Vivian, either. Was that all heat of the moment, too?"

Murphy rubbed his hand across his face. "I didn't kill Vivian."

"So tell me who did."

"I don't know." He set down the beer bottle. "I went into the lobby after dinner. Fontaine and Nate were out there, screaming at each other. It wasn't hard to figure out what had happened. Then the door opened to the ladies room and I saw Vivian. I went in and told her we would lose clients when word got out of what she had done. But she just laughed. Stood there in front of the mirror, playing with her hair. Said getting caught was half the fun. I grabbed her arm, spun her around, and slapped her." He stared off into empty space, watching the scene replay in his brain.

"So that's how she got the bruise on her face."

"I guess. She screamed at me, using some pretty creative profanity. I got out of there fast." He closed his eyes and put a hand behind his neck, kneading the tense muscles.

"But you waited for her," I said. "Followed her to the parking lot and shot her."

He frowned as he arched his neck. "Never happened."

"Come on, Murph. We both know you have a gun."

"Mine's not a match. The police have my bullets from that parking deck thing with Syska. After I left Vivian, I went back to the table and talked basketball with Judge Edmonton the rest of the night."

"You had plenty of time to kill her."

He picked up his beer. "You really think I could sit around calmly discussing a zone defense right after I shot Vivian in the head?"

I grabbed my coat and stood up. "I never thought you could steal from our clients, but you did."

"Where are you going?"

"I've heard enough. I'm leaving."

He grabbed my arm. "Robbie, I didn't kill her."

"I don't believe you." I moved toward the door.

"Robbie, wait," he called out as he followed me.

I had to get away. Now that I knew about Vivian, Murph would kill me, too. Barreling through the crowd, my head down, I shoved open the door and raced outside, colliding with someone standing on the sidewalk.

"Hey. Watch out," a familiar voice said.

I looked up. "Shep?"

"Robbie, what are you doing here?" He put his hand on my shoulder. "Are you all right? You look pretty rattled. Although I guess you have every right to be, considering everything that happened in St. Martin. The story was all over the news."

I glanced behind me into the restaurant. Murphy had faded into the crowd, but I knew he was still in there somewhere. "Shep, I have to talk to you."

"Sure." He pulled open the door. "Let's see if we can get a table."

I shook my head. "It's too crowded. How about if we just walk for a minute? This shouldn't take long."

"Of course. Lead the way."

# CHAPTER 41

THE WIND HAD PICKED UP, sending heavy clouds scuttling through the darkening sky. I pulled my coat tightly around me as I walked beside Shep, trying to figure out how to tell him that someone he'd worked with for over twenty years was a murderer.

He spoke before I could sort through my jumbled thoughts. "Robbie, if you've come to ask for your job back, I think it's too soon. Edgar Nelson is still furious with you. We need more time for all of this to blow over. To get him settled with a new advisor. Make sure he's going to keep his money with us."

"That wasn't why I wanted to talk to you." I stopped. "Shep, I think Murphy killed Vivian."

He frowned as he studied my face. "That's absurd. You can't believe that."

"It's true," I insisted. "She found out he was manipulating the books. Hiding his losses in other clients' accounts. Pulling out their cash to buy more Bovender."

"That's a pretty serious accusation, Robbie," he said, his breath smoky in the frosty air. "You have any proof? Something to back this up?"

"Yes, I have proof. And Murphy admitted it. Not the murder," I said quickly. "But the part about manipulating the accounts, dumping in Bovender."

We walked in silence to the bottom of the hill. On the corner was a music spot popular with the millennial crowd. A noisy line had formed in the street, eager fans waiting to get in to see the band.

"I need to hear more about this." Shep turned to the left, toward a pedestrian bridge that arched high over the river, its railing wrapped with tiny white lights that twinkled like earthbound stars. "Let's go this way. It's quieter."

I followed him onto the bridge, stepping carefully around the few icy patches that still remained on the wooden slats. He stopped midway across the river. From here the cityscape was beautiful. Neon logos shone brightly from the tops of tall office buildings. Lampposts glowed along the brick walkway that lined the shore.

"Now what's this about Murphy?" Shep asked. "I don't believe for a minute that he killed Vivian."

I had to lay the groundwork, to explain what had driven Murphy to an action that seemed incredible. "He's falsified trades, Shep. Taking cash from other clients and putting it in his accounts. It's been going on for months."

"Why would he do that?"

"Trying to hide his clients' losses. You know a lot of clients have dropped him. And he was afraid he'd lose more when they saw his weak performance numbers. That he'd be out of a job."

Shep shrugged. "It's been a tough couple of years. We've all been losing clients. You've lost a few yourself."

"But I haven't put in fake trades. All that Bovender he's been buying? He did it to keep his son on the basketball team. He skimmed cash out of other advisors' accounts."

Shep shoved his hands deep into his pockets. "Murphy's been with me a long time. I can't believe he'd do something like that."

"This Bovender thing just derailed him," I said. "You know how crazy he's been about that. Buying all the way down."

He shook his head. "Murphy convinced us that the Bovender situation was a terrific buying opportunity. We just have to wait a bit."

"But don't you understand, Shep, what he's been doing? He was careful to pick clients that never paid much attention to their statements. And if somebody did notice and call to complain, he'd say it was a computer error and reverse the trade."

He frowned. "You said you had proof?"

I nodded. "I've gone back through the paper trail for my accounts, comparing it to what's in our computer systems. It's easy to see what he's been doing, once you know what to look for. Vivian found out about it when Edgar Nelson complained about the losses in his account. She and Murphy fought about it at the ball. She threatened to tell you about it. So Murphy killed her."

Shep stared down at the muddy river as it slapped against the concrete pilings of the bridge.

"Shep, we've got to report this to the police. And to the regulators."

He turned toward me. "Let's not rush into this. We'll talk about it tomorrow in the office. See how we can fix it."

"How can you possibly fix this? He's cheated our clients. He killed Vivian."

"Calm down, Robbie. I don't believe he killed Vivian. And our clients will be a whole lot happier if we just fix this thing in-house, without involving the regulators. They'll shut us down if we report this. Freeze all the assets. And that won't be good for anybody."

"But we have to report it. He broke the law."

"No. I can't do that to Murphy. He's been my friend, my partner, for a long time."

"Then I'll report it. I'm sorry. He's my friend, too. But there's no way we can keep quiet about this." I started back toward the shore.

He grabbed my arm. "You're just like Vivian, you know. Both of you so young. So idealistic. So sure you know the right thing to do."

"I don't think there's any question about what's the right thing to do."

"That's what she said. I told her we had already worked to fix those accounts. That I just needed a little more time. But she was determined to report us to the regulators. Just like you."

My eyes grew wide. "You mean you already knew what Murphy was doing with those accounts? How he was hiding his losses?"

His laugh was bitter. "Of course. Where do you think he got the idea?"

The idea was too horrific to process. Shep was a legend in the investment community, known not only for his outstanding financial performance, but also for his integrity, his community service, his compassion. "No. You would never do that."

"The firm was in danger of going under. We had lost too many accounts."

I tried to pull away from him as I realized what he was saying, but he tightened his grip on my arm.

"I went out to the parking lot to reason with her. To persuade her to give us more time to fix the accounts, to put everything back the way it had been before. But she wouldn't listen."

"Oh my God, Shep. You killed her."

"Don't you understand? Vince Crandall and I started with nothing. We created one of the best wealth management firms in the Southeast. I couldn't let her destroy it." His eyes held that pained look I knew so well, the overwhelming emptiness of losing what you loved the most. He had that same look the day after the murder, when I thought it was Vivian he grieved for. His wife thought it too, telling me at the memorial service about his nightmares, and her fears that he and Vivian had been having an affair. But I realized it wasn't Vivian he had been mourning. It was Fairburn, Crandall, the business he spent his entire life building. He knew it was lost forever as soon as he pulled that trigger and left Vivian to die in the parking lot. "It was an accident," he said. "A horrible accident. I pulled the gun out just to scare her. She didn't believe I would use it. I never meant to. But then, it just went off."

We stood there for a moment in silence. I wanted to believe him. To think that he was not capable of such a monstrous act. But I knew he would do anything to save Fairburn, Crandall. And that included killing me.

He pulled a gun from his pocket. "I can't let you go."

"Put the gun away, Shep. Nobody needs to get hurt here."

"Funny. That's what Vivian said." He waved the gun in my face. "I'm sorry. I wish this could all be different."

"Someone will hear the shot. You'll never get away with it."

He glanced back toward Lynley's. "No one is paying any attention to us."

I jerked my arm free and backed away from him, trying to put some distance between us. "Don't do this."

He started slowly toward me, his gun thrust out in front of him.

I stepped backward, almost losing my balance on the icy bridge. "Stop." There was no one to help me. Nowhere to go. I could never get off this bridge before he shot me. I slid my hand into my purse and pulled out my Glock.

He looked surprised, then smiled. "Put the gun down," he said in a condescending tone. "You know you can't do this."

I firmed up my stance, feet separated, knees slightly bent. "Stop."

He took another step forward.

I lined up my shot through the sight at the top of the gun, aiming at the center of his chest. The webbing of my right hand was tight up against the handle, my left hand wrapped around the bottom to steady the gun. "For the love of God, Shep, please stop."

He rushed toward me.

I pulled the trigger.

He screamed and grabbed his elbow, dropping his gun.

It skittered to the far side of the bridge. That gun was the murder weapon, the one thing that would prove me innocent. I couldn't let it fall into the river. I hurried toward it and leaned down.

Shep's foot caught me just below the knees. My body hit hard on the wooden planks and my gun slid across the ice. I squirmed on my belly across the slippery bridge, my fingers scratching for it.

He yanked at my ankles. I thrashed out wildly to break his grip, then pushed myself to my feet.

He shoved me back against the railing, his hands on my shoulders, my back forced into a painful arch. My head dropped down toward the river. The earth swirled crazily as the water became my sky and the glowing names on the buildings marched backwards.

Shep leaned over me, his face just above mine, his mouth twisted into a desperate sneer.

Curling my fingers around the railing for leverage, I suddenly jerked upward and smacked my head hard into his. There was a satisfying crunch as the cartilage of his nose shattered. He cried out and staggered backwards.

I collapsed onto the wooden planks of the bridge, grateful to feel something solid beneath me.

He came toward me again and kicked out hard with his foot, the toe of his shoe digging into my stomach. I clenched my arms over my torso as bright spots flashed in my eyes and waves of nausea rippled through me.

He jabbed out his foot again. I grabbed his ankle and pushed up hard, throwing him off balance, back toward the railing.

The wood collapsed with a loud crack as his weight slammed against it.

He screamed, his hands clutching desperately at empty air, as he dropped down into the river below.

# CHAPTER 42

"ARE YOU SURE YOU'RE READY for this?" Fontaine asked.

The noisy crowd lined up impatiently at the black iron gate, spilling along my front sidewalk and out into the street, gesturing toward the house as they waited.

"Absolutely." I peered calmly out the window. Months of dealing with aggressive reporters, all eager to ferret out the details of the Fairburn, Crandall scandal, had honed my crowd management skills. This group did not scare me.

But then again, this was no angry mob. These were friends, clients and prospects, all invited to celebrate the grand opening of the new asset management firm that Fontaine and I had created. The first floor of my house was now the home of our new company, with a reception area, conference rooms and offices.

"It's time," I said. "Let's open the door and let them in."

It had been a tough road to get Hastings Bay Capital up and running. Fairburn, Crandall imploded after Shep, whom the police plucked from the icy river after I called 911, was indicted for securities fraud and the murder of Vivian Sutherland. The firm's assets were frozen while the regulators conducted a thorough investigation. Murphy and Darius rushed to make a deal, eager to spill their guts to avoid a long prison term. All three were barred for life from the securities industry. And Fairburn, Crandall, the firm that Shep had spent his entire life to build, was shut down.

All the employees scrambled to find new positions. Gibson Tyler pressed me to come to work for Wadsworth Capital. I thought about it a long time, and almost accepted his offer. But then I decided it was time to start the business I had always dreamed of. I wanted to manage money without worrying about sales quotas or the endless bickering of a dysfunctional investment committee.

While everyone else at Fairburn, Crandall was furiously working contacts to find a new job, I talked with my clients, reassuring them, explaining their options, setting up a strategy for how to handle their investments. And I spent long hours at the computer, doing fundamental and technical analysis on my stocks, getting back in sync with the market, feeling once more the rhythms and patterns that made all the pieces fit together.

The despair and guilt that had caused me so much confusion after the deaths of Rolfe and Jason gradually faded away. I knew I couldn't bring my family back. Couldn't change any of the horrible things that had happened in the past. But I needed to move forward, to focus on my future.

Ana, my lawyer, was one of the first through the door. "I can't believe how fantastic this all looks." She gestured toward the oriental rugs, brass-studded leather chairs and large flat-screen monitors in our reception area. "When you started it was all scaffolding and sheets of heavy plastic. To tell you the truth, I wasn't sure you could pull it off."

I had plenty of doubts of my own. Between the reporters and the SEC, the FBI, the U.S. attorney's office and the IRS, I almost gave up a number of times. But Fontaine stuck with me, drawing on her dad's expertise and contacts to help with our business plan. He gave us tips on outsourcing and setting up strategic alliances. And Fontaine used her considerable selling skills to bring in a lot of new money.

Judge Edmonton stood on my crowded front porch and ran his finger along the small brass plaque attached to the right of the door. "Hastings Bay Capital," he said. "Looks good. I guess it's all official now."

"Absolutely. And I couldn't have done without you and Barbara. Thank you so much for your confidence."

"It's well deserved. Anyone who can go through what you have in the past year and come out standing can certainly handle my investments. You're one tough woman."

Fontaine and I spent the next few hours mingling with the crowd as the caterers passed out champagne and hors d'oeuvres. The celebration was finally winding down when Luddy Driscoll stepped up on the porch. He looked tired, his face thinner and more chiseled than ever.

"Looks like your new venture is a big success," he said. "Congratulations."

He had rushed to my house the night Shep went off that icy bridge, crazy with fear that I had been injured, holding me so close I could feel the rapid beat of his heart. But I pushed him away, determined not to betray Rolfe again. For a while Luddy continued to update me on the Fairburn, Crandall investigation. But I was always slightly aloof, keeping our conversations short. His calls gradually tapered off. I had not seen him in months.

"Thanks," I said. "And I hear you've done well yourself. A big promotion from your coverage of the Fairburn, Crandall meltdown, right? That was a terrific interview you did with Shep."

He nodded. "He's an interesting guy. We keep in touch."

"Does he still blame me for what happened?"

"No. He knows it's his own fault. The firm just got too big. And once Vince Crandall left, he couldn't manage it. Everything was spinning out of control long before you got there."

"So he doesn't hold a grudge? I'm glad to hear it."

"I didn't say that. That bullet you planted in his elbow absolutely destroyed his golf game. There's no way he'll ever swing a club again."

"I wouldn't think he would be playing much golf in prison."

"Probably not," he agreed.

I gestured to the door. "Come on in. Have some champagne."

He shook his head. "No. I can't stay. I'm working on a story."

"Oh." We stood there awkwardly for a few minutes, uncertain what to say to each other. "Well, then," I said finally, "thanks for stopping by."

I expected him to walk away, but he waited as several clients came out to the porch, thanking me for a wonderful party, hugging me and wishing me luck.

Finally it was just the two of us. "I wanted to see if you had plans for Saturday night," he said. "There's a terrific new Italian restaurant, Leonora's, that just opened up. Our food editor gave it rave reviews. How about we check it out?"

There was no way I wanted to get back into a complicated relationship with Luddy. My heart still belonged to Rolfe. "I'm sorry," I said, shaking my head. "There's just so much to do to get the firm up and running."

He raised an eyebrow, challenging me. "It's just dinner. You have to eat sometime."

"Maybe some other time," I said, hoping he would get the hint that I wasn't interested. "When things are more settled."

"Of course." He started down the steps, then turned back, his expression wistful. "You know, sometimes you have to let go of the past and move on."

"Luddy, I..."

"When you're ready to do that," he said, "you give me a call."

I watched as he walked away, shoulders slumped, hands in his pockets, that hangdog posture he always assumed when he felt defeated. I felt guilty for rejecting him. Luddy had believed in me when Gutierrez was so convinced I was guilty. Had run interference with the press when they badgered me day and night after the Fairburn, Crandall scandal broke. And had portrayed me in his articles as the heroine who had uncovered Shep and Murphy's fraudulent scheme and saved Fairburn, Crandall's clients.

I hesitated. Rolfe was the one great love of my life. I could never feel that way about anyone ever again. I twisted my charm bracelet around my wrist, feeling the Eiffel tower charm, the gondola, the Mickey Mouse ears, all those precious memories of Rolfe and Jason and the life we had together. But pushing Luddy away would not bring them back.

Maybe it was time to leave the bracelet in my jewelry drawer. To accept the changes in my life. To start making new memories. "Luddy?"

He turned back. "Yes?"

As he said, it was just dinner. "Saturday night," I said. "Leonora's. Meet you there at eight?"

His smile started slowly at the corners of his mouth, then traveled upwards to crinkle the edges of his face. Those cynical eyes, usually so suspicious, were suddenly lit up with an emotion I'd never seen there before -- hope. Hope that we could start over again as friends, without any of the negative emotions that tied us to our past. Hope that maybe, just maybe, our friendship might deepen into something more.

He squared his shoulders and pulled his hands from his pockets, ready for the challenge. "See you then."